Robert Louis Stevenson

Robert Louis Stevenson:

AN ANTHOLOGY

Selected by Jorge Luis Borges and Adolfo Bioy Casares

Edited by Kevin MacNeil

First published in paperback in Great Britain in
2017 by Polygon, an imprint of Birlinn Ltd

West Newington House
10 Newington Road
Edinburgh
EH9 1QS

www.polygonbooks.co.uk

ISBN 978 1 84697 407 6

British Library Cataloguing-in-Publication Data
A catalogue record for this book is available
on request from the British Library.

Typeset by Biblichor Ltd, Edinburgh

Printed by Clays Ltd, St Ives plc

CONTENTS

INTRODUCTION

'I like hourglasses, maps, eighteenth-century typefaces, etymologies, the taste of coffee, and the prose of Robert Louis Stevenson.'

Jorge Luis Borges

'Borges created his precursors, even Stevenson.'

Rivka Galchen

Introduction

Kevin MacNeil

This anthology does not build a notional bridge between the litera-
tures of Scotland and Argentina so much as shed light on a tangible,
pleasing and under-recognised connection that already exists. It
might seem unlikely that there is a direct literary link between nine-
teenth-century Scotland's Robert Louis Stevenson (1850–94), and
twentieth-century Argentina's genre-bending metafictionalists Jorge
Luis Borges (1899–1986) and Adolfo Bioy Casares (1914–99), but
such a relationship does exist, as this introduction will demonstrate.
All three are internationally renowned authors; in many parts of the
world Stevenson and Borges, in particular, are household names. I shall
concentrate largely on the fascinating Stevenson–Borges dynamic.

The anthology you hold in your hands, published here for the
first time, was a long-cherished project of Borges and Bioy, possibly
conceived earlier but planned in the late 1960s, as Professor Daniel
Balderston affirms in 'A Projected Stevenson Anthology (Buenos
Aires, 1968–1970)', the essay that first alerted me to the ideas behind
the book, and which made me want to bring it into physical being.
Over and above earning great renown as authors in their own right,
Borges and Bioy had been successfully publishing anthologies with
Emecé Editores for years and they planned a series of *sumas*, anthologies of work by writers whom Borges and Bioy admired, but this
endeavour was never to see the light of day (likely for economic
reasons). For the Stevenson *suma*, they got as far as choosing the
contents and naming a translator. It is highly probable that Borges

would have taken the lead on writing the introduction. In the 1980s Borges attempted to revive the idea of publishing the RLS anthology – he had by now translated Stevenson's Fables himself – but again the anthology was not realised, likely because of the economic downturn Argentina suffered at the time.

It is tempting to think that Borges, who often cited or praised imaginary books, would have appreciated the journey this book has taken, flitting between an intangible reality and a physical one: the essays and fictions contained herein first existed within Stevenson's mind; they were then given physical form in books and magazines; Borges and Bioy conceived their anthology but did not live to see it come into physical existence; now it is published and so has finally become a tangible object, ready for absorption or reabsorption into the reader's mind.

The anthology as Borges and Bioy envisaged it was to be a collection of their favourite Stevenson essays, stories and fables. (Beneath their original list is an arrow pointing towards an additional one: *The Ebb-Tide*, *The Master of Ballantrae* and *Weir of Hermiston*. Perhaps the anthologists considered including excerpts from these novels, but they also knew that the book was already going to be about 350 pages long, including introduction.) At any rate, this is a book of wisdom and entertainment, of the practical and the fabulous, of ideas and expressions that are ultimately more timeless than dated, and which are more intriguing than ever when viewed through a Borgesian prism.

That the first part of the anthology places emphasis on Stevenson's essays is not the surprise it might initially seem. We'll come back to the subject of Stevenson's reputation, but for the moment it is enough to say that the essays in this volume, some of them quite obscure, deserve to be more widely read. All three authors were contemplative characters who thought deeply about fundamental issues such as identity, time, the nature of truth, meaning, morality and wisdom, not to mention the purposes and techniques of literature. As Clare Harman notes in her biography of Stevenson:

In his hands, the personal essay seemed to be coming to perfection in an amazing combination of high polish and novel directness, while aphorisms poured from his young mouth straight into the dictionaries of quotations.

It is a shame – and a curious one – that the personal essay is somewhat undervalued in this country. To observe or experience the route an intelligent, articulate mind travels when openly exploring vital issues is something of a privilege. This is especially true in the case of a writer like Stevenson, as engaging and eloquent as he is provocative (all these adjectives apply equally to Borges). The essays in this volume are erudite, stimulating and immensely quotable. Their appeal to Borges and Bioy is self-evident.

In his preface to the first edition of *A Universal History of Infamy*, Borges wrote:

> The exercises in narrative prose that make up this book . . . stem, I believe, from my rereadings of Stevenson and Chesterton.

Those 'exercises' – fictionalised accounts of real-life rebels, scoundrels and criminals – point towards a fascination, shared by all three authors, with the darker sides of life. Bioy, Stevenson and Borges were raised in well-to-do families and the latter two in particular harboured an enduring compulsion to investigate the edgier parts of town and the more shadowy parts of the psyche. Stevenson's youthful shenanigans in Edinburgh's Old Town drove his parents to despair (he contrasted his childhood piety with his 'precocious depravity'); Borges relished visiting the less respectable *barrios*.

Borges's inner life, like Stevenson's, was one of huge adventure and finely tuned perception. Both writers had been avid readers as children (Stevenson called the family nurse, who helped instil in him a love of stories, 'my second mother, my first wife'; Borges said, 'I think if I were asked to name the chief event of my life, I should say my father's library. In fact, I sometimes think I have never strayed outside that library'). Both had protective mothers and would always feel an attraction towards the brave, the audacious, the transgressive.

The extent to which physical limitations catalysed in Stevenson and Borges this admiration for the courageous is debatable. Stevenson suffered from real and perceived ailments throughout his life, and died tragically young; Borges, who endured an anxiety over incipient blindness, finally did go blind in the 1950s. 'My friends lost their faces,' he said. 'I live in the centre of a luminous mist.' In that same decade Borges was appointed as Director of the National Library – remarkably, the third blind man to hold such a position. Surrounded by 900,000 books he couldn't read, Borges, well aware of the irony, commented that God 'gave me books and night at the same time'.

Borges wrote panegyrics to ancestors of his who conducted themselves boldly in battle, such as Colonel Manuel Isidiro Suárez, his maternal great-grandfather, who fought at Junin in 1824 and earned praise from the liberator, Simón Bolívar. In contrast to such heroism, Borges, self-deprecating at the best of times, called himself cowardly and bookish, a man of fiction rather than a man of action. Questions of what it means to be a man or a gentleman, and how being a writer does or does not evidence those qualities, run throughout much of Stevenson's and Borges's prose writings and are evident in the titles of some of the essays in this volume.

That essay-writing was of great importance to Stevenson is clear from this anthology: that it was crucial to Borges is evident from his fiction and non-fiction. As the eminent Mexican poet Octavio Paz wrote: 'He [Borges] cultivated three genres: the essay, the poem and the short story. The division is arbitrary. His essays read like stories, his stories are poems; and his poems make us think as though they were essays.'

If it seems like Stevenson had a more profound influence on Borges than on Bioy, that is because this was the case. And it's reasonable to say that Borges had a stronger influence on Bioy than Bioy had on Borges; Bioy once said that an evening spent collaborating with Borges was the equivalent of a year of solitary writing. Works by Stevenson and H.G. Wells were literally the first books that Borges handled and the affinity Borges felt for Stevenson is implicit and explicit in his prose, poetry, talks and interviews.

Near life-long friends, Borges and Bioy, in a happy analogue to the doubleness that exists in their own writing and, of course, in Stevenson's, often merged into the same writer. They wrote, for example, detective stories, screenplays and fantastic fiction under the pseudonym H. Bustos Dumecq. (Some of their friends smilingly called this dual writer 'Biorges'.) Stevenson also collaborated – with poet and critic W.E. Henley, with wife Fanny and with stepson Lloyd Osbourne – but it is fair to say that both he and Borges achieved their finest, most influential and most original work when writing solo.

Borges once wrote that the primary tropes of fantastic literature are but four in number – the work within the work, the journey through time, the interplay of reality and dream, and the double. The latter two elements are especially pertinent in Stevenson's and Borges's lives and literary output. Stevenson wrote to F.H. Myers, a founder of the Society for Psychical Research, of which Stevenson was a member, that when feverish he felt he had 'two consciousnesses'. Duality features in many of Stevenson's works – *The Master of Ballantrae*, 'Markheim', *Catriona*, etc., with the most famous example being the *Strange Case of Dr Jekyll and Mr Hyde*, which Borges considered first and foremost a detective story. Borges liked to point out that the two names in the title implicitly persuade the reader from the start that we are dealing with two different characters. (In a review of a movie version of Jekyll and Hyde (the third most-filmed story of all time), Borges once suggested that the best way to make a film version work would be to have two different actors playing the respective title roles.) Doubles feature in many of Borges's writings, including 'The Theologians', 'The South' and 'The Shape of the Sword'. In 'The Theologians', two enemies discover that they are the same man. Borges was more likely to make a coward the ultimate hero of a story than to use a traditional protagonist. Almost every story in Borges's later work *Dr Brodie's Report* (the name echoing a famous Stevenson connection) is about two characters in opposition to each other. Borges believed human beings embodied the heroic and the tragic – being both dreamer and dream at once. Balderston notes:

> Both writers are fascinated by the motif of the double because of its usefulness in creating characters who can be identified by opposition to one another, that is, defined from the outside, without recurring to a specious psychology.

Borges occasionally wrote of himself as a character – as Stevenson sometimes does in his essays – not in a manner that is self-involved or egotistical but analytical and born of genuine intellectual inquiry. For example, Borges the rather shy librarian considers Borges the internationally famous writer and ends up wondering which of the two is writing down those very thoughts at that point in time.

Borges said:

> I am interested in the feeling I get every morning when I wake up and find that I am Borges . . . It is something deep down within myself – the fact that I feel constrained to be a particular individual, living in a particular city, in a particular time, and so on. This might be thought of as a variation of the Jekyll and Hyde motif. Stevenson thought of the division in ethical terms, but here the division is hardly ethical . . . There is always this idea of the split personality.

He was later to intensify and refine his ideas on identity, as we shall see.

As noted, Borges and Bioy were excellent anthologists, especially with regard to tales of crime and the fantastic. Their anthology sometimes known in English as *Extraordinary Tales*, for example, is itself extraordinary, bringing together compelling narratives from diverse cultures in a book that raises tantalising metaphysical and literary questions – and does so in a highly readable manner. One of the stories included is 'Faith, Half-Faith and No Faith at All', also featured in this anthology. In a brief but telling Preliminary Note, Borges and Bioy wrote:

> One of the many pleasures which literature has to offer is that of the narrative . . . The essence of narrative is to be found, we venture to think, in the present pieces; the rest is episodic illustration, psychological analysis, fortunate or inopportune verbal adornment.

The latter phrase could have been written by Stevenson, whose lively essay 'A Gossip on Romance', included in this volume, was well known to both Argentine authors. Bioy and Borges were contemptuous of narratives that did not have a meaningful story to tell. All three authors engaged with the fantastic to explore aspects of reality. In

'Some Gentlemen in Fiction', Stevenson conceded – in a manner some considered virtually blasphemous – that characters are 'only strings of words and parts of books'. To which Borges later responded: 'Achilles and Peer Gynt, Robinson Crusoe and Don Quixote may be reduced to it. The powerful men who ruled the earth, as well: Alexander is one string of words, Attila another'. This is a good example of Borges taking an idea from Stevenson and developing it in such a way that we read Stevenson with renewed insight. For Borges, the act of reading can encourage readers to interrogate the relationship between reality and imagination, between possibility and experience.

In 'A Humble Remonstrance', a rich and layered essay that constituted a response to Henry James's 'The Art of Fiction', Stevenson wrote:

> Life is monstrous [one of Borges's favourite adjectives], infinite, illogical, abrupt and poignant; a work of art, in comparison, is neat, finite, self-contained, rational, flowing and emasculate. Life imposes by brute energy, like inarticulate thunder; art catches the ear, among the far louder noises of experience, like an air artificially made by a discreet musician.

I think it likely that this quotation influenced the thinking of writer Mary Burchard Orvis, who stated:

> All good fiction has form, no matter how modern or surrealistic. Indeed, the particular value of fiction over raw experience is that it imposes a pattern or a meaning upon life. Life is frustrating, chaotic, illogical, fantastic, and more often than not, apparently meaningless; full of useless suffering, pain, tragedy . . . yet man . . . craves order . . . If he turns to fiction, he wants some sort of organisation, meaning and pattern.

Whether fiction imposes meaning or reveals it is an enormous question (one worthy of a book in itself). Stevenson and Borges attempt to negotiate an apparently meaningless universe by use of creativity (writing, dreaming, reading, interpreting), by contemplating the means through which an ethical compass might be calibrated, by asking and attempting to answer the great questions of being, identity, causality, creation and infinity. The essays and narratives in this anthology bear witness to these aspirations. In 'A Humble Remonstrance', Stevenson compares a work of art with geometry, an analogy that also surfaces in a number of Borges's writings. Many of Borges's stories centre on powerful, complex ideas brought to life – ideas which are deepened and developed through action and dynamism rather than static characterisation, and which bear an uneasy, stubborn and disquieting relationship to the real world. The same can be said for the best of Stevenson's work, including 'The Suicide Club', 'The Bottle Imp', and the fables.

That 'The Suicide Club' – three interconnected detective-fiction stories that create a larger narrative – would greatly appeal to the duo who wrote detective stories together and loved the genre is natural. Bioy and Borges also liked to create connections between their narratives – literary in-jokes, references to obscure or non-existent authors and books, and so on. On a trip to London Bioy once tried to get hold of a title Borges wrote about in 'The Approach to Al-Mu'tasim', unaware that the book had been invented by his friend.

'The Bottle Imp', one of Stevenson's most beloved stories, was partly inspired by a Richard John Smith melodrama first staged in London in 1828, and which in turn had been based on a German folk-tale. Stevenson considered it 'in its ingenuity and imaginative qualities singularly like the Hawaiian tales'. When it was translated into Samoan in 1891 (the same year it appeared in English), Stevenson was disconcerted to note that Samoan visitors to his house would ask him earnestly, 'Where is the bottle?' The trope of the coin is also to be found in Borges's fantastic story 'The Zahir', where it initially implies free-will, but soon becomes a conduit to a disturbing meditation on dream and reality.

Borges suggests that writers rewrite previous writers without truly realising it. In his narrative 'The Circular Ruins', a man dreams about a son until the son becomes real; the man then discovers he, too, is someone's dream. This story is essentially a fable on creativity; we come to understand that we owe a debt of influence to those who went before us and that we are not in control of things in the ways we might think or wish. Borges, who was very familiar with Stevenson's essay 'A Chapter on Dreams', said this story came to him as a dream, and that furthermore he considered reading to be a form of dreaming in that it is a private, internal experience only somewhat tied to the external world. The relationship between dream and reality, between creativity and actuality, is key. Discussing 'The Circular Ruins', Borges said, 'The whole story is about a dream, and, while writing it down, my everyday affairs – my job at the municipal library, going to the movies, dining with friends – were like a dream. For the space of that week, the one thing real to me was the story.'

Furthermore, referencing Schopenhauer, Borges highlights the idea that life and dreams are pages of the same book: reading them consecutively is living, flicking through them is dreaming. Fiction can seem to have a life of its own, and both Stevenson and Borges are intrigued by the ways in which life and literature interrelate. Stevenson seems to prefigure Pablo Picasso's dictum that 'Art is a lie that makes us realise truth' (which seems nowhere more true than in fiction, for the best and most lasting of fictions surely reveal bigger truths). These truths can seem unpredictable or unsettling in Stevenson's fables and Borges's stories alike. This is partly because both authors allow room for the reader to engage with the mysterious, with contingencies that *seem* acausal or impossible in life – coincidences, contradictions and the otherworldly. Borges often takes existential arguments to dizzying conclusions. Stevenson and Borges, in Balderston's words, 'find the highest achievements of the art of fiction to be those in which a story is suggested by a text but left to be completed by the imaginative reader'. This approach allows a reader to feel involved in the story in an insightful and pleasurable manner; we feel absorbed by and into the text, actively subsumed by the narrative process.

The art of reading allows us to cast off our selves and assume a different persona – perhaps even to become the author. In some ways, when we read Stevenson we become Stevenson. Alastair Reid, the Scottish poet and essayist who was a friend to and translator of Borges, paraphrased Borges's thoughts:

We are physical beings, rooted in the physical cycle of life-and-death. Yet we are also users of language, fiction-makers, and language and fictions are not, like us, subject to natural laws. Through them, we are able to cross over into a timeless dimension, to bring into being alternate worlds, to enjoy the full freedom of the imaginable.

Good readers, Borges believed, are rarer than good writers. Borges and Stevenson allow the reader's imagination to participate in the creation of the narrative. As Reid put it:

We are all *ficcioneros* – inveterate fiction-makers – it is through our fictions, private and public, that we make sense of our world, and find some equilibrium in it, it is through our fictions that we create ourselves.

Borges, like Stevenson, was a reader of Carlyle, who posited the notion that history was a story we read and write and which writes us. To Borges, we are in fact the authors, readers and protagonists of an infinite narrative – trying to negotiate our own meanings and those of others, while underneath all our superficial differences we are one person: nobody. This kind of radical thinking – seeded in Stevenson and others and brought to fruition in Borges – is lively, creative and provocative.

Stevenson and Borges were both enamoured with succinctness. 'There is but one art – to omit', wrote Stevenson. Borges famously didn't write novels because, in a sense, he had too much to say; it was more productive to write brief, dense stories and short, fertile essays. Borges condensed novels into ideas contained within a sentence, often contemplating instead the non-existent book. 'Why,' he reasoned, 'take five hundred pages to develop an idea whose oral demonstration fits into a few minutes?' Some have ascribed Borges's lack of superfluous detail to his myopia, but I think it is also attributable to stylistic choice, by way of Stevenson's essays and artistic practices.

Another thing they have in common is that the quantity of material they wrote is much greater than is generally supposed. Stevenson scholar Roger G. Swearingen identifies more than 350 projects the author embarked on in his short life, incorporating essays, novels, short stories and plays, and not counting his many letters. Borges wrote 1,000 pages of stories, more than 500 pages of poetry, a couple of dozen works of (often idiosyncratic) translation, 1,200 essays, hundreds of prologues as well as film and book reviews, capsule biographies, and more. In Borges's published works alone there are more than one hundred references to Stevenson.

Among the most condensed of Stevenson's writings are the fables. Stevenson was entranced by fables and a comment in a letter suggests he may have started writing his own as early as 1874. But this is by no means certain, and if true, would mean he worked on the fables on and off for two decades. Edmund Gosse, by contrast, claims he began them in Bournemouth in 1887, after completing the *Strange Case of Dr Jekyll and Mr Hyde*. Stevenson planned to publish a collection of his fables with Longman, but died before he could honour the contract. It is known that Fanny, Stevenson's wife, did not like the fables – she considered them 'aberrations' – and her influence may have stalled their publication. In fact, though they are overlooked and undervalued, the fables are a rich and vital element of Stevenson's literary legacy. Stevenson believed that just as tastes evolved, so must fables. And indeed there is something very modern about their unwillingness to yield to simplistic moralising. Serious, lyrical, nuanced, the fables ask deep questions about purpose and meaning. Some critics have described the fables as being like early examples of existentialist or Kafka-esque writing and it is no surprise that they appealed to Borges and Bioy. The aforementioned Borges story 'The Circular Ruins' may have been partly inspired by 'The Song of the Morrow', concerned as they both are with time, recurrence, doubling and multiplying, and circularity. Many of Borges's stories read like fables – pared back, resonant, transcendent. Perhaps because of their combination of narrative momentum, engagement with greater meaning and lean and graceful writing, they are simply a joy to read.

One of the Stevenson fables that intrigued Borges was 'Faith, Half-Faith and No Faith at All'. The eminent scholar R.H. Blyth (once tutor to Crown Prince, later Emperor, Akihito of Japan) offers an unusual interpretation. He equates Faith, the priest, with the man who believes (or professes to believe) in revealed religion. Half-Faith is the virtuous, perhaps sanctimonious, person who talks of qualities like beauty, goodness and truth. No Faith, says Blyth, 'is the man who lives by Zen'. It is not accurate to describe either Stevenson or Borges as Buddhists, but here emerges another fascinating connection. Blyth and others have noted unwitting aspects of Buddhism in Stevenson's writing – in these fables and in his works that reveal human nature as being more contradictory and more malleable than one might wish to believe. The connection between Borges and Buddhism is fascinating. 'Time passing,' wrote Borges, 'is a severing of selves, each one trapped in a past monad.' He wrote a book on Buddhism and lectured on the subject.

Borges said, 'There are two men whom I love personally, as if I had known them. If I had to draw up a list of friends, I would include not only my personal friends, my physical friends, but I would also include Stevenson and [fellow Scottish author] Andrew Lang. Although they might not approve of my stuff, I think they would like the idea of being liked for their work by a mere South American, divided from them in time and space.' He often spoke of Stevenson as a 'major writer', no matter what his interlocutor thought.

An unenviable element all three authors share is that they have been, at times, somewhat misunderstood. Stevenson has been dismissed as a 'mere' children's author or perceived as no more than a minor author. Borges and Bioy are sometimes considered to be the drily intellectual, detached or narrowly in-joking authors of works that are more interested in metaphysical complexities than in human beings. This, too, is an erroneous view.

Stevenson's reputation has fluctuated (as Borges's has, to a lesser extent). Richard Dury notes four distinct periods: lifetime reception; height of esteem (1894–1914); revision; reinstatement. The death notice in the *Illustrated London News* of 22 December 1894 shows how highly regarded Stevenson was: 'He is gone, our Prince of storytellers – such a Prince . . . with the insatiable taste for weird adventure, for diablerie, for a strange mixture of metaphysics and romance.' Ever since the sensational success of *Strange Case of Dr Jekyll and Mr Hyde,* Stevenson had been in demand. He commanded considerable fees from magazines such as *Scribner's* for some of the essays in this volume. Following his death, serious critics elevated his work and dreamy readers romanticised the noble Bohemian invalid who died young. Jack London, who visited Stevenson's grave in 1908, wrote to a friend: 'I do join you, heartily, in admiration of Robert Louis Stevenson. What an example he was of application and self-development! As a storyteller there isn't his equal; the same thing might almost be said of his essays.'

During the revisionist period, Stevenson was often treated with disdain, and was as good as expelled from the literary canon. In 1924 Leonard Woolf published an essay entitled 'The Fall of Stevenson', in which he wrote: 'there never has been a more head-long fall in a writer's reputation ... A false style tells most fatally against a writer when, as with Stevenson, he has nothing original to say.' This is hardly justified. And yet an aversion towards Stevenson's writings became strangely commonplace for a while. Edwin Muir, Stevenson's compatriot, wrote in 1931: 'Stevenson has simply fallen out of the procession. He is still read by the vulgar, but he has joined the band of writers on whom, by tacit consent, the serious critics have nothing to say.'

In the twenty-first century, however, critics are once again taking a more enlightened and understanding approach to Stevenson. He has been included in the *Norton Anthology of English Literature* (after being omitted from the first seven editions of that influential anthology) and is hailed by some critics as anticipating elements of modernism and postmodernism. It is tempting to wonder how Stevenson's reputation might have been rehabilitated, at least in the Spanish-speaking world, had the present anthology appeared as and when Borges and Bioy had first (or indeed subsequently) tried to publish it. Perhaps it is enough that writers as diverse as Isak Dinesen, Italo Calvino, Vladimir Nabokov, Kurt Vonnegut and Margaret Atwood have voiced their admiration for Stevenson.

To some extent, Borges's reputation has also been contradictory. Never easy to categorise at the best of times, Borges described himself as 'a Conservative', but his opinions were, as befitted his sense of self, changeable. He was anti-Fascist, anti-Communist, anti-Marxist, anti-Peronist. When he worked at the Miguel Cané municipal library (for which he procured many great works of literature in the English language, books by Stevenson among them), he was unceremoniously relieved of his duties because of political remarks he made and was instead appointed poultry inspector (!); he resigned immediately. Borges's reputation within Argentina received a major boost when, in 1961, he was jointly awarded the Prix International with Samuel Beckett. This prize also lead to greater recognition internationally and Borges came to be treated with reverence on the world stage. In some places Borges was perceived to be something of a counter-cultural figure; his image (on a book) appears in the infamous Donald Cammell/Nicolas Roeg film *Performance*, which Cammell claims was influenced by the Argentine. Borges was later to stir up controversy by making strong statements against Marxist and Communist writers, and it is reasonable to acknowledge that Borges's divisive political viewpoints had a bearing on his standing as a writer. When, in July 1985, Borges attended a trial and discovered that 'gentlemen' with whom he had lunched were responsible for the kidnapping, the torture and the 'disappearing' of many thousands of innocent citizens, he had to leave the courtroom, feeling physically sick.

Many people know and are bemused by his assessment of the Falklands/Malvinas conflict ('Two bald men fighting over a comb') but less well known and less well understood is his declaration that General Galtieri and Margaret Thatcher were one and the same person.

Writers who evidence such a profound eccentricity of thought often make for compelling reading. Borges, like Stevenson, combines tenacity and magic to create narratives that alter the way we read the world, each other, and literature itself. One of Borges's wittiest, strangest and most unshakeable stories is 'Pierre Menard, Author of *Don Quixote*'. Melding fantasy, humour and erudition, the short essayistic tale concerns Menard's ambition to rewrite *Don Quixote*, word for word, from scratch. It's not about plagiarism, though, for the narrator considers Menard's version to be richer and more successful than the Cervantes 'original', because it can be contextualised in the light of everything that has happened in the world since 1605, and because the style of writing, while natural to Cervantes, is archaic and challenging to Menard. The meaning of a text, then, is dependent upon the reader and on the context of the work.

The Borges essay 'Kafka and His Precursors' considers a logical paradox with profound implications. (It is in relation to this essay that the term 'Borgesian conundrum' has arisen.) Borges analyses six elements, from Zeno's paradox to Robert Browning's poem 'Fears and Scruples', that apply to his developing theory around the question of whether the writer writes the story or the story writes him/her. Borges indicates that the six narratives – which all pre-date Kafka – have, in fact, been proleptically influenced by *him*. Borges declares:

> If I am not mistaken, the heterogeneous pieces I have enumerated resemble Kafka; if I am not mistaken, not all of them resemble each other. The second fact is the more significant. In each of these texts we find Kafka's idiosyncrasy to a greater or lesser degree, but if Kafka had never written a line, we would not perceive this quality; in other words, it would not exist . . . In the critics' vocabulary, the word 'precursor' is indispensable, but it should be cleansed of all connotation of polemics or rivalry. The fact is that every writer *creates* his own precursors. His work modifies our conception of the past, as it will modify the future.

We can take a similarly innovative approach to the works of Shakespeare, Dickinson, Borges himself . . . or Stevenson.

In this way, Borges and Bioy Casares inform, reorientate and revitalise our reading of Robert Louis Stevenson. Perhaps, thanks to them, we can encounter a richer Stevenson, one whose contribution to world literature is not easily dismissed but is, rather, more lastingly assured.

Kevin MacNeil
Stirling and Buenos Aires
June 2017

ESSAYS

Lay Morals

The following chapters of a projected treatise on Ethics were drafted at Edinburgh in the spring of 1879. They are unrevised, and must not be taken as representing, either as to matter or form, their author's final thoughts; but they contain much that is essentially characteristic of his mind.

* * * * *

We inhabit a dead ember swimming wide in the blank of space, dizzily spinning as it swims, and lighted up from several million miles away by a more horrible hell-fire than was ever conceived by the theological imagination. Yet the dead ember is a green, commodious dwelling-place; and the reverberation of this hell-fire ripens flower and fruit and mildly warms us on summer eves upon the lawn.

I

THE PROBLEM of education is twofold: first to know, and then to utter. Every one who lives any semblance of an inner life thinks more nobly and profoundly than he speaks; and the best of teachers can impart only broken images of the truth which they perceive. Speech which goes from one to another between two natures, and, what is worse, between two experiences, is doubly relative. The speaker buries his meaning; it is for the hearer to dig it up again; and all speech, written or spoken, is in a dead language until it finds a willing and prepared hearer. Such, moreover, is the complexity of life, that when we condescend upon details in our advice, we may be sure we condescend on error; and the best of education is to throw out some magnanimous hints. No man was ever so poor that he could express all he has in him by words, looks, or actions; his true knowledge is eternally incommunicable, for it is a knowledge of himself; and his best wisdom comes to him by no process of the mind, but in a supreme self-dictation, which keeps varying from hour to hour in its dictates with the variation of events and circumstances.

A few men of picked nature, full of faith, courage, and contempt for others, try earnestly to set forth as much as they can grasp of this inner law; but the vast majority, when they come to advise the young, must be content to retail certain doctrines which have been already retailed to them in their own youth. Every generation has to educate another which it has brought upon the stage. People who readily accept the responsibility of parentship, having very different matters in their eye, are apt to feel rueful when that responsibility falls due. What are they to tell the child about life and conduct, subjects on which they have themselves so few and such confused opinions? Indeed, I do not know; the least said, perhaps, the soonest mended; and yet the child keeps asking, and the parent must find some words to say in his own defence. Where does he find them? and what are they when found?

As a matter of experience, and in nine hundred and ninety-nine cases out of a thousand, he will instil into his wide-eyed brat three bad things: the terror of public opinion, and, flowing from that as a fountain, the desire of wealth and applause. Besides these, or what might be deduced as corollaries from these, he will teach not much else of any effective value: some dim notions of divinity, perhaps, and book-keeping, and how to walk through a quadrille.

But, you may tell me, the young people are taught to be Christians. It may be want of penetration, but I have not yet been able to perceive it. As an honest man, whatever we teach, and be it good or evil, it is not the doctrine of Christ. What he taught (and in this he is like all other teachers worthy of the name) was not a code of rules, but a ruling spirit; not truths, but a spirit of truth; not views, but a view. What he showed us was an attitude of mind. Towards the many considerations on which conduct is built, each man stands in a certain relation. He takes life on a certain principle. He has a compass in his spirit which points in a certain direction. It is the attitude, the relation, the point of the compass, that is the whole body and gist of what he has to teach us; in this, the details are comprehended; out of this the specific precepts issue, and by this, and this only, can they be explained and applied.

And thus, to learn aright from any teacher, we must first of all, like a historical artist, think ourselves into sympathy with his position and, in the technical phrase, create his character. A historian confronted with some ambiguous politician, or an actor charged with a part, have but one pre-occupation; they must search all round and upon every side, and grope for some central conception which is to explain and justify the most extreme details; until that is found, the politician is an enigma, or perhaps a quack, and the part a tissue of fustian sentiment and big words; but once that is found, all enters into a plan, a human nature appears, the politician or the stage-king is understood from point to point, from end to end. This is a degree of trouble which will be gladly taken by a very humble artist; but not even the terror of eternal fire can teach a business man to bend his imagination to such athletic efforts. Yet without this, all is vain; until we understand the whole, we shall understand none of the parts; and otherwise we have no more than broken images and scattered words; the meaning remains buried; and the language in which our prophet speaks to us is a dead language in our ears.

Take a few of Christ's sayings and compare them with our current doctrines.

'Ye cannot,' he says, 'serve God and Mammon.' Cannot? And our whole system is to teach us how we can!

'The children of this world are wiser in their generation than the children of light.' Are they? I had been led to understand the reverse: that the Christian merchant, for example, prospered exceedingly in his affairs; that honesty was the best policy; that an author of repute had written a conclusive treatise 'How to make the best of both worlds.' Of both worlds indeed! Which am I to believe then—Christ or the author of repute?

'Take no thought for the morrow.' Ask the Successful Merchant; interrogate your own heart; and you will have to admit that this is not only a silly but an immoral position. All we believe, all we hope, all we honour in ourselves or our contemporaries, stands condemned in this one sentence, or, if you take the other view, condemns the sentence as unwise and inhumane. We are not then of the 'same mind that was in Christ.' We disagree with Christ. Either Christ meant nothing, or else he or we must be in the wrong. Well, says Thoreau, speaking of some texts from the New Testament, and finding a strange echo of another style which the reader may recognise: 'Let but one of these sentences be rightly read from any pulpit in the land, and there would not be left one stone of that meeting-house upon another.'

It may be objected that these are what are called 'hard sayings'; and that a man, or an education, may be very sufficiently Christian although it leave some of these sayings upon one side. But this is a very gross delusion. Although truth is difficult to state, it is both easy and agreeable to receive, and the mind runs out to meet it ere the phrase be done. The universe, in relation to what any man can say of it, is plain, patent and staringly comprehensible. In itself, it is a great and travailing ocean, unsounded, unvoyageable, an eternal mystery to man; or, let us say, it is a monstrous and impassable mountain, one side of which, and a few near slopes and foothills, we can dimly study with these mortal eyes. But what any man can say of it, even in his highest utterance, must have relation to this little and plain corner, which is no less visible to us than to him. We are looking on the same map; it will go hard if we cannot follow the demonstration. The longest and most abstruse flight of a philosopher becomes clear and shallow, in the flash of a moment, when we suddenly perceive the aspect and drift of his intention. The longest argument is but a finger pointed; once we get our own finger rightly parallel, and we see what the man meant, whether it be a new star or an old street-lamp. And briefly, if a saying is hard to understand, it is because we are thinking of something else.

But to be a true disciple is to think of the same things as our prophet, and to think of different things in the same order. To be of the same mind with another is to see all things in the same perspective; it is not to agree in a few indifferent matters near at hand and not much debated; it is to follow him in his farthest flights, to see the force of his hyperboles, to stand so exactly in the centre of his vision that whatever he may express, your eyes will light at once on the original, that whatever he may see to declare, your mind will at once accept. You do not belong to the school of any philosopher, because you agree with him that theft is, on the whole, objectionable, or that the sun is overhead at noon. It is by the hard sayings that disciple-ship is tested. We are all agreed about the middling and indifferent parts of knowledge and morality; even the most soaring spirits too often take them tamely upon trust. But the man, the philosopher or the moralist, does not stand upon these chance adhesions; and the purpose of any system looks towards those extreme points where it steps valiantly beyond tradition and returns with some covert hint of things outside. Then only can you be certain that the words are not words of course, nor mere echoes of the past; then only are you sure that if he be indicating anything at all, it is a star and not a street-lamp; then only do you touch the heart of the mystery, since it was for these that the author wrote his book.

Now, every now and then, and indeed surprisingly often, Christ finds a word that transcends all common-place morality; every now and then he quits the beaten track to pioneer the unexpressed, and throws out a pregnant and magnanimous hyperbole; for it is only by some bold poetry of thought that men can be strung up above the level of everyday conceptions to take a broader look upon experience or accept some higher principle of conduct. To a man who is of the same mind that was in Christ, who stands at some centre not too far from his, and looks at the world and conduct from some not dissimilar or, at least, not opposing attitude—or, shortly, to a man who is of Christ's philosophy—every such saying should come home with a thrill of joy and corroboration; he should feel each one below his feet as another sure foundation in the flux of time and chance; each should be another proof that in the torrent of the years and generations, where doctrines and great armaments and empires are swept away and swallowed, he stands immovable, holding by the eternal stars. But alas! at this juncture of the ages it is not so with us; on each and every such occasion our whole fellowship of Christians falls back in disapproving wonder and implicitly denies the saying. Christians! the farce is impudently broad. Let us stand up in the sight of Heaven and confess. The ethics that we hold are those of Benjamin Franklin. Honesty is the best policy, is perhaps a hard saying; it is certainly one by which a wise man of these days will not too curiously direct his steps; but I think it shows a glimmer of meaning to even our most dimmed intelligences; I think we perceive a principle behind it; I think, without hyperbole, we are of the same mind that was in Benjamin Franklin.

II

BUT, I may be told, we teach the ten commandments, where a world of morals lies condensed, the very pith and epitome of all ethics and religion; and a young man with these precepts engraved upon his mind must follow after profit with some conscience and Christianity of method. A man cannot go very far astray who neither dishonours his parents, nor kills, nor commits adultery, nor steals, nor bears false witness; for these things, rightly thought out, cover a vast field of duty.

Alas! what is a precept? It is at best an illustration; it is case law at the best which can be learned by precept. The letter is not only dead, but killing; the spirit which underlies, and cannot be uttered, alone is true and helpful. This is trite to sickness; but familiarity has a cunning disenchantment; in a day or two she can steal all beauty from the mountain tops; and the most startling words begin to fall dead upon the ear after several repetitions. If you see a thing too often, you no longer see it; if you hear a thing too often, you no longer hear it. Our attention requires to be surprised; and to carry a fort by assault, or to gain a thoughtful hearing from the ruck of mankind, are feats of about an equal difficulty and must be tried by not dissimilar means. The whole Bible has thus lost its message for the common run of hearers; it has become mere words of course; and the parson may bawl himself scarlet and beat the pulpit like a thing possessed, but his hearers will continue to nod; they are strangely at peace, they know all he has to say; ring the old bell as you choose, it is still the old bell and it cannot startle their composure. And so with this byword about the letter and the spirit. It is quite true, no doubt; but it has no meaning in the world to any man of us. Alas! it has just this meaning, and neither more nor less: that while the spirit is true, the letter is eternally false.

The shadow of a great oak lies abroad upon the ground at noon, perfect, clear, and stable like the earth. But let a man set himself to mark out the boundary with cords and pegs, and were he never so nimble and never so exact, what with the multiplicity of the leaves and the progression of the shadow as it flees before the travelling sun, long ere he has made the circuit the whole figure will have changed. Life may be compared, not to a single tree, but to a great and complicated forest; circumstance is more swiftly changing than a shadow, language much more inexact than the tools of a surveyor; from day to day the trees fall and are renewed; the very essences are fleeting as we look; and the whole world of leaves is swinging tempest-tossed among the winds of time. Look now for your shadows. O man of formulae, is this a place for you? Have you fitted the spirit to a single case? Alas, in the cycle of the ages when shall such another be proposed for the judgment of man? Now when the sun shines and the winds blow, the wood is filled with an innumerable multitude of shadows, tumultuously tossed and changing; and at every gust the whole carpet leaps and becomes new. Can you or your heart say more?

Look back now, for a moment, on your own brief experience of life; and although you lived it feelingly in your own person, and had every step of conduct burned in by pains and joys upon your memory, tell me what definite lesson does experience hand on from youth to manhood, or from both to age? The settled tenor which first strikes the eye is but the shadow of a delusion. This is gone; that never truly was; and you yourself are altered beyond recognition. Times and men and circumstances change about your changing character, with a speed of which no earthly hurricane affords an image. What was the best yesterday, is it still the best in this changed theatre of a tomorrow? Will your own Past truly guide you in your own violent and unexpected Future? And if this be questionable, with what humble, with what hopeless eyes, should we not watch other men driving beside us on their unknown careers, seeing with unlike eyes, impelled by different gales, doing and suffering in another sphere of things?

And as the authentic clue to such a labyrinth and change of scene, do you offer me these two score words? these five bald prohibitions? For the moral precepts are no more than five; the first four deal rather with matters of observance than of conduct; the tenth, Thou shalt not covet, stands upon another basis, and shall be spoken of ere long. The Jews, to whom they were first given, in the course of years began to find these precepts insufficient; and made an addition of no less than six hundred and fifty others! They hoped to make a pocket-book of reference on morals, which should stand to life in some such relation, say, as Hoyle stands in to the scientific game of whist. The comparison is just, and condemns the design; for those who play by rule will never be more than tolerable players; and you and I would like to play our game in life to the noblest and the most divine advantage. Yet if the Jews took a petty and huckstering view of conduct, what view do we take ourselves, who callously leave youth to go forth into the enchanted forest, full of spells and dire chimeras, with no guidance more complete than is afforded by these five precepts?

Honour thy father and thy mother. Yes, but does that mean to obey? and if so, how long and how far? Thou shall not kill. Yet the very intention and purport of the prohibition may be best fulfilled by killing. Thou shall not commit adultery. But some of the ugliest adulteries are committed in the bed of marriage and under the sanction of religion and law. Thou shalt not bear false witness. How? by speech or by silence also? or even by a smile? Thou shalt not steal. Ah, that indeed! But what is to steal?

To steal? It is another word to be construed; and who is to be our guide? The police will give us one construction, leaving the word only that least minimum of meaning without which society would fall in pieces; but surely we must take some higher sense than this; surely we hope more than a bare subsistence for mankind; surely we wish mankind to prosper and go on from strength to strength, and ourselves to live rightly in the eye of some more exacting potentate than a policeman. The approval or the disapproval of the police must be eternally indifferent to a man who is both valorous and good. There is extreme discomfort, but no shame, in the condemnation of the law. The law represents that modicum of morality which can be squeezed out of the ruck of mankind; but what is that to me, who aim higher and seek to be my own more stringent judge? I observe with pleasure that no brave man has ever given a rush for such considerations. The Japanese have a nobler and more sentimental feeling for this social bond into which we all are born when we come

into the world, and whose comforts and protection we all indiffer-
ently share throughout our lives:—but even to them, no more than
to our Western saints and heroes, does the law of the state supersede
the higher law of duty. Without hesitation and without remorse,
they transgress the stiffest enactments rather than abstain from
doing right. But the accidental superior duty being thus fulfilled,
they at once return in allegiance to the common duty of all citizens;
and hasten to denounce themselves; and value at an equal rate their
just crime and their equally just submission to its punishment.

The evading of the police will not long satisfy an active conscience
or a thoughtful head. But to show you how one or the other may
trouble a man, and what a vast extent of frontier is left unridden by
this invaluable eighth commandment, let me tell you a few pages out
of a young man's life.

He was a friend of mine; a young man like others; generous,
flighty, as variable as youth itself, but always with some high motions
and on the search for higher thoughts of life. I should tell you at once
that he thoroughly agrees with the eighth commandment. But he got
hold of some unsettling works, the New Testament among others,
and this loosened his views of life and led him into many perplexities. As he was the son of a man in a certain position, and well off,
my friend had enjoyed from the first the advantages of education,
nay, he had been kept alive through a sickly childhood by constant
watchfulness, comforts, and change of air; for all of which he was
indebted to his father's wealth.

At college he met other lads more diligent than himself, who
followed the plough in summer-time to pay their college fees in
winter; and this inequality struck him with some force. He was at
that age of a conversible temper, and insatiably curious in the
aspects of life; and he spent much of his time scraping acquaintance
with all classes of man—and woman-kind. In this way he came
upon many depressed ambitions, and many intelligences stunted
for want of opportunity; and this also struck him. He began to
perceive that life was a handicap upon strange, wrong-sided principles; and not, as he had been told, a fair and equal race. He began to
tremble that he himself had been unjustly favoured, when he saw all
the avenues of wealth, and power, and comfort closed against so

many of his superiors and equals, and held unwearyingly open before so idle, so desultory, and so dissolute a being as himself. There sat a youth beside him on the college benches, who had only one shirt to his back, and, at intervals sufficiently far apart, must stay at home to have it washed. It was my friend's principle to stay away as often as he dared; for I fear he was no friend to learning. But there was something that came home to him sharply, in this fellow who had to give over study till his shirt was washed, and the scores of others who had never an opportunity at all. If one of these could take his place, he thought; and the thought tore away a bandage from his eyes. He was eaten by the shame of his discoveries, and despised himself as an unworthy favourite and a creature of the back-stairs of Fortune. He could no longer see without confusion one of these brave young fellows battling up-hill against adversity. Had he not filched that fellow's birthright? At best was he not coldly profiting by the injustice of society, and greedily devouring stolen goods? The money, indeed, belonged to his father, who had worked, and thought, and given up his liberty to earn it; but by what justice could the money belong to my friend, who had, as yet, done nothing but help to squander it? A more sturdy honesty, joined to a more even and impartial temperament, would have drawn from these considerations a new force of industry, that this equivocal position might be brought as swiftly as possible to an end, and some good services to mankind justify the appropriation of expense. It was not so with my friend, who was only unsettled and discouraged, and filled full of that trumpeting anger with which young men regard injustices in the first blush of youth; although in a few years they will tamely acquiesce in their existence, and knowingly profit by their complications. Yet all this while he suffered many indignant pangs. And once, when he put on his boots, like any other unripe donkey, to run away from home, it was his best consolation that he was now, at a single plunge, to free himself from the responsibility of this wealth that was not his, and do battle equally against his fellows in the warfare of life.

Some time after this, falling into ill-health, he was sent at great expense to a more favourable climate; and then I think his perplexities were thickest. When he thought of all the other young men of singular promise, upright, good, the prop of families, who must remain at home to die, and with all their possibilities be lost to life and mankind; and how he, by one more unmerited favour, was chosen out from all these others to survive; he felt as if there were no life, no labour, no devotion of soul and body, that could repay and justify these partialities. A religious lady, to whom he communicated these reflections, could see no force in them whatever. 'It was God's will,' said she. But he knew it was by God's will that Joan of Arc was burnt at Rouen, which cleared neither Bedford nor Bishop Cauchon; and again, by God's will that Christ was crucified outside Jerusalem, which excused neither the rancour of the priests nor the timidity of Pilate. He knew, moreover, that although the possibility of this favour he was now enjoying issued from his circumstances, its acceptance was the act of his own will; and he had accepted it greedily, longing for rest and sunshine.

And hence this allegation of God's providence did little to relieve his scruples. I promise you he had a very troubled mind. And I would not laugh if I were you, though while he was thus making mountains out of what you think molehills, he were still (as perhaps he was) contentedly practising many other things that to you seem black as Hell. Every man is his own judge and mountain-guide through life. There is an old story of a mote and a beam, apparently not true, but worthy perhaps of some consideration. I should, if I were you, give some consideration to these scruples of his, and if I were he, I should do the like by yours; for it is not unlikely that there may be something under both. In the meantime you must hear how my friend acted. Like many invalids, he supposed that he would die. Now, should he die, he saw no means of repaying this huge loan which, by the hands of his father, mankind had advanced him for his sickness. In that case it would be lost money. So he determined that the advance should be as small as possible; and, so long as he continued to doubt his recovery, lived in an upper room, and grudged himself all but necessaries. But so soon as he began to perceive a change for the better, he felt justified in spending more freely, to speed and brighten his return to health, and trusted in the future to lend a help to mankind, as mankind, out of its treasury, had lent a help to him.

I do not say but that my friend was a little too curious and partial in his view; nor thought too much of himself and too little of his parents; but I do say that here are some scruples which tormented my friend in his youth, and still, perhaps, at odd times give him a prick in the midst of his enjoyments, and which after all have some foundation in justice, and point, in their confused way, to some more honourable honesty within the reach of man. And at least, is not this an unusual gloss upon the eighth commandment? And what sort of comfort, guidance, or illumination did that precept afford my friend throughout these contentions? 'Thou shalt not steal.' With all my heart! But am I stealing?

The truly quaint materialism of our view of life disables us from pursuing any transaction to an end. You can make no one understand that his bargain is anything more than a bargain, whereas in point of fact it is a link in the policy of mankind, and either a good or an evil to the world. We have a sort of blindness which prevents us from seeing anything but sovereigns. If one man agrees to give another so many shillings for so many hours' work, and then wilfully gives him a certain proportion of the price in bad money and only the remainder in good, we can see with half an eye that this man is a thief. But if the other spends a certain proportion of the hours in smoking a pipe of tobacco, and a certain other proportion in looking at the sky, or the clock, or trying to recall an air, or in meditation on his own past adventures, and only the remainder in downright work such as he is paid to do, is he, because the theft is one of time and not of money,—is he any the less a thief? The one gave a bad shilling, the other an imperfect hour; but both broke the bargain, and each is a thief. In piecework, which is what most of us do, the case is none the less plain for being even less material. If you forge a bad knife, you have wasted some of mankind's iron, and then, with unrivalled cynicism, you pocket some of mankind's money for your trouble. Is there any man so blind who cannot see that this is theft? Again, if you carelessly cultivate a farm, you have been playing fast and loose with mankind's resources against hunger; there will be less bread in consequence, and for lack of that bread somebody will die next winter: a grim consideration. And you must not hope to shuffle out of blame because you got less money for your less quantity of bread; for although a theft be partly punished, it is none the less a theft for that. You took the farm against competitors; there were others ready to shoulder the responsibility and be answerable for the tale of loaves; but it was you who took it. By the act you came under a tacit bargain with mankind to cultivate that farm with your best endeavour; you were under no superintendence, you were on parole; and you have broke your bargain, and to all who look closely, and yourself among the rest if you have moral eyesight, you are a thief. Or take the case of men of letters. Every piece of work which is not as good as you can make it, which you have palmed off imperfect, meagrely thought, niggardly in execution, upon mankind who is your paymaster on parole and in a sense your pupil, every hasty or slovenly or untrue performance, should rise up against you in the court of your own heart and condemn you for a thief. Have you a salary? If you trifle with your health, and so render yourself less capable for duty, and still touch, and still greedily pocket the emolument—what are you but a thief? Have you double accounts?

Do you by any time-honoured juggle, deceit, or ambiguous process, gain more from those who deal with you than it you were bargaining and dealing face to face in front of God?—what are you but a thief? Lastly, if you fill an office, or produce an article, which, in your heart of hearts, you think a delusion and a fraud upon mankind, and still draw your salary and go through the sham manoeuvres of this office, or still book your profits and keep on flooding the world with these injurious goods?—though you were old, and bald, and the first at church, and a baronet, what are you but a thief? These may seem hard words and mere curiosities of the intellect, in an age when the spirit of honesty is so sparingly cultivated that all business is conducted upon lies and so-called customs of the trade, that not a man bestows two thoughts on the utility or honourableness of his pursuit. I would say less if I thought less. But looking to my own reason and the right of things, I can only avow that I am a thief myself, and that I passionately suspect my neighbours of the same guilt.

Where did you hear that it was easy to be honest? Do you find that in your Bible? Easy! It is easy to be an ass and follow the multitude like a blind, besotted bull in a stampede; and that, I am well aware, is what you and Mrs Grundy mean by being honest. But it will not bear the stress of time nor the scrutiny of conscience. Even before the lowest of all tribunals,—before a court of law, whose business it is, not to keep men right, or within a thousand miles of right, but to withhold them from going so tragically wrong that they will pull down the whole jointed fabric of society by their misdeeds— even before a court of law, as we begin to see in these last days, our easy view of following at each other's tails, alike to good and evil, is beginning to be reproved and punished, and declared no honesty at all, but open theft and swindling; and simpletons who have gone on through life with a quiet conscience may learn suddenly, from the lips of a judge, that the custom of the trade may be a custom of the Devil. You thought it was easy to be honest. Did you think it was easy to be just and kind and truthful? Did you think the whole duty of aspiring man was as simple as a horn-pipe? and you could walk through life like a gentleman and a hero, with no more concern than it takes to go to church or to address a circular? And yet all this time you had the eighth commandment! and, what makes it richer, you would not have broken it for the world!

The truth is, that these commandments by themselves are of little use in private judgment. If compression is what you want, you have their whole spirit compressed into the golden rule; and yet there expressed with more significance, since the law is there spiritually and not materially stated. And in truth, four out of these ten commands, from the sixth to the ninth, are rather legal than ethical. The police-court is their proper home. A magistrate cannot tell whether you love your neighbour as yourself, but he can tell more or less whether you have murdered, or stolen, or committed adultery, or held up your hand and testified to that which was not; and these things, for rough practical tests, are as good as can be found. And perhaps, therefore, the best condensation of the Jewish moral law is in the maxims of the priests, 'neminem laedere' and 'suum cuique tribuere.' But all this granted, it becomes only the more plain that they are inadequate in the sphere of personal morality; that while they tell the magistrate roughly when to punish, they can never direct an anxious sinner what to do.

Only Polonius, or the like solemn sort of ass, can offer us a succinct proverb by way of advice, and not burst out blushing in our faces. We grant them one and all and for all that they are worth; it is something above and beyond that we desire. Christ was in general a great enemy to such a way of teaching; we rarely find him meddling with any of these plump commands but it was to open them out, and lift his hearers from the letter to the spirit. For morals are a personal affair; in the war of righteousness every man fights for his own hand; all the six hundred precepts of the Mishna cannot shake my private judgment; my magistracy of myself is an indefeasible charge, and my decisions absolute for the time and case. The moralist is not a judge of appeal, but an advocate who pleads at my tribunal. He has to show not the law, but that the law applies. Can he convince me? then he gains the cause. And thus you find Christ giving various counsels to varying people, and often jealously careful to avoid definite precept. Is he asked, for example, to divide a heritage? He refuses: and the best advice that he will offer is but a paraphrase of that tenth commandment which figures so strangely among the rest. Take heed, and beware of covetousness. If you complain that this is vague, I have failed to carry you along with me in my argument.

For no definite precept can be more than an illustration, though its truth were resplendent like the sun, and it was announced from Heaven by the voice of God. And life is so intricate and changing, that perhaps not twenty times, or perhaps not twice in the ages, shall we find that nice consent of circumstances to which alone it can apply.

III

ALTHOUGH THE world and life have in a sense become commonplace to our experience, it is but in an external torpor; the true sentiment slumbers within us; and we have but to reflect on ourselves or our surroundings to rekindle our astonishment. No length of habit can blunt our first surprise. Of the world I have but little to say in this connection; a few strokes shall suffice. We inhabit a dead ember swimming wide in the blank of space, dizzily spinning as it swims, and lighted up from several million miles away by a more horrible hell-fire than was ever conceived by the theological imagination. Yet the dead ember is a green, commodious dwelling-place; and the reverberation of this hell-fire ripens flower and fruit and mildly warms us on summer eves upon the lawn. Far off on all hands other dead embers, other flaming suns, wheel and race in the apparent void; the nearest is out of call, the farthest so far that the heart sickens in the effort to conceive the distance. Shipwrecked seamen on the deep, though they bestride but the truncheon of a boom, are safe and near at home compared with mankind on its bullet. Even to us who have known no other, it seems a strange, if not an appalling, place of residence.

But far stranger is the resident, man, a creature compact of wonders that, after centuries of custom, is still wonderful to himself. He inhabits a body which he is continually outliving, discarding and renewing. Food and sleep, by an unknown alchemy, restore his spirits and the freshness of his countenance. Hair grows on him like grass; his eyes, his brain, his sinews, thirst for action; he joys to see and touch and hear, to partake the sun and wind, to sit down and intently ponder on his astonishing attributes and situation, to rise up and run, to perform the strange and revolting round of physical functions. The sight of a flower, the note of a bird, will often move him deeply; yet he looks unconcerned on the impassable distances and portentous bonfires of the universe. He comprehends, he designs, he tames nature, rides the sea, ploughs, climbs the air in a balloon, makes vast inquiries, begins interminable labours, joins himself into federations and populous cities, spends his days to deliver the ends of the earth or to benefit unborn posterity; and yet knows himself for a piece of unsurpassed fragility and the creature of a few days. His sight, which conducts him, which takes notice of the farthest stars, which is miraculous in every way and a thing defying explanation or belief, is yet lodged in a piece of jelly, and can be extinguished with a touch. His heart, which all through life so indomitably, so athletically labours, is but a capsule, and may be stopped with a pin. His whole body, for all its savage energies, its leaping and its winged desires, may yet be tamed and conquered by a draught of air or a sprinkling of cold dew. What he calls death, which is the seeming arrest of everything, and the ruin and hateful transformation of the visible body, lies in wait for him outwardly in a thousand accidents, and grows up in secret diseases from within. He is still learning to be a man when his faculties are already beginning to decline; he has not yet understood himself or his position before he inevitably dies. And yet this mad, chimerical creature can take no thought of his last end, lives as though he were eternal, plunges with his vulnerable body into the shock of war, and daily affronts death with unconcern. He cannot take a step without pain or pleasure. His life is a tissue of sensations, which he distinguishes as they seem to come more directly from himself or his surroundings. He is conscious of himself as a joyer or a sufferer, as that which craves, chooses, and is satisfied; conscious of his surroundings as it were of an inexhaustible purveyor, the source of aspects, inspirations, wonders, cruel knocks and transporting caresses. Thus he goes on his way, stumbling among delights and agonies.

Matter is a far-fetched theory, and materialism is without a root in man. To him everything is important in the degree to which it moves him. The telegraph wires and posts, the electricity speeding from clerk to clerk, the clerks, the glad or sorrowful import of the message, and the paper on which it is finally brought to him at home, are all equally facts, all equally exist for man. A word or a thought can wound him as acutely as a knife of steel. If he thinks he is loved, he will rise up and glory to himself, although he be in a distant land and short of necessary bread. Does he think he is not loved?—he may have the woman at his beck, and there is not a joy for him in all the world. Indeed, if we are to make any account of this figment of reason, the distinction between material and immaterial, we shall conclude that the life of each man as an individual is immaterial, although the continuation and prospects of mankind as a race turn upon material conditions. The physical business of each man's body is transacted for him; like a sybarite, he has attentive valets in his own viscera; he breathes, he sweats, he digests without an effort, or so much as a consenting volition; for the most part he even eats, not with a wakeful consciousness, but as it were between two thoughts. His life is centred among other and more important considerations; touch him in his honour or his love, creatures of the imagination which attach him to mankind or to an individual man or woman; cross him in his piety which connects his soul with Heaven; and he turns from his food, he loathes his breath, and with a magnanimous emotion cuts the knots of his existence and frees himself at a blow from the web of pains and pleasures.

It follows that man is twofold at least; that he is not a rounded and autonomous empire; but that in the same body with him there dwell other powers tributary but independent. If I now behold one walking in a garden, curiously coloured and illuminated by the sun, digesting his food with elaborate chemistry, breathing, circulating blood, directing himself by the sight of his eyes, accommodating his body by a thousand delicate balancings to the wind and the uneven surface of the path, and all the time, perhaps, with his mind engaged about America, or the dog-star, or the attributes of God—what am I to say, or how am I to describe the thing I see? Is that truly a man, in the rigorous meaning of the word? or is it not a man and something else? What, then, are we to count the centre-bit and axle of a being so variously compounded? It is a question much debated. Some read his history in a certain intricacy of nerve and the success of successive digestions; others find him an exiled piece of Heaven blown upon and determined by the breath of God; and both schools of theorists will scream like scalded children at a word of doubt. Yet either of these views, however plausible, is beside the question; either may be right; and I care not; I ask a more particular answer, and to a more immediate point. What is the man? There is Something that was before hunger and that remains behind after a meal. It may or may not be engaged in any given act or passion, but when it is, it changes, heightens, and sanctifies. Thus it is not engaged in lust, where satisfaction ends the chapter; and it is engaged in love, where no satisfaction can blunt the edge of the desire, and where age, sickness, or alienation may deface what was desirable without diminishing the sentiment. This something, which is the man, is a permanence which abides through the vicissitudes of passion, now overwhelmed and now triumphant, now unconscious of itself in the immediate distress of appetite or pain, now rising unclouded above all. So, to the man, his own central self fades and grows clear again amid the tumult of the senses, like a revolving Pharos in the night. It is forgotten; it is hid, it seems, for ever; and yet in the next calm hour he shall behold himself once more, shining and unmoved among changes and storm.

Mankind, in the sense of the creeping mass that is born and eats, that generates and dies, is but the aggregate of the outer and lower sides of man. This inner consciousness, this lantern alternately obscured and shining, to and by which the individual exists and must order his conduct, is something special to himself and not common to the race. His joys delight, his sorrows wound him, according as this is interested or indifferent in the affair; according as they arise in an imperial war or in a broil conducted by the tributary chieftains of the mind. He may lose all, and this not suffer; he may lose what is materially a trifle, and this leap in his bosom with a cruel pang. I do not speak of it to hardened theorists: the living man knows keenly what it is I mean.

'Perceive at last that thou hast in thee something better and more divine than the things which cause the various effects, and, as it were, pull thee by the strings. What is that now in thy mind? is it fear, or suspicion, or desire, or anything of that kind?' Thus far Marcus Aurelius, in one of the most notable passages in any book. Here is a question worthy to be answered. What is in thy mind? What is the utterance of your inmost self when, in a quiet hour, it can be heard intelligibly? It is something beyond the compass of your thinking, inasmuch as it is yourself; but is it not of a higher spirit than you had dreamed betweenwhiles, and erect above all base considerations? This soul seems hardly touched with our infirmities; we can find in it certainly no fear, suspicion, or desire; we are only conscious—and that as though we read it in the eyes of someone else—of a great and unqualified readiness. A readiness to what? to pass over and look beyond the objects of desire and fear, for something else. And this something else? this something which is apart from desire and fear, to which all the kingdoms of the world and the immediate death of the body are alike indifferent and beside the point, and which yet regards conduct—by what name are we to call it? It may be the love of God; or it may be an inherited (and certainly well concealed) instinct to preserve self and propagate the race; I am not, for the moment, averse to either theory; but it will save time to call it righteousness. By so doing I intend no subterfuge to beg a question; I am indeed ready, and more than willing, to accept the rigid consequence, and lay aside, as far as the treachery of the reason will permit, all former meanings attached to the word righteousness. What is right is that for which a man's central self is ever ready to sacrifice immediate or distant interests; what is wrong is what the central self discards or rejects as incompatible with the fixed design of righteousness.

To make this admission is to lay aside all hope of definition. That which is right upon this theory is intimately dictated to each man by himself, but can never be rigorously set forth in language, and never, above all, imposed upon another. The conscience has, then, a vision like that of the eyes, which is incommunicable, and for the most part illuminates none but its possessor. When many people perceive the same or any cognate facts, they agree upon a word as symbol; and hence we have such words as tree, star, love, honour, or death; hence also we have this word right, which, like the others, we all understand, most of us understand differently, and none can express succinctly otherwise. Yet even on the straitest view, we can make some steps towards comprehension of our own superior thoughts. For it is an incredible and most bewildering fact that a man, through life, is on variable terms with himself; he is aware of tiffs and reconciliations; the intimacy is at times almost suspended, at times it is renewed again with joy. As we said before, his inner self or soul appears to him by successive revelations, and is frequently obscured.

It is from a study of these alternations that we can alone hope to discover, even dimly, what seems right and what seems wrong to this veiled prophet of ourself.

All that is in the man in the larger sense, what we call impression as well as what we call intuition, so far as my argument looks, we must accept. It is not wrong to desire food, or exercise, or beautiful surroundings, or the love of sex, or interest which is the food of the mind. All these are craved; all these should be craved; to none of these in itself does the soul demur; where there comes an undeniable want, we recognise a demand of nature. Yet we know that these natural demands may be superseded; for the demands which are common to mankind make but a shadowy consideration in comparison to the demands of the individual soul. Food is almost the first prerequisite; and yet a high character will go without food to the ruin and death of the body rather than gain it in a manner which the spirit disavows. Pascal laid aside mathematics; Origen doctored his body with a knife; every day someone is thus mortifying his dearest interests and desires, and, in Christ's words, entering maim into the Kingdom of Heaven. This is to supersede the lesser and less harmonious affections by renunciation; and though by this ascetic path we may get to Heaven, we cannot get thither a whole and perfect man. But there is another way, to supersede them by reconciliation, in which the soul and all the faculties and senses pursue a common route and share in one desire. Thus, man is tormented by a very imperious physical desire; it spoils his rest, it is not to be denied; the doctors will tell you, not I, how it is a physical need, like the want of food or slumber. In the satisfaction of this desire, as it first appears, the soul sparingly takes part; nay, it oft unsparingly regrets and disapproves the satisfaction. But let the man learn to love a woman as far as he is capable of love; and for this random affection of the body there is substituted a steady determination, a consent of all his powers and faculties, which supersedes, adopts, and commands the other.

The desire survives, strengthened, perhaps, but taught obedience and changed in scope and character. Life is no longer a tale of betrayals and regrets; for the man now lives as a whole; his consciousness now moves on uninterrupted like a river; through all the extremes and ups and downs of passion, he remains approvingly conscious of himself.

Now to me, this seems a type of that rightness which the soul demands. It demands that we shall not live alternately with our opposing tendencies in continual see-saw of passion and disgust, but seek some path on which the tendencies shall no longer oppose, but serve each other to a common end. It demands that we shall not pursue broken ends, but great and comprehensive purposes, in which soul and body may unite like notes in a harmonious chord. That were indeed a way of peace and pleasure, that were indeed a heaven upon earth. It does not demand, however, or, to speak in measure, it does not demand of me, that I should starve my appetites for no purpose under heaven but as a purpose in itself; or, in a weak despair, pluck out the eye that I have not yet learned to guide and enjoy with wisdom. The soul demands unity of purpose, not the dismemberment of man; it seeks to roll up all his strength and sweetness, all his passion and wisdom, into one, and make of him a perfect man exulting in perfection. To conclude ascetically is to give up, and not to solve, the problem. The ascetic and the creeping hog, although they are at different poles, have equally failed in life. The one has sacrificed his crew; the other brings back his seamen in a cock-boat, and has lost the ship. I believe there are not many sea-captains who would plume themselves on either result as a success.

But if it is righteousness thus to fuse together our divisive impulses and march with one mind through life, there is plainly one thing more unrighteous than all others, and one declension which is irretrievable and draws on the rest. And this is to lose consciousness of oneself. In the best of times, it is but by flashes, when our whole nature is clear, strong and conscious, and events conspire to leave us free, that we enjoy communion with our soul. At the worst, we are so fallen and passive that we may say shortly we have none. An arctic torpor seizes upon men.

Although built of nerves, and set adrift in a stimulating world, they develop a tendency to go bodily to sleep; consciousness becomes engrossed among the reflex and mechanical parts of life; and soon loses both the will and power to look higher considerations in the face. This is ruin; this is the last failure in life; this is temporal damnation, damnation on the spot and without the form of judgment. 'What shall it profit a man if he gain the whole world and lose himself?'

It is to keep a man awake, to keep him alive to his own soul and its fixed design of righteousness, that the better part of moral and religious education is directed; not only that of words and doctors, but the sharp ferule of calamity under which we are all God's scholars till we die. If, as teachers, we are to say anything to the purpose, we must say what will remind the pupil of his soul; we must speak that soul's dialect; we must talk of life and conduct as his soul would have him think of them. If, from some conformity between us and the pupil, or perhaps among all men, we do in truth speak in such a dialect and express such views, beyond question we shall touch in him a spring; beyond question he will recognise the dialect as one that he himself has spoken in his better hours; beyond question he will cry, 'I had forgotten, but now I remember; I too have eyes, and I had forgot to use them! I too have a soul of my own, arrogantly upright, and to that I will listen and conform.' In short, say to him anything that he has once thought, or been upon the point of thinking, or show him any view of life that he has once clearly seen, or been upon the point of clearly seeing; and you have done your part and may leave him to complete the education for himself.

Now, the view taught at the present time seems to me to want greatness; and the dialect in which alone it can be intelligibly uttered is not the dialect of my soul. It is a sort of postponement of life; nothing quite is, but something different is to be; we are to keep our eyes upon the indirect from the cradle to the grave. We are to regulate our conduct not by desire, but by a politic eye upon the future; and to value acts as they will bring us money or good opinion; as they will bring us, in one word, profit. We must be what is called respectable, and offend no one by our carriage; it will not do to make oneself conspicuous—who knows? even in virtue? says the Christian parent! And we must be what is called prudent and make money; not only because it is pleasant to have money, but because that also is a part of respectability, and we cannot hope to be received in society without decent possessions. Received in society! as if that were the Kingdom of Heaven! There is dear

Mr So-and-so;—look at him!—so much respected—so much looked up to—quite the Christian merchant! And we must cut our conduct as strictly as possible after the pattern of Mr So-and-so; and lay our whole lives to make money and be strictly decent. Besides these holy injunctions, which form by far the greater part of a youth's training in our Christian homes, there are at least two other doctrines. We are to live just now as well as we can, but scrape at last into Heaven, where we shall be good. We are to worry through the week in a lay, disreputable way, but, to make matters square, live a different life on Sunday.

The train of thought we have been following gives us a key to all these positions, without stepping aside to justify them on their own ground. It is because we have been disgusted fifty times with physical squalls, and fifty times torn between conflicting impulses, that we teach people this indirect and tactical procedure in life, and to judge by remote consequences instead of the immediate face of things. The very desire to act as our own souls would have us, coupled with a pathetic disbelief in ourselves, moves us to follow the example of others; perhaps, who knows? they may be on the right track; and the more our patterns are in number, the better seems the chance; until, if we be acting in concert with a whole civilised nation, there are surely a majority of chances that we must be acting right. And again, how true it is that we can never behave as we wish in this tormented sphere, and can only aspire to different and more favourable circumstances, in order to stand out and be ourselves wholly and rightly! And yet once more, if in the hurry and pressure of affairs and passions you tend to nod and become drowsy, here are twenty-four hours of Sunday set apart for you to hold counsel with your soul and look around you on the possibilities of life.

This is not, of course, all that is to be, or even should be, said for these doctrines. Only, in the course of this chapter, the reader and I have agreed upon a few catchwords, and been looking at morals on a certain system; it was a pity to lose an opportunity of testing the catchwords, and seeing whether, by this system as well as by others, current doctrines could show any probable justification. If the doctrines had come too badly out of the trial, it would have condemned the system. Our sight of the world is very narrow; the mind but a pedestrian instrument; there's nothing new under the sun, as Solomon says, except the man himself; and though that changes the aspect of everything else, yet he must see the same things as other people, only from a different side.

And now, having admitted so much, let us turn to criticism.

If you teach a man to keep his eyes upon what others think of him, unthinkingly to lead the life and hold the principles of the majority of his contemporaries, you must discredit in his eyes the one authoritative voice of his own soul. He may be a docile citizen; he will never be a man. It is ours, on the other hand, to disregard this babble and chattering of other men better and worse than we are, and to walk straight before us by what light we have. They may be right; but so, before heaven, are we. They may know; but we know also, and by that knowledge we must stand or fall. There is such a thing as loyalty to a man's own better self; and from those who have not that, God help me, how am I to look for loyalty to others? The most dull, the most imbecile, at a certain moment turn round, at a certain point will hear no further argument, but stand unflinching by their own dumb, irrational sense of right. It is not only by steel or fire, but through contempt and blame, that the martyr fulfils the calling of his dear soul. Be glad if you are not tried by such extremities. But although all the world ranged themselves in one line to tell you 'This is wrong', be you your own faithful vassal and the ambassador of God—throw down the glove and answer 'This is right.' Do you think you are only declaring yourself? Perhaps in some dim way, like a child who delivers a message not fully understood, you are opening wider the straits of prejudice and preparing mankind for some truer and more spiritual grasp of truth; perhaps, as you stand forth for your own judgment, you are covering a thousand weak ones with your body; perhaps, by this declaration alone, you have avoided the guilt of false witness against humanity and the little ones unborn. It is good, I believe, to be respectable, but much nobler to respect oneself and utter the voice of God. God, if there be any God, speaks daily in a new language by the tongues of men; the thoughts and habits of each fresh generation and each new-coined spirit throw another light upon the universe and contain another commentary on the printed Bibles; every scruple, every true dissent, every glimpse of something new, is a letter of God's alphabet; and though there is a grave responsibility for all who speak, is there none for those who unrighteously keep silence and conform? Is not that also to conceal and cloak God's counsel? And how should we regard the man of science who suppressed all facts that would not tally with the orthodoxy of the hour?

Wrong? You are as surely wrong as the sun rose this morning round the revolving shoulder of the world. Not truth, but truthfulness, is the good of your endeavour. For when will men receive that first part and prerequisite of truth, that, by the order of things, by the greatness of the universe, by the darkness and partiality of man's experience, by the inviolate secrecy of God, kept close in His most open revelations, every man is, and to the end of the ages must be, wrong? Wrong to the universe; wrong to mankind; wrong to God. And yet in another sense, and that plainer and nearer, every man of men, who wishes truly, must be right. He is right to himself, and in the measure of his sagacity and candour. That let him do in all sincerity and zeal, not sparing a thought for contrary opinions; that, for what it is worth, let him proclaim. Be not afraid; although he be wrong, so also is the dead, stuffed Dagon he insults. For the voice of God, whatever it is, is not that stammering, inept tradition which the people holds. These truths survive in travesty, swamped in a world of spiritual darkness and confusion; and what a few comprehend and faithfully hold, the many, in their dead jargon, repeat, degrade, and misinterpret.

So far of Respectability; what the Covenanters used to call 'rank conformity': the deadliest gag and wet blanket that can be laid on men. And now of Profit. And this doctrine is perhaps the more redoubtable, because it harms all sorts of men; not only the heroic and self-reliant, but the obedient, cowlike squadrons. A man, by this doctrine, looks to consequences at the second, or third, or fiftieth turn. He chooses his end, and for that, with wily turns and through a great sea of tedium, steers this mortal bark. There may be political wisdom in such a view; but I am persuaded there can spring no great moral zeal. To look thus obliquely upon life is the very recipe for moral slumber. Our intention and endeavour should be directed, not on some vague end of money or applause, which shall come to us by a ricochet in a month or a year, or twenty years, but on the act itself;

not on the approval of others, but on the rightness of that act. At every instant, at every step in life, the point has to be decided, our soul has to be saved, Heaven has to be gained or lost. At every step our spirits must applaud, at every step we must set down the foot and sound the trumpet. 'This have I done,' we must say; 'right or wrong, this have I done, in unfeigned honour of intention, as to myself and God.' The profit of every act should be this, that it was right for us to do it. Any other profit than that, if it involved a kingdom or the woman I love, ought, if I were God's upright soldier, to leave me untempted.

It is the mark of what we call a righteous decision, that it is made directly and for its own sake. The whole man, mind and body, having come to an agreement, tyrannically dictates conduct. There are two dispositions eternally opposed: that in which we recognise that one thing is wrong and another right, and that in which, not seeing any clear distinction, we fall back on the consideration of consequences. The truth is, by the scope of our present teaching, nothing is thought very wrong and nothing very right, except a few actions which have the disadvantage of being disrespectable when found out; the more serious part of men inclining to think all things rather wrong, the more jovial to suppose them right enough for practical purposes. I will engage my head, they do not find that view in their own hearts; they have taken it up in a dark despair; they are but troubled sleepers talking in their sleep. The soul, or my soul at least, thinks very distinctly upon many points of right and wrong, and often differs flatly with what is held out as the thought of corporate humanity in the code of society or the code of law. Am I to suppose myself a monster? I have only to read books, the Christian Gospels for example, to think myself a monster no longer; and instead I think the mass of people are merely speaking in their sleep.

It is a commonplace, enshrined, if I mistake not, even in school copy-books, that honour is to be sought and not fame. I ask no other admission; we are to seek honour, upright walking with our own conscience every hour of the day, and not fame, the consequence, the far-off reverberation of our footsteps. The walk, not the rumour of the walk, is what concerns righteousness. Better disrespectable honour than dishonourable fame. Better useless or seemingly hurtful honour, than dishonour ruling empires and filling the mouths of thousands. For the man must walk by what he sees, and leave the issue with God who made him and taught him by the fortune of his life. You would not dishonour yourself for money; which is at least tangible; would you do it, then, for a doubtful forecast in politics, or another person's theory in morals?

So intricate is the scheme of our affairs, that no man can calculate the bearing of his own behaviour even on those immediately around him, how much less upon the world at large or on succeeding generations! To walk by external prudence and the rule of consequences would require, not a man, but God. All that we know to guide us in this changing labyrinth is our soul with its fixed design of righteousness, and a few old precepts which commend themselves to that. The precepts are vague when we endeavour to apply them; consequences are more entangled than a wisp of string, and their confusion is unrestingly in change; we must hold to what we know and walk by it. We must walk by faith, indeed, and not by knowledge.

You do not love another because he is wealthy or wise or eminently respectable: you love him because you love him; that is love, and any other only a derision and grimace. It should be the same with all our actions. If we were to conceive a perfect man, it should be one who was never torn between conflicting impulses, but who, on the absolute consent of all his parts and faculties, submitted in every action of his life to a self-dictation as absolute and unreasoned as that which bids him love one woman and be true to her till death. But we should not conceive him as sagacious, ascetical, playing off his appetites against each other, turning the wing of public respectable immorality instead of riding it directly down, or advancing toward his end through a thousand sinister compromises and considerations. The one man might be wily, might be adroit, might be wise, might be respectable, might be gloriously useful; it is the other man who would be good.

The soul asks honour and not fame; to be upright, not to be successful; to be good, not prosperous; to be essentially, not outwardly, respectable. Does your soul ask profit? Does it ask money? Does it ask the approval of the indifferent herd? I believe not. For my own part, I want but little money, I hope; and I do not want to be decent at all, but to be good.

I V

WE HAVE spoken of that supreme self-dictation which keeps varying from hour to hour in its dictates with the variation of events and circumstances. Now, for us, that is ultimate. It may be founded on some reasonable process, but it is not a process which we can follow or comprehend. And moreover the dictation is not continuous, or not continuous except in very lively and well-living natures; and betweenwhiles we must brush along without it. Practice is a more intricate and desperate business than the toughest theorising; life is an affair of cavalry, where rapid judgment and prompt action are alone possible and right. As a matter of fact, there is no one so upright but he is influenced by the world's chatter; and no one so headlong but he requires to consider consequences and to keep an eye on profit. For the soul adopts all affections and appetites without exception, and cares only to combine them for some common purpose which shall interest all. Now, respect for the opinion of others, the study of consequences, and the desire of power and comfort, are all undeniably factors in the nature of man; and the more undeniably since we find that, in our current doctrines, they have swallowed up the others and are thought to conclude in themselves all the worthy parts of man. These, then, must also be suffered to affect conduct in the practical domain, much or little according as they are forcibly or feebly present to the mind of each.

Now, a man's view of the universe is mostly a view of the civilised society in which he lives. Other men and women are so much more grossly and so much more intimately palpable to his perceptions, that they stand between him and all the rest; they are larger to his eye than the sun, he hears them more plainly than thunder, with them, by them, and for them, he must live and die. And hence the laws that affect his intercourse with his fellow-men, although merely customary and the creatures of a generation, are more clearly and continually before his mind than those which bind him into the eternal system of things, support him in his upright progress on this

whirling ball, or keep up the fire of his bodily life. And hence it is
that money stands in the first rank of considerations and so powerfully affects the choice. For our society is built with money for
mortar; money is present in every joint of circumstance; it might be
named the social atmosphere, since, in society, it is by that alone that
men continue to live, and only through that or chance that they can
reach or affect one another. Money gives us food, shelter, and
privacy; it permits us to be clean in person, opens for us the doors of
the theatre, gains us books for study or pleasure, enables us to help
the distresses of others, and puts us above necessity so that we can
choose the best in life. If we love, it enables us to meet and live with
the loved one, or even to prolong her health and life; if we have scruples, it gives us an opportunity to be honest; if we have any bright
designs, here is what will smooth the way to their accomplishment.
Penury is the worst slavery, and will soon lead to death.

But money is only a means; it presupposes a man to use it. The
rich can go where he pleases, but perhaps please himself nowhere.
He can buy a library or visit the whole world, but perhaps has neither
patience to read nor intelligence to see. The table may be loaded and
the appetite wanting; the purse may be full, and the heart empty. He
may have gained the world and lost himself; and with all his wealth
around him, in a great house and spacious and beautiful demesne,
he may live as blank a life as any tattered ditcher. Without an appetite, without an aspiration, void of appreciation, bankrupt of desire
and hope, there, in his great house, let him sit and look upon his
fingers. It is perhaps a more fortunate destiny to have a taste for
collecting shells than to be born a millionaire. Although neither is to
be despised, it is always better policy to learn an interest than to
make a thousand pounds; for the money will soon be spent, or
perhaps you may feel no joy in spending it; but the interest remains
imperishable and ever new. To become a botanist, a geologist, a
social philosopher, an antiquary, or an artist, is to enlarge one's
possessions in the universe by an incalculably higher degree, and by
a far surer sort of property, than to purchase a farm of many acres.
You had perhaps two thousand a year before the transaction; perhaps
you have two thousand five hundred after it. That represents your
gain in the one case. But in the other, you have thrown down a

barrier which concealed significance and beauty. The blind man has learned to see. The prisoner has opened up a window in his cell and beholds enchanting prospects; he will never again be a prisoner as he was; he can watch clouds and changing seasons, ships on the river, travellers on the road, and the stars at night; happy prisoner! his eyes have broken jail! And again he who has learned to love an art or science has wisely laid up riches against the day of riches; if prosperity come, he will not enter poor into his inheritance; he will not slumber and forget himself in the lap of money, or spend his hours in counting idle treasures, but be up and briskly doing; he will have the true alchemic touch, which is not that of Midas, but which transmutes dead money into living delight and satisfaction. *Être et pas avoir*—to be, not to possess—that is the problem of life. To be wealthy, a rich nature is the first requisite and money but the second. To be of a quick and healthy blood, to share in all honourable curiosities, to be rich in admiration and free from envy, to rejoice greatly in the good of others, to love with such generosity of heart that your love is still a dear possession in absence or unkindness—these are the gifts of fortune which money cannot buy and without which money can buy nothing. For what can a man possess, or what can he enjoy, except himself? If he enlarge his nature, it is then that he enlarges his estates. If his nature be happy and valiant, he will enjoy the universe as if it were his park and orchard.

But money is not only to be spent; it has also to be earned. It is not merely a convenience or a necessary in social life; but it is the coin in which mankind pays his wages to the individual man. And from this side, the question of money has a very different scope and application. For no man can be honest who does not work. Service for service. If the farmer buys corn, and the labourer ploughs and reaps, and the baker sweats in his hot bakery, plainly you who eat must do something in your turn. It is not enough to take off your hat, or to thank God upon your knees for the admirable constitution of society and your own convenient situation in its upper and more ornamental stories. Neither is it enough to buy the loaf with a sixpence; for then you are only changing the point of the inquiry; and you must first have bought the sixpence. Service for service: how have you bought your sixpences? A man of spirit desires certainty in a thing of such a nature; he must see to it that there is some reciprocity between him and mankind; that he pays his expenditure in service; that he has not a lion's share in profit and a drone's in labour; and is not a sleeping partner and mere costly incubus on the great mercantile concern of mankind.

Services differ so widely with different gifts, and some are so inappreciable to external tests, that this is not only a matter for the private conscience, but one which even there must be leniently and trustfully considered. For remember how many serve mankind who do no more than meditate; and how many are precious to their friends for no more than a sweet and joyous temper. To perform the function of a man of letters it is not necessary to write; nay, it is perhaps better to be a living book. So long as we love we serve; so long as we are loved by others, I would almost say that we are indispensable; and no man is useless while he has a friend. The true services of life are inestimable in money, and are never paid. Kind words and caresses, high and wise thoughts, humane designs, tender behaviour to the weak and suffering, and all the charities of man's existence, are neither bought nor sold.

Yet the dearest and readiest, if not the most just, criterion of a man's services, is the wage that mankind pays him or, briefly, what he earns. There at least there can be no ambiguity. St Paul is fully and freely entitled to his earnings as a tentmaker, and Socrates fully and freely entitled to his earnings as a sculptor, although the true business of each was not only something different, but something which remained unpaid. A man cannot forget that he is not superintended, and serves mankind on parole. He would like, when challenged by his own conscience, to reply: 'I have done so much work, and no less, with my own hands and brain, and taken so much profit, and no more, for my own personal delight.' And though St Paul, if he had possessed a private fortune, would probably have scorned to waste his time in making tents, yet of all sacrifices to public opinion none can be more easily pardoned than that by which a man, already spiritually useful to the world, should restrict the field of his chief usefulness to perform services more apparent, and possess a livelihood that neither stupidity nor malice could call in question. Like all sacrifices to public opinion and mere external decency, this would certainly be wrong; for the soul should rest contented with its own approval and indissuadably pursue its own calling. Yet, so grave and delicate is the question, that a man may well hesitate before he decides it for himself; he may well fear that he sets too high a valuation on his own endeavours after good; he may well condescend upon a humbler duty, where others than himself shall judge the service and proportion the wage.

And yet it is to this very responsibility that the rich are born. They can shuffle off the duty on no other; they are their own paymasters on parole; and must pay themselves fair wages and no more. For I suppose that in the course of ages, and through reform and civil war and invasion, mankind was pursuing some other and more general design than to set one or two Englishmen of the nineteenth century beyond the reach of needs and duties. Society was scarce put together, and defended with so much eloquence and blood, for the convenience of two or three millionaires and a few hundred other persons of wealth and position. It is plain that if mankind thus acted and suffered during all these generations, they hoped some benefit, some ease, some wellbeing, for themselves and their descendants; that if they supported law and order, it was to secure fair-play for all; that if they denied themselves in the present, they must have had some designs upon the future. Now, a great hereditary fortune is a miracle of man's wisdom and mankind's forbearance; it has not only been amassed and handed down, it has been suffered to be amassed and handed down; and surely in such a consideration as this, its possessor should find only a new spur to activity and honour, that with all this power of service he should not prove unserviceable, and that this mass of treasure should return in benefits upon the race. If he had twenty, or thirty, or a hundred thousand at his banker's, or if all Yorkshire or all California were his to manage or to sell, he would still be morally penniless, and have the world to begin like Whittington, until he had found some way of serving mankind. His wage is physically in his own hand; but, in honour, that wage must still be earned. He is only steward on parole of what is called his fortune. He must honourably perform his stewardship. He must estimate his own services and allow himself a salary in proportion, for that will be one among his functions. And while he will then be free to spend that salary, great or little, on his own private pleasures, the rest of his fortune he but holds and disposes under trust for mankind; it is not his, because he has not earned it; it cannot be his, because his services have already been paid; but year by year it is his to distribute, whether to help individuals whose birthright and outfit have been swallowed up in his, or to further public works and institutions.

At this rate, short of inspiration, it seems hardly possible to be both rich and honest; and the millionaire is under a far more continuous temptation to thieve than the labourer who gets his shilling daily for despicable toils. Are you surprised? It is even so. And you repeat it every Sunday in your churches. 'It is easier for a camel to pass through the eye of a needle than for a rich man to enter the Kingdom of God.' I have heard this and similar texts ingeniously explained away and brushed from the path of the aspiring Christian by the tender Great-heart of the parish. One excellent clergyman told us that the 'eye of a needle' meant a low, Oriental postern through which camels could not pass till they were unloaded—which is very likely just; and then went on, bravely confounding the 'Kingdom of God' with Heaven, the future paradise, to show that of course no rich person could expect to carry his riches beyond the grave—which, of course, he could not and never did. Various greedy sinners of the congregation drank in the comfortable doctrine with relief. It was worth the while having come to church that Sunday morning! All was plain. The Bible, as usual, meant nothing in particular; it was merely an obscure and figurative school-copybook; and if a man were only respectable, he was a man after God's own heart.

Alas! I fear not. And though this matter of a man's services is one for his own conscience, there are some cases in which it is difficult to restrain the mind from judging. Thus I shall be very easily persuaded that a man has earned his daily bread; and if he has but a friend or two to whom his company is delightful at heart, I am more than persuaded at once. But it will be very hard to persuade me that any one has earned an income of a hundred thousand. What he is to his friends, he still would be if he were made penniless tomorrow; for as to the courtiers of luxury and power, I will neither consider them friends, nor indeed consider them at all. What he does for mankind there are most likely hundreds who would do the same, as effectually for the race and as pleasurably to themselves, for the merest fraction of this monstrous wage. Why it is paid, I am, therefore, unable to conceive, and as the man pays it himself, out of funds in his detention, I have a certain backwardness to think him honest.

At least, we have gained a very obvious point: that what a man spends upon himself, he shall have earned by services to the race. Thence flows a principle for the outset of life, which is a little different from that taught in the present day. I am addressing the middle and the upper classes; those who have already been fostered and prepared for life at some expense; those who have some choice before them, and can pick professions; and above all, those who are what is called independent, and need do nothing unless pushed by honour or ambition. In this particular the poor are happy; among them, when a lad comes to his strength, he must take the work that offers, and can take it with an easy conscience. But in the richer classes the question is complicated by the number of opportunities and a variety of considerations. Here, then, this principle of ours comes in helpfully. The young man has to seek, not a road to wealth, but an opportunity of service; not money, but honest work. If he has some strong propensity, some calling of nature, some over-weening interest in any special field of industry, inquiry, or art, he will do right to obey the impulse; and that for two reasons: the first external, because there he will render the best services; the second personal, because a demand of his own nature is to him without appeal whenever it can be satisfied with the consent of his other faculties and appetites. If he has no such elective taste, by the very principle on which he chooses any pursuit at all he must choose the most honest and serviceable, and not the most highly remunerated. We have here an external problem, not from or to ourself, but flowing from the constitution of society; and we have our own soul with its fixed design of righteousness. All that can be done is to present the problem in proper terms, and leave it to the soul of the individual. Now, the problem to the poor is one of necessity: to earn wherewithal to live, they must find remunerative labour. But the problem to the rich is one of honour: having the wherewithal, they must find serviceable labour. Each has to earn his daily bread: the one, because he has not yet got it to eat; the other, who has already eaten it, because he has not yet earned it.

Of course, what is true of bread is true of luxuries and comforts, whether for the body or the mind. But the consideration of luxuries leads us to a new aspect of the whole question, and to a second proposition no less true, and maybe no less startling, than the last.

At the present day, we, of the easier classes, are in a state of surfeit and disgrace after meat. Plethora has filled us with indifference; and we are covered from head to foot with the callosities of habitual opulence. Born into what is called a certain rank, we live, as the saying is, up to our station. We squander without enjoyment, because our fathers squandered. We eat of the best, not from delicacy, but from brazen habit. We do not keenly enjoy or eagerly desire the presence of a luxury; we are unaccustomed to its absence. And not only do we squander money from habit, but still more pitifully waste it in ostentation. I can think of no more melancholy disgrace for a creature who professes either reason or pleasure for his guide, than to spend the smallest fraction of his income upon that which he does not desire; and to keep a carriage in which you do not wish to drive, or a butler of whom you are afraid, is a pathetic kind of folly. Money, being a means of happiness, should make both parties happy when it changes hands; rightly disposed, it should be twice blessed in its employment; and buyer and seller should alike have their twenty shillings' worth of profit out of every pound.

Benjamin Franklin went through life an altered man, because he once paid too dearly for a penny whistle. My concern springs usually from a deeper source, to wit, from having bought a whistle when I did not want one. I find I regret this, or would regret it if I gave myself the time, not only on personal but on moral and philanthropical considerations. For, first, in a world where money is wanting to buy books for eager students and food and medicine for pining children, and where a large majority are starved in their most immediate desires, it is surely base, stupid, and cruel to squander money when I am pushed by no appetite and enjoy no return of genuine satisfaction. My philanthropy is wide enough in scope to include myself; and when I have made myself happy, I have at least one good argument that I have acted rightly; but where that is not so, and I have bought and not enjoyed, my mouth is closed, and I conceive that I have robbed the poor. And, second, anything I buy or use which I do not sincerely want or cannot vividly enjoy, disturbs the balance of supply and demand, and contributes to remove industrious hands from the production of what is useful or pleasurable and to keep them busy upon ropes of sand and things that are a weariness to the flesh. That extravagance is truly sinful, and a very silly sin to boot, in which we impoverish mankind and ourselves. It is another question for each man's heart. He knows if he can enjoy what he buys and uses; if he cannot, he is a dog in the manger; nay, if he cannot, I contend he is a thief, for nothing really belongs to a man which he cannot use. Proprietor is connected with propriety; and that only is the man's which is proper to his wants and faculties.

A youth, in choosing a career, must not be alarmed by poverty. Want is a sore thing, but poverty does not imply want. It remains to be seen whether with half his present income, or a third, he cannot, in the most generous sense, live as fully as at present. He is a fool who objects to luxuries; but he is also a fool who does not protest against the waste of luxuries on those who do not desire and cannot enjoy them. It remains to be seen, by each man who would live a true life to himself and not a merely specious life to society, how many luxuries he truly wants and to how many he merely submits as to a social propriety; and all these last he will immediately forswear. Let him do this, and he will be surprised to find how little money it requires to keep him in complete contentment and activity of mind and senses. Life at any level among the easy classes is conceived upon a principle of rivalry, where each man and each household must ape the tastes and emulate the display of others. One is delicate in eating, another in wine, a third in furniture or works of art or dress; and I, who care nothing for any of these refinements, who am perhaps a plain athletic creature and love exercise, beef, beer, flannel shirts and a camp bed, am yet called upon to assimilate all these other tastes and make these foreign occasions of expenditure my own. It may be cynical: I am sure I shall be told it is selfish; but I will spend my money as I please and for my own intimate personal gratification, and should count myself a nincompoop indeed to lay out the colour of a halfpenny on any fancied social decency or duty. I shall not wear gloves unless my hands are cold, or unless I am born with a delight in them.

Dress is my own affair, and that of one other in the world; that, in fact and for an obvious reason, of any woman who shall chance to be in love with me. I shall lodge where I have a mind. If I do not ask society to live with me, they must be silent; and even if I do, they have no further right but to refuse the invitation! There is a kind of idea abroad that a man must live up to his station, that his house, his table, and his toilette, shall be in a ratio of equivalence, and equally imposing to the world. If this is in the Bible, the passage has eluded my inquiries. If it is not in the Bible, it is nowhere but in the heart of the fool.

Throw aside this fancy. See what you want, and spend upon that; distinguish what you do not care about, and spend nothing upon that. There are not many people who can differentiate wines above a certain and that not at all a high price. Are you sure you are one of these? Are you sure you prefer cigars at sixpence each to pipes at some fraction of a farthing? Are you sure you wish to keep a gig? Do you care about where you sleep, or are you not as much at your ease in a cheap lodging as in an Elizabethan manor-house? Do you enjoy fine clothes? It is not possible to answer these questions without a trial; and there is nothing more obvious to my mind, than that a man who has not experienced some ups and downs, and been forced to live more cheaply than in his father's house, has still his education to begin. Let the experiment be made, and he will find to his surprise that he has been eating beyond his appetite up to that hour; that the cheap lodging, the cheap tobacco, the rough country clothes, the plain table, have not only no power to damp his spirits, but perhaps give him as keen pleasure in the using as the dainties that he took, betwixt sleep and waking, in his former callous and somnambulous submission to wealth.

The true Bohemian, a creature lost to view under the imaginary Bohemians of literature, is exactly described by such a principle of life. The Bohemian of the novel, who drinks more than is good for him and prefers anything to work, and wears strange clothes, is for

the most part a respectable Bohemian, respectable in disrespectability, living for the outside, and an adventurer. But the man I mean
lives wholly to himself, does what he wishes, and not what is thought
proper, buys what he wants for himself, and not what is thought
proper, works at what he believes he can do well and not what will
bring him in money or favour. You may be the most respectable of
men, and yet a true Bohemian. And the test is this: a Bohemian, for
as poor as he may be, is always open-handed to his friends; he knows
what he can do with money and how he can do without it, a far rarer
and more useful knowledge; he has had less, and continued to live in
some contentment; and hence he cares not to keep more, and shares
his sovereign or his shilling with a friend. The poor, if they are generous, are Bohemian in virtue of their birth. Do you know where
beggars go? Not to the great houses where people sit dazed among
their thousands, but to the doors of poor men who have seen the
world; and it was the widow who had only two mites, who cast half
her fortune into the treasury.

But a young man who elects to save on dress or on lodging, or
who in any way falls out of the level of expenditure which is common
to his level in society, falls out of society altogether. I suppose the
young man to have chosen his career on honourable principles; he
finds his talents and instincts can be best contented in a certain
pursuit; in a certain industry, he is sure that he is serving mankind
with a healthy and becoming service; and he is not sure that he
would be doing so, or doing so equally well, in any other industry
within his reach. Then that is his true sphere in life; not the one in
which he was born to his father, but the one which is proper to his
talents and instincts. And suppose he does fall out of society, is that
a cause of sorrow? Is your heart so dead that you prefer the recognition of many to the love of a few? Do you think society loves you?
Put it to the proof. Decline in material expenditure, and you will
find they care no more for you than for the Khan of Tartary. You
will lose no friends. If you had any, you will keep them. Only those
who were friends to your coat and equipage will disappear; the smiling faces will disappear as by enchantment; but the kind hearts will
remain steadfastly kind. Are you so lost, are you so dead, are you so
little sure of your own soul and your own footing upon solid fact,

that you prefer before goodness and happiness the countenance of sundry diners-out, who will flee from you at a report of ruin, who will drop you with insult at a shadow of disgrace, who do not know you and do not care to know you but by sight, and whom you in your turn neither know nor care to know in a more human manner? Is it not the principle of society, openly avowed, that friendship must not interfere with business; which being paraphrased, means simply that a consideration of money goes before any consideration of affection known to this cold-blooded gang, that they have not even the honour of thieves, and will rook their nearest and dearest as readily as a stranger? I hope I would go as far as most to serve a friend; but I declare openly I would not put on my hat to do a pleasure to society. I may starve my appetites and control my temper for the sake of those I love; but society shall take me as I choose to be, or go without me. Neither they nor I will lose; for where there is no love, it is both laborious and unprofitable to associate.

But it is obvious that if it is only right for a man to spend money on that which he can truly and thoroughly enjoy, the doctrine applies with equal force to the rich and to the poor, to the man who has amassed many thousands as well as to the youth precariously beginning life. And it may be asked, Is not this merely preparing misers, who are not the best of company? But the principle was this: that which a man has not fairly earned, and, further, that which he cannot fully enjoy, does not belong to him, but is a part of mankind's treasure which he holds as steward on parole. To mankind, then, it must be made profitable; and how this should be done is, once more, a problem which each man must solve for himself, and about which none has a right to judge him. Yet there are a few considerations which are very obvious and may here be stated.

Mankind is not only the whole in general, but every one in particular. Every man or woman is one of mankind's dear possessions; to his or her just brain, and kind heart, and active hands, mankind intrusts some of its hopes for the future; he or she is a possible well-spring of good acts and source of blessings to the race. This money which you do not need, which, in a rigid sense, you do not want, may therefore be returned not only in public benefactions to the race, but in private kindnesses.

Your wife, your children, your friends stand nearest to you, and should be helped the first. There at least there can be little imposture, for you know their necessities of your own knowledge. And consider, if all the world did as you did, and according to their means extended help in the circle of their affections, there would be no more crying want in times of plenty and no more cold, mechanical charity given with a doubt and received with confusion. Would not this simple rule make a new world out of the old and cruel one which we inhabit?

* * * * *

[After two more sentences the fragment breaks off.]

On Morality

There is no eternal Thou Shalt Not inscribed upon man's nature; only rumours in the market-place varying from age to age, praising tomorrow what they yesterday condemned.

THE WORD morality is so old and so important that we begin to pay it an idolatrous adoration. We are like infants that have planted money; it has been buried so long; there must certainly be some increase; the word is so old and venerable, it must surely have acquired a more august significance. In both we are right; if the coins lie buried long enough, they are become antiquities to be treasured in museums; if the word has been long enough familiar in men's minds, it has acquired the more authority upon their action. In both we are wrong; the sixpence is still only a sixpence; it is not a shilling; though it may now be sold for half-a-crown; and the word even to this day, even when it rules us with the prestige of inherited familiarity, has yet gained no more divine sanction, but still rehearses the humble story of its birth. Morality—from *mos*, that which is customary, that which is accepted, 'good form,' the 'correct thing' in our particular day or nation—it must still seem strange, that so poor a name should have been chosen for our whole science of right and wrong, of all that is most passionate, most sad, and most noble in the tragedy of man: a plain word of what we call truth is always so untrue to subjective emotions, seems always indeed so calumnious of life. And yet still, after all these centuries, there is no more in the word than we put in it. And in one sense there is less. Follow the opinions of a single and a very narrow race from the day of Jacob's remarkable enterprise on Shechem, to the day when Gamaliel stood up and said . . .

We see there through what an orbit morality runs, and the two attitudes of man to his *mores:* his savage trust in them, his civilised dubiety:—in the morning of a nation's life, unflinching loyalty to its own customs; in the evening, curiosity as to those of others, which 'may be of God' also. So that here we find the word has actually declined in force; but at the same time we find another idea springing up concurrently.

The love of approval, the need of human countenance, the ape-like trick of imitating that which we admire, the childish propensity to repeat the same act or the same form of words once used, among low races continually breed fresh customs. They grow up, without much or any thought of use; accident and aesthetic taste led to their acceptance, the ape-like part of man to their perpetuation: and the individual savage was born to the whole mass, and followed the manners of his tribe for the same reason that he spoke its dialect. They were his by birth, and he enquired no further. To men of other parentage, inheriting other customs, he could be justly tolerant, at least, if they were neighbours. Thus the half-breed Indian, if he were a high-minded man, although preferring the habits of his mother tribe, held himself bound to be a Christian. It was his duty (quite apart from intellectual assent) to offer a brave type of the paternal race, and not to tamper with but shiningly to fulfil its least tradition.

Such being the growth of morals, such their original sanction, it might even seem strange that any should have proved of use. But it is to be observed that even in those days there were leaders of men; the great law-giver, mythical hero, had, doubtless, many avatars; and the Survival of the Fittest was at work. Such being their growth and sanction, it is very plain that at least, of all this mountain-heap of customs, many must be useless and some harmful. And here we see the task of a progressive civilisation. The civilised man, though he has still much of the habitual loyalty, struggles beyond. International religions—Christianity, Islam, and the like—and still more the mighty intellectual labours and monumental example of the Roman Empire, have widened his moral prospect. He conceives himself no longer as the child of a sect nor yet wholly as the subject of a nation, but in a great and growing measure as a member of the general race. With an enfranchised criticism,—in these days at least tending to be hostile—he considers his inheritance of morals; has already discarded many that appeared harmful, or only inert and cumbersome; and would probably (if he knew how) eliminate all but what are needful to preserve the peace. Superstition has changed place; he no longer believes in the sanctity of any particular custom, but he has made a new idol in the place of that. He conceives of morals as being only partly customary, and that part the worse. He deludes himself with a fairy tale that when the body of law and custom shall be dead, the soul of morality will be disengaged and made perfect; that a man may plough up his orchard, and come round again next week and enjoy the shade and gather apples.

II

This singular notion, it is well to brush away. There is no eternal *Thou Shalt Not* inscribed upon man's nature; only rumours in the market-place varying from age to age, praising tomorrow what they yesterday condemned. There is no Arabian tale so fantastic as the history of right and wrong and perhaps no action conceivable that has not (at one time or other) figured under both categories. If there be anything we can condemn (today and in our race) without after-thought or hesitation, it is the wanton infliction of suffering. Yet it was no degraded race that recognised elaborate cruelty for a duty. And once so recognised, it became one. The Mohawk, when he tortured his prisoners, or was tortured himself, through days of agony not to be narrated, was no less consciously (and no less surely) in the Kingdom of Heaven, than you when you rattle pence into the missionary box. That was right for him; to this business, he brought, with a whole heart, his moral forces: the noblest part of him found exercise among horrors that we sicken to remember. The Jesuit missionary, coming to a new field of labour, rejoiced to find already planted in men's hearts the root and rudiment of all religion: the doctrine of a future life of bliss for those who have done well. Yet a little, and he was proportionately cast down by a new discovery: that what his penitents meant by doing well was to kill their enemies— and eat them. And the same organ, the same bundle of inherited propensities, the same human conscience, supported the Father in his laborious and peaceful exile, and applauded the Carib at his inhu-man banquet. To multiply instances were only to waste space; historic inquiry, international comparison, will furnish them alike, and by the shipload to the dullest. The notions of right and wrong, in so far as they attach to specific acts, are the creatures of mere fashion, like our boots and bonnets. Such a fashion once set, the soul of contem-porary man clings about it and will die for it; once overthrown, and the souls of his descendants are astonished to read of his delusion.

III

Yet the notion is general and not confined to Jacobins, that all *mores* may be overthrown, and morality survive; that the soul of the matter will not merely be unharmed but really embellished by the brutal murder of the body. And the elegant superstition stands (like all the rest) on some foundation. The most amazing fact in man—his indestructible willingness to do what he thinks right instead of what he thinks agreeable—alike precedes and outlasts the creeds in which it looks for sanction.

It is not wonderful if he think highly of this moral instinct, and, in one sense, too highly. For as a guide, it is stone blind, and as a teacher, it is dumb. Incurable courtier of the day, it curtseys to all fashions; dull soldier of fortune, it will still serve under the nearest captain. Yet here we seem to go too far; for the conscience often revolts from the contemporary doctrine, and the reformer and the martyr (of whom we are going to have plenty to say further on) make a noble mark on the pages of man's history. It is true our inheritance is twofold, tribal or national on the one hand, individual on the other. The race or nation inherits from millions of ascendents a body of rigid laws and a general and fluid sense of what is fitting. The individual man inherits no law, but a special sense of what is fitting. The law is always lagging in the rear; the individual and the general sense are always at some odds. It is a three-cornered duel; a triangular conflict of authorities in which man's soul, being in the midst, receives the mauling. Leave law aside, for that is a question by itself; and which of the other two, supposing them to differ, shall a man obey? On the one side, the manners, eminently respectable of his race and period; on the other, the instinct τὸ καλόν of himself. On the one his inherited voice; on the other, his inherited and instilled gregariousness and love of approbation. To the thoughtful man, his special sense will appear to speak with more authority; it takes him on his bed at night and poisons solitude when his life truly passes. With the man of words, the good sleeper, the good fellow, the grasper of hands, the general sense will usually triumph; for such a one lives in the light of the camp-fire and by the countenance of admiring comrades. And in either case, the conscience having come through tribulation, will clap its wings and crow for victory: equally pleased, being indeed a buzzard of an attribute.

'What is truth?' It was Pilate's momentous question: the conservative's eternal question to the reformer. What is truth? And what is your truth, the little cranny, the little flaw in the coincidence between your personal, and the tribal, sense of right? Is it worth dying for? Is it worth proclaiming? Are you sure it will repay mankind for the bursting of ties, the disconsecration of catch-words, the enfranchisement of appetites? Lord Bacon, whom asses suppose to be the author of the plays of Shakespeare, had so little weighed the bearing of the question, had so imperfectly conceived the drama of the scene, that he must write of 'jesting Pilate'. It was tragic jesting; Pilate was straining every nerve to save his prisoner; pleading with him like the sceptical eclectic that the Roman was, and pleading in vain as he must always do with perfect faith. The martyr and the reformer, types of the individual conscience in revolt from the collective, answer quite unshaken by the question. They think it worth while to die for an egg on the antipodes; and for that we honour them without reserve. They think it worth while to crack the mortar of society and loose the bonds of habitual assent; and here we sometimes wonder. What a man does with his life is largely his own affair; and we know the best he can do with it is to lay it down. What he does to that weak fabric of manners in which we live is a more serious matter. Ancient consent, inherited propensities, the fear of disaffected countenances on the street, these are fragile business. So long as we suppose manners to be the shadow of an eternal something else, they are no more sacred than the morning papers. So soon as we understand them for the ground and bond of man's association, the terms of his surrender to society, the best that he has yet agreed to recognise, the spoken word (not always pertinent) in which his aspirations after righteousness take voice—even the reformer will begin to hesitate. 'All things are lawful to me,' said Paul waxing exceeding bold, but even that revolutionary thinker allowed that all were not expedient. Man stands between his two guides the authoritative choice in his own bosom, the external consent or compromise of his age and nation, both inherited, both stark irrational, both (if we reflect upon it) sacred. If he cross his conscience, certain intimate dishonour, possible personal degradation: if he defy the sense of his contemporaries, certain outward disrepute and possible public hurt. And if the public hurt is to be considered the more tenderly, yet we must not minimise the disrepute. It is good to bear unpopularity; but the sense that suffers is the probable root of all our virtues. And the man who has no sensitive need of public countenance, the man who offends his neighbours without pain, is of the blood of criminals. And there is nothing (it is worth while to observe) on which the New Testament blows so directly hot and cold as on this difficulty. Christ with his sweeping 'Let the dead bury their dead,' Paul with his timid concern for the weak brother.

The Ethics of Crime

A crime properly is any act which shocks the popular conscience.

THERE IS no subject on which public opinion seems more lax and self-destructive. Crime is originally a legal term; already in Latin it has lost its legal strictness, but the base of the idea remained as it still remains today in English. Today what we have to complain of is a certain vagueness, the direct legacy of the eighteenth century and its *reductio ad absurdum*, the French Revolution. The word has been Jacobinised; the idea had also been in this way: A crime properly is any act which shocks the popular conscience. It is not simply an infringement of the law, many of whose provisions are explicitly municipal, lack an emotional sanction, and may be broken without offending public sentiment, as today by the poacher and yesterday by the smuggler. Crime (to reach the full meaning of the word) should at once break the letter of the law and offend against the sanctities of life; as matricide, or rape; acts which the law forbids and by which the public conscience is revolted. There are days when it will seem a virtue to be finding at least these. The corrupt management of a bank is committing a worse act to the enlightened mind than any single murder. All sinful acts run to murder. Murder is a distinction without a difference. Two strands are in the word as we use it today: a legal or emotional, and it is from this circumstance that sometimes the emotional element is present, and not the legal. A sin is not a crime, because the law regards it not: and the mass of men (all indeed but the puritans) have retained wit enough to perceive that the law should not regard it. Yet the sin may awaken as much public horror as the crime. To many of us the desertion of the Soudan appeared an act of monstrous iniquity; it shocked us; above all, when the people of that country came to be personified for English immigrants in the beloved figure of Gordon, it spoke more to our hearts and consciences than any dozens of murders. But it was not a crime, for it broke no positive enactment. This is a case from yesterday; today there are some others who are shocked by Mr Balfour's rule in Ireland; it stirs them to the very seat of generous indignation. But Mr Balfour is administering, not breaking, the law; and his worst acts (supposing any of them to be bad) are not crimes.

And, sometimes again, the legal element is present and not the emotional. Suppose that during those long months while Gordon waited in Soudan, a thought had occurred to some zealot in that part of the nation, which felt as I confess I did, that there was an offence against loyalty. Suppose that it had occurred to him, that on the death of some conspicuous minister, the ministry would be apt to fall, and that which succeeded it was certain to move with greater vigour in the business of the rescue; and suppose him led on (as men so easily are) by this course of reasoning; suppose him to play the part of the free justice; and suppose (true to his premises) the ministry had fallen and Gordon and the immigrants were saved. The zealot act had thus (on our hypothesis) the happiest conse-quence; a life fallen, but how many had been spared! the sanctity of human life had been broken, but the sanctity of human pledge corroborated by a declaratory act. Many people in England had thrown up their caps at such a consummation; and for the fortunate deed had lacked the emotional element of a crime. For all that, the law would have been broken, and it would have been a sad day for England, if judge, jury, and hangman had not done their part. Equally today, there is no lack of Irish patriots (unless fame belies them) who think of Mr Balfour as an imaginary personage was supposed to think of Gladstone; indeed, fame belies them, if they do not pass from thought to action; and if their hopes for Ireland be justified, the death of the Irish secretary would be a gain to that section of the human race. Let us suppose him killed, and let us suppose as we did in the other case, that all the hopes of the assassin are instantly realised, and Ireland becomes at once happy, virtuous, and free. For the Irish and the party, this deed will lack the emotional element of a crime; it will seem instead a providential disposition. But as the law will have been broken; and if the judge, the jury, and the hangman fail of their offices, it will be an ill day for Ireland, and England, and the world.

The emotional element is the personal; the legal is the national. The first represents my feeling; the second is the best means I can collect as to the feeling of mankind at large. If there be a majority against a law, it can be instantly repealed. Until it is repealed, I am bound to regard it as the voice of my fellow-citizens. Am I bound to prefer it? Here law and religion, the sanctity of the human conscience and the sanctity of human ties, come into direct collision. I believe it to be right; the law, the mouthpiece of generations of mankind, declares it to be wrong. It is an act of some presumption to back my own opinion against that of so many, but presumption is not uncommon nor always wrong. *Ipsi dixi;* but perhaps after all it is I who am in the right. It may be proper to commit murder; it may be proper (for aught I can see) to commit rape, circumstances vary so infinitely, consciences read them in such varying lights. And we have all (except the puritans and, to some extent, the Jacobins) agreed that a man's conscience is autonomous; we have but reserved the right to interfere and (what we somewhat uprighteously call) to punish him; we tell him, little Mr Chucks, in the most gentlemanly manner in the world: 'My dear little fellow, you have done one person quite right; and your conscience is, no doubt, an admirable conscience; but as its dictates render you a public nuisance in our community, one must seclude or make an end of you.' The man, in short, is quite right emotionally, to have murdered Mr Balfour; and we are legally quite right to hang him.

Pulvis Et Umbra

We behold space sown with rotatory islands, suns and worlds and the shards and wrecks of systems: some, like the sun, still blazing; some rotting, like the earth; others, like the moon, stable in desolation.

WE LOOK for some reward of our endeavours and are disappointed; not success, not happiness, not even peace of conscience, crowns our ineffectual efforts to do well. Our frailties are invincible, our virtues barren; the battle goes sore against us to the going down of the sun. The canting moralist tells us of right and wrong; and we look abroad, even on the face of our small earth, and find them change with every climate, and no country where some action is not honoured for a virtue and none where it is not branded for a vice; and we look in our experience, and find no vital congruity in the wisest rules, but at the best a municipal fitness. It is not strange if we are tempted to despair of good. We ask too much. Our religions and moralities have been trimmed to flatter us, till they are all emasculate and sentimentalised, and only please and weaken. Truth is of a rougher strain. In the harsh face of life, faith can read a bracing gospel. The human race is a thing more ancient than the ten commandments; and the bones and revolutions of the Kosmos, in whose joints we are but moss and fungus, more ancient still.

I

Of the Kosmos in the last resort, science reports many doubtful things and all of them appalling. There seems no substance to this solid globe on which we stamp: nothing but symbols and ratios. Symbols and ratios carry us and bring us forth and beat us down; gravity that swings the incommensurable suns and worlds through space, is but a figment varying inversely as the squares of distances; and the suns and worlds themselves, imponderable figures of abstraction, NH_3, and H_2O. Consideration dares not dwell upon this view; that way madness lies; science carries us into zones of speculation, where there is no habitable city for the mind of man.

But take the Kosmos with a grosser faith, as our senses give it us. We behold space sown with rotatory islands, suns and worlds and the shards and wrecks of systems: some, like the sun, still blazing; some rotting, like the earth; others, like the moon, stable in desolation. All of these we take to be made of something we call matter: a thing which no analysis can help us to conceive; to whose incredible properties no familiarity can reconcile our minds. This stuff, when not purified by the lustration of fire, rots uncleanly into something we call life; seized through all its atoms with a pediculous malady; swelling in tumours that become independent, sometimes even (by an abhorrent prodigy) locomotory; one splitting into millions, millions cohering into one, as the malady proceeds through varying stages. This vital putrescence of the dust, used as we are to it, yet strikes us with occasional disgust, and the profusion of worms in a piece of ancient turf, or the air of a marsh darkened with insects, will sometimes check our breathing so that we aspire for cleaner places. But none is clean: the moving sand is infected with lice; the pure spring, where it bursts out of the mountain, is a mere issue of worms; even in the hard rock the crystal is forming.

In two main shapes this eruption covers the countenance of the earth: the animal and the vegetable: one in some degree the inversion of the other: the second rooted to the spot; the first coming detached out of its natal mud, and scurrying abroad with the myriad feet of insects or towering into the heavens on the wings of birds: a thing so inconceivable that, if it be well considered, the heart stops. To what passes with the anchored vermin, we have little clue, doubtless they have their joys and sorrows, their delights and killing agonies: it appears not how. But of the locomotory, to which we ourselves belong, we can tell more. These share with us a thousand miracles: the miracles of sight, of hearing, of the projection of sound, things that bridge space; the miracles of memory and reason, by which the present is conceived, and when it is gone, its image kept living in the brains of man and brute; the miracle of reproduction, with its imperious desires and staggering consequences. And to put the last touch upon this mountain mass of the revolting and the inconceivable, all these prey upon each other, lives tearing other lives in pieces, cramming them inside themselves, and by that summary process, growing fat: the vegetarian, the whale, perhaps the tree, not less than the lion of the desert; for the vegetarian is only the eater of the dumb.

Meanwhile our rotatory island loaded with predatory life, and more drenched with blood, both animal and vegetable, than ever mutinied ship, scuds through space with unimaginable speed, and turns alternate cheeks to the reverberation of a blazing world, ninety million miles away.

II

What a monstrous spectre is this man, the disease of the agglutinated dust, lifting alternate feet or lying drugged with slumber; killing, feeding, growing, bringing forth small copies of himself; grown upon with hair like grass, fitted with eyes that move and glitter in his face; a thing to set children screaming;—and yet looked at nearlier, known as his fellows know him, how surprising are his attributes! Poor soul, here for so little, cast among so many hardships, filled with desires so incommensurate and so inconsistent, savagely surrounded, savagely descended, irremediably condemned to prey upon his fellow lives: who should have blamed him had he been of a piece with his destiny and a being merely barbarous? And we look and behold him instead filled with imperfect virtues: infinitely childish, often admirably valiant, often touchingly kind; sitting down, amidst his momentary life, to debate of right and wrong and the attributes of the deity; rising up to do battle for an egg or die for an idea; singling out his friends and his mate with cordial affection; bringing forth in pain, rearing with long-suffering solicitude, his young. To touch the heart of his mystery, we find, in him one thought, strange to the point of lunacy: the thought of duty; the thought of something owing to himself, to his neighbour, to his God: an ideal of decency, to which he would rise if it were possible; a limit of shame, below which, if it be possible, he will not stoop. The design in most men is one of conformity; here and there, in picked natures, it transcends itself and soars on the other side, arming martyrs with independence; but in all, in their degrees, it is a bosom thought:— Not in man alone, for we trace it in dogs and cats whom we know fairly well, and doubtless some similar point of honour sways the elephant, the oyster, and the louse, of whom we know so little:—But in man, at least, it sways with so complete an empire that merely selfish things come second, even with the selfish: that appetites are starved, fears are conquered, pains supported; that almost the dullest shrinks from the reproof of a glance, although it were a child's; and all but the most cowardly stand amid the risks of war; and the more noble, having strongly conceived an act as due to their ideal, affront and embrace death. Strange enough if, with their singular origin and perverted practice, they think they are to be rewarded in some future life: stranger still, if they are persuaded of the contrary, and think this blow, which they solicit, will strike them senseless for eternity. I shall be reminded what a tragedy of misconception and misconduct man at large presents: of organised injustice, cowardly violence and treacherous crime; and of the damning imperfections of the best. They cannot be too darkly drawn. Man is indeed marked for failure in his efforts to do right. But where the best consistently miscarry, how tenfold more remarkable that all should continue to strive; and surely we should find it both touching and inspiriting, that in a field from which success is banished, our race should not cease to labour.

If the first view of this creature, stalking in his rotatory isle, be a thing to shake the courage of the stoutest, on this nearer sight, he startles us with an admiring wonder. It matters not where we look, under what climate we observe him, in what stage of society, in what depth of ignorance, burthened with what erroneous morality; by camp-fires in Assiniboia, the snow powdering his shoulders, the wind plucking his blanket, as he sits, passing the ceremonial calumet and uttering his grave opinions like a Roman senator; in ships at sea, a man inured to hardship and vile pleasures, his brightest hope a fiddle in a tavern and a bedizened trull who sells herself to rob him, and he for all that simple, innocent, cheerful, kindly like a child, constant to toil, brave to drown, for others; in the slums of cities, moving among indifferent millions to mechanical employments, without hope of change in the future, with scarce a pleasure in the present, and yet true to his virtues, honest up to his lights, kind to his neighbours, tempted perhaps in vain by the bright gin-palace, perhaps long-suffering with the drunken wife that ruins him; in India (a woman this time) kneeling with broken cries and streaming tears, as she drowns her child in the sacred river; in the brothel, the discard of society, living mainly on strong drink, fed with affronts, a fool, a thief, the comrade of thieves, and even here keeping the point of honour and the touch of pity, often repaying the world's scorn with service, often standing firm upon a scruple, and at a certain cost, rejecting riches:—everywhere some virtue cherished or affected, everywhere some decency of thought and carriage, everywhere the ensign of man's ineffectual goodness:—ah! if I could show you this! if I could show you these men and women, all the world over, in every stage of history, under every abuse of error, under every circumstance of failure, without hope, without help, without thanks, still obscurely fighting the lost fight of virtue, still clinging, in the brothel or on the scaffold, to some rag of honour, the poor jewel of their souls! They may seek to escape, and yet they cannot; it is not alone their privilege and glory, but their doom; they are condemned to some nobility; all their lives long, the desire of good is at their heels, the implacable hunter.

Of all earth's meteors, here at least is the most strange and consoling: that this ennobled lemur, this hair-crowned bubble of the dust, this inheritor of a few years and sorrows, should yet deny himself his rare delights, and add to his frequent pains, and live for an ideal, however misconceived. Nor can we stop with man. A new doctrine, received with screams a little while ago by canting moralists, and still not properly worked into the body of our thoughts, lights us a step farther into the heart of this rough but noble universe. For nowadays the pride of man denies in vain his kinship with the original dust. He stands no longer like a thing apart. Close at his heels we see the dog, prince of another genus: and in him too, we see dumbly testified the same cultus of an unattainable ideal, the same constancy in failure. Does it stop with the dog? We look at our feet where the ground is blackened with the swarming ant: a creature so small, so far from us in the hierarchy of brutes, that we can scarce trace and scarce comprehend his doings; and here also, in his ordered politics and rigorous justice, we see confessed the law of duty and the fact of individual sin. Does it stop, then, with the ant? Rather this desire of well-doing and this doom of frailty run through all the grades of life: rather is this earth, from the frosty top of Everest to the next margin of the internal fire, one stage of ineffectual virtues and one temple of pious tears and perseverance. The whole creation groaneth and travaileth together. It is the common and the god-like law of life. The browsers, the biters, the barkers, the hairy coats of field and forest, the squirrel in the oak, the thousand-footed creeper in the dust, as they share with us the gift of life, share with us the love of an ideal: strive like us—like us are tempted to grow weary of the struggle—to do well; like us receive at times unmerited refreshment, visitings of support, returns of courage; and are condemned like us to be crucified between that double law of the members and the will. Are they like us, I wonder, in the timid hope of some reward, some sugar with the drug? do they, too, stand aghast at unrewarded virtues, at the sufferings of those whom, in our partiality, we take to be just, and the prosperity of such as, in our blindness, we call wicked? It may be, and yet God knows what they should look for. Even while they look, even while they repent, the foot of man treads them by thousands in the dust, the yelping hounds burst upon their trail, the bullet speeds, the knives are heating in the den of the vivisectionist; or the dew falls, and the generation of a day is blotted out. For these are creatures, compared with whom our weakness is strength, our ignorance wisdom, our brief span eternity.

And as we dwell, we living things, in our isle of terror and under the imminent hand of death, God forbid it should be man the erected, the reasoner, the wise in his own eyes—God forbid it should be man that wearies in well-doing, that despairs of unrewarded effort, or utters the language of complaint. Let it be enough for faith, that the whole creation groans in mortal frailty, strives with unconquerable constancy: Surely not all in vain.

On the Choice of a Profession

Thus it is, that, out of men, we make bankers.

YOU WRITE to me, my dear sir, requesting advice at one of the most momentous epochs in a young man's life. You are about to choose a profession; and with a diffidence highly pleasing at your age, you would be glad, you say, of some guidance in the choice. There is nothing more becoming than for youth to seek counsel: nothing more becoming to age than to be able to give it; and in a civilisation old and complicated like ours, where practical persons boast of a kind of practical philosophy superior to all others, you would very naturally expect to find all such questions systematically answered. For the dicta of the Practical Philosophy, you come to me. What, you ask, are the principles usually followed by the wise in the like critical junctures? There, I confess, you pose me on the threshold. I have examined my own recollections; I have interrogated others; and with all the will in the world to serve you better, I fear I can only tell you that the wise, in these circumstances, act upon no principles whatever. This is disappointing to you; it was painful to myself; but if I am to declare the truth as I see it, I must repeat that wisdom has nothing to do with the choice of a profession.

We all know what people say, and very foolish it usually is. The question is to get inside of these flourishes, and discover what it is they think and ought to say: to perform, in short, the Socratic Operation.—The more ready-made answers there are to any question, the more abstruse it becomes; for those of whom we make the enquiry have the less need of consideration before they reply. The world being more or less beset with Anxious Enquirers of the Socratic persuasion, it is the object of a Liberal Education to equip people with a proper number of these answers by way of passport; so they can pass swimmingly to and fro on their affairs without the trouble of thinking. How should a banker know his own mind? It takes him all his time to manage his bank. If you saw a company of pilgrims, walking as if for a wager, each with his teeth set; and if you happened to ask them one after another: Whither they were going?

and from each you were to receive the same answer: that positively they were all in such a hurry, they had never found leisure to enquire into the nature of their errand:—confess, my dear sir, you would be startled at the indifference they exhibited. Am I going too far, if I say, that this is the condition of the large majority of our fellow-men and almost all our fellow-women?

I stop a banker.

'My good fellow,' I say, 'give me a moment.'

'I have not a moment to spare,' says he.

'Why?' I enquire.

'I must be banking,' he replies. 'I am so busily engaged in banking all day long that I have hardly leisure for my meals.'

'And what,' I continue my interrogatory, 'is banking?'

'Sir,' says he, 'it is my business.'

'Your business?' I repeat. 'And what is a man's business?'

'Why,' cries the banker, 'a man's business is his duty.' And with that he breaks away from me, and I see him skimming to his avocations.

But this is a sort of answer that provokes reflection. Is a man's business his duty? Or perhaps should not his duty be his business? If it is not my duty to conduct a bank (and I contend that it is not) is it the duty of my friend the banker? Who told him it was? Is it in the Bible? Is he sure that banks are a good thing? Might it not have been his duty to stand aside, and let someone else conduct the bank? Or perhaps ought he not to have been a ship-captain instead? All of these perplexing queries may be summed up under one head: the grave problem which my friend offers to the world: Why is he a Banker?

Well, why is it? There is one principal reason, I conceive: that the man was trapped. Education, as practised, is a form of harnessing with the friendliest intentions. The fellow was hardly in trousers before they whipped him into school; hardly done with school before they smuggled him into an office; it is ten to one they have had him married into the bargain; and all this before he has had time so much as to imagine that there may be any other practicable course. Drum, drum, drum; you must be in time for school; you must do your Cornelius Nepos; you must keep your hands clean;

you must go to parties—a young man should make friends; and, finally—you must take this opening in a bank. He has been used to caper to this sort of piping from the first; and he joins the regiment of bank clerks for precisely the same reason as he used to go to the nursery at the stroke of eight. Then at last, rubbing his hands with a complacent smile, the parent lays his conjuring pipe aside. The trick is performed, ladies and gentlemen; the wild ass's colt is broken in; and now sits diligently scribing. Thus it is, that, out of men, we make bankers.

You have doubtless been present at the washing of sheep, which is a brisk, high-handed piece of manoeuvring, in its way; but what is it, as a subject of contemplation, to the case of the poor young animal, Man, turned loose into this roaring world, herded by robustious guardians, taken with the panic before he has wit enough to apprehend its cause, and soon flying with all his heels in the van of the general stampede? It may be that in after years, he shall fall upon a train of reflection, and begin narrowly to scrutinise the reasons that decided his path and his continued mad activity in that direction. And perhaps he may be very well pleased at the retrospect, and see fifty things that might have been worse, for one that would have been better; and even supposing him to take the other cue, bitterly to deplore the circumstances in which he is placed and bitterly to reprobate the jockeying that got him into them, the fact is, it is too late to indulge such whims. It is too late, after the train has started, to debate the needfulness of this particular journey: the door is locked, the express goes tearing overland at sixty miles an hour; he had better betake himself to sleep or the daily paper, and discourage unavailing thought. He sees many pleasant places out of the window: cottages in a garden, angles by the riverside, balloons voyaging the sky; but as for him, he is booked for all his natural days, and must remain a banker to the end.

If the juggling only began with school-time, if even the domineering friends and counsellors had made a choice of their own, there might still be some pretension to philosophy in the affair. But no. They too were trapped; they are but tame elephants unwittingly ensnaring others, and were themselves ensnared by tame elephants of an older domestication. We have all learned our tricks in captivity, to the spiriting of Mrs Grundy and a system of rewards and punishments. The crack of the whip and the trough of fodder: the cut direct and an invitation to dinner: the gallows and the Shorter Catechism: a pat upon the head and a stinging lash on the reverse: these are the elements of education and the principles of the Practical Philosophy. Sir Thomas Browne, in the earlier part of the seventeenth century, had already apprehended the staggering fact that geography is a considerable part of orthodoxy; and that a man who, when born in London, makes a conscientious Protestant, would have made an equally conscientious Hindu if he had first seen daylight in Benares. This is but a small part, however important, of the things that are settled for us by our place of birth. An Englishman drinks beer and tastes his liquor in the throat; a Frenchman drinks wine and tastes it in the front of the mouth. Hence, a single beverage lasts the Frenchman all afternoon; and the Englishman cannot spend above a very short time in a café, but he must swallow half a bucket. The Englishman takes a cold tub every morning in his bedroom; the Frenchman has an occasional hot bath. The Englishman has an unlimited family and will die in harness; the Frenchman retires upon a competency with three children at the outside. So this imperative national tendency follows us through all the privacies of life, dictates our thoughts, and attends us to the grave. We do nothing, we say nothing, we wear nothing, but it is stamped with the Queen's Arms. We are English down to our boots and into our digestions. There is not a dogma of all those by which we lead young men, but we get it ourselves, between sleep and waking, between death and life, in a complete abeyance of the reasoning part.

'But how, sir,' (you will ask) 'is there then no wisdom in the world? And when my admirable father was this day urging me, with the most affecting expressions, to decide on an industrious, honest and lucrative employment—?' Enough, sir; I follow your thoughts, and will answer them to the utmost of my ability. Your father, for whom I entertain a singular esteem is, I am proud to believe, a professing Christian: the Gospel, therefore, is or ought to be his rule of conduct. Now, I am of course ignorant to the terms employed by your father; but I quote here from a very urgent letter, written by another parent, who was a man of sense, integrity, great energy, and a Christian persuasion, and who has perhaps set forth the common view with a certain innocent openness of his own:

'You are now come to that time of life,' he writes to his son, 'and have reason within yourself to consider the absolute necessity of making provision for the time when it will be asked, Who is this man? Is he doing any good in the world? Has he the means of being "One of us"? I beseech you,' he goes on, rising in emotion, and appealing to his son by name, 'I beseech you do not trifle with this till it actually comes upon you. Bethink yourself and bestir yourself as a man. This is the time—' and so forth. This gentleman has candour; he is perspicacious, and has to deal apparently with a perspicacious pick-logic of a son; and hence the startling perspicacity of the document. But, my dear sir, what a principle of life! To 'do good in the world' is to be received into a society apart from personal affection. I could name many forms of evil vastly more exhilarating whether in prospect or enjoyment. If I scraped money, believe me, it should be for some more cordial purpose. And then, scraping money? It seems to me as if he had forgotten the Gospel. This is a view of life not quite the same as the Christian, which the old gentleman professed and sincerely studied to practise. But upon this point, I dare dilate no further. Suffice it to say, that looking round me on the manifestations of this Christian society of ours, I have been often tempted to exclaim: What, then, is Antichrist?

A wisdom, at least, which professes one set of propositions and yet acts upon another, can be no very entire or rational ground of conduct. Doubtless, there is much in this question of money; and for my part, I believe no young man ought to be at peace till he is self-supporting, and has an open, clear life of it on his own foundation. But here a consideration occurs to me of, as I must consider, startling originality. It is this: That there are two sides to this question as well as to so many others. Make more?—Aye, or spend less? There is no absolute call upon a man to make any specific income, unless, indeed, he has set his immortal soul on being 'One of us'.

A thoroughly respectable income is as much as a man spends. A luxurious income, or true opulence, is something more than a man spends. Raise the income, lower the expenditure, and, my dear sir, surprising as it seems, we have the same result. But I hear you remind

me, with pursed lips, of privations—of hardships. Alas! Sir, there are
privations upon either side; the banker has to sit all day in his bank,
a serious privation; can you not conceive that the landscape painter,
whom I take to be the meanest and most lost among contemporary
men, truly and deliberately prefers the privations upon his side—to
wear no gloves, to drink beer, to live on chops or even on potatoes,
and lastly, not to be 'One of us'—truly and deliberately prefers his
privations to those of the banker? I can. Yes, sir, I repeat those words;
I can. Believe me, there are Rivers in Bohemia!—but there is nothing
so hard to get people to understand as this: That they pay for their
money; and nothing so difficult to make them remember as this:
That money, when they have it, is for most of them, at least, only a
cheque to purchase pleasure with. How then if a man gets pleasure
in following an art? He might gain more cheques by following
another; but then, although there is a difference in cheques, the
amount of pleasure is the same. He gets some of his directly; unlike
the bank clerk, he is having his fortnight's holiday, and doing what
delights him, all the year.

All these patent truisms have a very strange air, when written
down. But that, my dear sir, is no fault of mine or of the truisms.
There they are. I beseech you, do not trifle with them. Bethink yourself like a man. This is the time.

But, you say, all this is very well; it does not help me to a choice.
Once more, sir, you have me; it does not. What shall I say? A choice,
let us remember, is almost more of a negative than a positive. You
embrace one thing; but you refuse a thousand. The most liberal
profession imprisons many energies and starves many affections. If
you are in a bank, you cannot be much upon the sea. You cannot be
both a first-rate violinist and a first-rate painter: you must lose in the
one art if you persist in following both. If you are sure of your preference, follow it. If not—nay, my dear sir, it is not for me or any man
to go beyond this point. God made you; not I. I cannot even make
you over again. I have heard of a schoolmaster, whose speciality it
was to elicit the bent of each pupil: poor schoolmaster, poor pupils!
As for me, if you have nothing indigenous in your own heart, no
living preference, no fine, human scorn, I leave you to the tide; it
will sweep you somewhere. Have you but a grain of inclination, I

will help you. If you wish to be a costermonger, be it, shame the devil; and I will stand the donkey. If you wish to be nothing, once more I leave you to the tide. I regret profoundly, my dear young sir, not only for you in whom I see such a lively promise of the future, but for the sake of your admirable and truly worthy father and your no less excellent mamma, that my remarks should seem no more conclusive. I can give myself this praise, that I have kept back nothing; but this, alas! is a subject on which there is little to put forward. It will probably not much matter what you decide upon doing; for most men seem to sink at length to the degree of stupor necessary for contentment in their different estates. Yes, sir, this is what I have observed. Most men are happy, and most men dishonest. Their mind sinks to the proper level; their honour easily accepts the custom of the trade. I wish you may find degeneration no more painful than your neighbours, soon sink into apathy, and be long spared in a state of respectable somnambulism, from the grave to which we haste.

Gentlemen

A quality of exquisite aptitude marks out the gentlemanly act; without an element of wit, we can be only gentlemen by negatives.

WHAT DO we mean today by that common phrase, a gentleman? By the lights of history, from *gens, gentilis*, it should mean a man of family, 'one of a kent house', one of notable descent: thus embodying an ancient stupid belief and implying a modern scientific theory. The ancient and stupid belief came to the ground, with a prodigious dust and the collapse of several polities, in the latter half of the last century. There followed upon this an interregnum, during which it was believed that all men were born 'free and equal', and that it really did not matter who your father was. Man has always been nobly irrational, bandaging his eyes against the facts of life, feeding himself on the wind of ambitious falsehood, counting his stock to be the children of the gods; and yet perhaps he never showed in a more touching light than when he embraced this boyish theory. Freedom we now know for a thing incompatible with corporate life and a blessing probably peculiar to the solitary robber; we know besides that every advance in richness of existence, whether moral or material, is paid for by a loss of liberty; that liberty is man's coin in which he pays his way; that luxury and knowledge and virtue, and love and the family affections, are all so many fresh fetters on the naked and solitary freeman. And the ancient stupid belief having come to the ground and the dust of its fall subsided, behold the modern scientific theory beginning to rise very nearly on the old foundation; and individuals no longer (as was fondly imagined) springing into life from God knows where, incalculable, untrammelled, abstract, equal to one another—but issuing modestly from a race; with virtues and vices, fortitudes and frailties, ready made; the slaves of their inheritance of blood; eternally unequal. So that we in the present, and yet more our scientific descendants in the future, must use, when we desire to praise a character, the old expression, gentleman, in nearly the old sense: one of a happy strain of blood, one fortunate in the descent from brave and self-respecting ancestors, whether clowns or counts.

And yet plainly this is of but little help. The intricacy of descent defies prediction; so that even the heir of a hundred sovereigns may

be born a brute or a vulgarian. We may be told that a picture is an
heirloom; that does not tell us what the picture represents. All qualities are inherited, and all characters; but which are the qualities that
belong to the gentleman? what is the character that earns and
deserves that honourable style?

II

The current ideas vary with every class, and need scarce be combated,
need scarce be mentioned save for the love of fun. In one class, and
not long ago, he was regarded as a gentleman who kept a gig. He is a
gentleman in one house who does not eat peas with his knife; in
another who is not to be discountenanced by any created form of
butler. In my own case I have learned to move among pompous
menials without much terror, never without much respect. In the
narrow sense, and so long as they publicly tread the boards of their
profession, it would be difficult to find more finished gentlemen;
and it would often be a matter of grave thought with me, sitting in
my club, to compare the bearing of the servants with that of those on
whom they waited. There could be no question which were the
better gentlemen. And yet I was hurried into no democratic theories; for I saw the members' part was the more difficult to play, I saw
that to serve was a more graceful attitude than to be served, I knew
besides that much of the servants' gentility was *ad hoc* and would be
laid aside with their livery jackets; and to put the matter in a nutshell,
that some of the members would have made very civil footmen and
many of the servants intolerable members. For all that, one of the
prettiest gentlemen I ever knew was a servant. A gentleman he
happened to be, even in the old stupid sense, only on the wrong side
of the blanket; and a man besides of much experience, having served
in the Guards' Club, and been valet to old Cooke of the *Saturday
Review*, and visited the States with Madame Sinico (I think it was)
and Portugal with Madame Someone-else, so that he had studied,
at least from the chair-backs, many phases of society. It chanced he
was waiter in a hotel where I was staying with my mother; it was
midwinter and we were the only guests; all afternoons, he and I
passed together on a perfect equality in the smoking-room; and at

meal-time, he waited on my mother and me as a servant. Now here was a trial of manners from which few would have come forth successful. To take refuge in a frozen bearing would have been the timid, the inelegant, resource of almost all. My friend was much more bold; he joined in the talk, he ventured to be jocular, he pushed familiarity to the nice margin, and yet still preserved the indefinable and proper distance of the English servant, and yet never embarrassed, never even alarmed, the comrade with whom he had just been smoking a pipe. It was a masterpiece of social dexterity—on artificial lines no doubt, and dealing with difficulties that should never have existed, that exist much less in France, and that will exist nowhere long—but a masterpiece for all that, and one that I observed with despairing admiration, as I have watched Sargent paint.

I say these difficulties should never have existed; for the whole relation of master and servant is today corrupt and vulgar. At home in England it is the master who is degraded; here in the States, by a triumph of inverted tact, the servant often so contrives that he degrades himself. He must be above his place; and it is the mark of a gentleman to be at home. He thinks perpetually of his own dignity; it is the proof of a gentleman to be jealous of the dignity of others. He is ashamed of his trade, which is the essence of vulgarity. He is paid to do certain services; yet he does them so gruffly that any man of spirit would resent them if they were gratuitous favours; and this (if he will reflect upon it tenderly) is so far from the genteel as to be not even coarsely honest. Yet we must not blame the man for these mistakes; the vulgarity is in the air. There is a tone in popular literature much to be deplored; deprecating service, like a disgrace; honouring those who are ashamed of it; honouring even (I speak not without book) such as prefer to live by the charity of poor neighbours instead of blacking the shoes of the rich. Blacking shoes is counted (in these works) a thing specially disgraceful. To the philosophic mind, it will seem a less exceptionable trade than to deal in stocks, and one in which it is more easy to be honest than to write books. Why, then, should it be marked out for reprobation by the popular authors? It is taken, I think, for a type; inoffensive in itself, it stands for many disagreeable household duties; disagreeable to fulfil, I had nearly said shameful to impose; and with the dullness of their tribe, the popular authors transfer the shame to the wrong party. Truly, in this matter there seems a lack of gentility somewhere; a lack of refinement, of reserve, of common modesty; a strain of the spirit of those ladies in the past, who did not hesitate to bathe before a footman. And one thing at least is easy to prophesy, not many years will have gone by before those shall be held the most 'elegant' gentlemen, and those the most 'refined' ladies, who wait (in a dozen particulars) upon themselves. But the shame is for the masters only. The servant stands quite clear. He has one of the easiest parts to play upon the face of earth; he must be far misled, if he so grossly fails in it.

III

It is a fairly common accomplishment to behave with decency in one character and among those to whom we are accustomed and with whom we have been brought up. The trial of gentility lies in some such problem as that of my waiter's, in foreign travel, or in some sudden and sharp change of class. I once sailed on the emigrant side from the Clyde to New York; among my fellow-passengers I passed generally as a mason, for the excellent reason that there was a mason on board *who happened to know*; and this fortunate event enabled me to mix with these working people on a footing of equality. I thus saw them at their best, using their own civility; while I, on the other hand, stood naked to their criticism. The workmen were at home, I was abroad, I was the shoe-black in the drawing-room, the Huron at Versailles; and I used to have hot and cold fits, lest perchance I made a beast of myself in this new environment. I had no allowances to hope for; I could not plead that I was 'only a gentleman after all', for I was known to be a mason; and I must stand and fall by my transplanted manners on their own intrinsic decency. It chanced there was a Welsh blacksmith on board, who was not only well-mannered himself and a judge of manners, but a fellow besides of an original mind. He had early diagnosed me for a masquerader and a person out of place; and as we had grown intimate upon the voyage, I carried him my troubles. How did I behave? Was I, upon this crucial test, at all a gentleman? I might have asked eight hundred thousand blacksmiths (if Wales or the world contain so many) and they would have held my question for a mockery; but Jones was a man of genuine perception, thought a long time before he answered, looking at me comically and reviewing (I could see) the events of the voyage, and then told me that 'on the whole' I did 'pretty well'. Mr Jones was a humane man and very much my friend, and he could get no further than 'on the whole' and 'pretty well'. I was chagrined at the moment for myself; on a larger basis of experience, I am now only concerned for my class. My co-equals would have done but little better, and many of them worse. Indeed, I have never seen a sight more pitiable than that of the current gentleman unbending; unless it were the current lady! It is these stiff-necked condescensions, it is that grace-less assumption, that make the diabolic element in times of riot. A man may be willing to starve in silence like a hero; it is a rare man indeed who can accept the unspoken slights of the unworthy, and not be embittered. There was a visit paid to the steerage quarters on this same voyage, by a young gentleman and two young ladies; and as I was by that time pretty well accustomed to the workman's standard, I had a chance to see my own class from below. God help them, poor creatures! As they ambled back to their saloon, they left behind, in the minds of my companions, and in my mind also, an image and an influence that might well have set them weeping, could they have guessed its nature. I spoke a few lines past of a shoe-black in a drawing-room; it is what I never saw; but I did see that young gentleman and these young ladies on the forward deck, and the picture remains with me, and the offence they managed to convey is not forgotten.

IV

And yet for all this ambiguity, for all these imperfect examples, we know clearly what we mean by the word. When we meet a gentle-man of another class, through all contrariety of habits, the essentials of the matter stand confessed: I never had a doubt of Jones. More than that, we recognise the type in books; the actors of history, the characters of fiction, bear the mark upon their brow; at a word, by a bare act, we discern and segregate the mass, this one a gentleman, the others not. To take but the last hundred years, Scott, Gordon, Wellington in his cold way, Grant in his plain way, Shelley for all his follies, these were clearly gentlemen; Napoleon, Byron, Lockhart, these were as surely cads, and the two first cads of a rare water.

Let us take an anecdote of Grant and one of Wellington. On the day of the capitulation, Lee wore his presentation sword; it was the first thing Grant observed, and from that moment he had but one thought: how to avoid taking it. A man, who should perhaps have had the nature of an angel, but assuredly not the special virtues of the gentleman, might have received the sword, and no more words about it: he would have done well in a plain way. One who wished to be a gentleman, and knew not how, might have received and returned it: he would have done infamously ill, he would have proved himself a cad; taking the stage for himself, leaving to his adversary confusion of countenance and the ungraceful posture of the man condemned to offer thanks. Grant, without a word said, added to the terms this article: 'All officers to retain their side-arms'; and the problem was solved and Lee kept his sword, and Grant went down to posterity, not perhaps a fine gentleman, but a great one. And now for Wellington. The tale is on a lower plane, is elegant rather than noble; yet it is a tale of a gentleman too, and raises besides a pleasant and instructive question. Wellington and Marshal Marmont were adversaries (it will not have been forgotten) in one of the prettiest recorded acts of military fencing, the campaign of Salamanca: it was a brilliant business on both sides, just what Count Tolstoi ought to study before he writes again upon the inutility of generals; indeed, it was so very brilliant on the Marshal's part that on the last day, in one of those extremes of cleverness that come so near stupidity, he fairly over-reached himself, was taken 'in flagrant delict', was beaten like a sack, and had his own arm shot off as a reminder not to be so clever the next time. It appears he was incurable; a more distinguished example of the same precipitate, ingenious blundering will be present to the minds of all—his treachery in 1814; and even the tale I am now telling shows, on a lilliputian scale, the man's besetting weakness. Years after Salamanca, the two generals met, and the Marshal (willing to be agreeable) asked the Duke his opinion of the battle. With that promptitude, wit, and willingness to spare pain which make so large a part of the armoury of the gentleman, Wellington had his answer ready, impossible to surpass on its own ground: 'I early

perceived your excellency had been wounded.' And you see what a
pleasant position he had created for the Marshal, who had no more
to do than just to bow and smile and take the stage at his leisure. But
here we come to our problem. The Duke's answer (whether true or
false) created a pleasant position for the Marshal. But what sort of
position had the Marshal's question created for the Duke? and had
not Marmont the manoeuvrer once more manoeuvred himself into a
false position? I conceive so. It is the man who has gained the victory,
not the man who has suffered the defeat, who finds his ground
embarrassing. The vanquished has an easy part, it is easy for him to
make a handsome reference; but how hard for the victor to make a
handsome reply! An unanswerable compliment is the social bludg-
eon; and Marmont (with the most graceful intentions in the world)
had propounded one of the most desperate. Wellington escaped
from his embarrassment by a happy and courtly inspiration. Grant,
I imagine, since he had a genius for silence, would have found some
means to hold his peace. Lincoln, with his half-tact and unhappy
readiness, might have placed an appropriate anecdote and raised a
laugh; not an unkindly laugh, for he was a kindly man; but under the
circumstances the best-natured laugh would have been death to
Marmont. Shelley (if we can conceive him to have gained a battle at
all) would have blushed and stammered, feeling the Marshal's false
position like some grossness of his own; and when the blush had
communicated itself to the cheeks of his unlucky questioner, some
stupid, generous word (such as I cannot invent for him) would have
found its way to his lips and set them both at ease. Byron? well, he
would have managed to do wrong; I have too little sympathy for that
unmatched vulgarian to create his part. Napoleon? that would have
depended: had he been angry, he would have left all competitors
behind in cruel coarseness: had he been in a good humour, it might
have been the other way. For this man, the very model of a cad, was
so well served with truths by the clear insight of his mind, and with
words by his great though shallow gift of literature, that he has left
behind him one of the most gentlemanly utterances on record:
'*Madame, respectez le fardeau.*' And he could do the right thing too,
as well as say it; and any character in history might envy him that
moment when he gave his sword, the sword of the world-subduer, to

his old, loyal enemy, Macdonald. A strange thing to consider two
generations of a Skye family, and two generations of the same virtue,
fidelity to the defeated: the father braving the rains of the Hebrides
with the tattered beggar-lad that was his rightful sovereign; the son,
in that princely house of Fontainebleau, himself a marshal of the
Empire, receiving from the gratitude of one whom he had never
feared and who had never loved him, the tool and symbol of the
world's most splendid domination. I am glad, since I deal with the
name of gentlemen, to touch for one moment on its nobler sense,
embodied, on the historic scale and with epic circumstance, in the
lives of these Macdonalds. Nor is there any man but must be
conscious of a thrill of gratitude to Napoleon, for his worthy recognition of the worthiest virtue. Yes, that was done *like* a gentleman;
and yet in our hearts we must think that it was done by a performer.
For to feel precisely what it is to be a gentleman and what it is to be
a cad, we have but to study Napoleon's attitude after Trafalgar, and
compare it with that beautiful letter of Louis the Fourteenth's in
which he acknowledges the news of Blenheim. We hear much about
the Sun-king nowadays, and Michelet is very sad reading about his
government, and Thackeray was very droll about his wig; but when
we read this letter from the vainest king in Europe smarting under
the deadliest reverse, we know that at least he was a gentleman. In
the battle, Tallard had lost his son, Louis the primacy of Europe; it is
only with the son the letter deals. Poor Louis! if his wig had been
twice as great, and his sins twice as numerous, here is a letter to
throw wide the gates of Heaven for his entrance. I wonder what
would Louis have said to Marshal Marmont? Something infinitely
condescending; for he was too much of a king to be quite a gentleman. And Marcus Aurelius, how would he have met the question?
With some reference to the gods no doubt, uttered not quite without
a twang; for the good emperor and great gentleman of Rome was of
the Methodists of his day and race.

And now to make the point at which I have been aiming. The
perfectly straightforward person who should have said to Marmont,
'I was uncommonly glad to get you beaten,' would have done the
next best to Wellington who had the inspiration of graceful speech;
just as the perfectly straightforward person who should have taken

Lee's sword and kept it, would have done the next best to Grant who had the inspiration of the truly graceful act. Lee would have given up his sword and preserved his dignity; Marmont might have laughed, his pride need not have suffered. Not to try to spare people's feelings is so much kinder than to try in a wrong way; and not to try to be a gentleman at all is so much more gentlemanly than to try and fail! So that this gift, or grace, or virtue, resides not so much in conduct as in knowledge; not so much in refraining from the wrong, as in knowing the precisely right. A quality of exquisite aptitude marks out the gentlemanly act; without an element of wit, we can be only gentlemen by negatives.

V

More and more, as our knowledge widens, we have to reply to those who ask for a definition: 'I can't give you that, but I will tell you a story.' We cannot say what a thing will be, nor what it ought to be; but we can say what it has been, and how it came to be what it is: History instead of Definition. It is this which (if we continue teachable) will make short work of all political theories; it is on this we must fall back to explain our word, gentleman.

The life of our fathers was highly ceremonial; a man's steps were counted; his acts, his gestures were prescribed; marriage, sale, adoption, and not only legal contracts, but the simplest necessary movements, must be all conventionally ordered and performed to rule. Life was a rehearsed piece; and only those who had been drilled in the rehearsals could appear with decency in the performance. A gentile man, one of a dominant race, hereditary priest, hereditary leader, was, by the circumstances of his birth and education, versed in this symbolic etiquette. Whatever circumstance arose, he would be prepared to utter the sacramental word, to perform the ceremonial act. For every exigence of family or tribal life, peace or war, marriage or sacrifice, fortune or mishap, he stood easily waiting, like the well-graced actor for his cue. The clan that he guided would be safe from shame, it would be ensured from loss; for the man's attitude would be always becoming, his bargains legal, and his sacrifices pleasing to the gods. It is from this gentile man, the priest, the chief,

the expert in legal forms and attitudes, the bulwark and the ornament of his tribe, that our name of gentleman descends. So much of
the sense still clings to it, it still points the man who, in every circumstance of life, knows what to do and how to do it gracefully; so much
of its sense it has lost, for this grace and knowledge are no longer of
value in practical affairs; so much of a new sense it has taken on, for
as well as the nicest fitness, it now implies a punctual loyalty of word
and act. And note the word loyalty; here is a parallel advance from
the proficiency of the gentile man to the honour of the gentleman,
and from the sense of legality to that of loyalty. With the decay of the
ceremonial element in life, the gentleman has lost some of his prestige, I had nearly said some of his importance; and yet his part is the
more difficult to play. It is hard to preserve the figures of a dance
when many of our partners dance at random. It is easy to be a gentleman in a very stiff society, where much of our action is prescribed; it
is hard indeed in a very free society where (as it seems) almost any
word or act must come by inspiration. The rehearsed piece is at an
end; we are now floundering through an impromptu charade. Far
more of ceremonial remains (to be sure) traditional in the terms of
our association, far more hereditary in the texture of brains, than is
dreamed by the superficial; it is our fortress against many perils, the
cement of states, the meeting ground of classes. But much of life
comes up for the first time, unrehearsed, and must be acted on upon
the instant. Knowledge there can here be none; the man must invent
an attitude, he must be inspired with speech; and the most perfect
gentleman is he who, in these irregular cases, acts and speaks with
most aplomb and fitness. His tact simulates knowledge; to see him
so easy and secure and graceful you would think he had been
through it all before; you would think he was the gentile man of old,
repeating for the thousandth time, upon some public business, the
sacramental words and ceremonial gestures of his race.

Lastly, the club footman, so long as he is in his livery jacket, appears
the perfect gentleman and visibly out-shines the members; and the
same man, in the public-house, among his equals, becomes perhaps
plain and dull, perhaps even brutal. He has learned the one part of
service perfectly; there he has knowledge, he shines in the prepared
performance; outside of that he must rely on tact, and sometimes

flounders sadly in the unrehearsed charade. The gentleman, again, may be put to open shame as he changes from one country, or from one rank of society to another. The footman was a gentleman only *ad hoc*; the other (at the most) *ad hoec*; and when he has got beyond his knowledge, he begins to flounder in the charade. Even so the gentile man was only gentile among those of his own gens and their subordinates and neighbours; in a distant city, he too was peregrine and inexpert, and must become the client of another, or find his bargains insecure and be excluded from the service of the gods.

Some Gentlemen in Fiction

At bottom, what we hate or love is doubtless some projection of the author; the personal atmosphere is doubtless his; and when we think we know Hamlet, we know but a side of his creator.

I

TO MAKE a character at all—so to select, so to describe a few acts, a few speeches, perhaps (though this is quite superfluous) a few details of physical appearance, as that these shall all cohere and strike in the reader's mind a common note of personality—there is no more delicate enterprise, success is nowhere less comprehensible than here. We meet a man, we find his talk to have been racy; and yet if every word were taken down by shorthand, we should stand amazed at its essential insignificance. Physical presence, the speaking eye, the inimitable commentary of the voice, it was in these the spell resided; and these are all excluded from the pages of the novel. There is one writer of fiction whom I have the advantage of knowing; and he confesses to me that his success in this matter (small though it be) is quite surprising to himself. 'In one of my books,' he writes, 'and in one only, the characters took the bit in their mouth; all at once, they became detached from the flat paper, they turned their backs on me and walked off bodily; and from that time, my task was stenographic—it was they who spoke, it was they who wrote the remainder of the story. When this miracle of genesis occurred, I was thrilled with joyous surprise; I felt a certain awe—shall we call it superstitious? And yet how small a miracle it was; with what a partial life were my characters endowed; and when all was said, how little did I know of them! It was a form of words that they supplied me with; it was in a form of words that they consisted; beyond and behind was nothing.' The limitation, which this writer felt and which he seems to have deplored, can be remarked in the work of even literary princes. I think it was Hazlitt who declared that, if the names were dropped at press, he could restore any speech in Shakespeare to the proper speaker; and I daresay we could all pick out the words of Nym or Pistol, Caius or Evans; but not even Hazlitt could do the like for the great leading characters, who yet are cast in a more delicate mould, and appear before us far more subtly and far more fully differentiated, than these easy-going ventriloquial puppets. It is just when the obvious expedients of the barrel-organ vocabulary, the droll mispronunciation or the racy dialect, are laid aside, that the true masterpieces are wrought (it would seem) from nothing. Hamlet speaks in character, I potently believe it, and yet see not how. He speaks at least as no man ever spoke in life, and very much as many other heroes do in the same volume; now uttering the noblest verse, now prose of the most cunning workmanship; clothing his opinions throughout in that amazing dialect, Shakespearese. The opinions themselves, again, though they are true and forcible and reinforced with excellent images, are not peculiar either to Hamlet, or to any man or class or period; in their admirable generality of appeal resides their merit; they might figure, and they would be applauded, in almost any play and in the mouth of almost any noble and considerate character.— The only hint that is given as to his physical man—I speak for myself—is merely shocking, seems merely erroneous, and is perhaps best explained away upon the theory that Shakespeare had Burbage more directly in his eye than Hamlet. As for what the Prince does and what he refrains from doing, all acts and passions are strangely impersonal. A thousand characters, as different among themselves as night from day, should yet, under the like stress of circumstance, have trodden punctually in the footprints of Hamlet and each other. Have you read *André Cornélis?* in which M. Bourget handled over again but yesterday the theme of *Hamlet*, even as Godwin had already rehandled part of it in *Caleb Williams*. You can see the character M. Bourget means with quite sufficient clearness; it is not a masterpiece, but it is adequately indicated; and the character is proper to the part, these acts and passions fit him like a glove, he carries the tale, not with so good a grace as Hamlet, but with equal nature. Well, the two personalities are fundamentally distinct: they breathe upon us out of different worlds; in face, in touch, in the subtle atmosphere by which we recognise an individual, in all that goes to build up a character—or at least that shadowy thing, a character in a book—they are even opposed: the same fate involves them, they behave on the same lines, and they have not one hair in common. What, then, remains of Hamlet? and by what magic does he stand forth in our brains, *teres atque rotundus*, solid to the touch, a man to praise, to blame, to pity, ay, and to love?

At bottom, what we hate or love is doubtless some projection of the author; the personal atmosphere is doubtless his; and when we think we know Hamlet, we know but a side of his creator. It is a good old comfortable doctrine, which our fathers have taken for a pillow, which has served as a cradle for ourselves; and yet, in some of its applications, it brings us face to face with difficulties. I said last month that we could tell a gentleman in a novel. Let us continue to take Hamlet. Manners vary, they invert themselves, from age to age; Shakespeare's gentlemen are not quite ours, there is no doubt their talk would raise a flutter in a modern tea-party; but in the old pious phrase, they have the root of the matter. All the most beautiful traits of the gentleman adorn this character of Hamlet: it was the side on which Salvini seized, which he so attractively displayed, with which he led theatres captive; it is the side, I think, by which the Prince endears himself to readers. It is true there is one staggering scene, the great scene with his mother. But we must regard this as the author's lost battle; here it was that Shakespeare failed: what to do with the Queen, how to depict her, how to make Hamlet use her, these (as we know) were his miserable problem; it beat him; he faced it with an indecision worthy of his hero; he shifted, he shuffled with it; in the end, he may be said to have left his paper blank. One reason why we do not more generally recognise this failure of Shakespeare's is because we have most of us seen the play performed; and managers, by what seems a stroke of art, by what is really (I dare say) a fortunate necessity, smuggle the problem out of sight—the play, too, for the matter of that; but the glamour of the footlights and the charm of that little strip of fiddlers' heads and elbows, conceal the conjuring. This stroke of art (let me call it so) consists in casting the Queen as an old woman. Thanks to the footlights and the fiddlers' heads, we never pause to inquire why the King should have pawned his soul for this college-bedmaker in masquerade; and thanks to the absurdity of the whole position, and that unconscious unchivalry of audiences (ay, and of authors also) to old women, Hamlet's monstrous conduct passes unobserved or unresented. Were the Queen cast as she should be, a woman still young and beautiful, had she been coherently written by Shakespeare, and were she played with any spirit, even an audience would rise.

But the scene is simply false, effective on the stage, untrue of any son or any mother; in judging the character of Hamlet, it must be left upon one side; and in all other relations we recognise the Prince for a gentleman.

Now, if the personal charm of any verbal puppet be indeed only an emanation from its author, may we conclude, since we feel Hamlet to be a gentleman, that Shakespeare was one too? An instructive parallel occurs. There were in England two writers of fiction, contemporaries, rivals in fame, opposites in character; one descended from a great house, easy, generous, witty, debauched, a favourite in the tap-room and the hunting field, yet withal a man of a high practical intelligence, a distinguished public servant, an ornament of the bench: the other, sprung from I know not whence—but not from kings—buzzed about by second-rate women, and their fit companion, a tea-bibber in parlours, a man of painful propriety, with all the narrowness and much of the animosity of the backshop and the dissenting chapel. Take the pair, they seem like types: Fielding, with all his faults, was undeniably a gentleman; Richardson, with all his genius and his virtues, as undeniably was not. And now turn to their works. In *Tom Jones*, a novel of which the respectable profess that they could stand the dulness if it were not so blackguardly, and the more honest admit they could forgive the blackguardism if it were not so dull—in *Tom Jones*, with its voluminous bulk and troops of characters, there is no shadow of a gentleman, for Allworthy is only ink and paper. In *Joseph Andrews*, I fear I have always confined my reading to the parson; and Mr Adams, delightful as he is, has no pretension 'to the genteel'. In *Amelia*, things get better; all things get better; it is one of the curiosities of literature that Fielding, who wrote one book that was engaging, truthful, kind, and clean, and another book that was dirty, dull, and false, should be spoken of, the world over, as the author of the second and not the first, as the author of *Tom Jones*, not of *Amelia*. And in *Amelia*, sure enough, we find some gentlefolk; Booth and Dr Harrison will pass in a crowd, I dare not say they will do more. It is very differently that one must speak of Richardson's creations. With Sir Charles Grandison I am unacquainted—there are many impediments in this brief life of man; I have more than once, indeed, reconnoitred the first volume with a flying party, but always decided not to break ground before the place till my siege guns came up; and it's an odd thing—I have been all these years in the field, and that powerful artillery is still miles in the rear. The day it overtakes me, Baron Gibbon's fortress shall be beat about his ears, and my flag be planted on the formidable ramparts of the second part of *Faust*. Clarendon, too— But why should I continue this confession? Let the reader take up the wondrous tale himself, and run over the books that he has tried, and failed withal, and vowed to try again, and now beholds, as he goes about a library, with secret compunction. As to Sir Charles at least, I have the report of spies; and by the papers in the office of my Intelligence Department, it would seem he was a most accomplished baronet. I am the more ready to credit these reports, because the spies are persons thoroughly accustomed to the business; and because my own investigation of a kindred quarter of the globe (*Clarissa Harlowe*) has led me to set a high value on the Richardsonians. Lovelace—in spite of his abominable misbehaviour—Colonel Morden and my Lord M— are all gentlemen of undisputed quality. They more than pass muster, they excel; they have a gallant, a conspicuous carriage; they roll into the book, four in hand, in gracious attitudes. The best of Fielding's gentlemen had scarce been at their ease in M— Hall; Dr Harrison had seemed a plain, honest man, a trifle below his company; and poor Booth (supposing him to have served in Colonel Morden's corps and to have travelled in the post-chaise along with his commandant) had been glad to slink away with Mowbray and crack a bottle in the butler's room.

So that here, on the terms of our theory, we have an odd inversion, tempting to the cynic.

II

Just the other day, there were again two rival novelists in England: Thackeray and Dickens; and the case of the last is, in this connection, full of interest. Here was a man and an artist, the most strenuous, one of the most endowed; and for how many years he laboured in vain to create a gentleman! With all his watchfulness of men and manners, with all his fiery industry, with his exquisite native gift of characterisation, with his clear knowledge of what he meant to do, there was yet something lacking. In part after part, novel after novel, a whole menagerie of characters, the good, the bad, the droll, and the tragic, came at his beck like slaves about an Oriental despot; there was only one who stayed away: the gentleman. If this ill fortune had persisted it might have shaken man's belief in art and industry. But years were given and courage was continued to the indefatigable artist; and at length, after so many and such lamentable failures, success began to attend upon his arms. David Copperfield scrambled through on hands and knees; it was at least a negative success; and Dickens, keenly alive to all he did, must have heaved a sigh of infinite relief. Then came the evil days, the days of *Dombey* and *Dorrit*, from which the lover of Dickens willingly averts his eyes; and when that temporary blight had passed away, and the artist began with a more resolute arm to reap the aftermath of his genius, we find him able to create a Carton, a Wrayburn, a Twemlow. No mistake about these three; they are all gentlemen: the sottish Carton, the effete Twemlow, the insolent Wrayburn, all have doubled the cape.

There were never in any book three perfect sentences on end; there was never a character in any volume but it somewhere tripped. We are like dancing dogs and preaching women: the wonder is not that we should do it well, but that we should do it at all. And Wrayburn, I am free to admit, comes on one occasion to the dust. I mean, of course, the scene with the old Jew. I will make you a present of the Jew for a cardboard figure; but that is neither here nor there: the ineffectuality of the one presentment does not mitigate the grossness, the baseness, the inhumanity of the other. In this scene, and in one other (if I remember aright) where it is echoed, Wrayburn combines the wit of the omnibus-cad with the good feeling of the Andaman Islander: in all the remainder of the book, throughout a thousand perils, playing (you would say) with difficulty, the author swimmingly steers his hero on the true course. The error stands by itself, and it is striking to observe the moment of its introduction. It follows immediately upon one of the most dramatic passages in fiction, that in which Bradley Headstone barks his knuckles on the churchyard wall. To handle Bradley (one of Dickens's superlative achievements) were a thing impossible to almost any man but his creator; and even to him, we may be sure, the effort was exhausting. Dickens was a weary man when he had barked the schoolmaster's knuckles, a weary man and an excited; but the tale of bricks had to be finished, the monthly number waited; and under the false inspiration of irritated nerves, the scene of Wrayburn and the Jew was written and sent forth; and there it is, a blot upon the book and a buffet to the reader.

I make no more account of this passage than of that other in *Hamlet*: a scene that has broken down, the judicious reader cancels for himself. And the general tenor of Wrayburn, and the whole of Carton and Twemlow, are beyond exception. Here, then, we have a man who found it for years an enterprise beyond his art to draw a gentleman, and who in the end succeeded. Is it because Dickens was not a gentleman himself that he so often failed? and if so, then how did he succeed at last? Is it because he was a gentleman that he succeeded? and if so, what made him fail? I feel inclined to stop this paper here, after the manner of conundrums, and offer a moderate reward for a solution. But the true answer lies probably deeper than did ever plummet sound. And mine (such as it is) will hardly appear to the reader to disturb the surface.

These verbal puppets (so to call them once again) are things of a divided parentage: the breath of life may be an emanation from their maker, but they themselves are only strings of words and parts of books; they dwell in, they belong to, literature; convention, technical artifice, technical gusto, the mechanical necessities of the art, these are the flesh and blood with which they are invested. If we look only at Carton and Wrayburn, both leading parts, it must strike us at once that both are most ambitiously attempted; that Dickens was not content to draw a hero and a gentleman plainly and quietly; that, after all his ill-success, he must still handicap himself upon these fresh adventures, and make Carton a sot, and sometimes a cantankerous sot, and Wrayburn insolent to the verge, and sometimes beyond the verge, of what is pardonable. A moment's thought will show us this was in the nature of his genius, and a part of his literary method. His fierce intensity of design was not to be slaked with any academic portraiture; not all the arts of individualisation could perfectly content him; he must still seek something more definite and more express than nature. All artists, it may be properly argued, do the like; it is their method to discard the middling and the insignificant, to disengage the charactered and the precise. But it is only a class of artists that pursue so singly the note of personality; and is it not possible that such a preoccupation may disable men from representing gentlefolk? The gentleman passes in the stream of the day's manners, inconspicuous. The lover of the individual may find him scarce worth drawing. And even if he draw him, on what will his attention centre but just upon those points in which his model exceeds or falls short of his subdued ideal—but just upon those points in which the gentleman is not genteel? Dickens, in an hour of irritated nerves, and under the pressure of the monthly number, defaced his Wrayburn. Observe what he sacrifices. The ruling passion strong in his hour of weakness, he sacrifices dignity, decency, the essential human beauties of his hero; he still preserves the dialect, the shrill note of personality, the mark of identification. Thackeray, under the strain of the same villainous system, would have fallen upon the other side; his gentleman would still have been a gentleman, he would have only ceased to be an individual figure.

There are incompatible ambitions. You cannot paint a Vandyke and keep it a Franz Hals.

III

I have preferred to conclude my inconclusive argument before I touched on Thackeray. Personally, he scarce appeals to us as the ideal gentleman; if there were nothing else, perpetual nosing after snobbery at least suggests the snob; but about the men he made, there can be no such question of reserve. And whether because he was himself a gentleman in a very high degree, or because his methods were in a very high degree suited to this class of work, or from the common operation of both causes, a gentleman came from his pen by the gift of nature. He could draw him as a character part, full of pettiness, tainted with vulgarity, and yet still a gentleman, in the inimitable Major Pendennis. He could draw him as the full-blown hero in Colonel Esmond. He could draw him—the next thing to the work of God—human and true and noble and frail, in Colonel Newcome. If the art of being a gentleman were forgotten, like the art of staining glass, it might be learned anew from that one character. It is learned there, I dare to say, daily. Mr Andrew Lang, in a graceful attitude of melancholy, denies the influence of books. I think he forgets his philosophy; for surely there go two elements to the determination of conduct: heredity, and experience—that which is given to us at birth, that which is added and cancelled in the course of life; and what experience is more formative, what step of life is more efficient, than to know and weep for Colonel Newcome? And surely he forgets himself; for I call to mind other pages, beautiful pages, from which it may be gathered that the language of *The Newcomes* sings still in his memory, and its gospel is sometimes not forgotten. I call it a gospel: it is the best I know. Error and suffering and failure and death, those calamities that our contemporaries paint upon so vast a scale—they are all depicted here, but in a more true proportion. We may return, before this picture, to the simple and ancient faith. We may be sure (although we know not why) that we give our lives, like coral insects, to build up insensibly, in the twilight of the seas of time, the reef of righteousness. And we may be sure (although we see not how) it is a thing worth doing.

The Morality of
the Profession of Letters

Those who write have to see that each man's knowledge is, as near as they can make it, answerable to the facts of life; that he shall not suppose himself an angel or a monster; nor take this world for a hell; nor be suffered to imagine that all rights are concentred in his own caste or country, or all veracities in his own parochial creed.

THE PROFESSION of letters has been lately debated in the public prints; and it has been debated, to put the matter mildly, from a point of view that was calculated to surprise high-minded men, and bring a general contempt on books and reading. Some time ago, in particular, a lively, pleasant, popular writer devoted an essay, lively and pleasant like himself, to a very encouraging view of the profession. We may be glad that his experience is so cheering, and we may hope that all others, who deserve it, shall be as handsomely rewarded; but I do not think we need be at all glad to have this question, so important to the public and ourselves, debated solely on the ground of money. The salary in any business under heaven is not the only, nor indeed the first, question. That you should continue to exist is a matter for your own consideration; but that your business should be first honest, and second useful, are points in which honour and morality are concerned. If the writer to whom I refer succeeds in persuading a number of young persons to adopt this way of life with an eye set singly on the livelihood, we must expect them in their works to follow profit only, and we must expect in consequence, if he will pardon me the epithets, a slovenly, base, untrue, and empty literature. Of that writer himself I am not speaking: he is diligent, clean, and pleasing; we all owe him periods of entertainment, and he has achieved an amiable popularity which he has adequately deserved. But the truth is, he does not, or did not when he first embraced it, regard his profession from this purely mercenary side. He went into it, I shall venture to say, if not with any noble design, at least in the ardour of a first love; and he enjoyed its practice long before he paused to calculate the wage. The other day an author was complimented on a piece of work, good in itself and exceptionally good for him, and replied, in terms unworthy of a commercial traveller, that as the book was not briskly selling he did not give a copper farthing for its merit. It must not be supposed that the person to whom this answer was addressed received it as a profession of faith;

he knew, on the other hand, that it was only a whiff of irritation; just as we know, when a respectable writer talks of literature as a way of life, like shoemaking, but not so useful, that he is only debating one aspect of a question, and is still clearly conscious of a dozen others more important in themselves and more central to the matter in hand. But while those who treat literature in this penny-wise and virtue-foolish spirit are themselves truly in possession of a better light, it does not follow that the treatment is decent or improving, whether for themselves or others. To treat all subjects in the highest, the most honourable, and the pluckiest spirit, consistent with the fact, is the first duty of a writer. If he be well paid, as I am glad to hear he is, this duty becomes the more urgent, the neglect of it the more disgraceful. And perhaps there is no subject on which a man should speak so gravely as that industry, whatever it may be, which is the occupation or delight of his life; which is his tool to earn or serve with; and which, if it be unworthy, stamps himself as a mere incubus of dumb and greedy bowels on the shoulders of labouring humanity. On that subject alone even to force the note might lean to virtue's side. It is to be hoped that a numerous and enterprising generation of writers will follow and surpass the present one; but it would be better if the stream were stayed, and the roll of our old, honest English books were closed, than that esurient bookmakers should continue and debase a brave tradition, and lower, in their own eyes, a famous race. Better that our serene temples were deserted than filled with trafficking and juggling priests.

There are two just reasons for the choice of any way of life: the first is inbred taste in the chooser; the second some high utility in the industry selected. Literature, like any other art, is singularly interesting to the artist; and, in a degree peculiar to itself among the arts, it is useful to mankind. These are the sufficient justifications for any young man or woman who adopts it as the business of his life. I shall not say much about the wages. A writer can live by his writing. If not so luxuriously as by other trades, then less luxuriously. The nature of the work he does all day will more affect his happiness than the quality of his dinner at night. Whatever be your calling, and however much it brings you in the year, you could still, you know, get more by cheating. We all suffer ourselves to be too much concerned about a little poverty; but such considerations should not move us in the choice of that which is to be the business and justification of so great a portion of our lives; and like the missionary, the patriot, or the philosopher, we should all choose that poor and brave career in which we can do the most and best for mankind. Now Nature, faithfully followed, proves herself a careful mother. A lad, for some liking to the jingle of words, betakes himself to letters for his life; by-and-by, when he learns more gravity, he finds that he has chosen better than he knew; that if he earns little, he is earning it amply; that if he receives a small wage, he is in a position to do considerable services; that it is in his power, in some small measure, to protect the oppressed and to defend the truth. So kindly is the world arranged, such great profit may arise from a small degree of human reliance on oneself, and such, in particular, is the happy star of this trade of writing, that it should combine pleasure and profit to both parties, and be at once agreeable, like fiddling, and useful, like good preaching.

This is to speak of literature at its highest; and with the four great elders who are still spared to our respect and admiration, with Carlyle, Ruskin, Browning, and Tennyson before us, it would be cowardly to consider it at first in any lesser aspect. But while we cannot follow these athletes, while we may none of us, perhaps, be very vigorous, very original, or very wise, I still contend that, in the humblest sort of literary work, we have it in our power either to do great harm or great good. We may seek merely to please; we may seek, having no higher gift, merely to gratify the idle nine days' curiosity of our contemporaries; or we may essay, however feebly, to instruct. In each of these we shall have to deal with that remarkable art of words which, because it is the dialect of life, comes home so easily and powerfully to the minds of men; and since that is so, we contribute, in each of these branches, to build up the sum of sentiments and appreciations which goes by the name of Public Opinion or Public Feeling. The total of a nation's reading, in these days of daily papers, greatly modifies the total of the nation's speech; and the speech and reading, taken together, form the efficient educational medium of youth. A good man or woman may keep a youth some little while in clearer air; but the contemporary atmosphere is all-powerful in the end on the average of mediocre characters. The copious Corinthian baseness of the American reporter or the Parisian *chroniquear*, both so lightly readable, must exercise an incalculable influence for ill; they touch upon all subjects, and on all with the same ungenerous hand; they begin the consideration of all, in young and unprepared minds, in an unworthy spirit; on all, they supply some pungency for dull people to quote. The mere body of this ugly matter overwhelms the rare utterances of good men; the sneering, the selfish, and the cowardly are scattered in broad sheets on every table, while the antidote, in small volumes, lies unread upon the shelf. I have spoken of the American and the French, not because they are so much baser, but so much more readable, than the English; their evil is done more effectively, in America for the masses, in French for the few that care to read; but with us as with them, the duties of literature are daily neglected, truth daily perverted and suppressed, and grave subjects daily degraded in the treatment. The journalist is not reckoned an important officer; yet judge of the good he might do, the harm he does; judge of it by one instance only: that when we find two journals on the reverse sides of politics each, on the same day, openly garbling a piece of news for the interest of its own party, we smile at the discovery (no discovery now!) as over a good joke and pardonable stratagem. Lying so open is scarce lying, it is true; but one of the things that we profess to teach our young is a respect for truth; and I cannot think this piece of education will be crowned with any great success, so long as some of us practise and the rest openly approve of public falsehood.

There are two duties incumbent upon any man who enters on the business of writing: truth to the fact and a good spirit in the treat-ment. In every department of literature, though so low as hardly to deserve the name, truth to the fact is of importance to the education and comfort of mankind, and so hard to preserve, that the faithful trying to do so will lend some dignity to the man who tries it. Our judgments are based upon two things: first, upon the original pref-erences of our soul; but, second, upon the mass of testimony to the nature of God, man, and the universe which reaches us, in divers manners, from without. For the most part these divers manners are reducible to one, all that we learn of past times and much that we learn of our own reaching us through the medium of books or papers, and even he who cannot read learning from the same source at second-hand and by the report of him who can. Thus the sum of the contemporary knowledge or ignorance of good and evil is, in large measure, the handiwork of those who write. Those who write have to see that each man's knowledge is, as near as they can make it, answerable to the facts of life; that he shall not suppose himself an angel or a monster; nor take this world for a hell; nor be suffered to imagine that all rights are concentred in his own caste or country, or all veracities in his own parochial creed. Each man should learn what is within him, that he may strive to mend; he must be taught what is without him, that he may be kind to others. It can never be wrong to tell him the truth; for, in his disputable state, weaving as he goes his theory of life, steering himself, cheering or reproving others, all facts are of the first importance to his conduct; and even if a fact shall discourage or corrupt him, it is still best that he should know it; for it is in this world as it is, and not in a world made easy by educational suppressions, that he must win his way to shame or glory. In one word, it must always be foul to tell what is false; and it can never be safe to suppress what is true. The very fact that you omit may be the fact which somebody was wanting, for one man's meat is another man's poison, and I have known a person who was cheered by the perusal of *Candide*. Every fact is a part of that great puzzle we must set together; and none that comes directly in a writer's path but has some nice relations, unperceivable by him, to the totality and bearing of the subject under hand. Yet there are certain classes of fact eternally more necessary than others, and it is with these that literature must first bestir itself. They are not hard to distinguish, nature once more easily leading us; for the necessary, because the efficacious, facts are those which are most interesting to the natural mind of man. Those which are coloured, picturesque, human, and rooted in morality, and those, on the other hand, which are clear, indisputable, and a part of science, are alone vital in importance, seizing by their interest, or useful to communicate. So far as the writer merely narrates, he should principally tell of these. He should tell of the kind and wholesome and beautiful elements of our life; he should tell unsparingly of the evil and sorrow of the present, to move us with instances: he should tell of wise and good people in the past, to excite us by example; and of these he should tell soberly and truthfully, not glossing faults, that we may neither grow discouraged with ourselves nor exacting to our neighbours. So the body of contemporary literature, ephemeral and feeble in itself, touches in the minds of men the springs of thought and kindness, and supports them (for those who will go at all are easily supported) on their way to what is true and right. And if, in any degree, it does so now, how much more might it do so if the writers chose! There is not a life in all the records of the past but, properly studied, might lend a hint and a help to some contemporary. There is not a juncture in today's affairs but some useful word may yet be said of it. Even the reporter has an office, and, with clear eyes and honest language, may unveil injustices and point the way to progress. And for a last word: in all narration there is only one way to be clever, and that is to be exact. To be vivid is a secondary quality which must presuppose the first; for vividly to convey a wrong impression is only to make failure conspicuous.

But a fact may be viewed on many sides; it may be chronicled with rage, tears, laughter, indifference, or admiration, and by each of these the story will be transformed to something else. The newspapers that told of the return of our representatives from Berlin, even if they had not differed as to the facts, would have sufficiently differed by their spirits; so that the one description would have been a second ovation, and the other a prolonged insult. The subject makes but a trifling part of any piece of literature, and the view of the writer is itself a fact more important because less disputable than the others. Now this spirit in which a subject is regarded, important in all kinds of literary work, becomes all-important in works of fiction, meditation, or rhapsody; for there it not only colours but itself chooses the facts; not only modifies but shapes the work. And hence, over the far larger proportion of the field of literature, the health or disease of the writer's mind or momentary humour forms not only the leading feature of his work, but is, at bottom, the only thing he can communicate to others. In all works of art, widely speaking, it is first of all the author's attitude that is narrated, though in the attitude there be implied a whole experience and a theory of life. An author who has begged the question and reposes in some narrow faith cannot, if he would, express the whole or even many of the sides of this various existence; for, his own life being maim, some of them are not admitted in his theory, and were only dimly and unwillingly recognised in his experience. Hence the smallness, the triteness, and the inhumanity in works of merely sectarian religion; and hence we find equal although unsimilar limitation in works inspired by the spirit of the flesh or the despicable taste for high society. So that the first duty of any man who is to write is intellectual. Designedly or not, he has so far set himself up for a leader of the minds of men; and he must see that his own mind is kept supple, charitable, and bright. Everything but prejudice should find a voice through him; he should see the good in all things; where he has even a fear that he does not wholly understand, there he should be wholly silent; and he should recognise from the first that he has only one tool in his workshop, and that tool is sympathy.

The second duty, far harder to define, is moral. There are a thousand different humours in the mind, and about each of them, when it is uppermost, some literature tends to be deposited. Is this to be allowed? Not certainly in every case, and yet perhaps in more than rigourists would fancy. It were to be desired that all literary work, and chiefly works of art, issued from sound, human, healthy, and potent impulses, whether grave or laughing, humorous, romantic, or religious. Yet it cannot be denied that some valuable books are partially insane; some, mostly religious, partially inhuman; and very many tainted with morbidity and impotence. We do not loathe a masterpiece although we gird against its blemishes. We are not, above all, to look for faults, but merits. There is no book perfect, even in design; but there are many that will delight, improve, or encourage the reader. On the one hand, the Hebrew psalms are the only religious poetry on earth; yet they contain sallies that savour rankly of the man of blood. On the other hand, Alfred de Musset had a poisoned and a contorted nature; I am only quoting that generous and frivolous giant, old Dumas, when I accuse him of a bad heart; yet, when the impulse under which he wrote was purely creative, he could give us works like *Carmosine* or *Fantasio*, in which the last note of the romantic comedy seems to have been found again to touch and please us. When Flaubert wrote *Madame Bovary*, I believe he thought chiefly of a somewhat morbid realism; and behold! the book turned in his hands into a masterpiece of appalling morality. But the truth is, when books are conceived under a great stress, with a soul of ninefold power, nine times heated and electrified by effort, the conditions of our being are seized with such an ample grasp, that, even should the main design be trivial or base, some truth and beauty cannot fail to be expressed. Out of the strong comes forth sweetness; but an ill thing poorly done is an ill thing top and bottom. And so this can be no encouragement to knock-kneed, feeble-wristed scribes, who must take their business conscientiously or be ashamed to practise it.

Man is imperfect; yet, in his literature, he must express himself and his own views and preferences; for to do anything else is to do a far more perilous thing than to risk being immoral: it is to be sure of being untrue. To ape a sentiment, even a good one, is to travesty a sentiment; that will not be helpful. To conceal a sentiment, if you are sure you hold it, is to take a liberty with truth. There is probably no point of view possible to a sane man but contains some truth and, in the true connection, might be profitable to the race. I am not afraid of the truth, if any one could tell it me, but I am afraid of parts of it impertinently uttered. There is a time to dance and a time to mourn; to be harsh as well as to be sentimental; to be ascetic as well as to glorify the appetites; and if a man were to combine all these extremes into his work, each in its place and proportion, that work would be the world's masterpiece of morality as well as of art. Partiality is immorality; for any book is wrong that gives a misleading picture of the world and life. The trouble is that the weakling must be partial; the work of one proving dank and depressing; of another, cheap and vulgar; of a third, epileptically sensual; of a fourth, sourly ascetic. In literature as in conduct, you can never hope to do exactly right. All you can do is to make as sure as possible; and for that there is but one rule. Nothing should be done in a hurry that can be done slowly. It is no use to write a book and put it by for nine or even ninety years; for in the writing you will have partly convinced yourself; the delay must precede any beginning; and if you meditate a work of art, you should first long roll the subject under the tongue to make sure you like the flavour, before you brew a volume that shall taste of it from end to end; or if you propose to enter on the field of controversy, you should first have thought upon the question under all conditions, in health as well as in sickness, in sorrow as well as in joy. It is this nearness of examination necessary for any true and kind writing, that makes the practice of the art a prolonged and noble education for the writer.

There is plenty to do, plenty to say, or to say over again, in the meantime. Any literary work which conveys faithful facts or pleasing impressions is a service to the public. It is even a service to be thankfully proud of having rendered. The slightest novels are a blessing to those in distress, not chloroform itself a greater. Our fine old sea-captain's life was justified when Carlyle soothed his mind with *The King's Own* or *Newton Forster*. To please is to serve; and so far from its being difficult to instruct while you amuse, it is difficult to do the one thoroughly without the other. Some part of the writer or his life will crop out in even a vapid book; and to read a novel that was conceived with any force is to multiply experience and to exercise the sympathies. Every article, every piece of verse, every essay, every *entre-filet*, is destined to pass, however swiftly, through the minds of some portion of the public, and to colour, however transiently, their thoughts. When any subject falls to be discussed, some scribbler on a paper has the invaluable opportunity of beginning its discussion in a dignified and human spirit; and if there were enough who did so in our public press, neither the public nor the Parliament would find it in their minds to drop to meaner thoughts. The writer has the chance to stumble, by the way, on something pleasing, something interesting, something encouraging, were it only to a single reader. He will be unfortunate, indeed, if he suit no one. He has the chance, besides, to stumble on something that a dull person shall be able to comprehend; and for a dull person to have read anything and, for that once, comprehended it, makes a marking epoch in his education.

Here, then, is work worth doing and worth trying to do well. And so, if I were minded to welcome any great accession to our trade, it should not be from any reason of a higher wage, but because it was a trade which was useful in a very great and in a very high degree;

which every honest tradesman could make more serviceable to mankind in his single strength; which was difficult to do well and possible to do better every year; which called for scrupulous thought on the part of all who practised it, and hence became a perpetual education to their nobler natures; and which, pay it as you please, in the large majority of the best cases will still be underpaid. For surely, at this time of day in the nineteenth century, there is nothing that an honest man should fear more timorously than getting and spending more than he deserves.

A Note on Realism

We talk of bad and good. Everything, indeed, is good which is conceived with honesty and executed with communicative ardour.

STYLE IS the invariable mark of any master; and for the student who does not aspire so high as to be numbered with the giants, it is still the one quality in which he may improve himself at will. Passion, wisdom, creative force, the power of mystery or colour, are allotted in the hour of birth, and can be neither learned nor simulated. But the just and dexterous use of what qualities we have, the proportion of one part to another and to the whole, the elision of the useless, the accentuation of the important, and the preservation of a uniform character from end to end—these, which taken together constitute technical perfection, are to some degree within the reach of industry and intellectual courage. What to put in and what to leave out; whether some particular fact be organically necessary or purely ornamental; whether, if it be purely ornamental, it may not weaken or obscure the general design; and finally, whether, if we decide to use it, we should do so grossly and notably, or in some conventional disguise: are questions of plastic style continually rearising. And the sphinx that patrols the highways of executive art has no more unanswerable riddle to propound.

In literature (from which I must draw my instances) the great change of the past century has been effected by the admission of detail. It was inaugurated by the romantic Scott; and at length, by the semi-romantic Balzac and his more or less wholly unromantic followers, bound like a duty on the novelist. For some time it signified and expressed a more ample contemplation of the conditions of man's life; but it has recently (at least in France) fallen into a merely technical and decorative stage, which it is, perhaps, still too harsh to call survival. With a movement of alarm, the wiser or more timid begin to fall a little back from these extremities; they begin to aspire after a more naked, narrative articulation; after the succinct, the dignified, and the poetic; and as a means to this, after a general lightening of this baggage of detail. After Scott we beheld the starveling story—once, in the hands of Voltaire, as abstract as a parable

—begin to be pampered upon facts. The introduction of these details developed a particular ability of hand; and that ability, childishly indulged, has led to the works that now amaze us on a railway journey. A man of the unquestionable force of M. Zola spends himself on technical successes. To afford a popular flavour and attract the mob, he adds a steady current of what I may be allowed to call the rancid. That is exciting to the moralist; but what more particularly interests the artist is this tendency of the extreme of detail, when followed as a principle, to degenerate into mere *feux-de-joie* of literary tricking. The other day even M. Daudet was to be heard babbling of audible colours and visible sounds.

This odd suicide of one branch of the realists may serve to remind us of the fact which underlies a very dusty conflict of the critics. All representative art, which can be said to live, is both realistic and ideal; and the realism about which we quarrel is a matter purely of externals. It is no especial cultus of nature and veracity, but a mere whim of veering fashion, that has made us turn our back upon the larger, more various, and more romantic art of yore. A photographic exactitude in dialogue is now the exclusive fashion; but even in the ablest hands it tells us no more—I think it even tells us less—than Moliere, wielding his artificial medium, has told to us and to all time of Alceste or Orgon, Dorine or Chrysale. The historical novel is forgotten. Yet truth to the conditions of man's nature and the conditions of man's life, the truth of literary art, is free of the ages. It may be told us in a carpet comedy, in a novel of adventure, or a fairy tale. The scene may be pitched in London, on the sea-coast of Bohemia, or away on the mountains of Beulah. And by an odd and luminous accident, if there is any page of literature calculated to awake the envy of M. Zola, it must be that Troilus and Cressida which Shakespeare, in a spasm of unmanly anger with the world, grafted on the heroic story of the siege of Troy.

This question of realism, let it then be clearly understood, regards not in the least degree the fundamental truth, but only the technical method, of a work of art. Be as ideal or as abstract as you please, you will be none the less veracious; but if you be weak, you run the risk of being tedious and inexpressive; and if you be very strong and honest, you may chance upon a masterpiece.

A work of art is first cloudily conceived in the mind; during the period of gestation it stands more clearly forward from these swaddling mists, puts on expressive lineaments, and becomes at length that most faultless, but also, alas! that incommunicable product of the human mind, a perfected design. On the approach to execution all is changed. The artist must now step down, don his working clothes, and become the artisan. He now resolutely commits his airy conception, his delicate Ariel, to the touch of matter; he must decide, almost in a breath, the scale, the style, the spirit, and the particularity of execution of his whole design.

The engendering idea of some works is stylistic; a technical preoccupation stands them instead of some robuster principle of life. And with these the execution is but play; for the stylistic problem is resolved beforehand, and all large originality of treatment wilfully foregone. Such are the verses, intricately designed, which we have learnt to admire, with a certain smiling admiration, at the hands of Mr Lang and Mr Dobson; such, too, are those canvases where dexterity or even breadth of plastic style takes the place of pictorial nobility of design. So, it may be remarked, it was easier to begin to write *Esmond* than *Vanity Fair*, since, in the first, the style was dictated by the nature of the plan; and Thackeray, a man probably of some indolence of mind, enjoyed and got good profit of this economy of effort. But the case is exceptional. Usually in all works of art that have been conceived from within outwards, and generously nourished from the author's mind, the moment in which he begins to execute is one of extreme perplexity and strain.

Artists of indifferent energy and an imperfect devotion to their own ideal make this ungrateful effort once for all; and, having formed a style, adhere to it through life. But those of a higher order cannot rest content with a process which, as they continue to employ it, must infallibly degenerate towards the academic and the cut-and-dried. Every fresh work in which they embark is the signal for a fresh engagement of the whole forces of their mind; and the changing views which accompany the growth of their experience are marked by still more sweeping alterations in the manner of their art. So that criticism loves to dwell upon and distinguish the varying periods of a Raphael, a Shakespeare, or a Beethoven.

It is, then, first of all, at this initial and decisive moment when execution is begun, and thenceforth only in a less degree, that the ideal and the real do indeed, like good and evil angels, contend for the direction of the work. Marble, paint, and language, the pen, the needle, and the brush, all have their grossnesses, their ineffable impotences, their hours, if I may so express myself, of insubordination. It is the work and it is a great part of the delight of any artist to contend with these unruly tools, and now by brute energy, now by witty expedient, to drive and coax them to effect his will. Given these means, so laughably inadequate, and given the interest, the intensity, and the multiplicity of the actual sensation whose effect he is to render with their aid, the artist has one main and necessary resource which he must, in every case and upon any theory, employ. He must, that is, suppress much and omit more. He must omit what is tedious or irrelevant, and suppress what is tedious and necessary. But such facts as, in regard to the main design, subserve a variety of purposes, he will perforce and eagerly retain. And it is the mark of the very highest order of creative art to be woven exclusively of such. There, any fact that is registered is contrived a double or a treble debt to pay, and is at once an ornament in its place, and a pillar in the main design. Nothing would find room in such a picture that did not serve, at once, to complete the composition, to accentuate the scheme of colour, to distinguish the planes of distance, and to strike the note of the selected sentiment; nothing would be allowed in such a story that did not, at the same time, expedite the progress of the fable, build up the characters, and strike home the moral or the philosophical design. But this is unattainable. As a rule, so far from building the fabric of our works exclusively with these, we are thrown into a rapture if we think we can muster a dozen or a score of them, to be the plums of our confection. And hence, in order that the canvas may be filled or the story proceed from point to point, other details must be admitted. They must be admitted, alas! upon a doubtful title; many without marriage robes. Thus any work of art, as it proceeds towards completion, too often—I had almost written always—loses in force and poignancy of main design. Our little air is swamped and dwarfed among hardly relevant orchestration; our little passionate story drowns in a deep sea of descriptive eloquence or slipshod talk.

But again, we are rather more tempted to admit those particulars which we know we can describe; and hence those most of all which, having been described very often, have grown to be conventionally treated in the practice of our art. These we choose, as the mason chooses the acanthus to adorn his capital, because they come naturally to the accustomed hand. The old stock incidents and accessories, tricks of workmanship and schemes of composition (all being admirably good, or they would long have been forgotten) haunt and tempt our fancy, offer us ready-made but not perfectly appropriate solutions for any problem that arises, and wean us from the study of nature and the uncompromising practice of art. To struggle, to face nature, to find fresh solutions, and give expression to facts which have not yet been adequately or not yet elegantly expressed, is to run a little upon the danger of extreme self-love.

Difficulty sets a high price upon achievement; and the artist may easily fall into the error of the French naturalists, and consider any fact as welcome to admission if it be the ground of brilliant handiwork; or, again, into the error of the modern landscape-painter, who is apt to think that difficulty overcome and science well displayed can take the place of what is, after all, the one excuse and breath of art—charm. A little further, and he will regard charm in the light of an unworthy sacrifice to prettiness, and the omission of a tedious passage as an infidelity to art.

We have now the matter of this difference before us. The idealist, his eye singly fixed upon the greater outlines, loves rather to fill up the interval with detail of the conventional order, briefly touched, soberly suppressed in tone, courting neglect. But the realist, with a fine intemperance, will not suffer the presence of anything so dead as a convention; he shall have all fiery, all hotpressed from nature, all charactered and notable, seizing the eye. The style that befits either of these extremes, once chosen, brings with it its necessary disabilities and dangers. The immediate danger of the realist is to sacrifice the beauty and significance of the whole to local dexterity, or, in the insane pursuit of completion, to immolate his readers under facts; but he comes in the last resort, and as his energy declines, to discard all design, abjure all choice, and, with scientific thoroughness, steadily to communicate matter which is not worth learning. The danger of the idealist is, of course, to become merely null and lose all grip of fact, particularity, or passion.

We talk of bad and good. Everything, indeed, is good which is conceived with honesty and executed with communicative ardour. But though on neither side is dogmatism fitting, and though in every case the artist must decide for himself, and decide afresh and yet afresh for each succeeding work and new creation; yet one thing may be generally said, that we of the last quarter of the nineteenth century, breathing as we do the intellectual atmosphere of our age, are more apt to err upon the side of realism than to sin in quest of the ideal. Upon that theory it may be well to watch and correct our own decisions, always holding back the hand from the least appearance of irrelevant dexterity, and resolutely fixed to begin no work that is not philosophical, passionate, dignified, happily mirthful, or, at the last and least, romantic in design.

A Gossip on Romance

The words, if the book be eloquent, should run thenceforward in our ears like the noise of breakers, and the story, if it be a story, repeat itself in a thousand coloured pictures to the eye.

IN ANYTHING fit to be called by the name of reading, the process itself should be absorbing and voluptuous; we should gloat over a book, be rapt clean out of ourselves, and rise from the perusal, our mind filled with the busiest, kaleidoscopic dance of images, incapable of sleep or of continuous thought. The words, if the book be eloquent, should run thenceforward in our ears like the noise of breakers, and the story, if it be a story, repeat itself in a thousand coloured pictures to the eye. It was for this last pleasure that we read so closely, and loved our books so dearly, in the bright, troubled period of boyhood. Eloquence and thought, character and conversation, were but obstacles to brush aside as we dug blithely after a certain sort of incident, like a pig for truffles. For my part, I liked a story to begin with an old wayside inn where, 'towards the close of the year 17—', several gentlemen in three-cocked hats were playing bowls. A friend of mine preferred the Malabar coast in a storm, with a ship beating to windward, and a scowling fellow of Herculean proportions striding along the beach; he, to be sure, was a pirate. This was further afield than my home-keeping fancy loved to travel, and designed altogether for a larger canvas than the tales that I affected. Give me a highwayman and I was full to the brim; a Jacobite would do, but the highwayman was my favourite dish. I can still hear that merry clatter of the hoofs along the moonlit lane; night and the coming of day are still related in my mind with the doings of John Rann or Jerry Abershaw; and the words 'post-chaise', the 'great North road', 'ostler', and 'nag' still sound in my ears like poetry. One and all, at least, and each with his particular fancy, we read storybooks in childhood, not for eloquence or character or thought, but for some quality of the brute incident. That quality was not mere bloodshed or wonder. Although each of these was welcome in its place, the charm for the sake of which we read depended on something different from either. My elders used to read novels aloud; and I can still remember four different passages which I heard, before I was ten, with the same keen and lasting pleasure. One I discovered long afterwards to be the admirable opening of *What Will He Do with It*: it was no wonder I was pleased with that. The other three still remain unidentified. One is a little vague; it was about a dark, tall house at night, and people groping on the stairs by the light that escaped from the open door of a sickroom. In another, a lover left a ball, and went walking in a cool, dewy park, whence he could watch the lighted windows and the figures of the dancers as they moved. This was the most sentimental impression I think I had yet received, for a child is somewhat deaf to the sentimental. In the last, a poet, who had been tragically wrangling with his wife, walked forth on the sea-beach on a tempestuous night and witnessed the horrors of a wreck. Different as they are, all these early favourites have a common note—they have all a touch of the romantic.

Drama is the poetry of conduct, romance the poetry of circumstance. The pleasure that we take in life is of two sorts—the active and the passive. Now we are conscious of a great command over our destiny; anon we are lifted up by circumstance, as by a breaking wave, and dashed we know not how into the future. Now we are pleased by our conduct, anon merely pleased by our surroundings. It would be hard to say which of these modes of satisfaction is the more effective, but the latter is surely the more constant. Conduct is three parts of life, they say; but I think they put it high. There is a vast deal in life and letters both which is not immoral, but simply a-moral; which either does not regard the human will at all, or deals with it in obvious and healthy relations; where the interest turns, not upon what a man shall choose to do, but on how he manages to do it; not on the passionate slips and hesitations of the conscience, but on the problems of the body and of the practical intelligence, in clean, open-air adventure, the shock of arms or the diplomacy of life. With such material as this it is impossible to build a play, for the serious theatre exists solely on moral grounds, and is a standing proof of the dissemination of the human conscience. But it is possible to build, upon this ground, the most joyous of verses, and the most lively, beautiful, and buoyant tales.

One thing in life calls for another; there is a fitness in events and places. The sight of a pleasant arbour puts it in our mind to sit there.

One place suggests work, another idleness, a third early rising and long rambles in the dew. The effect of night, of any flowing water, of lighted cities, of the peep of day, of ships, of the open ocean, calls up in the mind an army of anonymous desires and pleasures. Something, we feel, should happen; we know not what, yet we proceed in quest of it. And many of the happiest hours of life fleet by us in this vain attendance on the genius of the place and moment. It is thus that tracts of young fir, and low rocks that reach into deep soundings, particularly torture and delight me. Something must have happened in such places, and perhaps ages back, to members of my race; and when I was a child I tried in vain to invent appropriate games for them, as I still try, just as vainly, to fit them with the proper story. Some places speak distinctly. Certain dank gardens cry aloud for a murder; certain old houses demand to be haunted; certain coasts are set apart for shipwreck. Other spots again seem to abide their destiny, suggestive and impenetrable, 'miching mallecho.' The inn at Burford Bridge, with its arbours and green garden and silent, eddying river—though it is known already as the place where Keats wrote some of his *Endymion* and Nelson parted from his Emma—still seems to wait the coming of the appropriate legend. Within these ivied walls, behind these old green shutters, some further business smoulders, waiting for its hour. The old Hawes Inn at the Queen's Ferry makes a similar call upon my fancy. There it stands, apart from the town, beside the pier, in a climate of its own, half inland, half marine—in front, the ferry bubbling with the tide and the guardship swinging to her anchor; behind, the old garden with the trees. Americans seek it already for the sake of Lovel and Oldbuck, who dined there at the beginning of *The Antiquary*. But you need not tell me—that is not all; there is some story, unrecorded or not yet complete, which must express the meaning of that inn more fully. So it is with names and faces; so it is with incidents that are idle and inconclusive in themselves, and yet seem like the beginning of some quaint romance, which the all-careless author leaves untold. How many of these romances have we not seen determine at their birth; how many people have met us with a look of meaning in their eye, and sunk at once into trivial acquaintances; to how many places have we not drawn near, with express intimations—'here my destiny awaits me'—and we have but dined there and passed on! I have lived both at the Hawes and Burford in a perpetual flutter, on the heels, as it seemed, of some adventure that should justify the place; but though the feeling had me to bed at night and called me again at morning in one unbroken round of pleasure and suspense, nothing befell me in either worth remark. The man or the hour had not yet come; but some day, I think, a boat shall put off from the Queen's Ferry, fraught with a dear cargo, and some frosty night a horseman, on a tragic errand, rattle with his whip upon the green shutters of the inn at Burford.

Now, this is one of the natural appetites with which any lively literature has to count. The desire for knowledge, I had almost added the desire for meat, is not more deeply seated than this demand for fit and striking incident. The dullest of clowns tells, or tries to tell, himself a story, as the feeblest of children uses invention in his play; and even as the imaginative grown person, joining in the game, at once enriches it with many delightful circumstances, the great creative writer shows us the realisation and the apotheosis of the day-dreams of common men. His stories may be nourished with the realities of life, but their true mark is to satisfy the nameless longings of the reader, and to obey the ideal laws of the day-dream. The right kind of thing should fall out in the right kind of place; the right kind of thing should follow; and not only the characters talk aptly and think naturally, but all the circumstances in a tale answer one to another like notes in music. The threads of a story come from time to time together and make a picture in the web; the characters fall from time to time into some attitude to each other or to nature, which stamps the story home like an illustration.

Crusoe recoiling from the footprint, Achilles shouting over against the Trojans, Ulysses bending the great bow, Christian running with his fingers in his ears, these are each culminating moments in the legend, and each has been printed on the mind's eye for ever. Other things we may forget; we may forget the words, although they are beautiful; we may forget the author's comment, although perhaps it was ingenious and true; but these epoch-making scenes, which put the last mark of truth upon a story and fill up, at one blow, our capacity for sympathetic pleasure, we so adopt into the very bosom of our mind that neither time nor tide can efface or weaken the impression. This, then, is the plastic part of literature: to embody character, thought, or emotion in some act or attitude that shall be remarkably striking to the mind's eye. This is the highest and hardest thing to do in words; the thing which, once accomplished, equally delights the schoolboy and the sage, and makes, in its own right, the quality of epics. Compared with this, all other purposes in literature, except the purely lyrical or the purely philosophic, are bastard in nature, facile of execution, and feeble in result. It is one thing to write about the inn at Burford, or to describe scenery with the word-painters; it is quite another to seize on the heart of the suggestion and make a country famous with a legend. It is one thing to remark and to dissect, with the most cutting logic, the complications of life, and of the human spirit; it is quite another to give them body and blood in the story of Ajax or of Hamlet. The first is literature, but the second is something besides, for it is likewise art.

English people of the present day are apt, I know not why, to look somewhat down on incident, and reserve their admiration for the clink of teaspoons and the accents of the curate. It is thought clever to write a novel with no story at all, or at least with a very dull one. Reduced even to the lowest terms, a certain interest can be communicated by the art of narrative; a sense of human kinship stirred; and a kind of monotonous fitness, comparable to the words and air of Sandy's Mull, preserved among the infinitesimal occurrences recorded. Some people work, in this manner, with even a strong touch. Mr Trollope's inimitable clergymen naturally arise to the mind in this connection. But even Mr Trollope does not confine himself to chronicling small beer.

Mr Crawley's collision with the Bishop's wife, Mr. Melnotte dallying in the deserted banquet-room, are typical incidents, epically conceived, fitly embodying a crisis. Or again look at Thackeray. If Rawdon Crawley's blow were not delivered, *Vanity Fair* would cease to be a work of art. That scene is the chief ganglion of the tale; and the discharge of energy from Rawdon's fist is the reward and consolation of the reader. The end of Esmond is a yet wider excursion from the author's customary fields; the scene at Castlewood is pure Dumas; the great and wily English borrower has here borrowed from the great, unblushing French thief; as usual, he has borrowed admirably well, and the breaking of the sword rounds off the best of all his books with a manly, martial note. But perhaps nothing can more strongly illustrate the necessity for marking incident than to compare the living fame of Robinson Crusoe with the discredit of Clarissa Harlowe. *Clarissa* is a book of a far more startling import, worked out, on a great canvas, with inimitable courage and unflagging art. It contains wit, character, passion, plot, conversations full of spirit and insight, letters sparkling with unstrained humanity; and if the death of the heroine be somewhat frigid and artificial, the last days of the hero strike the only note of what we now call Byronism, between the Elizabethans and Byron himself. And yet a little story of a shipwrecked sailor, with not a tenth part of the style nor a thousandth part of the wisdom, exploring none of the arcana of humanity and deprived of the perennial interest of love, goes on from edition to edition, ever young, while *Clarissa* lies upon the shelves unread. A friend of mine, a Welsh blacksmith, was twenty-five years old and could neither read nor write, when he heard a chapter of *Robinson* read aloud in a farm kitchen. Up to that moment he had sat content, huddled in his ignorance, but he left that farm another man. There were day-dreams, it appeared, divine day-dreams, written and printed and bound, and to be bought for money and enjoyed at pleasure. Down he sat that day, painfully learned to read Welsh, and returned to borrow the book. It had been lost, nor could he find another copy but one that was in English. Down he sat once more, learned English, and at length, and with entire delight, read *Robinson*. It is like the story of a love-chase. If he had heard a letter from *Clarissa*, would he have been fired with the same chivalrous ardour? I wonder. Yet *Clarissa* has every quality that can be shown in prose, one alone excepted—pictorial or picture-making romance. While *Robinson* depends, for the most part and with the overwhelming majority of its readers, on the charm of circumstance.

In the highest achievements of the art of words, the dramatic and the pictorial, the moral and romantic interest, rise and fall together by a common and organic law. Situation is animated with passion, passion clothed upon with situation. Neither exists for itself, but each inheres indissolubly with the other. This is high art;

and not only the highest art possible in words, but the highest art of all, since it combines the greatest mass and diversity of the elements of truth and pleasure. Such are epics, and the few prose tales that have the epic weight. But as from a school of works, aping the creative, incident and romance are ruthlessly discarded, so may character and drama be omitted or subordinated to romance. There is one book, for example, more generally loved than Shakespeare, that captivates in childhood, and still delights in age—I mean *The Arabian Nights*—where you shall look in vain for moral or for intellectual interest. No human face or voice greets us among that wooden crowd of kings and genies, sorcerers and beggarmen. Adventure, on the most naked terms, furnishes forth the entertainment and is found enough. Dumas approaches perhaps nearest of any modern to these Arabian authors in the purely material charm of some of his romances.

The early part of *Monte Cristo*, down to the finding of the treasure, is a piece of perfect story-telling; the man never breathed who shared these moving incidents without a tremor; and yet Faria is a thing of packthread and Dantès little more than a name. The sequel is one long-drawn error, gloomy, bloody, unnatural and dull; but as for these early chapters, I do not believe there is another volume extant where you can breathe the same unmingled atmosphere of romance. It is very thin and light to be sure, as on a high mountain; but it is brisk and clear and sunny in proportion.

I saw the other day, with envy, an old and a very clever lady setting forth on a second or third voyage into *Monte Cristo*. Here are stories which powerfully affect the reader, which can be reperused at any age, and where the characters are no more than puppets. The bony fist of the showman visibly propels them; their springs are an open secret; their faces are of wood, their bellies filled with bran; and yet we thrillingly partake of their adventures. And the point may be illustrated still further. The last interview between Lucy and Richard Feveril is pure drama; more than that, it is the strongest scene, since Shakespeare, in the English tongue. Their first meeting by the river, on the other hand, is pure romance; it has nothing to do with character; it might happen to any other boy or maiden, and be none the less delightful for the change.

And yet I think he would be a bold man who should choose between these passages. Thus, in the same book, we may have two scenes, each capital in its order: in the one, human passion, deep calling unto deep, shall utter its genuine voice; in the second, according circumstances, like instruments in tune, shall build up a trivial but desirable incident, such as we love to prefigure for ourselves; and in the end, in spite of the critics, we may hesitate to give the preference to either. The one may ask more genius—I do not say it does; but at least the other dwells as clearly in the memory.

True romantic art, again, makes a romance of all things. It reaches into the highest abstraction of the ideal; it does not refuse the most pedestrian realism. *Robinson Crusoe* is as realistic as it is romantic; both qualities are pushed to an extreme, and neither suffers. Nor does romance depend upon the material importance of the incidents. To deal with strong and deadly elements, banditti, pirates, war and murder, is to conjure with great names, and, in the event of failure, to double the disgrace. The arrival of Haydn and Consuelo at the Canon's villa is a very trifling incident; yet we may read a dozen boisterous stories from beginning to end, and not receive so fresh and stirring an impression of adventure. It was the scene of Crusoe at the wreck, if I remember rightly, that so bewitched my blacksmith. Nor is the fact surprising.

Every single article the castaway recovers from the hulk is 'a joy for ever' to the man who reads of them. They are the things that should be found, and the bare enumeration stirs the blood. I found a glimmer of the same interest the other day in a new book, *The Sailor's Sweetheart*, by Mr Clark Russell. The whole business of the brig *Morning Star* is very rightly felt and spiritedly written; but the clothes, the books and the money satisfy the reader's mind like things to eat. We are dealing here with the old cut-and-dry, legitimate interest of treasure trove.

But even treasure trove can be made dull. There are few people who have not groaned under the plethora of goods that fell to the lot of the Swiss Family Robinson, that dreary family. They found article after article, creature after creature, from milk kine to pieces of ordnance, a whole consignment; but no informing taste had presided over the selection, there was no smack or relish in the invoice; and these riches left the fancy cold. The box of goods in Verne's *Mysterious Island* is another case in point: there was no gusto and no glamour about that; it might have come from a shop. But the two hundred and seventy-eight Australian sovereigns on board the *Morning Star* fell upon me like a surprise that I had expected; whole vistas of secondary stories, besides the one in hand, radiated forth from that discovery, as they radiate from a striking particular in life; and I was made for the moment as happy as a reader has the right to be.

To come at all at the nature of this quality of romance, we must bear in mind the peculiarity of our attitude to any art. No art produces illusion; in the theatre we never forget that we are in the theatre; and while we read a story, we sit wavering between two minds, now merely clapping our hands at the merit of the performance, now condescending to take an active part in fancy with the characters. This last is the triumph of romantic story-telling: when the reader consciously plays at being the hero, the scene is a good scene. Now in character-studies the pleasure that we take is critical; we watch, we approve, we smile at incongruities, we are moved to sudden heats of sympathy with courage, suffering or virtue. But the characters are still themselves, they are not us; the more clearly they are depicted, the more widely do they stand away from us, the more imperiously do they thrust us back into our place as a spectator. I cannot identify myself with Rawdon Crawley or with Eugène de Rastignac, for I have scarce a hope or fear in common with them. It is not character but incident that woos us out of our reserve.

Something happens as we desire to have it happen to ourselves; some situation, that we have long dallied with in fancy, is realised in the story with enticing and appropriate details. Then we forget the characters; then we push the hero aside; then we plunge into the tale in our own person and bathe in fresh experience; and then, and then only, do we say we have been reading a romance. It is not only pleasurable things that we imagine in our day-dreams; there are lights in which we are willing to contemplate even the idea of our own death; ways in which it seems as if it would amuse us to be cheated, wounded or calumniated. It is thus possible to construct a story, even of tragic import, in which every incident, detail and trick of

circumstance shall be welcome to the reader's thoughts. Fiction is to
the grown man what play is to the child; it is there that he changes
the atmosphere and tenor of his life; and when the game so chimes
with his fancy that he can join in it with all his heart, when it pleases
him with every turn, when he loves to recall it and dwells upon its
recollection with entire delight, fiction is called romance.

Walter Scott is out and away the king of the romantics. *The Lady
of the Lake* has no indisputable claim to be a poem beyond the inher-
ent fitness and desirability of the tale. It is just such a story as a man
would make up for himself, walking, in the best health and temper,
through just such scenes as it is laid in. Hence it is that a charm
dwells undefinable among these slovenly verses, as the unseen
cuckoo fills the mountains with his note; hence, even after we have
flung the book aside, the scenery and adventures remain present to
the mind, a new and green possession, not unworthy of that beautiful name, *The Lady of the Lake*, or that direct, romantic opening—one
of the most spirited and poetical in literature—'The stag at eve had
drunk his fill.' The same strength and the same weaknesses adorn
and disfigure the novels. In that ill-written, ragged book, *The Pirate*,
the figure of Cleveland—cast up by the sea on the resounding fore-
land of Dunrossness—moving, with the blood on his hands and the
Spanish words on his tongue, among the simple islanders—singing
a serenade under the window of his Shetland mistress—is conceived
in the very highest manner of romantic invention. The words of his
song, 'Through groves of palm', sung in such a scene and by such a
lover, clench, as in a nutshell, the emphatic contrast upon which the
tale is built. In *Guy Mannering*, again, every incident is delightful to
the imagination; and the scene when Harry Bertram lands at
Ellangowan is a model instance of romantic method.

'I remember the tune well,' he says, 'though I cannot guess what
should at present so strongly recall it to my memory.' He took his
flageolet from his pocket and played a simple melody. Apparently
the tune awoke the corresponding associations of a damsel. She
immediately took up the song—

> 'Are these the links of Forth, she said;
> Or are they the crooks of Dee,

    Or the bonny woods of Warroch Head
    That I so fain would see?'

'By heaven!' said Bertram, 'it is the very ballad.'

On this quotation two remarks fall to be made. First, as an instance of modern feeling for romance, this famous touch of the flageolet and the old song is selected by Miss Braddon for omission. Miss Braddon's idea of a story, like Mrs Todgers's idea of a wooden leg, were something strange to have expounded. As a matter of personal experience, Meg's appearance to old Mr Bertram on the road, the ruins of Derncleugh, the scene of the flageolet, and the Dominie's recognition of Harry, are the four strong notes that continue to ring in the mind after the book is laid aside. The second point is still more curious. The reader will observe a mark of excision in the passage as quoted by me. Well, here is how it runs in the original: 'a damsel, who, close behind a fine spring about half-way down the descent, and which had once supplied the castle with water, was engaged in bleaching linen'. A man who gave in such copy would be discharged from the staff of a daily paper. Scott has forgotten to prepare the reader for the presence of the 'damsel'; he has forgotten to mention the spring and its relation to the ruin; and now, face to face with his omission, instead of trying back and starting fair, crams all this matter, tail foremost, into a single shambling sentence. It is not merely bad English, or bad style; it is abominably bad narrative besides.

Certainly the contrast is remarkable; and it is one that throws a strong light upon the subject of this paper. For here we have a man of the finest creative instinct touching with perfect certainty and charm the romantic junctures of his story; and we find him utterly careless, almost, it would seem, incapable, in the technical matter of style, and not only frequently weak, but frequently wrong in points of drama. In character parts, indeed, and particularly in the Scotch, he was delicate, strong and truthful; but the trite, obliterated features of too many of his heroes have already wearied two generations of readers. At times his characters will speak with something far beyond propriety with a true heroic note; but on the next page they will be wading wearily forward with an ungrammatical and undramatic rigmarole of words. The man who could conceive and write the character of Elspeth of the Craigburnfoot, as Scott has conceived and written it, had not only splendid romantic, but splendid tragic gifts. How comes it, then, that he could so often fob us off with languid, inarticulate twaddle?

It seems to me that the explanation is to be found in the very quality of his surprising merits. As his books are play to the reader, so were they play to him. He conjured up the romantic with delight, but he had hardly patience to describe it. He was a great day-dreamer, a seer of fit and beautiful and humorous visions, but hardly a great artist; hardly, in the manful sense, an artist at all. He pleased himself, and so he pleases us. Of the pleasures of his art he tasted fully; but of its toils and vigils and distresses never man knew less. A great romantic—an idle child.

A Humble Remonstrance

Life is monstrous, infinite, illogical, abrupt and poignant; a work of art, in comparison, is neat, finite, self-contained, rational, flowing and emasculate. Life imposes by brute energy, like inarticulate thunder; art catches the ear, among the far louder noises of experience, like an air artificially made by a discreet musician.

WE HAVE recently enjoyed a quite peculiar pleasure: hearing, in some detail, the opinions, about the art they practise, of Mr Walter Besant and Mr Henry James; two men certainly of very different calibre: Mr James so precise of outline, so cunning of fence, so scrupulous of finish, and Mr Besant so genial, so friendly, with so persuasive and humorous a vein of whim: Mr James the very type of the deliberate artist, Mr Besant the impersonation of good nature. That such doctors should differ will excite no great surprise; but one point in which they seem to agree fills me, I confess, with wonder. For they are both content to talk about the 'art of fiction'; and Mr Besant, waxing exceedingly bold, goes on to oppose this so-called 'art of fiction' to the 'art of poetry'. By the art of poetry he can mean nothing but the art of verse, an art of handicraft, and only comparable with the art of prose. For that heat and height of sane emotion which we agree to call by the name of poetry, is but a libertine and vagrant quality; present, at times, in any art, more often absent from them all; too seldom present in the prose novel, too frequently absent from the ode and epic. Fiction is the same case; it is no substantive art, but an element which enters largely into all the arts but architecture. Homer, Wordsworth, Phidias, Hogarth, and Salvini, all deal in fiction; and yet I do not suppose that either Hogarth or Salvini, to mention but these two, entered in any degree into the scope of Mr Besant's interesting lecture or Mr James's charming essay. The art of fiction, then, regarded as a definition, is both too ample and too scanty. Let me suggest another; let me suggest that what both Mr James and Mr Besant had in view was neither more nor less than the art of narrative.

But Mr Besant is anxious to speak solely of 'the modern English novel', the stay and bread-winner of Mr Mudie; and in the author of the most pleasing novel on that roll, *All Sorts and Conditions of Men*, the desire is natural enough. I can conceive, then, that he would hasten to propose two additions, and read thus: the art of fictitious narrative in prose.

Now the fact of the existence of the modern English novel is not to be denied; materially, with its three volumes, leaded type, and gilded lettering, it is easily distinguishable from other forms of literature; but to talk at all fruitfully of any branch of art, it is needful to build our definitions on some more fundamental ground then binding. Why, then, are we to add 'in prose'? *The Odyssey* appears to me the best of romances; *The Lady of the Lake* to stand high in the second order; and Chaucer's tales and prologues to contain more of the matter and art of the modern English novel than the whole treasury of Mr Mudie. Whether a narrative be written in blank verse or the Spenserian stanza, in the long period of Gibbon or the chipped phrase of Charles Reade, the principles of the art of narrative must be equally observed. The choice of a noble and swelling style in prose affects the problem of narration in the same way, if not to the same degree, as the choice of measured verse; for both imply a closer synthesis of events, a higher key of dialogue, and a more picked and stately strain of words. If you are to refuse *Don Juan*, it is hard to see why you should include *Zanoni* or (to bracket works of very different value) *The Scarlet Letter*; and by what discrimination are you to open your doors to *The Pilgrim's Progress* and close them on *The Faery Queen*? To bring things closer home, I will here propound to Mr Besant a conundrum. A narrative called *Paradise Lost* was written in English verse by one John Milton; what was it then? It was next translated by Chateaubriand into French prose; and what was it then?

Lastly, the French translation was, by some inspired compatriot of George Gilfillan (and of mine), turned bodily into an English novel; and, in the name of clearness, what was it then?

But, once more, why should we add 'fictitious'? The reason why is obvious. The reason why not, if something more recondite, does not want for weight. The art of narrative, in fact, is the same, whether it is applied to the selection and illustration of a real series of events or of an imaginary series. Boswell's *Life of Johnson* (a work of cunning and inimitable art) owes its success to the same technical manoeuvres as (let us say) *Tom Jones*: the clear conception of certain characters of man, the choice and presentation of certain incidents out of a great number that offered, and the invention (yes, invention) and preservation of a certain key in dialogue. In which these things are done with the more art—in which with the greater air of nature—readers will differently judge. Boswell's is, indeed, a very special case, and almost a generic; but it is not only in Boswell, it is in every biography with any salt of life, it is in every history where events and men, rather than ideas, are presented—in Tacitus, in Carlyle, in Michelet, in Macaulay—that the novelist will find many of his own methods most conspicuously and adroitly handled. He will find besides that he, who is free—who has the right to invent or steal a missing incident, who has the right, more precious still, of wholesale omission—is frequently defeated, and, with all his advantages, leaves a less strong impression of reality and passion. Mr James utters his mind with a becoming fervour on the sanctity of truth to the novelist; on a more careful examination truth will seem a word of very debateable propriety, not only for the labours of the novelist, but for those of the historian. No art—to use the daring phrase of Mr James—can successfully 'compete with life'; and the art that seeks to do so is condemned to perish *montibus aviis*. Life goes before us, infinite in complication; attended by the most various and surprising meteors; appealing at once to the eye, to the ear, to the mind—the seat of wonder, to the touch—so thrillingly delicate, and to the belly—so imperious when starved. It combines and employs in its manifestation the method and material, not of one art only, but of all the arts, Music is but an arbitrary trifling with a few of life's majestic chords; painting is but a shadow of its pageantry of light and colour; literature does but drily indicate that wealth of incident, of moral obligation, of virtue, vice, action, rapture and agony, with which it teems. To 'compete with life', whose sun we cannot look upon, whose passions and diseases waste and slay us—to compete with the flavour of wine, the beauty of the dawn, the scorching of fire, the bitterness of death and separation—here is, indeed, a projected escalade of heaven; here are, indeed, labours for a Hercules in a dress coat, armed with a pen and a dictionary to depict the passions, armed with a tube of superior flake-white to paint the portrait of the insufferable sun. No art is true in this sense: none can 'compete with life': not even history, built indeed of indisputable facts, but these facts robbed of their vivacity and sting; so that even when we read of the sack of a city or the fall of an empire, we are surprised, and justly commend the author's talent, if our pulse be quickened. And mark, for a last differentia, that this quickening of the pulse is, in almost every case, purely agreeable; that these phantom reproductions of experience, even at their most acute, convey decided pleasure; while experience itself, in the cockpit of life, can torture and slay.

What, then, is the object, what the method, of an art, and what the source of its power? The whole secret is that no art does 'compete with life'. Man's one method, whether he reasons or creates, is to half-shut his eyes against the dazzle and confusion of reality. The arts, like arithmetic and geometry, turn away their eyes from the gross, coloured and mobile nature at our feet, and regard instead a certain figmentary abstraction. Geometry will tell us of a circle, a thing never seen in nature; asked about a green circle or an iron circle, it lays its hand upon its mouth. So with the arts. Painting, ruefully comparing sunshine and flake-white, gives up truth of colour, as it had already given up relief and movement; and instead of vying with nature, arranges a scheme of harmonious tints. Literature, above all in its most typical mood, the mood of narrative, similarly flees the direct challenge and pursues instead an independent and creative aim. So far as it imitates at all, it imitates not life but speech: not the facts of human destiny, but the emphasis and the suppressions with which the human actor tells of them.

The real art that dealt with life directly was that of the first men who told their stories round the savage camp-fire. Our art is occupied, and bound to be occupied, not so much in making stories true as in making them typical; not so much in capturing the lineaments of each fact, as in marshalling all of them towards a common end. For the welter of impressions, all forcible but all discreet, which life presents, it substitutes a certain artificial series of impressions, all indeed most feebly represented, but all aiming at the same effect, all eloquent of the same idea, all chiming together like consonant notes in music or like the graduated tints in a good picture. From all its chapters, from all its pages, from all its sentences, the well-written novel echoes and re-echoes its one creative and controlling thought; to this must every incident and character contribute; the style must have been pitched in unison with this; and if there is anywhere a word that looks another way, the book would be stronger, clearer, and (I had almost said) fuller without it. Life is monstrous, infinite, illogical, abrupt and poignant; a work of art, in comparison, is neat, finite, self-contained, rational, flowing and emasculate. Life imposes by brute energy, like inarticulate thunder; art catches the ear, among the far louder noises of experience, like an air artificially made by a discreet musician. A proposition of geometry does not compete with life; and a proposition of geometry is a fair and luminous parallel for a work of art. Both are reasonable, both untrue to the crude fact; both inhere in nature, neither represents it.

The novel, which is a work of art, exists, not by its resemblances to life, which are forced and material, as a shoe must still consist of leather, but by its immeasurable difference from life, which is designed and significant, and is both the method and the meaning of the work.

The life of man is not the subject of novels, but the inexhaustible magazine from which subjects are to be selected; the name of these is legion; and with each new subject—for here again I must differ by the whole width of heaven from Mr James—the true artist will vary his method and change the point of attack. That which was in one case an excellence, will become a defect in another; what was the making of one book, will in the next be impertinent or dull. First each novel, and then each class of novels, exists by and for itself. I will take, for instance, three main classes, which are fairly distinct: first, the novel of adventure, which appeals to certain almost sensual and quite illogical tendencies in man; second, the novel of character, which appeals to our intellectual appreciation of man's foibles and mingled and inconstant motives; and third, the dramatic novel, which deals with the same stuff as the serious theatre, and appeals to our emotional nature and moral judgment.

And first for the novel of adventure. Mr James refers, with singular generosity of praise, to a little book about a quest for hidden treasure; but he lets fall, by the way, some rather startling words. In this book he misses what he calls the 'immense luxury' of being able to quarrel with his author. The luxury, to most of us, is to lay by our judgment, to be submerged by the tale as by a billow, and only to awake, and begin to distinguish and find fault, when the piece is over and the volume laid aside. Still more remarkable is Mr James's reason. He cannot criticise the author, as he goes, 'because,' says he, comparing it with another work, 'I have been a child, but I have never been on a quest for buried treasure.' Here is, indeed, a wilful paradox; for if he has never been on a quest for buried treasure, it can be demonstrated that he has never been a child. There never was a child (unless Master James) but has hunted gold, and been a pirate, and a military commander, and a bandit of the mountains; but has fought, and suffered shipwreck and prison, and imbrued its little hands in gore, and gallantly retrieved the lost battle, and triumphantly protected innocence and beauty. Elsewhere in his essay Mr James has protested with excellent reason against too narrow a conception of experience; for the born artist, he contends, the 'faintest hints of life' are converted into revelations; and it will be found true, I believe, in a majority of cases, that the artist writes with more gusto and effect of those things which he has only wished to do, than of those which he has done. Desire is a wonderful telescope, and *Pisgah* the best observatory. Now, while it is true that neither Mr James nor the author of the work in question has ever, in the fleshly sense, gone questing after gold, it is probable that both have ardently desired and fondly imagined the details of such a life in youthful day-dreams; and the author, counting upon that, and well aware (cunning and low-minded man!) that this class of interest, having been frequently treated, finds a readily accessible and beaten road to the sympathies of the reader, addressed himself throughout to the building up and circumstantiation of this boyish dream. Character to the boy is a sealed book; for him, a pirate is a beard, a pair of wide trousers and a liberal complement of pistols. The author, for the sake of circumstantiation and because he was himself more or less grown up, admitted character, within certain limits, into his design; but only within certain limits. Had the same puppets figured in a scheme of another sort, they had been drawn to very different purpose; for in this elementary novel of adventure, the characters need to be presented with but one class of qualities—the warlike and formidable. So as they appear insidious in deceit and fatal in the combat, they have served their end. Danger is the matter with which this class of novel deals; fear, the passion with which it idly trifles; and the characters are portrayed only so far as they realise the sense of danger and provoke the sympathy of fear. To add more traits, to be too clever, to start the hare of moral or intellectual interest while we are running the fox of material interest, is not to enrich but to stultify your tale. The stupid reader will only be offended, and the clever reader lose the scent.

The novel of character has this difference from all others: that it requires no coherency of plot, and for this reason, as in the case of *Gil Blas*, it is sometimes called the novel of adventure. It turns on the humours of the persons represented; these are, to be sure, embodied in incidents, but the incidents themselves, being tributary, need not march in a progression; and the characters may be statically shown. As they enter, so they may go out; they must be consistent, but they need not grow. Here Mr James will recognise the note of much of his own work: he treats, for the most part, the statics of character, studying it at rest or only gently moved; and, with his usual delicate and just artistic instinct, he avoids those stronger passions which would deform the attitudes he loves to study, and change his sitters from the humorists of ordinary life to the brute forces and bare types of more emotional moments. In his recent *Author of Beltraffio*, so just in conception, so nimble and neat in workmanship, strong passion is indeed employed; but observe that it is not displayed. Even in the heroine the working of the passion is suppressed; and the great struggle, the true tragedy, the *scène-à-faire* passes unseen behind the panels of a locked door. The delectable invention of the young visitor is introduced, consciously or not, to this end: that Mr James, true to his method, might avoid the scene of passion. I trust no reader will suppose me guilty of undervaluing this little masterpiece. I mean merely that it belongs to one marked class of novel, and that it would have been very differently conceived and treated had it belonged to that other marked class, of which I now proceed to speak.

I take pleasure in calling the dramatic novel by that name, because it enables me to point out by the way a strange and peculiarly English misconception. It is sometimes supposed that the drama consists of incident. It consists of passion, which gives the actor his opportunity; and that passion must progressively increase, or the actor, as the piece proceeded, would be unable to carry the audience from a lower to a higher pitch of interest and emotion. A good serious play must therefore be founded on one of the passionate cruces of life, where duty and inclination come nobly to the grapple; and the same is true of what I call, for that reason, the dramatic novel. I will instance a few worthy specimens, all of our own day and language; Meredith's *Rhoda Fleming*, that wonderful and painful book, long out of print, and hunted for at bookstalls like an Aldine; Hardy's *Pair of Blue Eyes*; and two of Charles Reade's, *Griffith Gaunt* and *The Double Marriage*, originally called *White Lies*, and founded (by an accident quaintly favourable to my nomenclature) on a play by Maquet, the partner of the great Dumas. In this kind of novel the closed door of *The Author of Beltraffio* must be broken open; passion must appear upon the scene and utter its last word; passion is the be-all and the end-all, the plot and the solution, the protagonist and the *deus ex machina* in one. The characters may come anyhow upon the stage: we do not care; the point is, that, before they leave it, they shall become transfigured and raised out of themselves by passion. It may be part of the design to draw them with detail; to depict a full-length character, and then behold it melt and change in the furnace of emotion. But there is no obligation of the sort; nice portraiture is not required; and we are content to accept mere abstract types, so they be strongly and sincerely moved. A novel of this class may be even great, and yet contain no individual figure; it may be great, because it displays the workings of the perturbed heart and the impersonal utterance of passion; and with an artist of the second class it is, indeed, even more likely to be great, when the issue has thus been narrowed and the whole force of the writer's mind directed to passion alone. Cleverness again, which has its fair field in the novel of character, is debarred all entry upon this more solemn theatre. A far-fetched motive, an ingenious evasion of the issue, a witty instead of a passionate turn, offend us like an insincerity. All should be plain, all straightforward to the end. Hence it is that, in Rhoda Fleming, Mrs Lovell raises such resentment in the reader; her motives are too flimsy, her ways are too equivocal, for the weight and strength of her surroundings. Hence the hot indignation of the reader when Balzac, after having begun the *Duchesse de Langeais* in terms of strong if somewhat swollen passion, cuts the knot by the derangement of the hero's clock.

Such personages and incidents belong to the novel of character; they are out of place in the high society of the passions; when the passions are introduced in art at their full height, we look to see them, not baffled and impotently striving, as in life, but towering above circumstance and acting substitutes for fate.

And here I can imagine Mr James, with his lucid sense, to intervene. To much of what I have said he would apparently demur; in much he would, somewhat impatiently, acquiesce. It may be true; but it is not what he desired to say or to hear said. He spoke of the finished picture and its worth when done; I, of the brushes, the palette, and the north light. He uttered his views in the tone and for the ear of good society; I, with the emphasis and technicalities of the obtrusive student. But the point, I may reply, is not merely to amuse the public, but to offer helpful advice to the young writer. And the young writer will not so much be helped by genial pictures of what an art may aspire to at its highest, as by a true idea of what it must be on the lowest terms. The best that we can say to him is this: Let him choose a motive, whether of character or passion; carefully construct his plot so that every incident is an illustration of the motive, and every property employed shall bear to it a near relation of congruity or contrast; avoid a sub-plot, unless, as sometimes in Shakespeare, the sub-plot be a reversion or complement of the main intrigue; suffer not his style to flag below the level of the argument; pitch the key of conversation, not with any thought of how men talk in parlours, but with a single eye to the degree of passion he may be called on to express; and allow neither himself in the narrative nor any character in the course of the dialogue, to utter one sentence that is not part and parcel of the business of the story or the discussion of the problem involved. Let him not regret if this shortens his book; it will be better so; for to add irrelevant matter is not to lengthen but to bury. Let him not mind if he miss a thousand qualities, so that he keeps unflaggingly in pursuit of the one he has

chosen. Let him not care particularly if he miss the tone of conversation, the pungent material detail of the day's manners, the
reproduction of the atmosphere and the environment. These
elements are not essential: a novel may be excellent, and yet have
none of them; a passion or a character is so much the better depicted
as it rises clearer from material circumstance. In this age of the
particular, let him remember the ages of the abstract, the great
books of the past, the brave men that lived before Shakespeare and
before Balzac. And as the root of the whole matter, let him bear in
mind that his novel is not a transcript of life, to be judged by its
exactitude; but a simplification of some side or point of life, to stand
or fall by its significant simplicity. For although, in great men, working upon great motives, what we observe and admire is often their
complexity, yet underneath appearances the truth remains
unchanged: that simplification was their method, and that simplicity is their excellence.

II

Since the above was written another novelist has entered repeatedly
the lists of theory: one well worthy of mention, Mr W. D. Howells;
and none ever couched a lance with narrower convictions. His own
work and those of his pupils and masters singly occupy his mind; he
is the bondslave, the zealot of his school; he dreams of an advance in
art like what there is in science; he thinks of past things as radically
dead; he thinks a form can be outlived: a strange immersion in his
own history; a strange forgetfulness of the history of the race!
Meanwhile, by a glance at his own works (could he see them with the
eager eyes of his readers) much of this illusion would be dispelled.
For while he holds all the poor little orthodoxies of the day—no
poorer and no smaller than those of yesterday or tomorrow, poor
and small, indeed, only so far as they are exclusive—the living quality of much that he has done is of a contrary, I had almost said of a
heretical, complexion. A man, as I read him, of an originally strong
romantic bent—a certain glow of romance still resides in many of his
books, and lends them their distinction. As by accident he runs out
and revels in the exceptional; and it is then, as often as not, that his

reader rejoices—justly, as I contend. For in all this excessive eager-
ness to be centrally human, is there not one central human thing that
Mr Howells is too often tempted to neglect: I mean himself?

A poet, a finished artist, a man in love with the appearances of life,
a cunning reader of the mind, he has other passions and aspirations
than those he loves to draw. And why should he suppress himself
and do such reverence to the Lemuel Barkers? The obvious is not of
necessity the normal; fashion rules and deforms; the majority fall
tamely into the contemporary shape, and thus attain, in the eyes of
the true observer, only a higher power of insignificance; and the
danger is lest, in seeking to draw the normal, a man should draw the
null, and write the novel of society instead of the romance of man.

A Chapter on Dreams

Not an hour, not a mood, not a glance of the eye, can we revoke; it is all gone, past conjuring.

THE PAST is all of one texture—whether feigned or suffered—whether acted out in three dimensions, or only witnessed in that small theatre of the brain which we keep brightly lighted all night long, after the jets are down, and darkness and sleep reign undisturbed in the remainder of the body. There is no distinction on the face of our experiences; one is vivid indeed, and one dull, and one pleasant, and another agonising to remember; but which of them is what we call true, and which a dream, there is not one hair to prove. The past stands on a precarious footing; another straw split in the field of metaphysic, and behold us robbed of it.

There is scarce a family that can count four generations but lays a claim to some dormant title or some castle and estate: a claim not prosecutable in any court of law, but flattering to the fancy and a great alleviation of idle hours. A man's claim to his own past is yet less valid. A paper might turn up (in proper story-book fashion) in the secret drawer of an old ebony secretary, and restore your family to its ancient honours, and reinstate mine in a certain West Indian islet (not far from St Kitts, as beloved tradition hummed in my young ears) which was once ours, and is now unjustly someone else's, and for that matter (in the state of the sugar trade) is not worth anything to anybody. I do not say that these revolutions are likely; only no man can deny that they are possible; and the past, on the other baud, is, lost for ever: our old days and deeds, our old selves, too, and the very world in which these scenes were acted, all brought down to the same faint residuum as a last night's dream, to some incontinuous images, and an echo in the chambers of the brain. Not an hour, not a mood, not a glance of the eye, can we revoke; it is all gone, past conjuring.

And yet conceive us robbed of it, conceive that little thread of memory that we trail behind us broken at the pocket's edge; and in what naked nullity should we be left! for we only guide ourselves, and only know ourselves, by these air-painted pictures of the past.

Upon these grounds, there are some among us who claim to have lived longer and more richly than their neighbours; when they lay asleep they claim they were still active; and among the treasures of memory that all men review for their amusement, these count in no second place the harvests of their dreams. There is one of this kind whom I have in my eye, and whose case is perhaps unusual enough to be described. He was from a child an ardent and uncomfortable dreamer. When he had a touch of fever at night, and the room swelled and shrank, and his clothes, hanging on a nail, now loomed up instant to the bigness of a church, and now drew away into a horror of infinite distance and infinite littleness, the poor soul was very well aware of what must follow, and struggled hard against the approaches of that slumber which was the beginning of sorrows.

But his struggles were in vain; sooner or later the night-hag would have him by the throat, and pluck him strangling and screaming, from his sleep. His dreams were at times commonplace enough, at times very strange, at times they were almost formless: he would be haunted, for instance, by nothing more definite than a certain hue of brown, which he did not mind in the least while he was awake, but feared and loathed while he was dreaming; at times, again, they took on every detail of circumstance, as when once he supposed he must swallow the populous world, and awoke screaming with the horror of the thought. The two chief troubles of his very narrow existence— the practical and everyday trouble of school tasks and the ultimate and airy one of Hell and judgment—were often confounded together into one appalling nightmare. He seemed to himself to stand before the Great White Throne; he was called on, poor little devil, to recite some form of words, on which his destiny depended; his tongue stuck, his memory was blank, Hell gaped for him; and he would awake, clinging to the curtain-rod with his knees to his chin.

These were extremely poor experiences, on the whole; and at that time of life my dreamer would have very willingly parted with his power of dreams. But presently, in the course of his growth, the cries and physical contortions passed away, seemingly for ever; his visions were still for the most part miserable, but they were more constantly supported; and he would awake with no more extreme symptom than a flying heart, a freezing scalp, cold sweats, and the speechless midnight fear. His dreams, too, as befitted a mind better stocked with particulars, became more circumstantial, and had more the air and continuity of life. The look of the world beginning to take hold on his attention, scenery came to play a part in his sleeping as well as in his waking thoughts, so that he would take long, uneventful journeys and see strange towns and beautiful places as he lay in bed. And, what is more significant, an odd taste that he had for the Georgian costume and for stories laid in that period of English history, began to rule the features of his dreams; so that he masqueraded there in a three-cornered hat and was much engaged with Jacobite conspiracy between the hour for bed and that for breakfast. About the same time, he began to read in his dreams—tales, for the most part, and for the most part after the manner of G. P. R. James, but so incredibly more vivid and moving than any printed book, that he has ever since been malcontent with literature.

And then, while he was yet a student, there came to him a dream-adventure which he has no anxiety to repeat; he began, that is to say, to dream in sequence and thus to lead a double life—one of the day, one of the night—one that he had every reason to believe was the true one, another that he had no means of proving to be false. I should have said he studied, or was by way of studying, at Edinburgh College, which (it may be supposed) was how I came to know him. Well, in his dream-life, he passed a long day in the surgical theatre, his heart in his mouth, his teeth on edge, seeing monstrous malformations and the abhorred dexterity of surgeons. In a heavy, rainy, foggy evening he came forth into the South Bridge, turned up the High Street, and entered the door of a tall LAND, at the top of which he supposed himself to lodge. All night long, in his wet clothes, he climbed the stairs, stair after stair in endless series, and at every second flight a flaring lamp with a reflector. All night long, he brushed by single persons passing downward—beggarly women of the street, great, weary, muddy labourers, poor scarecrows of men, pale parodies of women—but all drowsy and weary like himself, and all single, and all brushing against him as they passed. In the end, out of a northern window, he would see day beginning to whiten over the Firth, give up the ascent, turn to descend, and in a breath be back again upon the streets, in his wet clothes, in the wet, haggard dawn, trudging to another day of monstrosities and operations. Time went quicker in the life of dreams, some seven hours (as near as he can guess) to one; and it went, besides, more intensely, so that the gloom of these fancied experiences clouded the day, and he had not shaken off their shadow ere it was time to lie down and to renew them. I cannot tell how long it was that he endured this discipline; but it was long enough to leave a great black blot upon his memory, long enough to send him, trembling for his reason, to the doors of a certain doctor; whereupon with a simple draught he was restored to the common lot of man.

The poor gentleman has since been troubled by nothing of the sort; indeed, his nights were for some while like other men's, now blank, now chequered with dreams, and these sometimes charming, sometimes appalling, but except for an occasional vividness, of no extraordinary kind. I will just note one of these occasions, ere I pass on to what makes my dreamer truly interesting. It seemed to him that he was in the first floor of a rough hill-farm. The room showed some poor efforts at gentility, a carpet on the floor, a piano, I think, against the wall; but, for all these refinements, there was no mistaking he was in a moorland place, among hillside people, and set in miles of heather. He looked down from the window upon a bare farmyard, that seemed to have been long disused.

A great, uneasy stillness lay upon the world. There was no sign of the farm-folk or of any live stock, save for an old, brown, curly dog of the retriever breed, who sat close in against the wall of the house and seemed to be dozing. Something about this dog disquieted the dreamer; it was quite a nameless feeling, for the beast looked right enough—indeed, he was so old and dull and dusty and broken-down, that he should rather have awakened pity; and yet the conviction came and grew upon the dreamer that this was no proper dog at all, but something hellish. A great many dozing summer flies hummed about the yard; and presently the dog thrust forth his paw, caught a fly in his open palm, carried it to his mouth like an ape, and looking suddenly up at the dreamer in the window, winked to him with one eye. The dream went on, it matters not how it went; it was a good dream as dreams go; but there was nothing in the sequel worthy of that devilish brown dog. And the point of interest for me

lies partly in that very fact: that having found so singular an incident, my imperfect dreamer should prove unable to carry the tale to
a fit end and fall back on indescribable noises and indiscriminate
horrors. It would be different now; he knows his business better!

For, to approach at last the point: This honest fellow had long
been in the custom of setting himself to sleep with tales, and so had
his father before him; but these were irresponsible inventions, told
for the teller's pleasure, with no eye to the crass public or the thwart
reviewer: tales where a thread might be dropped, or one adventure
quitted for another, on fancy's least suggestion. So that the little
people who manage man's internal theatre had not as yet received a
very rigorous training; and played upon their stage like children
who should have slipped into the house and found it empty, rather
than like drilled actors performing a set piece to a huge hall of faces.
But presently my dreamer began to turn his former amusement of
story-telling to (what is called) account; by which I mean that he
began to write and sell his tales. Here was he, and here were the little
people who did that part of his business, in quite new conditions.
The stories must now be trimmed and pared and set upon all fours,
they must run from a beginning to an end and fit (after a manner)
with the laws of life; the pleasure, in one word, had become a business; and that not only for the dreamer, but for the little people of
his theatre. These understood the change as well as he. When he lay
down to prepare himself for sleep, he no longer sought amusement,
but printable and profitable tales; and after he had dozed off in his
box-seat, his little people continued their evolutions with the same
mercantile designs. All other forms of dream deserted him but two:
he still occasionally reads the most delightful books, he still visits at
times the most delightful places; and it is perhaps worthy of note
that to these same places, and to one in particular, he returns at
intervals of months and years, finding new field-paths, visiting new
neighbours, beholding that happy valley under new effects of noon
and dawn and sunset. But all the rest of the family of visions is quite
lost to him: the common, mangled version of yesterday's affairs, the
raw-head-and-bloody-bones nightmare, rumoured to be the child
of toasted cheese—these and their like are gone; and, for the most
part, whether awake or asleep, he is simply occupied—he or his little

people—in consciously making stories for the market. This dreamer (like many other persons) has encountered some trifling vicissitudes of fortune. When the bank begins to send letters and the butcher to linger at the back gate, he sets to belabouring his brains after a story, for that is his readiest money-winner; and, behold! at once the little people begin to bestir themselves in the same quest, and labour all night long, and all night long set before him truncheons of tales upon their lighted theatre. No fear of his being frightened now; the flying heart and the frozen scalp are things by-gone; applause, growing applause, growing interest, growing exultation in his own cleverness (for he takes all the credit), and at last a jubilant leap to wakefulness, with the cry, 'I have it, that'll do!' upon his lips: with such and similar emotions he sits at these nocturnal dramas, with such outbreaks, like Claudius in the play, he scatters the performance in the midst. Often enough the waking is a disappointment: he has been too deep asleep, as I explain the thing; drowsiness has gained his little people, they have gone stumbling and maundering through their parts; and the play, to the awakened mind, is seen to be a tissue of absurdities. And yet how often have these sleepless Brownies done him honest service, and given him, as he sat idly taking his pleasure in the boxes, better tales than he could fashion for himself.

Here is one, exactly as it came to him. It seemed he was the son of a very rich and wicked man, the owner of broad acres and a most damnable temper. The dreamer (and that was the son) had lived much abroad, on purpose to avoid his parent; and when at length he returned to England, it was to find him married again to a young wife, who was supposed to suffer cruelly and to loathe her yoke. Because of this marriage (as the dreamer indistinctly understood) it was desirable for father and son to have a meeting; and yet both being proud and both angry, neither would condescend upon a visit. Meet they did accordingly, in a desolate, sandy country by the sea; and there they quarrelled, and the son, stung by some intolerable insult, struck down the father dead. No suspicion was aroused; the dead man was found and buried, and the dreamer succeeded to the broad estates, and found himself installed under the same roof with his father's widow, for whom no provision had been made. These two lived very much alone, as people may after a bereavement, sat down to table together, shared the long evenings, and grew daily better friends; until it seemed to him of a sudden that she was prying about dangerous matters, that she had conceived a notion of his guilt, that she watched him and tried him with questions. He drew back from her company as men draw back from a precipice suddenly discovered; and yet so strong was the attraction that he would drift again and again into the old intimacy, and again and again be startled back by some suggestive question or some inexplicable meaning in her eye. So they lived at cross purposes, a life full of broken dialogue, challenging glances, and suppressed passion; until, one day, he saw the woman slipping from the house in a veil, followed her to the station, followed her in the train to the seaside country, and out over the sandhills to the very place where the murder was done. There she began to grope among the bents, he watching her, flat upon his face; and presently she had something in her hand—I cannot remember what it was, but it was deadly evidence against the dreamer—and as she held it up to look at it, perhaps from the shock of the discovery, her foot slipped, and she hung at some peril on the brink of the tall sand-wreaths. He had no thought but to spring up and rescue her; and there they stood face to face, she with that deadly matter openly in her hand—his very presence on the spot another link of proof. It was plain she was about to speak, but this was more than he could bear—he could bear to be lost, but not to talk of it with his destroyer; and he cut her short with trivial conversation. Arm in arm, they returned together to the train, talking he knew not what, made the journey back in the same carriage, sat down to dinner, and passed the evening in the drawing-room as in the past. But suspense and fear drummed in the dreamer's bosom. 'She has not denounced me yet'—so his thoughts ran—'when will she denounce me? Will it be tomorrow?' And it was not tomorrow, nor the next day, nor the next; and their life settled back on the old terms, only that she seemed kinder than before, and that, as for him, the burthen of his suspense and wonder grew daily more unbearable, so that he wasted away like a man with a disease. Once, indeed, he broke all bounds of decency, seized an occasion when she was abroad, ransacked her room, and at last, hidden away among her jewels, found the damning evidence. There he stood, holding this thing, which was his life, in the hollow of his hand, and marvelling at her inconsequent behaviour, that she should seek, and keep, and yet not use it; and then the door opened, and behold herself. So, once more, they stood, eye to eye, with the evidence between them; and once more she raised to him a face brimming with some communication; and once more he shied away from speech and cut her off. But before he left the room, which he had turned upside down, he laid back his death warrant where he had found it; and at that, her face lighted up.

The next thing he heard, she was explaining to her maid, with some ingenious falsehood, the disorder of her things. Flesh and blood could bear the strain no longer; and I think it was the next morning (though chronology is always hazy in the theatre of the mind) that he burst from his reserve. They had been breakfasting together in one corner of a great, parqueted, sparely-furnished room of many windows; all the time of the meal she had tortured him with sly allusions; and no sooner were the servants gone, and these two protagonists alone together, than he leaped to his feet. She too sprang up, with a pale face; with a pale face, she heard him as he raved out his complaint: Why did she torture him so? she knew all, she knew he was no enemy to her; why did she not denounce him at once? what signified her whole behaviour? why did she torture him? and yet again, why did she torture him? And when he had done, she fell upon her knees, and with outstretched hands: 'Do you not understand?' she cried. 'I love you!'

Hereupon, with a pang of wonder and mercantile delight, the dreamer awoke. His mercantile delight was not of long endurance; for it soon became plain that in this spirited tale there were unmarketable elements; which is just the reason why you have it here so briefly told. But his wonder has still kept growing; and I think the reader's will also, if he consider it ripely. For now he sees why I speak of the little people as of substantive inventors and performers. To the end they had kept their secret. I will go bail for the dreamer (having excellent grounds for valuing his candour) that he had no guess whatever at the motive of the woman—the hinge of the whole well-invented plot—until the instant of that highly dramatic declaration. It was not his tale; it was the little people's! And observe: not only was the secret kept, the story was told with really guileful craftsmanship. The conduct of both actors is (in the cant phrase) psychologically correct, and the emotion aptly graduated up to the surprising climax. I am awake now, and I know this trade; and yet I cannot better it. I am awake, and I live by this business; and yet I could not outdo—could not perhaps equal—that crafty artifice (as of some old, experienced carpenter of plays, some Dennery or Sardou) by which the same situation is twice presented and the two actors twice brought face to face over the evidence, only once it is in her hand, once in his—and these in their due order, the least dramatic first. The more I think of it, the more I am moved to press upon the world my question: Who are the Little People? They are near connections of the dreamer's, beyond doubt; they share in his financial worries and have an eye to the bank-book; they share plainly in his training; they have plainly learned like him to build the scheme of a considerate story and to arrange emotion in progressive order; only I think they have more talent; and one thing is beyond doubt, they can tell him a story piece by piece, like a serial, and keep him all the while in ignorance of where they aim. Who are they, then? and who is the dreamer?

Well, as regards the dreamer, I can answer that, for he is no less a person than myself;—as I might have told you from the beginning, only that the critics murmur over my consistent egotism;—and as I am positively forced to tell you now, or I could advance but little farther with my story. And for the Little People, what shall I say they are but just my Brownies, God bless them! who do one-half my work for me while I am fast asleep, and in all human likelihood, do the rest for me as well, when I am wide awake and fondly suppose I do it for myself. That part which is done while I am sleeping is the Brownies' part beyond contention; but that which is done when I am up and about is by no means necessarily mine, since all goes to show the Brownies have a hand in it even then.

Here is a doubt that much concerns my conscience. For myself—what I call I, my conscious ego, the denizen of the pineal gland unless he has changed his residence since Descartes, the man with the conscience and the variable bank-account, the man with the hat and the boots, and the privilege of voting and not carrying his candidate at the general elections—I am sometimes tempted to suppose he is no story-teller at all, but a creature as matter of fact as any cheesemonger or any cheese, and a realist bemired up to the ears in actuality; so that, by that account, the whole of my published fiction should be the single-handed product of some Brownie, some Familiar, some unseen collaborator, whom I keep locked in a back garret, while I get all the praise and he but a share (which I cannot prevent him getting) of the pudding. I am an excellent adviser, something like Moliere's servant; I pull back and I cut down; and I dress the whole in the best words and sentences that I can find and make; I hold the pen, too; and I do the sitting at the table, which is about the worst of it; and when all is done, I make up the manuscript and pay for the registration; so that, on the whole, I have some claim to share, though not so largely as I do, in the profits of our common enterprise.

I can but give an instance or so of what part is done sleeping and what part awake, and leave the reader to share what laurels there are, at his own nod, between myself and my collaborators; and to do this I will first take a book that a number of persons have been polite enough to read, the *Strange Case of Dr. Jekyll and Mr. Hyde*

I had long been trying to write a story on this subject, to find a body, a vehicle, for that strong sense of man's double being which must at times come in upon and overwhelm the mind of every thinking creature. I had even written one, *The Travelling Companion*, which was returned by an editor on the plea that it was a work of genius and indecent, and which I burned the other day on the ground that it was not a work of genius, and that *Jekyll* had supplanted it. Then came one of those financial fluctuations to which (with an elegant modesty) I have hitherto referred in the third person. For two days I went about racking my brains for a plot of any sort; and on the second night I dreamed the scene at the window, and a scene afterward split in two, in which Hyde, pursued for some crime, took the powder and underwent the change in the presence of his pursuers. All the rest was made awake, and consciously, although I think I can trace in much of it the manner of my Brownies. The meaning of the tale is therefore mine, and had long pre-existed in my garden of

Adonis, and tried one body after another in vain; indeed, I do most of the morality, worse luck! and my Brownies have not a rudiment of what we call a conscience. Mine, too, is the setting, mine the characters. All that was given me was the matter of three scenes, and the central idea of a voluntary change becoming involuntary. Will it be thought ungenerous, after I have been so liberally ladling out praise to my unseen collaborators, if I here toss them over, bound hand and foot, into the arena of the critics? For the business of the powders, which so many have censured, is, I am relieved to say, not mine at all but the Brownies'. Of another tale, in case the reader should have glanced at it, I may say a word: the not very defensible story of *Olalla*. Here the court, the mother, the mother's niche, Olalla, Olalla's chamber, the meetings on the stair, the broken window, the ugly scene of the bite, were all given me in bulk and detail as I have tried to write them; to this I added only the external scenery (for in my dream I never was beyond the court), the portrait, the characters of Felipe and the priest, the moral, such as it is, and the last pages, such as, alas! they are. And I may even say that in this case the moral itself was given me; for it arose immediately on a comparison of the mother and the daughter, and from the hideous trick of atavism in the first. Sometimes a parabolic sense is still more undeniably present in a dream; sometimes I cannot but suppose my Brownies have been aping Bunyan, and yet in no case with what would possibly be called a moral in a tract; never with the ethical narrowness; conveying hints instead of life's larger limitations and that sort of sense which we seem to perceive in the arabesque of time and space.

For the most part, it will be seen, my Brownies are somewhat fantastic, like their stories hot and hot, full of passion and the picturesque, alive with animating incident; and they have no prejudice against the supernatural. But the other day they gave me a surprise, entertaining me with a love-story, a little April comedy, which I ought certainly to hand over to the author of *A Chance Acquaintance*, for he could write it as it should be written, and I am sure (although I mean to try) that I cannot.—But who would have supposed that a Brownie of mine should invent a tale for Mr Howells?

FICTIONS

The Suicide Club

There is every reason why I should not tell you my story. Perhaps that is just the reason why I am going to do so.

STORY OF THE YOUNG MAN
WITH THE CREAM TARTS

DURING HIS residence in London, the accomplished Prince Florizel of Bohemia gained the affection of all classes by the seduction of his manner and by a well-considered generosity. He was a remarkable man even by what was known of him; and that was but a small part of what he actually did. Although of a placid temper in ordinary circumstances, and accustomed to take the world with as much philosophy as any ploughman, the Prince of Bohemia was not without a taste for ways of life more adventurous and eccentric than that to which he was destined by his birth. Now and then, when he fell into a low humour, when there was no laughable play to witness in any of the London theatres, and when the season of the year was unsuitable to those field sports in which he excelled all competitors, he would summon his confidant and Master of the Horse, Colonel Geraldine, and bid him prepare himself against an evening ramble. The Master of the Horse was a young officer of a brave and even temerarious disposition. He greeted the news with delight, and hastened to make ready. Long practice and a varied acquaintance of life had given him a singular facility in disguise; he could adapt not only his face and bearing, but his voice and almost his thoughts, to those of any rank, character, or nation; and in this way he diverted attention from the Prince, and sometimes gained admission for the pair into strange societies. The civil authorities were never taken into the secret of these adventures; the imperturbable courage of the one and the ready invention and chivalrous devotion of the other had brought them through a score of dangerous passes; and they grew in confidence as time went on.

One evening in March they were driven by a sharp fall of sleet into an Oyster Bar in the immediate neighbourhood of Leicester

Square. Colonel Geraldine was dressed and painted to represent a person connected with the Press in reduced circumstances; while the Prince had, as usual, travestied his appearance by the addition of false whiskers and a pair of large adhesive eyebrows. These lent him a shaggy and weather-beaten air, which, for one of his urbanity, formed the most impenetrable disguise. Thus equipped, the commander and his satellite sipped their brandy and soda in security.

The bar was full of guests, both male and female; but though more than one of these offered to fall into talk with our adventurers, none of them promised to grow interesting upon a nearer acquaintance. There was nothing present but the lees of London and the commonplace of disrespectability; and the Prince had already fallen to yawning, and was beginning to grow weary of the whole excursion, when the swing doors were pushed violently open, and a young man, followed by a couple of commissionaires, entered the bar. Each of the commissionaires carried a large dish of cream tarts under a cover, which they at once removed; and the young man made the round of the company, and pressed these confections upon everyone's acceptance with an exaggerated courtesy. Sometimes his offer was laughingly accepted; sometimes it was firmly, or even harshly, rejected. In these latter cases the new-comer always ate the tart himself, with some more or less humourous commentary.

At last he accosted Prince Florizel.

'Sir,' said he, with a profound obeisance, proffering the tart at the same time between his thumb and forefinger, 'will you so far honour an entire stranger? I can answer for the quality of the pastry, having eaten two dozen and three of them myself since five o'clock.'

'I am in the habit,' replied the Prince, 'of looking not so much to the nature of a gift as to the spirit in which it is offered.'

'The spirit, sir,' returned the young man, with another bow, 'is one of mockery.'

'Mockery?' repeated Florizel. 'And whom do you propose to mock?'

'I am not here to expound my philosophy,' replied the other, 'but to distribute these cream tarts. If I mention that I heartily include myself in the ridicule of the transaction, I hope you will consider honour satisfied and condescend. If not, you will constrain me to eat my twenty-eighth, and I own to being weary of the exercise.'

'You touch me,' said the Prince, 'and I have all the will in the world to rescue you from this dilemma, but upon one condition. If my friend and I eat your cakes—for which we have neither of us any natural inclination—we shall expect you to join us at supper, by way of recompense.'

The young man seemed to reflect.

'I have still several dozen upon hand,' he said at last; 'and that will make it necessary for me to visit several more bars before my great affair is concluded. This will take some time; and if you are hungry—'

The Prince interrupted him with a polite gesture.

'My friend and I will accompany you,' he said: 'for we have already a deep interest in your very agreeable mode of passing an evening. And now that the preliminaries of peace are settled, allow me to sign the treaty for both.'

And the Prince swallowed the tart with the best grace imaginable.

'It is delicious,' said he.

'I perceive you are a connoisseur,' replied the young man.

Colonel Geraldine likewise did honour to the pastry; and every one in that bar having now either accepted or refused his delicacies, the young man with the cream tarts led the way to another and similar establishment. The two commissionaires, who seemed to have grown accustomed to their absurd employment, followed immediately after; and the Prince and the Colonel brought up the rear, arm in arm, and smiling to each other as they went. In this order the company visited two other taverns, where scenes were enacted of a like nature to that already described—some refusing, some accepting, the favours of this vagabond hospitality, and the young man himself eating each rejected tart.

On leaving the third saloon the young man counted his store. There were but nine remaining, three in one tray and six in the other.

'Gentlemen,' said he, addressing himself to his two new followers, 'I am unwilling to delay your supper. I am positively sure you must be hungry. I feel that I owe you a special consideration. And on this great day for me, when I am closing a career of folly by my most conspicuously silly action, I wish to behave handsomely to all who give me countenance. Gentlemen, you shall wait no longer. Although my constitution is shattered by previous excesses, at the risk of my life I liquidate the suspensory condition.'

With these words he crushed the nine remaining tarts into his mouth, and swallowed them at a single movement each. Then, turning to the commissionaires, he gave them a couple of sovereigns.

'I have to thank you,' said he, 'for your extraordinary patience.'

And he dismissed them with a bow apiece. For some seconds he stood looking at the purse from which he had just paid his assistants, then, with a laugh, he tossed it into the middle of the street, and signified his readiness for supper.

In a small French restaurant in Soho, which had enjoyed an exaggerated reputation for some little while, but had already begun to be forgotten, and in a private room up two pair of stairs, the three companions made a very elegant supper, and drank three or four bottles of champagne, talking the while upon indifferent subjects. The young man was fluent and gay, but he laughed louder than was natural in a person of polite breeding; his hands trembled violently, and his voice took sudden and surprising inflections, which seemed to be independent of his will. The dessert had been cleared away, and all three had lighted their cigars, when the Prince addressed him in these words:—

'You will, I am sure, pardon my curiosity. What I have seen of you has greatly pleased but even more puzzled me. And though I should be loath to seem indiscreet, I must tell you that my friend and I are persons very well worthy to be entrusted with a secret. We have many of our own, which we are continually revealing to improper ears. And if, as I suppose, your story is a silly one, you need have no delicacy with us, who are two of the silliest men in England. My name is Godall, Theophilus Godall; my friend is Major Alfred Hammersmith—or at least, such is the name by which he chooses to be known. We pass our lives entirely in the search for extravagant adventures; and there is no extravagance with which we are not capable of sympathy.'

'I like you, Mr Godall,' returned the young man; 'you inspire me with a natural confidence; and I have not the slightest objection to your friend, the Major; whom I take to be a nobleman in masquer-ade. At least, I am sure he is no soldier.'

The Colonel smiled at this compliment to the perfection of his art; and the young man went on in a more animated manner.

'There is every reason why I should not tell you my story. Perhaps that is just the reason why I am going to do so. At least, you seem so well prepared to hear a tale of silliness that I cannot find it in my heart to disappoint you. My name, in spite of your example, I shall keep to myself. My age is not essential to the narrative. I am descended from my ancestors by ordinary generation, and from them I inherited the very eligible human tenement which I still occupy and a fortune of three hundred pounds a year. I suppose they also handed on to me a hare-brain humour, which it has been my chief delight to indulge. I received a good education. I can play the violin nearly well enough to earn money in the orchestra of a penny gaff, but not quite. The same remark applies to the flute and the French horn. I learned enough of whist to lose about a hundred a year at that scientific game. My acquaintance with French was suffi-cient to enable me to squander money in Paris with almost the same facility as in London. In short, I am a person full of manly accom-plishments. I have had every sort of adventure, including a duel about nothing. Only two months ago I met a young lady exactly suited to my taste in mind and body; I found my heart melt; I saw that I had come upon my fate at last, and was in the way to fall in love. But when I came to reckon up what remained to me of my capi-tal, I found it amounted to something less than four hundred pounds! I ask you fairly—can a man who respects himself fall in love on four hundred pounds? I concluded, certainly not; left the presence of my charmer, and slightly accelerating my usual rate of expenditure, came this morning to my last eighty pounds. This I divided into two equal parts; forty I reserved for a particular purpose; the remaining forty I was to dissipate before the night. I have passed a very enter-taining day; and played many farces besides that of the cream tarts which procured me the advantage of your acquaintance; for I was determined, as I told you, to bring a foolish career to a still more foolish conclusion; and when you saw me throw my purse into the street, the forty pounds were at an end. Now you know me as well as

I know myself: a fool but consistent in his folly; and, as I will ask you to believe, neither a whimperer nor a coward.'

From the whole tone of the young man's statement it was plain that he harboured very bitter and contemptuous thoughts about himself. His auditors were led to imagine that his love affair was nearer his heart than he admitted, and that he had a design on his own life. The farce of the cream tarts began to have very much the air of a tragedy in disguise.

'Why, is this not odd,' broke out Geraldine, giving a look to Prince Florizel, 'that we three fellows should have met by the merest accident in so large a wilderness as London, and should be so nearly in the same condition?'

'How?' cried the young man. 'Are you, too, ruined? Is this supper a folly like my cream tarts? Has the Devil brought three of his own together for a last carouse?'

'The Devil, depend upon it, can sometimes do a very gentlemanly thing,' returned Prince Florizel; 'and I am so much touched by this coincidence, that, although we are not entirely in the same case, I am going to put an end to the disparity. Let your heroic treatment of the last cream tarts be my example.'

So saying, the Prince drew out his purse and took from it a small bundle of bank-notes.

'You see, I was a week or so behind you, but I mean to catch you up and come neck and neck into the winning-post,' he continued. 'This,' laying one of the notes upon the table, 'will suffice for the bill. As for the rest—'

He tossed them into the fire, and they went up the chimney in a single blaze.

The young man tried to catch his arm, but as the table was between them his interference came too late.

'Unhappy man,' he cried, 'you should not have burned them all! You should have kept forty pounds.'

'Forty pounds!' repeated the Prince. 'Why, in heaven's name, forty pounds?'

'Why not eighty?' cried the Colonel; 'for to my certain knowledge there must have been a hundred in the bundle.'

'It was only forty pounds he needed,' said the young man

gloomily. 'But without them there is no admission. The rule is strict. Forty pounds for each. Accursed life, where a man cannot even die without money!'

The Prince and the Colonel exchanged glances.

'Explain yourself,' said the latter. 'I have still a pocket-book tolerably well lined, and I need not say how readily I would share my wealth with Godall. But I must know to what end: you must certainly tell us what you mean.'

The young man seemed to awaken; he looked uneasily from one to the other, and his face flushed deeply.

'You are not fooling me?' he asked. 'You are indeed ruined men like me?'

'Indeed, I am for my part,' replied the Colonel.

'And for mine,' said the Prince, 'I have given you proof. Who but a ruined man would throw his notes into the fire? The action speaks for itself.'

'A ruined man—yes,' returned the other suspiciously, 'or else a millionaire.'

'Enough, sir,' said the Prince; 'I have said so, and I am not accustomed to have my word remain in doubt.'

'Ruined?' said the young man. 'Are you ruined, like me? Are you, after a life of indulgence, come to such a pass that you can only indulge yourself in one thing more? Are you'—he kept lowering his voice as he went on—'are you going to give yourselves that last indulgence? Are you going to avoid the consequences of your folly by the one infallible and easy path? Are you going to give the slip to the sheriff's officers of conscience by the one open door?'

Suddenly he broke off and attempted to laugh.

'Here is your health!' he cried, emptying his glass, 'and goodnight to you, my merry ruined men.'

Colonel Geraldine caught him by the arm as he was about to rise.

'You lack confidence in us,' he said, 'and you are wrong. To all your questions I make answer in the affirmative. But I am not so timid, and can speak the Queen's English plainly. We too, like yourself, have had enough of life, and are determined to die. Sooner or later, alone or together, we meant to seek out death and beard him where he lies ready. Since we have met you, and your case is more pressing, let it be tonight—and at once—and, if you will, all three together. Such a penniless trio,' he cried, 'should go arm in arm into the halls of Pluto, and give each other some countenance among the shades!'

Geraldine had hit exactly on the manners and intonations that became the part he was playing. The Prince himself was disturbed, and looked over at his confidant with a shade of doubt. As for the young man, the flush came back darkly into his cheek, and his eyes threw out a spark of light.

'You are the men for me!' he cried, with an almost terrible gayety. 'Shake hands upon the bargain!' (His hand was cold and wet.) 'You little know in what a company you will begin the march! You little know in what a happy moment for yourselves you partook of my cream tarts! I am only a unit, but I am a unit in an army. I know Death's private door. I am one of his familiars, and can show you into eternity without ceremony and yet without scandal.'

They called upon him eagerly to explain his meaning.

'Can you muster eighty pounds between you?' he demanded.

Geraldine ostentatiously consulted his pocket-book, and replied in the affirmative.

'Fortunate beings!' cried the young man. 'Forty pounds is the entry money of the Suicide Club.'

'The Suicide Club,' said the Prince, 'why, what the devil is that?'

'Listen,' said the young man; 'this is the age of conveniences, and I have to tell you of the last perfection of the sort. We have affairs in different places; and hence railways were invented. Railways separated us infallibly from our friends; and so telegraphs were made that we might communicate speedily at great distances. Even in hotels we have lifts to spare us a climb of some hundred steps. Now, we know that life is only a stage to play the fool upon as long as the part amuses us. There was one more convenience lacking to modern comfort; a decent, easy way to quit that stage; the back stairs to liberty; or, as I said this moment, Death's private door. This, my two fellow-rebels, is supplied by the Suicide Club. Do not suppose that you and I are alone, or even exceptional, in the highly reasonable desire that we profess. A large number of our fellow-men, who have grown heartily sick of the performance in which they are expected to join daily and all their lives long, are only kept from flight by one or two considerations. Some have families who would be shocked, or even blamed, if the matter became public; others have a weakness at heart and recoil from the circumstances of death. That is, to some extent, my own experience. I cannot put a pistol to my head and draw the trigger; for something stronger than myself withholds the act; and although I loathe life, I have not strength enough in my body to take hold of death and be done with it. For such as I, and for all who desire to be out of the coil without posthumous scandal, the Suicide Club has been inaugurated. How this has been managed, what is its history, or what may be its ramifications in other lands, I am myself uninformed; and what I know of its constitution, I am not at liberty to communicate to you. To this extent, however, I am at your service. If you are truly tired of life, I will introduce you tonight to a meeting; and if not tonight, at least some time within the week, you will be easily relieved of your existences. It is now (consulting his watch) eleven; by half-past, at latest, we must leave this place; so that you have half an hour before you to consider my proposal. It is more serious than a cream tart,' he added, with a smile; 'and I suspect more palatable.'

'More serious, certainly,' returned Colonel Geraldine; 'and as it is so much more so, will you allow me five minutes' speech in private with my friend, Mr Godall?'

'It is only fair,' answered the young man. 'If you will permit, I will retire.'

'You will be very obliging,' said the Colonel.

As soon as the two were alone—'What,' said Prince Florizel, 'is the use of this confabulation, Geraldine? I see you are flurried, whereas my mind is very tranquilly made up. I will see the end of this.'

'Your Highness,' said the Colonel turning pale; 'let me ask you to consider the importance of your life, not only to your friends, but to the public interest. "If not tonight," said this madman; but supposing that tonight some irreparable disaster were to overtake your Highness's person, what, let me ask you, what would be my despair, and what the concern and disaster of a great nation?'

'I will see the end of this,' repeated the Prince in his most deliberate tones; 'and have the kindness, Colonel Geraldine, to remember and respect your word of honour as a gentleman. Under no circumstances, recollect, nor without my special authority, are you to betray the incognito under which I choose to go abroad. These were my commands, which I now reiterate. And now,' he added, 'let me ask you to call for the bill.'

Colonel Geraldine bowed in submission; but he had a very white face as he summoned the young man of the cream tarts, and issued his directions to the waiter. The Prince preserved his undisturbed demeanour, and described a Palais Royal farce to the young suicide with great humour and gusto. He avoided the Colonel's appealing looks without ostentation, and selected another cheroot with more than usual care. Indeed, he was now the only man of the party who kept any command over his nerves.

The bill was discharged, the Prince giving the whole change of the note to the astonished waiter; and the three drove off in a four wheeler. They were not long upon the way before the cab stopped at the entrance to a rather dark court. Here all descended.

After Geraldine had paid the fare, the young man turned, and addressed Prince Florizel as follows:

'It is still time, Mr Godall, to make good your escape into thralldom. And for you too, Major Hammersmith. Reflect well before you take another step; and if your hearts say no—here are the crossroads.'

'Lead on, sir,' said the Prince. 'I am not the man to go back from a thing once said.'

'Your coolness does me good,' replied their guide. 'I have never seen anyone so unmoved at this conjuncture; and yet you are not the first whom I have escorted to this door. More than one of my friends has preceded me, where I knew I must shortly follow. But this is of no interest to you. Wait me here for only a few moments; I shall return as soon as I have arranged the preliminaries of your introduction.'

And with that the young man, waving his hand to his companions, turned into the court, entered a door-way and disappeared.

'Of all our follies,' said Colonel Geraldine in a low voice, 'this is the wildest and most dangerous.'

'I perfectly believe so,' returned the Prince.

'We have still,' pursued the Colonel, 'a moment to ourselves. Let me beseech your Highness to profit by the opportunity and retire. The consequences of this step are so dark, and may be so grave, that I feel myself justified in pushing a little farther than usual the liberty which your Highness is so condescending as to allow me in private.'

'Am I to understand that Colonel Geraldine is afraid?' asked his Highness, taking his cheroot from his lips, and looking keenly into the other's face.

'My fear is certainly not personal,' replied the other proudly; 'of that your Highness may rest well assured.'

'I had supposed as much,' returned the Prince, with undisturbed good humour; 'but I was unwilling to remind you of the difference in our stations. No more—no more,' he added, seeing Geraldine about to apologise, 'you stand excused.'

And he smoked placidly, leaning against a railing, until the young man returned.

'Well,' he asked, 'has our reception been arranged?'

'Follow me,' was the reply. 'The President will see you in the cabinet. And let me warn you to be frank in your answers. I have stood your guarantee; but the club requires a searching inquiry before admission; for the indiscretion of a single member would lead to the dispersion of the whole society forever.'

The Prince and Geraldine put their heads together for a moment. 'Bear me out in this,' said the one; and 'Bear me out in that,' said the other; and by boldly taking up the characters of men with whom both were acquainted, they had come to an agreement in a twinkling, and were ready to follow their guide into the President's cabinet.

There were no formidable obstacles to pass. The outer door stood open; the door of the cabinet was ajar; and there, in a small but very high apartment, the young man left them once more.

'He will be here immediately,' he said with a nod, as he disappeared.

Voices were audible in the cabinet through the folding doors which formed one end; and now and then the noise of a champagne cork, followed by a burst of laughter, intervened among the sounds of conversation. A single tall window looked out upon the river and the embankment; and by the disposition of the lights they judged themselves not far from Charing Cross station. The furniture was scanty, and the coverings worn to the thread; and there was nothing movable except a hand-bell in the centre of a round table, and the hats and coats of a considerable party hung round the wall on pegs.

'What sort of a den is this?' said Geraldine.

'That is what I have come to see,' replied the Prince. 'If they keep live devils on the premises, the thing may grow amusing.'

Just then the folding door was opened no more than was necessary for the passage of a human body; and there entered at the same moment a louder buzz of talk, and the redoubtable President of the Suicide Club. The President was a man of fifty or upwards; large and rambling in his gait, with shaggy side-whiskers, a bald top to his head, and a veiled grey eye, which now and then emitted a twinkle. His mouth, which embraced a large cigar, he kept continually screwing round and round and from side to side, as he looked sagaciously and coldly at the strangers. He was dressed in light tweeds, with his neck very open, in a striped shirt collar; and carried a minute book under one arm.

'Good evening,' said he, after he had closed the door behind him. 'I am told you wish to speak with me.'

'We have a desire, sir, to join the Suicide Club,' replied the Colonel.

The President rolled his cigar about in his mouth.

'What is that?' he said abruptly.

'Pardon me,' returned the Colonel, 'but I believe you are the person best qualified to give us information on that point.'

'I?' cried the President. 'A Suicide Club? Come, come! this is a frolic for All Fools' Day. I can make allowances for gentlemen who get merry in their liquor; but let there be an end to this.'

'Call your club what you will,' said the Colonel, 'you have some company behind these doors, and we insist on joining it.'

'Sir,' returned the President, curtly, 'you have made a mistake. This is a private house, and you must leave it instantly.'

The Prince had remained quietly in his seat throughout this little colloquy; but now, when the Colonel looked over to him, as much as to say, 'Take your answer and come away, for God's sake!', he drew his cheroot from his mouth, and spoke—

'I have come here,' said he, 'upon the invitation of a friend of yours. He has doubtless informed you of my intention in thus intruding on your party. Let me remind you that a person in my circumstances has exceedingly little to bind him, and is not at all likely to tolerate much rudeness. I am a very quiet man, as a usual thing; but, my dear sir, you are either going to oblige me in the little matter of which you are aware, or you shall very bitterly repent that you ever admitted me to your antechamber.'

The President laughed aloud.

'That is the way to speak,' said he. 'You are a man who is a man. You know the way to my heart, and can do what you like with me. Will you,' he continued, addressing Geraldine, 'will you step aside for a few minutes? I shall finish first with your companion, and some of the club's formalities require to be fulfilled in private.'

With these words he opened the door of a small closet, into which he shut the Colonel.

'I believe in you,' he said to Florizel, as soon as they were alone; 'but are you sure of your friend?'

'Not so sure as I am of myself, though he has more cogent reasons,' answered Florizel, 'but sure enough to bring him here without alarm. He has had enough to cure the most tenacious man of life. He was cashiered the other day for cheating at cards.'

'A good reason, I daresay,' replied the President; 'at least, we have another in the same case, and I feel sure of him. Have you also been in the Service, may I ask?'

'I have,' was the reply; 'but I was too lazy, I left it early.'

'What is your reason for being tired of life?' pursued the President.

'The same, as near as I can make out,' answered the Prince; 'unadulterated laziness.'

The President started. 'D—n it,' said he, 'you must have something better than that.'

'I have no more money,' added Florizel. 'That is also a vexation, without doubt. It brings my sense of idleness to an acute point.'

The President rolled his cigar round in his mouth for some seconds, directing his gaze straight into the eyes of this unusual neophyte; but the Prince supported his scrutiny with unabashed good temper.

'If I had not a deal of experience,' said the President at last, 'I should turn you off. But I know the world; and this much anyway, that the most frivolous excuses for a suicide are often the toughest to stand by. And when I downright like a man, as I do you, sir, I would rather strain the regulation than deny him.'

The Prince and the Colonel, one after the other, were subjected to a long and particular interrogatory: the Prince alone; but Geraldine in the presence of the Prince, so that the President might observe the countenance of the one while the other was being warmly cross-examined. The result was satisfactory; and the President, after having booked a few details of each case, produced a form of oath to be accepted. Nothing could be conceived more passive than the obedience promised, or more stringent than the terms by which the juror bound himself. The man who forfeited a pledge so awful could scarcely have a rag of honour or any of the consolations of religion left to him. Florizel signed the document, but not without a shudder; the Colonel followed his example with an air of great depression. Then the President received the entry money; and without more ado, introduced the two friends into the smoking-room of the Suicide Club.

The smoking-room of the Suicide Club was the same height as the cabinet into which it opened, but much larger, and papered from top to bottom with an imitation of oak wainscot. A large and cheer- ful fire and a number of gas-jets illuminated the company. The Prince and his follower made the number up to eighteen. Most of the party were smoking, and drinking champagne; a feverish hilar- ity reigned, with sudden and rather ghastly pauses.

'Is this a full meeting?' asked the Prince.

'Middling,' said the President. 'By the way,' he added, 'if you have any money, it is usual to offer some champagne. It keeps up a good spirit, and is one of my own little perquisites.'

'Hammersmith,' said Florizel, 'I may leave the champagne to you.'

And with that he turned away and began to go round among the guests. Accustomed to play the host in the highest circles, he charmed and dominated all whom he approached; there was some- thing at once winning and authoritative in his address; and his extraordinary coolness gave him yet another distinction in this half maniacal society. As he went from one to another he kept both his eyes and ears open, and soon began to gain a general idea of the people among whom he found himself. As in all other places of resort, one type predominated: people in the prime of youth, with every show of intelligence and sensibility in their appearance, but with little promise of strength or the quality that makes success. Few were much above thirty, and not a few were still in their teens. They stood, leaning on tables and shifting on their feet; sometimes they smoked extraordinarily fast, and sometimes they let their cigars go out; some talked well, but the conversation of others was plainly the result of nervous tension, and was equally without wit or purport. As each new bottle of champagne was opened, there was a manifest improvement in gayety. Only two were seated—one in a chair in the recess of the window, with his head hanging and his hands plunged deep into his trouser pockets, pale, visibly moist with perspiration, saying never a word, a very wreck of soul and body; the other sat on the divan close by the chimney, and attracted notice by a trenchant dissimilarity from all the rest. He was probably upwards of forty, but he looked fully ten years older; and Florizel thought he had never seen a man more naturally hideous, nor one more ravaged by disease and ruinous excitements. He was no more than skin and bone, was partly paralysed, and wore spectacles of such unusual power, that his eyes appeared through the glasses greatly magnified and distorted in shape. Except the Prince and the President, he was the only person in the room who preserved the composure of ordinary life.

There was little decency among the members of the club. Some boasted of the disgraceful actions, the consequences of which had reduced them to seek refuge in death; and the others listened without disapproval. There was a tacit understanding against moral judgments; and whoever passed the club doors enjoyed already some of the immunities of the tomb. They drank to each other's memories, and to those of notable suicides in the past. They compared and developed their different views of death—some declaring that it was no more than blackness and cessation; others full of a hope that that very night they should be scaling the stars and commercing with the mighty dead.

'To the eternal memory of Baron Trenck, the type of suicides!' cried one. 'He went out of a small cell into a smaller, that he might come forth again to freedom.'

'For my part,' said a second, 'I wish no more than a bandage for my eyes and cotton for my ears. Only they have no cotton thick enough in this world.'

A third was for reading the mysteries of life in a future state; and a fourth professed that he would never have joined the club, if he had not been induced to believe in Mr Darwin.

'I could not bear,' said this remarkable suicide, 'to be descended from an ape.'

Altogether, the Prince was disappointed by the bearing and conversation of the members.

'It does not seem to me,' he thought, 'a matter for so much disturbance. If a man has made up his mind to kill himself, let him do it, in God's name, like a gentleman. This flutter and big talk is out of place.'

In the meanwhile Colonel Geraldine was a prey to the blackest apprehensions; the club and its rules were still a mystery, and he looked round the room for someone who should be able to set his mind at rest. In this survey his eye lighted on the paralytic person with the strong spectacles; and seeing him so exceedingly tranquil, he besought the President, who was going in and out of the room under a pressure of business, to present him to the gentleman on the divan.

The functionary explained the needlessness of all such formalities within the club, but nevertheless presented Mr Hammersmith to Mr Malthus.

Mr Malthus looked at the Colonel curiously, and then requested him to take a seat upon his right.

'You are a new-comer,' he said; 'and wish information? You have come to the proper source. It is two years since I first visited this charming club.'

The Colonel breathed again. If Mr Malthus had frequented the place for two years there could be little danger for the Prince in a single evening. But Geraldine was none the less astonished, and began to suspect a mystification.

'What!' cried he, 'two years! I thought—but indeed I see I have been made the subject of a pleasantry.'

'By no means,' replied Mr Malthus mildly. 'My case is peculiar. I am not, properly speaking, a suicide at all; but, as it were, an honorary member. I rarely visit the club twice in two months. My infirmity and the kindness of the President have procured me these little immunities, for which besides I pay at an advanced rate. Even as it is my luck has been extraordinary.'

'I am afraid,' said the Colonel, 'that I must ask you to be more explicit. You must remember that I am still most imperfectly acquainted with the rules of the club.'

'An ordinary member who comes here in search of death like yourself,' replied the paralytic, 'returns every evening until fortune favours him. He can, even if he is penniless, get board and lodging from the President: very fair, I believe, and clean, although, of course, not luxurious; that could hardly be, considering the exiguity (if I may so express myself) of the subscription. And then the President's company is a delicacy in itself.'

'Indeed!' cried Geraldine, 'he had not greatly prepossessed me.'

'Ah!' said Mr Malthus, 'you do not know the man: the drollest fellow! What stories! What cynicism! He knows life to admiration and, between ourselves, is probably the most corrupt rogue in Christendom.'

'And he also,' asked the Colonel, 'is a permanency—like yourself, if I may say so without offence?'

'Indeed, he is a permanency in a very different sense from me,' replied Mr Malthus. 'I have been graciously spared, but I must go at last. Now he never plays. He shuffles and deals for the club, and makes the necessary arrangements. That man, my dear Mr Hammersmith, is the very soul of ingenuity. For three years he has pursued in London his useful and, I think I may add, his artistic calling; and not so much as a whisper of suspicion has been once aroused. I believe him myself to be inspired. You doubtless remember the celebrated case, six months ago, of the gentleman who was accidentally poisoned in a chemist's shop? That was one of the least rich, one of the least racy, of his notions; but then, how simple! and how safe!'

'You astound me,' said the Colonel. 'Was that unfortunate gentleman one of the—' He was about to say 'victims'; but bethinking
himself in time, he substituted—'members of the club?'

In the same flash of thought it occurred to him that Mr. Malthus
himself had not at all spoken in the tone of one who is in love with
death; and he added hurriedly:

'But I perceive I am still in the dark. You speak of shuffling and
dealing; pray for what end? And since you seem rather unwilling to
die than otherwise, I must own that I cannot conceive what brings
you here at all.'

'You say truly that you are in the dark,' replied Mr Malthus with
more animation. 'Why, my dear sir, this club is the temple of intoxication. If my enfeebled health could support the excitement more
often, you may depend upon it I should be more often here. It
requires all the sense of duty engendered by a long habit of ill-health
and careful regimen, to keep me from excess in this, which is, I may
say, my last dissipation. I have tried them all, sir,' he went on, laying
his hand on Geraldine's arm, 'all without exception, and I declare to
you, upon my honour, there is not one of them that has not been
grossly and untruthfully overrated. People trifle with love. Now, I
deny that love is a strong passion. Fear is the strong passion; it is with
fear that you must trifle, if you wish to taste the intense joys of living.
Envy me—envy me, sir,' he added with a chuckle, 'I am a coward!'

Geraldine could scarcely repress a movement of repulsion for this
deplorable wretch; but he commanded himself with an effort, and
continued his inquiries.

'How, sir,' he asked, 'is the excitement so artfully prolonged? and
where is there any element of uncertainty?'

'I must tell you how the victim for every evening is selected,'
returned Mr Malthus; 'and not only the victim, but another member,
who is to be the instrument in the club's hands, and Death's high
priest for that occasion.'

'Good God!' said the Colonel, 'do they then kill each other?'

'The trouble of suicide is removed in that way,' returned Malthus
with a nod.

'Merciful heavens!' ejaculated the Colonel, 'and may you—may
I—may the—my friend, I mean—may any of us be pitched upon this

evening as the slayer of another man's body and immortal spirit? Can such things be possible among men born of women? Oh! infamy of infamies!'

He was about to rise in his horror, when he caught the Prince's eye. It was fixed upon him from across the room with a frowning and angry stare. And in a moment Geraldine recovered his composure.

'After all,' he added, 'why not? And since you say the game is interesting, *vogue la galère*—I follow the club!'

Mr Malthus had keenly enjoyed the Colonel's amazement and disgust. He had the vanity of wickedness; and it pleased him to see another man give way to a generous movement, while he felt himself, in his entire corruption, superior to such emotions.

'You now, after your first moment of surprise,' said he, 'are in a position to appreciate the delights of our society. You can see how it combines the excitement of a gaming-table, a duel, and a Roman amphitheatre. The Pagans did well enough; I cordially admire the refinement of their minds; but it has been reserved for a Christian country to attain this extreme, this quintessence, this absolute of poignancy. You will understand how vapid are all amusements to a man who has acquired a taste for this one. The game we play,' he continued, 'is one of extreme simplicity. A full pack—but I perceive you are about to see the thing in progress. Will you lend me the help of your arm? I am unfortunately paralysed.'

Indeed, just as Mr Malthus was beginning his description, another pair of folding-doors was thrown open, and the whole club began to pass, not without some hurry, into the adjoining room. It was similar in every respect to the one from which it was entered, but somewhat differently furnished. The centre was occupied by a long green table, at which the President sat shuffling a pack of cards with great particularity. Even with the stick and the Colonel's arm, Mr Malthus walked with so much difficulty that everyone was seated before this pair and the Prince, who had waited for them, entered the apartment; and, in consequence, the three took seats close together at the lower end of the board.

'It is a pack of fifty-two,' whispered Mr Malthus. 'Watch for the ace of spades, which is the sign of death, and the ace of clubs, which designates the official of the night. Happy, happy young men!' he added. 'You have good eyes, and can follow the game. Alas! I cannot tell an ace from a deuce across the table.'

And he proceeded to equip himself with a second pair of spectacles. 'I must at least watch the faces,' he explained.

The Colonel rapidly informed his friend of all that he had learned from the honorary member, and of the horrible alternative that lay before them. The Prince was conscious of a deadly chill and a contraction about his heart; he swallowed with difficulty, and looked from side to side like a man in a maze.

'One bold stroke,' whispered the Colonel, 'and we may still escape.'

But the suggestion recalled the Prince's spirits.

'Silence!' said he. 'Let me see that you can play like a gentleman for any stake, however serious.'

And he looked about him, once more to all appearance at his ease, although his heart beat thickly, and he was conscious of an unpleasant heat in his bosom. The members were all very quiet and intent; everyone was pale, but none so pale as Mr Malthus. His eyes protruded; his head kept nodding involuntarily upon his spine; his hands found their way, one after the other, to his mouth, where they made clutches at his tremulous and ashen lips. It was plain that the honorary member enjoyed his membership on very startling terms.

'Attention, gentlemen!' said the President.

And he began slowly dealing the cards about the table in the reverse direction, pausing until each man had shown his card. Nearly everyone hesitated; and sometimes you would see a player's fingers stumble more than once before he could turn over the momentous slip of pasteboard. As the Prince's turn drew nearer, he was conscious of a growing and almost suffocating excitement; but he had somewhat of the gambler's nature, and recognised almost with astonishment that there was a degree of pleasure in his sensations. The nine of clubs fell to his lot; the three of spades was dealt to Geraldine; and the queen of hearts to Mr Malthus, who was unable to suppress a sob of relief. The young man of the cream tarts almost immediately afterwards turned over the ace of clubs, and remained frozen with horror, the card still resting on his finger; he had not come there to kill, but to be killed; and the Prince, in his generous sympathy with his position, almost forgot the peril that still hung over himself and his friend.

The deal was coming round again, and still Death's card had not come out. The players held their respiration, and only breathed by gasps. The Prince received another club; Geraldine had a diamond; but when Mr Malthus turned up his card a horrible noise, like that of something breaking, issued from his mouth; and he rose from his seat and sat down again, with no sign of his paralysis. It was the ace of spades. The honorary member had trifled once too often with his terrors.

Conversation broke out again almost at once. The players relaxed their rigid attitudes, and began to rise from the table and stroll back by twos and threes into the smoking-room. The President stretched his arms and yawned, like a man who had finished his day's work. But Mr Malthus sat in his place, with his head in his hands, and his hands upon the table, drunk and motionless—a thing stricken down.

The Prince and Geraldine made their escape at once. In the cold night air their horror of what they had witnessed was redoubled.

'Alas!' cried the Prince, 'to be bound by an oath in such a matter! to allow this wholesale trade in murder to be continued with profit and impunity! If I but dared to forfeit my pledge!'

'That is impossible for your Highness,' replied the Colonel, 'whose honour is the honour of Bohemia. But I dare, and may with propriety, forfeit mine.'

'Geraldine,' said the Prince, 'if your honour suffers in any of the adventures into which you follow me, not only will I never pardon you, but—what I believe will much more sensibly affect you—I should never forgive myself.'

'I receive your Highness's commands,' replied the Colonel. 'Shall we go from this accursed spot?'

'Yes,' said the Prince. 'Call a cab in heaven's name, and let me try to forget in slumber the memory of this night's disgrace.'

But it was notable that he carefully read the name of the court before he left it.

The next morning, as soon as the Prince was stirring, Colonel Geraldine brought him a daily newspaper, with the following paragraph marked:—

'MELANCHOLY ACCIDENT.—This morning, about two o'clock, Mr. Bartholomew Malthus, of 16 Chepstow Place, Westbourne Grove, on his way home from a party at a friend's house, fell over the upper parapet in Trafalgar Square, fracturing his skull and breaking a leg and an arm. Death was instantaneous. Mr. Malthus, accompanied by a friend, was engaged in looking for a cab at the time of the unfortunate occurrence. As Mr. Malthus was paralytic, it is thought that his fall may have been occasioned by another seizure. The unhappy gentleman was well known in the most respectable circles, and his loss will be widely and deeply deplored.'

'If ever a soul went straight to Hell,' said Geraldine solemnly, 'it was that paralytic man's.'

The Prince buried his face in his hands, and remained silent.

'I am almost rejoiced,' continued the Colonel, 'to know that he is dead. But for our young man of the cream tarts I confess my heart bleeds.'

'Geraldine,' said the Prince, raising his face, 'that unhappy lad was last night as innocent as you and I; and this morning the guilt of blood is on his soul. When I think of the President, my heart grows sick within me. I do not know how it shall be done, but I shall have that scoundrel at my mercy as there is a God in Heaven. What an experience, what a lesson, was that game of cards!'

'One,' said the Colonel, 'never to be repeated.'

The Prince remained so long without replying, that Geraldine grew alarmed.

'You cannot mean to return,' he said. 'You have suffered too much, and seen too much horror already. The duties of your high position forbid the repetition of the hazard.'

'There is much in what you say,' replied Prince Florizel, 'and I am not altogether pleased with my own determination. Alas! in the clothes of the greatest potentate, what is there but a man? I never felt my weakness more acutely than now, Geraldine, but it is stronger than I. Can I cease to interest myself in the fortunes of the unhappy young man who supped with us some hours ago? Can I leave the President to follow his nefarious career unwatched? Can I begin an adventure so entrancing, and not follow it to an end? No,

Geraldine; you ask of the Prince more than the man is able to perform. Tonight, once more, we take our places at the table of the Suicide Club.'

Colonel Geraldine fell upon his knees.

'Will your Highness take my life?' he cried. 'It is his—his freely; but do not, O do not! let him ask me to countenance so terrible a risk.'

'Colonel Geraldine,' replied the Prince, with some haughtiness of manner, 'your life is absolutely your own. I only looked for obedience; and when that is unwillingly rendered, I shall look for that no longer. I add one word: your importunity in this affair has been sufficient.'

The Master of the Horse regained his feet at once. 'Your Highness,' he said, 'may I be excused in my attendance this afternoon? I dare not, as an honourable man, venture a second time into that fatal house until I have perfectly ordered my affairs. Your Highness shall meet, I promise him, with no more opposition from the most devoted and grateful of his servants.'

'My dear Geraldine,' returned Prince Florizel, 'I always regret when you oblige me to remember my rank. Dispose of your day as you think fit, but be here before eleven in the same disguise.'

The club, on this second evening, was not so fully attended; and when Geraldine and the Prince arrived, there were not above half-a-dozen persons in the smoking-room. His Highness took the President aside and congratulated him warmly on the demise of Mr Malthus.

'I like,' he said, 'to meet with capacity, and certainly find much of it in you. Your profession is of a very delicate nature, but I see you are well qualified to conduct it with success and secrecy.'

The President was somewhat affected by these compliments from one of his Highness's superior bearing. He acknowledged them almost with humility.

'Poor Malthy!' he added, 'I shall hardly know the club without him. The most of my patrons are boys, sir, and poetical boys, who are not much company for me. Not but what Malthy had some poetry, too; but it was of a kind that I could understand.'

'I can readily imagine you should find yourself in sympathy with Mr Malthus,' returned the Prince. 'He struck me as a man of a very original disposition.'

The young man of the cream tarts was in the room, but painfully depressed and silent. His late companions sought in vain to lead him into conversation.

'How bitterly I wish,' he cried, 'that I had never brought you to this infamous abode! Begone, while you are clean-handed. If you could have heard the old man scream as he fell, and the noise of his bones upon the pavement! Wish me, if you have any kindness to so fallen a being—wish the ace of spades for me tonight!'

A few more members dropped in as the evening went on, but the club did not muster more than the devil's dozen when they took their places at the table. The Prince was again conscious of a certain joy in his alarms; but he was astonished to see Geraldine so much more self-possessed than on the night before.

'It is extraordinary,' thought the Prince, 'that a will, made or unmade, should so greatly influence a young man's spirit.'

'Attention, gentlemen!' said the President, and he began to deal.

Three times the cards went all round the table, and neither of the marked cards had yet fallen from his hand. The excitement as he began the fourth distribution was overwhelming. There were just cards enough to go once more entirely round. The Prince, who sat second from the dealer's left, would receive, in the reverse mode of dealing practised at the club, the second last card. The third player turned up a black ace—it was the ace of clubs. The next received a diamond, the next a heart, and so on; but the ace of spades was still undelivered. At last Geraldine, who sat upon the Prince's left, turned his card; it was an ace, but the ace of hearts.

When Prince Florizel saw his fate upon the table in front of him, his heart stood still. He was a brave man, but the sweat poured off his face. There were exactly fifty chances out of a hundred that he was doomed. He reversed the card; it was the ace of spades. A loud roaring filled his brain, and the table swam before his eyes. He heard the player on his right break into a fit of laughter that sounded between mirth and disappointment; he saw the company rapidly dispersing, but his mind was full of other thoughts. He recognised how foolish, how criminal, had been his conduct. In perfect health, in the prime of his years, the heir to a throne, he had gambled away his future and that of a brave and loyal country. 'God,' he cried, 'God forgive me!' And with that, the confusion of his senses passed away, and he regained his self-possession in a moment.

To his surprise Geraldine had disappeared. There was no one in the card-room but his destined butcher consulting with the President, and the young man of the cream tarts, who slipped up to the Prince and whispered in his ear:

'I would give a million, if I had it, for your luck.'

His Highness could not help reflecting, as the young man departed, that he would have sold his opportunity for a much more moderate sum.

The whispered conference now came to an end. The holder of the ace of clubs left the room with a look of intelligence, and the President, approaching the unfortunate Prince, proffered him his hand.

'I am pleased to have met you, sir,' said he, 'and pleased to have been in a position to do you this trifling service. At least, you cannot complain of delay. On the second evening—what a stroke of luck!'

The Prince endeavoured in vain to articulate something in response, but his mouth was dry and his tongue seemed paralysed.

'You feel a little sickish?' asked the President, with some show of solicitude. 'Most gentlemen do. Will you take a little brandy?'

The Prince signified in the affirmative, and the other immediately filled some of the spirit into a tumbler.

'Poor old Malthy!' ejaculated the President, as the Prince drained the glass. 'He drank near upon a pint, and little enough good it seemed to do him!'

'I am more amenable to treatment,' said the Prince, a good deal revived. 'I am my own man again at once, as you perceive. And so, let me ask you, what are my directions?'

'You will proceed along the Strand in the direction of the City, and on the left-hand pavement, until you meet the gentleman who has just left the room. He will continue your instructions, and him you will have the kindness to obey; the authority of the club is vested in his person for the night. And now,' added the President, 'I wish you a pleasant walk.'

Florizel acknowledged the salutation rather awkwardly, and took his leave. He passed through the smoking-room, where the bulk of the players were still consuming champagne, some of which he had himself ordered and paid for; and he was surprised to find himself cursing them in his heart. He put on his hat and great coat in the cabinet, and selected his umbrella from a corner. The familiarity of these acts, and the thought that he was about them for the last time, betrayed him into a fit of laughter which sounded unpleasantly in his own ears. He conceived a reluctance to leave the cabinet, and turned instead to the window. The sight of the lamps and the darkness recalled him to himself.

'Come, come, I must be a man,' he thought, 'and tear myself away.'

At the corner of Box Court three men fell upon Prince Florizel and he was unceremoniously thrust into a carriage, which at once drove rapidly away. There was already an occupant.

'Will your Highness pardon my zeal?' said a well-known voice.

The Prince threw himself upon the Colonel's neck in a passion of relief.

'How can I ever thank you?' he cried. 'And how was this effected?'

Although he had been willing to march upon his doom, he was overjoyed to yield to friendly violence, and return once more to life and hope.

'You can thank me effectually enough,' replied the Colonel, 'by avoiding all such dangers in the future. And as for your second question, all has been managed by the simplest means. I arranged this afternoon with a celebrated detective. Secrecy has been promised and paid for. Your own servants have been principally engaged in the affair. The house in Box Court has been surrounded since nightfall, and this, which is one of your own carriages, has been awaiting you for nearly an hour.'

'And the miserable creature who was to have slain me—what of him?' inquired the Prince.

'He was pinioned as he left the club,' replied the Colonel, 'and now awaits your sentence at the Palace, where he will soon be joined by his accomplices.'

'Geraldine,' said the Prince, 'you have saved me against my explicit orders, and you have done well. I owe you not only my life, but a lesson; and I should be unworthy of my rank if I did not show myself grateful to my teacher. Let it be yours to choose the manner.'

There was a pause, during which the carriage continued to speed through the streets, and the two men were each buried in his own reflections. The silence was broken by Colonel Geraldine.

'Your Highness,' said he, 'has by this time a considerable body of prisoners. There is at least one criminal among the number to whom justice should be dealt. Our oath forbids us all recourse to law; and discretion would forbid it equally if the oath were loosened. May I inquire your Highness's intention?'

'It is decided,' answered Florizel; 'the President must fall in duel. It only remains to choose his adversary.'

'Your Highness has permitted me to name my own recompense,' said the Colonel. 'Will he permit me to ask the appointment of my brother? It is an honourable post, but I dare assure your Highness that the lad will acquit himself with credit.'

'You ask me an ungracious favour,' said the Prince, 'but I must refuse you nothing.'

The Colonel kissed his hand with the greatest affection; and at that moment the carriage rolled under the archway of the Prince's splendid residence.

An hour after, Florizel in his official robes, and covered with all the orders of Bohemia, received the members of the Suicide Club.

'Foolish and wicked men,' said he, 'as many of you as have been driven into this strait by the lack of fortune shall receive employment and remuneration from my officers. Those who suffer under a sense of guilt must have recourse to a higher and more generous Potentate than I. I feel pity for all of you, deeper than you can imagine; tomorrow you shall tell me your stories; and as you answer more frankly, I shall be the more able to remedy your misfortunes. As for you,' he added, turning to the President, 'I should only offend a person of your parts by any offer of assistance; but I have instead a piece of diversion to propose to you. Here,' laying his hand on the shoulder of Colonel Geraldine's young brother, 'is an officer of mine who desires to make a little tour upon the Continent; and I ask you, as a favour, to accompany him on this excursion. Do you,' he went on, changing his tone, 'do you shoot well with the pistol? Because you may have need of that accomplishment. When two men go travelling together, it is best to be prepared for all. Let me add that, if by any chance you should lose young Mr Geraldine upon the way, I shall always have another member of my household to place at your disposal; and I am known, Mr President, to have long eyesight, and as long an arm.'

With these words, said with much sternness, the Prince concluded his address. Next morning the members of the club were suitably provided for by his munificence, and the President set forth upon his travels, under the supervision of Mr Geraldine, and a pair of faithful and adroit lackeys, well trained in the Prince's household. Not content with this, discreet agents were put in possession of the house of Box Court, and all letters of visitors for the Suicide Club or its officials were to be examined by Prince Florizel in person.

Here (says my Arabian author) *ends* THE STORY OF THE YOUNG MAN WITH THE CREAM TARTS, *who is now a comfortable householder in Wigmore Street, Cavendish Square. The number, for obvious reasons, I suppress. Those who care to pursue the adventures of Prince Florizel and the President of the Suicide Club, may read the* HISTORY OF THE PHYSICIAN AND THE SARATOGA TRUNK.

STORY OF THE PHYSICIAN
AND THE SARATOGA TRUNK

MR SILAS Q. SCUDDAMORE was a young American of a simple and harmless disposition, which was the more to his credit as he came from New England—a quarter of the New World not precisely famous for those qualities. Although he was exceedingly rich, he kept a note of all his expenses in a little paper pocket-book; and he had chosen to study the attractions of Paris from the seventh storey of what is called a furnished hotel, in the Latin Quarter. There was a great deal of habit in his penuriousness; and his virtue, which was very remarkable among his associates, was principally founded upon diffidence and youth.

The next room to his was inhabited by a lady, very attractive in her air and very elegant in toilette, whom, on his first arrival, he had taken for a Countess. In course of time he had learned that she was known by the name of Madame Zéphyrine, and that whatever station she occupied in life it was not that of a person of title. Madame Zéphyrine, probably in the hope of enchanting the young American, used to flaunt by him on the stairs with a civil inclination, a word of course, and a knock-down look out of her black eyes, and disappear in a rustle of silk, and with the revelation of an admirable foot and ankle. But these advances, so far from encouraging Mr Scuddamore, plunged him into the depths of depression and bashfulness. She had come to him several times for a light, or to apologise for the imaginary depredations of her poodle; but his mouth was closed in the presence of so superior a being, his French promptly left him, and he could only stare and stammer until she was gone. The slenderness of their intercourse did not prevent him from throwing out insinuations of a very glorious order when he was safely alone with a few males.

The room on the other side of the American's—for there were three rooms on a floor in the hotel—was tenanted by an old English physician of rather doubtful reputation. Dr Noel, for that was his name, had been forced to leave London, where he enjoyed a large and increasing practice; and it was hinted that the police had been the instigators of this change of scene. At least he, who had made something of a figure in earlier life, now dwelt in the Latin Quarter in great simplicity and solitude, and devoted much of his time to study. Mr Scuddamore had made his acquaintance, and the pair would now and then dine together frugally in a restaurant across the street.

Silas Q. Scuddamore had many little vices of the more respectable order, and was not restrained by delicacy from indulging them in many rather doubtful ways. Chief among his foibles stood curiosity. He was a born gossip; and life, and especially those parts of it in which he had no experience, interested him to the degree of passion. He was a pert, invincible questioner, pushing his inquiries with equal pertinacity and indiscretion; he had been observed, when he took a letter to the post, to weigh it in his hand, to turn it over and over, and to study the address with care; and when he found a flaw in the partition between his room and Madame Zéphyrine's, instead of filling it up, he enlarged and improved the opening, and made use of it as a spy-hole on his neighbour's affairs.

One day, in the end of March, his curiosity growing as it was indulged, he enlarged the hole a little further, so that he might command another corner of the room. That evening, when he went as usual to inspect Madame Zéphyrine's movements, he was astonished to find the aperture obscured in an odd manner on the other side, and still more abashed when the obstacle was suddenly withdrawn and a titter of laughter reached his ears. Some of the plaster had evidently betrayed the secret of his spy-hole, and his neighbour had been returning the compliment in kind. Mr Scuddamore was moved to a very acute feeling of annoyance; he condemned Madame Zéphyrine unmercifully; he even blamed himself; but when he found, next day, that she had taken no means to baulk him of his favourite pastime, he continued to profit by her carelessness, and gratify his idle curiosity.

That next day Madame Zéphyrine received a long visit from a tall, loosely-built man of fifty or upwards, whom Silas had not hitherto seen. His tweed suit and coloured shirt, no less than his shaggy side-whiskers, identified him as a Britisher, and his dull grey eye affected Silas with a sense of cold. He kept screwing his mouth from side to side and round and round during the whole colloquy, which was carried on in whispers. More than once it seemed to the young New Englander as if their gestures indicated his own apartment; but the only thing definite he could gather by the most scrupulous attention was this remark made by the Englishman in a somewhat higher key, as if in answer to some reluctance or opposition.

'I have studied his taste to a nicety, and I tell you again and again you are the only woman of the sort that I can lay my hands on.'

In answer to this, Madame Zéphyrine sighed, and appeared by a gesture to resign herself, like one yielding to unqualified authority.

That afternoon the observatory was finally blinded, a wardrobe having been drawn in front of it upon the other side, and while Silas was still lamenting over this misfortune, which he attributed to the Britisher's malign suggestion, the concierge brought him up a letter in a female handwriting. It was conceived in French of no very rigorous orthography, bore no signature, and in the most encouraging terms invited the young American to be present in a certain part of the Bullier Ball at eleven o'clock that night. Curiosity and timidity fought a long battle in his heart; sometimes he was all virtue, sometimes all fire and daring; and the result of it was that, long before ten, Mr Silas Q. Scuddamore presented himself in unimpeachable attire at the door of the Bullier Ball Rooms, and paid his entry money with a sense of reckless deviltry that was not without its charm.

It was Carnival time, and the Ball was very full and noisy. The lights and the crowd at first rather abashed our young adventurer, and then, mounting to his brain with a sort of intoxication, put him in possession of more than his own share of manhood. He felt ready to face the Devil, and strutted in the ballroom with the swagger of a cavalier. While he was thus parading, he became aware of Madame Zéphyrine and her Britisher in conference behind a pillar. The cat-like spirit of eaves-dropping overcame him at once. He stole nearer and nearer on the couple from behind, until he was within earshot.

'That is the man,' the Britisher was saying; 'there—with the long blond hair—speaking to a girl in green.'

Silas identified a very handsome young fellow of small stature, who was plainly the object of this designation.

'It is well,' said Madame Zéphyrine. 'I shall do my utmost. But, remember, the best of us may fail in such a matter.'

'Tut!' returned her companion; 'I answer for the result. Have I not chosen you from thirty? Go; but be wary of the Prince. I cannot think what cursed accident has brought him here tonight. As if there were not a dozen balls in Paris better worth his notice than this riot of students and counter-jumpers! See him where he sits, more like a reigning Emperor at home than a Prince upon his holidays!'

Silas was again lucky. He observed a person of rather a full build, strikingly handsome, and of a very stately and courteous demeanour, seated at table with another handsome young man, several years his junior, who addressed him with conspicuous deference. The name of Prince struck gratefully on Silas's Republican hearing, and the aspect of the person to whom that name was applied exercised its usual charm upon his mind. He left Madame Zéphyrine and her Englishman to take care of each other, and threading his way through the assembly, approached the table which the Prince and his confidant had honoured with their choice.

'I tell you, Geraldine,' the former was saying, 'the action is madness. Yourself (I am glad to remember it) chose your brother for this perilous service, and you are bound in duty to have a guard upon his conduct. He has consented to delay so many days in Paris; that was already an imprudence, considering the character of the man he has to deal with; but now, when he is within eight and forty hours of his departure, when he is within two or three days of the decisive trial, I ask you, is this a place for him to spend his time? He should be in a gallery at practice; he should be sleeping long hours and taking moderate exercise on foot; he should be on a rigorous diet, without white wines or brandy. Does the dog imagine we are all playing comedy? The thing is deadly earnest, Geraldine.'

'I know the lad too well to interfere,' replied Colonel Geraldine, 'and well enough not to be alarmed. He is more cautious than you fancy, and of an indomitable spirit. If it had been a woman I should not say so much, but I trust the President to him and the two valets without an instant's apprehension.'

'I am gratified to hear you say so,' replied the Prince; 'but my mind is not at rest. These servants are well-trained spies, and already has not this miscreant succeeded three times in eluding their observation and spending several hours on end in private, and most likely dangerous, affairs? An amateur might have lost him by accident, but if Rudolph and Jérome were thrown off the scent, it must have been done on purpose, and by a man who had a cogent reason and exceptional resources.'

'I believe the question is now one between my brother and myself,' replied Geraldine, with a shade of offence in his tone.

'I permit it to be so, Colonel Geraldine,' returned Prince Florizel. 'Perhaps, for that very reason, you should be all the more ready to accept my counsels. But enough. That girl in yellow dances well.'

And the talk veered into the ordinary topics of a Paris ballroom in the Carnival.

Silas remembered where he was, and that the hour was already near at hand when he ought to be upon the scene of his assignation. The more he reflected the less he liked the prospect, and as at that moment an eddy in the crowd began to draw him in the direction of the door, he suffered it to carry him away without resistance. The eddy stranded him in a corner under the gallery, where his ear was immediately struck with the voice of Madame Zéphyrine. She was speaking in French with the young man of the blond locks who had been pointed out by the strange Britisher not half an hour before.

'I have a character at stake,' she said, 'or I would put no other condition than my heart recommends. But you have only to say so much to the porter, and he will let you go by without a word.'

'But why this talk of debt?' objected her companion.

'Heavens!' said she, 'do you think I do not understand my own hotel?'

And she went by, clinging affectionately to her companion's arm.

This put Silas in mind of his billet.

'Ten minutes hence,' thought he, 'and I may be walking with as beautiful a woman as that, and even better dressed—perhaps a real lady, possibly a woman of title.'

And then he remembered the spelling, and was a little downcast. 'But it may have been written by her maid,' he imagined.

The clock was only a few minutes from the hour, and this immediate proximity set his heart beating at a curious and rather disagreeable speed. He reflected with relief that he was in no way bound to put in an appearance. Virtue and cowardice were together, and he made once more for the door, but this time of his own accord, and battling against the stream of people which was now moving in a contrary direction. Perhaps this prolonged resistance wearied him, or perhaps he was in that frame of mind when merely to continue in the same determination for a certain number of minutes produces a reaction and a different purpose. Certainly, at least, he wheeled about for a third time, and did not stop until he had found a place of concealment within a few yards of the appointed place.

Here he went through an agony of spirit, in which he several times prayed to God for help, for Silas had been devoutly educated. He had now not the least inclination for the meeting; nothing kept him from flight but a silly fear lest he should be thought unmanly; but this was so powerful that it kept head against all other motives; and although it could not decide him to advance, prevented him from definitely running away. At last the clock indicated ten minutes past the hour. Young Scuddamore's spirit began to rise; he peered round the corner and saw no one at the place of meeting; doubtless his unknown correspondent had wearied and gone away. He became as bold as he had formerly been timid. It seemed to him that if he came at all to the appointment, however late, he was clear from the charge of cowardice. Nay, now he began to suspect a hoax, and actually complimented himself on his shrewdness in having suspected and out-manoeuvred his mystifiers. So very idle a thing is a boy's mind!

Armed with these reflections, he advanced boldly from his corner; but he had not taken above a couple of steps before a hand was laid upon his arm. He turned and beheld a lady cast in a very large mould and with somewhat stately features, but bearing no mark of severity in her looks.

'I see that you are a very self-confident lady-killer,' said she; 'for you make yourself expected. But I was determined to meet you. When a woman has once so far forgotten herself as to make the first advance, she has long ago left behind her all considerations of petty pride.'

Silas was overwhelmed by the size and attractions of his correspondent and the suddenness with which she had fallen upon him. But she soon set him at his ease. She was very towardly and lenient in her behaviour; she led him on to make pleasantries, and then applauded him to the echo; and in a very short time, between blandishments and a liberal imbibition of warm brandy, she had not only induced him to fancy himself in love, but to declare his passion with the greatest vehemence.

'Alas!' she said; 'I do not know whether I ought not to deplore this moment, great as is the pleasure you give me by your words. Hitherto I was alone to suffer; now, poor boy, there will be two. I am not my own mistress. I dare not ask you to visit me at my own house, for I am watched by jealous eyes. Let me see,' she added; 'I am older than you, although so much weaker; and while I trust in your courage and determination, I must employ my own knowledge of the world for our mutual benefit. Where do you live?'

He told her that he lodged in a furnished hotel, and named the street and number.

She seemed to reflect for some minutes, with an effort of mind.

'I see,' she said at last. 'You will be faithful and obedient, will you not?'

Silas assured her eagerly of his fidelity.

'Tomorrow night, then,' she continued, with an encouraging smile, 'you must remain at home all the evening; and if any friends should visit you, dismiss them at once on any pretext that most readily presents itself. Your door is probably shut by ten?' she asked.

'By eleven,' answered Silas.

'At a quarter past eleven,' pursued the lady, 'leave the house. Merely cry for the door to be opened, and be sure you fall into no talk with the porter, as that might ruin everything. Go straight to the corner where the Luxembourg Gardens join the Boulevard; there you will find me waiting you. I trust you to follow my advice from point to point: and remember, if you fail me in only one particular, you will bring the sharpest trouble on a woman whose only fault is to have seen and loved you.'

'I cannot see the use of all these instructions,' said Silas.

'I believe you are already beginning to treat me as a master,' she cried, tapping him with her fan upon the arm. 'Patience, patience! that should come in time. A woman loves to be obeyed at first, although afterwards she finds her pleasure in obeying. Do as I ask you, for heaven's sake, or I will answer for nothing. Indeed, now I think of it,' she added, with the manner of one who had just seen further into a difficulty, 'I find a better plan of keeping importunate visitors away. Tell the porter to admit no one for you, except a person who may come that night to claim a debt; and speak with some feeling, as though you feared the interview, so that he may take your words in earnest.'

'I think you may trust me to protect myself against intruders,' he said, not without a little pique.

'That is how I should prefer the thing arranged,' she answered, coldly. 'I know you men; you think nothing of a woman's reputation.'

Silas blushed and somewhat hung his head; for the scheme he had in view had involved a little vain-glorying before his acquaintances.

'Above all,' she added, 'do not speak to the porter as you come out.'

'And why?' said he. 'Of all your instructions, that seems to me the least important.'

'You at first doubted the wisdom of some of the others, which you now see to be very necessary,' she replied. 'Believe me, this also has its uses; in time you will see them; and what am I to think of your affection, if you refuse me such trifles at our first interview?'

Silas confounded himself in explanations and apologies; in the middle of these she looked up at the clock and clapped her hands together with a suppressed scream.

'Heavens!' she cried, 'is it so late? I have not an instant to lose. Alas, we poor women, what slaves we are! What have I not risked for you already?'

And after repeating her directions, which she artfully combined with caresses and the most abandoned looks, she bade him farewell and disappeared among the crowd.

The whole of the next day Silas was filled with a sense of great importance; he was now sure she was a countess; and when evening came he minutely obeyed her orders and was at the corner of the Luxembourg Gardens by the hour appointed. No one was there. He waited nearly half an hour, looking in the face of everyone who passed or loitered near the spot; he even visited the neighbouring corners of the Boulevard and made a complete circuit of the garden railings; but there was no beautiful countess to throw herself into his arms. At last, and most reluctantly, he began to retrace his steps towards his hotel. On the way he remembered the words he had heard pass between Madame Zéphyrine and the blond young man, and they gave him an indefinite uneasiness.

'It appears,' he reflected, 'that everyone has to tell lies to our porter.'

He rang the bell, the door opened before him, and the porter in his bed-clothes came to offer him a light.

'Has he gone?' inquired the porter.

'He? Whom do you mean?' asked Silas, somewhat sharply, for he was irritated by his disappointment.

'I did not notice him go out,' continued the porter, 'but I trust you paid him. We do not care, in this house, to have lodgers who cannot meet their liabilities.'

'What the devil do you mean?' demanded Silas, rudely. 'I cannot understand a word of this farrago.'

'The short blond young man who came for his debt,' returned the other. 'Him it is I mean. Who else should it be, when I had your orders to admit no one else?'

'Why, good God, of course he never came,' retorted Silas.

'I believe what I believe,' retorted the porter, putting his tongue into his cheek with a most roguish air.

'You are an insolent scoundrel,' cried Silas, and, feeling that he had made a ridiculous exhibition of asperity, and at the same time bewildered by a dozen alarms, he turned and began to run upstairs.

'Do you not want a light then?' cried the porter.

But Silas only hurried the faster, and did not pause until he had reached the seventh landing and stood in front of his own door. There he waited a moment to recover his breath, assailed by the worst forebodings and almost dreading to enter the room.

When at last he did so he was relieved to find it dark, and to all appearance untenanted. He drew a long breath. Here he was, home again in safety, and this should be his last folly as certainly as it had been his first. The matches stood on a little table by the bed, and he began to grope his way in that direction. As he moved, his apprehensions grew upon him once more, and he was pleased, when his foot encountered an obstacle, to find it nothing more alarming than a chair. At last he touched curtains. From the position of the window, which was faintly visible, he knew he must be at the foot of the bed, and had only to feel his way along it in order to reach the table in question.

He lowered his hand, but what he touched was not simply a counterpane—it was a counterpane with something underneath it like the outline of a human leg. Silas withdrew his arm and stood a moment petrified.

'What, what,' he thought, 'can this betoken?'

He listened intently, but there was no sound of breathing. Once more, with a great effort, he reached out the end of his finger to the spot he had already touched; but this time he leaped back half a yard, and stood shivering and fixed with terror. There was something in his bed. What it was he knew not, but there was something there.

It was some seconds before he could move. Then, guided by an instinct, he fell straight upon the matches, and keeping his back toward the bed, lighted a candle. As soon as the flame had kindled, he turned slowly round and looked for what he feared to see. Sure enough, there was the worst of his imaginations realised. The coverlid was drawn carefully up over the pillow, but it moulded the outline of a human body lying motionless; and when he dashed forward and flung aside the sheets, he beheld the blond young man whom he had seen in the Bullier Ball the night before, his eyes open and without speculation, his face swollen and blackened, and a thin stream of blood trickling from his nostrils.

Silas uttered a long tremulous wail, dropped the candle, and fell on his knees beside the bed.

Silas was awakened from the stupor into which his terrible discovery had plunged him, by a prolonged but discreet tapping at the door. It took him some seconds to remember his position; and when he hastened to prevent anyone from entering it was already too late. Dr Noel, in a tall night-cap, carrying a lamp which lighted up his long white countenance, sidling in his gait, and peering and cocking his head like some sort of bird, pushed the door slowly open, and advanced into the middle of the room.

'I thought I heard a cry,' began the Doctor, 'and fearing you might be unwell, I did not hesitate to offer this intrusion.'

Silas, with a flushed face and a fearful beating heart, kept between the Doctor and the bed; but he found no voice to answer.

'You are in the dark,' pursued the Doctor; 'and yet you have not even begun to prepare for rest. You will not easily persuade me against my own eyesight; and your face declares most eloquently that you require either a friend or a physician—which is it to be? Let me feel your pulse, for that is often a just reporter of the heart.'

He advanced to Silas, who still retreated before him backwards, and sought to take him by the wrist; but the strain on the young American's nerves had become too great for endurance. He avoided the Doctor with a febrile movement, and, throwing himself upon the floor, burst into a flood of weeping.

As soon as Dr Noel perceived the dead man in the bed his face darkened; and hurrying back to the door which he had left ajar, he hastily closed and double-locked it.

'Up!' he cried, addressing Silas in strident tones. 'This is no time for weeping. What have you done? How came this body in your room? Speak freely to one who may be helpful. Do you imagine I would ruin you? Do you think this piece of dead flesh on your pillow can alter in any degree the sympathy with which you have inspired me? Credulous youth, the horror with which blind and unjust law regards an action never attaches to the doer in the eyes of those who love him; and if I saw the friend of my heart return to me out of seas of blood he would be in no way changed in my affection. Raise yourself,' he said; 'good and ill are a chimera; there is naught in life except destiny, and however you may be circumstanced there is one at your side who will help you to the last.'

Thus encouraged, Silas gathered himself together, and in a broken voice, and helped out by the Doctor's interrogations, contrived at last to put him in possession of the facts. But the conversation between the Prince and Geraldine he altogether omitted, as he had understood little of its purport, and had no idea that it was in any way related to his own misadventure.

'Alas!' cried Dr Noel, 'I am much abused, or you have fallen innocently into the most dangerous hands in Europe. Poor boy, what a pit has been dug for your simplicity! into what a deadly peril have your unwary feet been conducted! This man,' he said, 'this Englishman, whom you twice saw, and whom I suspect to be the soul of the contrivance, can you describe him? Was he young or old? tall or short?'

But Silas, who, for all his curiosity, had not a seeing eye in his head, was able to supply nothing but meagre generalities, which it was impossible to recognise.

'I would have it a piece of education in all schools!' cried the Doctor angrily. 'Where is the use of eyesight and articulate speech if a man cannot observe and recollect the features of his enemy? I, who know all the gangs of Europe, might have identified him, and gained new weapons for your defence. Cultivate this art in future, my poor boy; you may find it of momentous service.'

'The future!' repeated Silas. 'What future is there left for me except the gallows?'

'Youth is but a cowardly season,' returned the Doctor; 'and a man's own troubles look blacker than they are. I am old, and yet I never despair.'

'Can I tell such a story to the police?' demanded Silas.

'Assuredly not,' replied the Doctor. 'From what I see already of the machination in which you have been involved, your case is desperate upon that side; and for the narrow eye of the authorities you are infallibly the guilty person. And remember that we only know a portion of the plot; and the same infamous contrivers have doubtless arranged many other circumstances which would be elicited by a police inquiry, and help to fix the guilt more certainly upon your innocence.'

'I am then lost, indeed!' cried Silas.

'I have not said so,' answered Dr Noel, 'for I am a cautious man.'

'But look at this!' objected Silas, pointing to the body. 'Here is this object in my bed: not to be explained, not to be disposed of, not to be regarded without horror.'

'Horror?' replied the Doctor. 'No. When this sort of clock has run down, it is no more to me than an ingenious piece of mechanism, to be investigated with the bistoury. When blood is once cold and stagnant, it is no longer human blood; when flesh is once dead, it is no longer that flesh which we desire in our lovers and respect in our friends. The grace, the attraction, the terror, have all gone from it with the animating spirit. Accustom yourself to look upon it with composure, for if my scheme is practicable you will have to live in constant proximity to that which now so greatly horrifies you.'

'Your scheme?' cried Silas. 'What is that? Tell me speedily, Doctor; for I have scarcely courage enough to continue to exist.'

Without replying, Dr Noel turned towards the bed, and proceeded to examine the corpse.

'Quite dead,' he murmured. 'Yes, as I had supposed, the pockets empty. Yes, and the name cut off the shirt. Their work has been done thoroughly and well. Fortunately he is of small stature.'

Silas followed these words with an extreme anxiety. At last the Doctor, his autopsy completed, took a chair and addressed the young American with a smile.

'Since I came into your room,' said he, 'although my ears and my tongue have been so busy, I have not suffered my eyes to remain idle. I noted a little while ago that you have there, in the corner, one of those monstrous constructions which your fellow-countrymen carry with them into all quarters of the globe—in a word, a Saratoga trunk. Until this moment I have never been able to conceive the utility of these erections; but then I began to have a glimmer. Whether it was for convenience in the slave trade, or to obviate the results of too ready an employment of the bowie-knife, I cannot bring myself to decide. But one thing I see plainly—the object of such a box is to contain a human body.'

'Surely,' cried Silas, 'surely this is not a time for jesting.'

'Although I may express myself with some degree of pleasantry,' replied the Doctor, 'the purport of my words is entirely serious. And the first thing we have to do, my young friend, is to empty your coffer of all it contains.'

Silas, obeying the authority of Doctor Noel, put himself at his disposition. The Saratoga trunk was soon gutted of its contents, which made a considerable litter on the floor; and then—Silas taking the heels and the Doctor supporting the shoulders—the body of the murdered man was carried from the bed, and, after some difficulty, doubled up and inserted whole into the empty box. With an effort on the part of both, the lid was forced down upon this unusual baggage, and the trunk was locked and corded by the Doctor's own hand, while Silas disposed of what had been taken out between the closet and a chest of drawers.

'Now,' said the Doctor, 'the first step has been taken on the way to your deliverance. Tomorrow or rather today, it must be your task to allay the suspicions of your porter, paying him all that you owe; while you may trust me to make the arrangements necessary to a safe conclusion. Meantime, follow me to my room, where I shall give you a safe and powerful opiate; for, whatever you do, you must have rest.'

The next day was the longest in Silas's memory; it seemed as if it would never be done. He denied himself to his friends, and sat in a corner with his eyes fixed upon the Saratoga trunk in dismal contemplation. His own former indiscretions were now returned upon him in kind; for the observatory had been once more opened, and he was conscious of an almost continual study from Madame Zéphyrine's apartment. So distressing did this become, that he was at last obliged to block up the spy-hole from his own side; and when he was thus secured from observation he spent a considerable portion of his time in contrite tears and prayer.

Late in the evening Dr Noel entered the room carrying in his hand a pair of sealed envelopes without address, one somewhat bulky, and the other so slim as to seem without enclosure.

'Silas,' he said, seating himself at the table, 'the time has now come for me to explain my plan for your salvation. Tomorrow morning, at an early hour, Prince Florizel of Bohemia returns to London, after having diverted himself for a few days with the Parisian Carnival. It was my fortune, a good while ago, to do Colonel Geraldine, his Master of the Horse, one of those services so common in my profession, which are never forgotten upon either side. I have no need to explain to you the nature of the obligation under which he was laid; suffice it to say that I knew him ready to serve me in any practicable manner. Now, it was necessary for you to gain London with your trunk unopened. To this the Custom House seemed to oppose a fatal difficulty; but I bethought me that the baggage of so considerable a person as the Prince, is, as a matter of courtesy, passed without examination by the officers of Custom. I applied to Colonel Geraldine, and succeeded in obtaining a favourable answer. Tomorrow, if you go before six to the hotel where the Prince lodges, your baggage will be passed over as a part of his, and you yourself will make the journey as a member of his suite.'

'It seems to me, as you speak, that I have already seen both the Prince and Colonel Geraldine; I even overheard some of their conversation the other evening at the Bullier Ball.'

'It is probable enough; for the Prince loves to mix with all societies,' replied the Doctor. 'Once arrived in London,' he pursued, 'your task is nearly ended. In this more bulky envelope I have given you a letter which I dare not address; but in the other you will find the designation of the house to which you must carry it along with your box, which will there be taken from you and not trouble you any more.'

'Alas!' said Silas, 'I have every wish to believe you; but how is it possible? You open up to me a bright prospect, but, I ask you, is my mind capable of receiving so unlikely a solution? Be more generous, and let me farther understand your meaning.'

The Doctor seemed painfully impressed.

'Boy,' he answered, 'you do not know how hard a thing you ask of me. But be it so. I am now inured to humiliation; and it would be strange if I refused you this, after having granted you so much. Know, then, that although I now make so quiet an appearance— frugal, solitary, addicted to study—when I was younger, my name was once a rallying-cry among the most astute and dangerous spirits of London; and while I was outwardly an object for respect and consideration, my true power resided in the most secret, terrible, and criminal relations. It is to one of the persons who then obeyed me that I now address myself to deliver you from your burden. They were men of many different nations and dexterities, all bound together by a formidable oath, and working to the same purposes; the trade of the association was in murder; and I who speak to you, innocent as I appear, was the chieftain of this redoubtable crew.'

'What?' cried Silas. 'A murderer? And one with whom murder was a trade? Can I take your hand? Ought I to so much as accept your services? Dark and criminal old man, would you make an accomplice of my youth and my distress?'

The Doctor bitterly laughed.

'You are difficult to please, Mr Scuddamore,' said he; 'but I now offer you your choice of company between the murdered man and the murderer. If your conscience is too nice to accept my aid, say so, and I will immediately leave you. Thenceforward you can deal with your trunk and its belongings as best suits your upright conscience.'

'I own myself wrong,' replied Silas. 'I should have remembered how generously you offered to shield me, even before I had convinced you of my innocence, and I continue to listen to your counsels with gratitude.'

'That is well,' returned the Doctor; 'and I perceive you are beginning to learn some of the lessons of experience.'

'At the same time,' resumed the New-Englander, 'as you confess yourself accustomed to this tragical business, and the people to whom you recommend me are your own former associates and friends, could you not yourself undertake the transport of the box, and rid me at once of its detested presence?'

'Upon my word,' replied the Doctor, 'I admire you cordially. If you do not think I have already meddled sufficiently in your concerns, believe me, from my heart I think the contrary. Take or leave my services as I offer them; and trouble me with no more words of gratitude, for I value your consideration even more lightly than I do your intellect. A time will come, if you should be spared to see a number of years in health and mind, when you will think differently of all this, and blush for your tonight's behaviour.'

So saying, the Doctor arose from his chair, repeated his directions briefly and clearly, and departed from the room without permitting Silas any time to answer.

The next morning Silas presented himself at the hotel, where he was politely received by Colonel Geraldine, and relieved, from that moment, of all immediate alarm about his trunk and its grisly contents. The journey passed over without much incident, although the young man was horrified to overhear the sailors and railway porters complaining among themselves about the unusual weight of the Prince's baggage. Silas travelled in a carriage with the valets, for Prince Florizel chose to be alone with his Master of the Horse. On board the steamer, however, Silas attracted his Highness's attention by the melancholy of his air and attitude as he stood gazing at the pile of baggage; for he was still full of disquietude about the future.

'There is a young man,' observed the Prince, 'who must have some cause for sorrow.'

'That,' replied Geraldine, 'is the American for whom I obtained permission to travel with your suite.'

'You remind me that I have been remiss in courtesy,' said Prince Florizel, and advancing to Silas, he addressed him with the most exquisite condescension in these words,

'I was charmed, young sir, to be able to gratify the desire you made known to me through Colonel Geraldine. Remember, if you please, that I shall be glad at any future time to lay you under a more serious obligation.'

And then he put some questions as to the political condition of America, which Silas answered with sense and propriety.

'You are still a young man,' said the Prince; 'but I observe you to be very serious for your years. Perhaps you allow your attention to be too much occupied with grave studies. But, perhaps, on the other hand, I am myself indiscreet and touch upon a painful subject.'

'I have certainly cause to be the most miserable of men,' said Silas; 'never has a more innocent person been more dismally abused.'

'I will not ask you for your confidence,' returned Prince Florizel. 'But do not forget that Colonel Geraldine's recommendation is an unfailing passport; and that I am not only willing, but possibly more able than many others, to do you a service.'

Silas was delighted with the amiability of this great personage; but his mind soon returned upon its gloomy preoccupations; for not even the favour of a Prince to a Republican can discharge a brooding spirit of its cares.

The train arrived at Charing Cross, where the officers of the Revenue respected the baggage of Prince Florizel in the usual manner. The most elegant equipages were in waiting; and Silas was driven, along with the rest, to the Prince's residence. There Colonel Geraldine sought him out, and expressed himself pleased to have been of any service to a friend of the physician's, for whom he professed a great consideration.

'I hope,' he added, 'that you will find none of your porcelain injured. Special orders were given along the line to deal tenderly with the Prince's effects.'

And then, directing the servants to place one of the carriages at the young gentleman's disposal, and at once to charge the Saratoga trunk upon the dickey, the Colonel shook hands and excused himself on account of his occupations in the princely household.

Silas now broke the seal of the envelope containing the address, and directed the stately footman to drive him to Box Court, opening off the Strand. It seemed as if the place were not at all unknown to the man, for he looked startled and begged a repetition of the order. It was with a heart full of alarms, that Silas mounted into the luxurious vehicle, and was driven to his destination. The entrance to Box Court was too narrow for the passage of a coach; it was a mere footway between railings, with a post at either end. On one of these posts was seated a man, who at once jumped down and exchanged a friendly sign with the driver, while the footman opened the door and inquired of Silas whether he should take down the Saratoga trunk, and to what number it should be carried.

'If you please,' said Silas. 'To number three.'

The footman and the man who had been sitting on the post, even with the aid of Silas himself, had hard work to carry in the trunk; and before it was deposited at the door of the house in question, the young American was horrified to find a score of loiterers looking on.

But he knocked with as good a countenance as he could muster up, and presented the other envelope to him who opened.

'He is not at home,' said he, 'but if you will leave your letter and return tomorrow early, I shall be able to inform you whether and when he can receive your visit. Would you like to leave your box?' he added.

'Dearly,' cried Silas; and the next moment he repented his precipitation, and declared, with equal emphasis, that he would rather carry the box along with him to the hotel.

The crowd jeered at his indecision and followed him to the carriage with insulting remarks; and Silas, covered with shame and terror, implored the servants to conduct him to some quiet and comfortable house of entertainment in the immediate neighbourhood.

The Prince's equipage deposited Silas at the Craven Hotel in Craven Street, and immediately drove away, leaving him alone with the servants of the inn. The only vacant room, it appeared, was a little den up four pairs of stairs, and looking towards the back. To this hermitage, with infinite trouble and complaint, a pair of stout porters carried the Saratoga trunk. It is needless to mention that Silas kept closely at their heels throughout the ascent, and had his heart in his mouth at every corner. A single false step, he reflected, and the box might go over the banisters and land its fatal contents, plainly discovered, on the pavement of the hall.

Arrived in the room, he sat down on the edge of his bed to recover from the agony that he had just endured; but he had hardly taken his position when he was recalled to a sense of his peril by the action of the boots, who had knelt beside the trunk, and was proceeding officiously to undo its elaborate fastenings.

'Let it be!' cried Silas. 'I shall want nothing from it while I stay here.'

'You might have let it lie in the hall, then,' growled the man; 'a thing as big and heavy as a church. What you have inside, I cannot fancy. If it is all money, you are a richer man than me.'

'Money?' repeated Silas, in a sudden perturbation. 'What do you mean by money? I have no money, and you are speaking like a fool.'

'All right, Captain,' retorted the boots with a wink. 'There's nobody will touch your lordship's money. I'm as safe as the bank,' he added;

'but as the box is heavy, I shouldn't mind drinking something to your lordship's health.'

Silas pressed two Napoleons upon his acceptance, apologising, at the same time, for being obliged to trouble him with foreign money, and pleading his recent arrival for excuse. And the man, grumbling with even greater fervour, and looking contemptuously from the money in his hand to the Saratoga trunk and back again from the one to the other, at last consented to withdraw.

For nearly two days the dead body had been packed into Silas's box; and as soon as he was alone the unfortunate New-Englander nosed all the cracks and openings with the most passionate attention. But the weather was cool, and the trunk still managed to contain his shocking secret.

He took a chair beside it, and buried his face in his hands, and his mind in the most profound reflection. If he were not speedily relieved, no question but he must be speedily discovered. Alone in a strange city, without friends or accomplices, if the Doctor's introduction failed him, he was indubitably a lost New-Englander. He reflected pathetically over his ambitious designs for the future; he should not now become the hero and spokesman of his native place of Bangor, Maine; he should not, as he had fondly anticipated, move on from office to office, from honour to honour; he might as well divest himself at once of all hope of being acclaimed President of the United States, and leaving behind him a statue, in the worst possible style of art, to adorn the Capitol at Washington. Here he was, chained to a dead Englishman doubled up inside a Saratoga trunk; whom he must get rid of, or perish from the rolls of national glory!

I should be afraid to chronicle the language employed by this young man to the Doctor, to the murdered man, to Madame Zéphyrine, to the boots of the hotel, to the Prince's servants, and, in a word, to all who had been ever so remotely connected with his horrible misfortune.

He slunk down to dinner about seven at night; but the yellow coffee-room appalled him, the eyes of the other diners seemed to rest on his with suspicion, and his mind remained upstairs with the Saratoga trunk. When the waiter came to offer him cheese, his nerves were already so much on edge that he leaped half-way out of his chair and upset the remainder of a pint of ale upon the table-cloth.

The fellow offered to show him the smoking-room when he had done; and although he would have much preferred to return at once to his perilous treasure, he had not the courage to refuse, and was shown downstairs to the black, gas-lit cellar, which formed, and possibly still forms, the divan of the Craven Hotel.

Two very sad betting men were playing billiards, attended by a moist, consumptive marker; and for the moment Silas imagined that these were the only occupants of the apartment. But at the next glance his eye fell upon a person smoking in the farthest corner, with lowered eyes and a most respectable and modest aspect. He knew at once that he had seen the face before; and in spite of the entire change of clothes, recognised the man whom he had found seated on a post at the entrance to Box Court, and who had helped him to carry the trunk to and from the carriage. The New-Englander simply turned and ran, nor did he pause until he had locked and bolted himself into his bedroom.

There, all night long, a prey to the most terrible imaginations, he watched beside the fatal boxful of dead flesh. The suggestion of the boots that his trunk was full of gold inspired him with all manner of new terrors, if he so much as dared to close an eye; and the presence in the smoking-room, and under an obvious disguise, of the loiterer from Box Court convinced him that he was once more the centre of obscure machination.

Midnight had sounded some time, when, impelled by uneasy suspicions, Silas opened his bedroom door and peered into the passage. It was dimly illuminated by a single jet of gas; and some distance off he perceived a man sleeping on the floor in the costume of an hotel under-servant. Silas drew near the man on tiptoe. He lay partly on his back, partly on his side, and his right forearm concealed his face from recognition. Suddenly, while the American was still bending over him, the sleeper removed his arm and opened his eyes, and Silas found himself once more face to face with the loiterer of Box Court.

'Goodnight, sir,' said the man, pleasantly.

But Silas was too profoundly moved to find an answer, and regained his room in silence.

Towards morning, worn out by apprehension, he fell asleep on his chair, with his head forward on the trunk. In spite of so constrained an attitude and such a grisly pillow, his slumber was sound and prolonged, and he was only awakened at a late hour and by a sharp tapping at the door.

He hurried to open, and found the boots without.

'You are the gentleman who called yesterday at Box Court?' he asked.

Silas, with a quaver, admitted that he had done so.

'Then this note is for you,' added the servant, proffering a sealed envelope.

Silas tore it open, and found inside the words: 'Twelve o'clock.'

He was punctual to the hour; the trunk was carried before him by several stout servants; and he was himself ushered into a room, where a man sat warming himself before the fire with his back towards the door. The sound of so many persons entering and leaving, and the scraping of the trunk as it was deposited upon the bare boards, were alike unable to attract the notice of the occupant; and Silas stood waiting, in an agony of fear, until he should deign to recognise his presence.

Perhaps five minutes had elapsed before the man turned leisurely about, and disclosed the features of Prince Florizel of Bohemia.

'So, sir,' he said with great severity, 'this is the manner in which you abuse my politeness. You join yourselves to persons of condition, I perceive, for no other purpose than to escape the consequences of your crimes; and I can readily understand your embarrassment when I addressed myself to you yesterday.'

'Indeed,' cried Silas, 'I am innocent of everything except misfortune.'

And in a hurried voice, and with the greatest ingenuousness, he recounted to the Prince the whole history of his calamity.

'I see I have been mistaken,' said his Highness, when he had heard him to an end. 'You are no other than a victim, and since I am not to punish you, you may be sure I shall do my utmost to help. And now,' he continued, 'to business. Open your box at once, and let me see what it contains.'

Silas changed colour.

'I almost fear to look upon it,' he exclaimed.

'Nay,' replied the Prince, 'have you not looked at it already? This is a form of sentimentality to be resisted. The sight of a sick man, whom we can still help, should appeal more directly to the feelings than that of a dead man who is equally beyond help or harm, love or hatred. Nerve yourself, Mr Scuddamore,' and then, seeing that Silas still hesitated, 'I do not desire to give another name to my request,' he added.

The young American awoke as if out of a dream, and with a shiver of repugnance addressed himself to loose the straps and open the lock of the Saratoga trunk. The Prince stood by, watching with a composed countenance and his hands behind his back. The body was quite stiff, and it cost Silas a great effort, both moral and physical, to dislodge it from its position, and discover the face.

Prince Florizel started back with an exclamation of painful surprise.

'Alas!' he cried, 'you little know, Mr Scuddamore, what a cruel gift you have brought me. This is a young man of my own suite, the brother of my trusted friend; and it was upon matters of my own service that he has thus perished at the hands of violent and treacherous men. Poor Geraldine,' he went on, as if to himself, 'in what words am I to tell you of your brother's fate? How can I excuse myself in your eyes, or in the eyes of God, for the presumptuous schemes that led him to this bloody and unnatural death? Ah, Florizel! Florizel! when will you learn the discretion that suits mortal life, and be no longer dazzled with the image of power at your disposal? Power!' he cried; 'who is more powerless? I look upon this young man whom I have sacrificed, Mr Scuddamore, and feel how small a thing it is to be a Prince.'

Silas was moved at the sight of his emotion. He tried to murmur some consolatory words, and burst into tears. The Prince, touched by his obvious intention, came up to him and took him by the hand.

'Command yourself,' said he. 'We have both much to learn, and we shall both be better men for today's meeting.'

Silas thanked him in silence, with an affectionate look.

'Write me the address of Doctor Noel on this piece of paper,' continued the Prince, leading him towards the table; 'and let me recommend you, when you are again in Paris, to avoid the society of that dangerous man. He has acted in this matter on a generous inspiration; that I must believe; had he been privy to young Geraldine's death he would never have despatched the body to the care of the actual criminal.'

'The actual criminal!' repeated Silas in astonishment.

'Even so,' returned the Prince. 'This letter, which the disposition of Almighty Providence has so strangely delivered into my hands, was addressed to no less a person than the criminal himself, the infamous President of the Suicide Club. Seek to pry no further in these perilous affairs, but content yourself with your own miraculous escape, and leave this house at once. I have pressing affairs, and must arrange at once about this poor clay, which was so lately a gallant and handsome youth.'

Silas took a grateful and submissive leave of Prince Florizel, but he lingered in Box Court until he saw him depart in a splendid carriage on a visit to Colonel Henderson, of the police. Republican as he was, the young American took off his hat with almost a sentiment of devotion to the retreating carriage. And the same night he started by rail on his return to Paris.

Here (observes my Arabian Author) *is the end of* THE STORY OF THE PHYSICIAN AND THE SARATOGA TRUNK. *Omitting some reflections on the power of Providence, highly pertinent in the original, but little suited to our occidental taste, I shall only add that Mr Scuddamore has already begun to mount the ladder of political fame, and by last advices was the Sheriff of his native town.*

THE ADVENTURE OF THE HANSOM CAB

LIEUTENANT BRACKENBURY RICH had greatly distin-
guished himself in one of the lesser Indian hill wars. He it was who
took the chieftain prisoner with his own hand; his gallantry was
universally applauded; and when he came home, prostrated by an
ugly sabre cut and a protracted jungle fever, society was prepared to
welcome the Lieutenant as a celebrity of minor lustre. But his was a
character remarkable for unaffected modesty; adventure was dear to
his heart, but he cared little for adulation; and he waited at foreign
watering-places and in Algiers until the fame of his exploits had run
through its nine days' vitality and begun to be forgotten. He arrived
in London at last, in the early season, with as little observation as he
could desire; and as he was an orphan and had none but distant
relatives who lived in the provinces, it was almost as a foreigner that
he installed himself in the capital of the country for which he had
shed his blood.

On the day following his arrival he dined alone at a military club.
He shook hands with a few old comrades, and received their congrat-
ulations; but as one and all had some engagement for the evening, he
found himself left entirely to his own resources. He was in full dress,
for he had entertained the notion of visiting a theatre. But the great
city was new to him; he had gone from a provincial school to a military college, and thence direct to the Eastern Empire; and he
promised himself a variety of delights in this world for exploration.
Swinging his cane, he took his way westward. It was a mild evening,
already dark, and now and then threatening rain. The succession of
faces in the lamp-light stirred the Lieutenant's imagination; and it
seemed to him as if he could walk for ever in that stimulating city
atmosphere and surrounded by the mystery of four million private
lives. He glanced at the houses, and marvelled what was passing

behind those warmly-lighted windows; he looked into face after face, and saw them each intent upon some unknown interest, criminal or kindly.

'They talk of war,' he thought, 'but this is the great battlefield of mankind.'

And then he began to wonder that he should walk so long in this complicated scene, and not chance upon so much as the shadow of an adventure for himself.

'All in good time,' he reflected. 'I am still a stranger, and perhaps wear a strange air. But I must be drawn into the eddy before long.'

The night was already well advanced, when a plump of cold rain fell suddenly out of the darkness. Brackenbury paused under some trees, and as he did so he caught sight of a hansom cabman making him a sign that he was disengaged. The circumstance fell in so happily to the occasion that he at once raised his cane in answer, and had soon ensconced himself in the London gondola.

'Where to, sir?' asked the driver.

'Where you please,' said Brackenbury.

And immediately, at a pace of surprising swiftness, the hansom drove off through the rain into a maze of villas. One villa was so like another, each with its front garden, and there was so little to distinguish the deserted lamp-lit streets and crescents through which the flying hansom took its way, that Brackenbury soon lost all idea of direction. He would have been contented to believe that the cabman was amusing himself by driving him round and round and in and out about a small quarter, but there was something businesslike in the speed which convinced him of the contrary. The man had an object in view, he was hastening towards a definite end; and Brackenbury was at once astonished at the fellow's skill in picking a way through such a labyrinth, and a little concerned to imagine what was the occasion of his hurry. He had heard tales of strangers falling ill in London. Did the driver belong to some bloody and treacherous association? and was he himself being whirled to a murderous death?

The thought had scarcely presented itself, when the cab swung sharply round a corner and pulled up before the garden gate of a villa in a long and wide road. The house was brilliantly lighted up.

Another hansom had just driven away, and Brackenbury could see a gentleman being admitted at the front door and received by several liveried servants. He was surprised that the cabman should have stopped so immediately in front of a house where a reception was being held; but he did not doubt it was the result of accident, and sat placidly smoking where he was, until he heard the trap thrown open over his head.

'Here we are, sir,' said the driver.

'Here!' repeated Brackenbury. 'Where?'

'You told me to take you where I pleased, sir,' returned the man with a chuckle, 'and here we are.'

It struck Brackenbury that the voice was wonderfully smooth and courteous for a man in so inferior a position; he remembered the speed at which he had been driven; and now it occurred to him that the hansom was more luxuriously appointed than the common run of public conveyances.

'I must ask you to explain,' said he. 'Do you mean to turn me out into the rain? My good man, I suspect the choice is mine.'

'The choice is certainly yours,' replied the driver; 'but when I tell you all, I believe I know how a gentleman of your figure will decide. There is a gentlemen's party in this house. I do not know whether the master be a stranger to London and without acquaintances of his own; or whether he is a man of odd notions. But certainly I was hired to kidnap single gentlemen in evening dress, as many as I pleased, but military officers by preference. You have simply to go in and say that Mr Morris invited you.'

'Are you Mr Morris?' inquired the Lieutenant.

'Oh, no,' replied the cabman. 'Mr Morris is the person of the house.'

'It is not a common way of collecting guests,' said Brackenbury; 'but an eccentric man might very well indulge the whim without any intention to offend. And suppose that I refuse Mr Morris's invitation,' he went on, 'what then?'

'My orders are to drive you back where I took you from,' replied the man, 'and set out to look for others up to midnight. Those who have no fancy for such an adventure, Mr Morris said, were not the guests for him.'

These words decided the Lieutenant on the spot.

'After all,' he reflected, as he descended from the hansom, 'I have not had long to wait for my adventure.'

He had hardly found footing on the sidewalk, and was still feeling in his pocket for the fare, when the cab swung about and drove off by the way it came at the former break-neck velocity. Brackenbury shouted after the man, who paid no heed, and continued to drive away; but the sound of his voice was overheard in the house, the door was again thrown open, emitting a flood of light upon the garden, and a servant ran down to meet him holding an umbrella.

'The cabman has been paid,' observed the servant in a very civil tone; and he proceeded to escort Brackenbury along the path and up the steps. In the hall several other attendants relieved him of his hat, cane, and paletot, gave him a ticket with a number in return, and politely hurried him up a stair adorned with tropical flowers, to the door of an apartment on the first story. Here a grave butler inquired his name, and announcing 'Lieutenant Brackenbury Rich', ushered him into the drawing-room of the house.

A young man, slender and singularly handsome, came forward and greeted him with an air at once courtly and affectionate. Hundreds of candles, of the finest wax, lit up a room that was perfumed, like the staircase, with a profusion of rare and beautiful flowering shrubs. A side-table was loaded with tempting viands. Several servants went to and fro with fruits and goblets of champagne. The company was perhaps sixteen in number, all men, few beyond the prime of life, and with hardly an exception, of a dashing and capable exterior. They were divided into two groups, one about a roulette board, and the other surrounding a table at which one of their number held a bank of baccarat.

'I see,' thought Brackenbury, 'I am in a private gambling saloon, and the cabman was a tout.'

His eye had embraced the details, and his mind formed the conclusion, while his host was still holding him by the hand; and to him his looks returned from this rapid survey. At a second view Mr Morris surprised him still more than on the first. The easy elegance of his manners, the distinction, amiability, and courage that appeared upon his features, fitted very ill with the Lieutenant's preconceptions on the subject of the proprietor of a hell; and the tone of his conversation seemed to mark him out for a man of position and merit. Brackenbury found he had an instinctive liking for his entertainer; and though he chid himself for the weakness he was unable to resist a sort of friendly attraction for Mr. Morris's person and character.

'I have heard of you, Lieutenant Rich,' said Mr Morris, lowering his tone; 'and believe me I am gratified to make your acquaintance. Your looks accord with the reputation that has preceded you from India. And if you will forget for a while the irregularity of your presentation in my house, I shall feel it not only an honour, but genuine pleasure besides. A man who makes a mouthful of barbarian cavaliers,' he added with a laugh, 'should not be appalled by a breach of etiquette, however serious.'

And he led him towards the sideboard and pressed him to partake of some refreshments.

'Upon my word,' the Lieutenant reflected, 'this is one of the pleasantest fellows and, I do not doubt, one of the most agreeable societies in London.'

He partook of some champagne, which he found excellent; and observing that many of the company were already smoking, he lit one of his own Manillas, and strolled up to the roulette board, where he sometimes made a stake and sometimes looked on smilingly on the fortune of others. It was while he was thus idling that he became aware of a sharp scrutiny to which the whole of the guests were subjected. Mr Morris went here and there, ostensibly busied on hospitable concerns; but he had ever a shrewd glance at disposal; not a man of the party escaped his sudden, searching looks; he took stock of the bearing of heavy losers, he valued the amount of the stakes, he paused behind couples who were deep in conversation; and, in a word, there was hardly a characteristic of anyone present but he seemed to catch and make a note of it. Brackenbury began to wonder if this were indeed a gambling hell: it had so much the air of a private inquisition. He followed Mr Morris in all his movements; and although the man had a ready smile, he seemed to perceive, as it were under a mask, a haggard, careworn, and preoccupied spirit. The fellows around him laughed and made their game; but Brackenbury had lost interest in the guests.

'This Morris,' thought he, 'is no idler in the room. Some deep purpose inspires him; let it be mine to fathom it.'

Now and then Mr Morris would call one of his visitors aside; and after a brief colloquy in an anteroom, he would return alone, and the visitors in question reappeared no more. After a certain number of repetitions, this performance excited Brackenbury's curiosity to a high degree. He determined to be at the bottom of this minor mystery at once; and strolling into the anteroom, found a deep window recess concealed by curtains of the fashionable green. Here he hurriedly ensconced himself; nor had he to wait long before the sound of steps and voices drew near him from the principal apartment. Peering through the division, he saw Mr Morris escorting a fat and ruddy personage, with somewhat the look of a commercial traveller, whom Brackenbury had already remarked for his coarse laugh and under-bred behaviour at the table. The pair halted immediately before the window, so that Brackenbury lost not a word of the following discourse:—

'I beg you a thousand pardons!' began Mr Morris, with the most conciliatory manner; 'and, if I appear rude, I am sure you will readily forgive me. In a place so great as London accidents must continually happen; and the best that we can hope is to remedy them with as small delay as possible. I will not deny that I fear you have made a mistake and honoured my poor house by inadvertence; for, to speak openly, I cannot at all remember your appearance. Let me put the question without unnecessary circumlocution—between gentlemen of honour a word will suffice—Under whose roof do you suppose yourself to be?'

'That of Mr Morris,' replied the other, with a prodigious display of confusion, which had been visibly growing upon him throughout the last few words.

'Mr John or Mr James Morris?' inquired the host.

'I really cannot tell you,' returned the unfortunate guest. 'I am not personally acquainted with the gentlemen, any more than I am with yourself.'

'I see,' said Mr Morris. 'There is another person of the same name farther down the street; and I have no doubt the policeman will be able to supply you with his number. Believe me, I felicitate myself on the misunderstanding which has procured me the pleasure of your company for so long; and let me express a hope that we may meet again upon a more regular footing. Meantime, I would not for the world detain you longer from your friends. John,' he added, raising his voice, 'will you see that the gentleman finds his great-coat?'

And with the most agreeable air Mr Morris escorted his visitor as far as the anteroom door, where he left him under conduct of the butler. As he passed the window, on his return to the drawing-room, Brackenbury could hear him utter a profound sigh, as though his mind was loaded with a great anxiety, and his nerves already fatigued with the task on which he was engaged.

For perhaps an hour the hansoms kept arriving with such frequency, that Mr Morris had to receive a new guest for every old one that he sent away, and the company preserved its number undiminished. But towards the end of that time the arrivals grew few and far between, and at length ceased entirely, while the process of elimination was continued with unimpaired activity. The drawing-room began to look empty: the baccarat was discontinued for lack of a banker; more than one person said goodnight of his own accord, and was suffered to depart without expostulation: and in the meanwhile Mr Morris redoubled in agreeable attentions to those who stayed behind. He went from group to group and from person to person with looks of the readiest sympathy and the most pertinent and pleasing talk; he was not so much like a host as like a hostess, and there was a feminine coquetry and condescension in his manner which charmed the hearts of all.

As the guests grew thinner, Lieutenant Rich strolled for a moment out of the drawing-room into the hall in quest of fresher air. But he had no sooner passed the threshold of the antechamber than he was brought to a dead halt by a discovery of the most surprising nature. The flowering shrubs had disappeared from the staircase; three large furniture wagons stood before the garden gate; the servants were busy dismantling the house upon all sides; and some of them had already donned their great-coats and were preparing to depart. It was like the end of a country ball, where everything has been supplied by contract. Brackenbury had indeed some matter for reflection. First, the guests, who were no real guests after all, had been dismissed; and now the servants, who could hardly be genuine servants, were actively dispersing.

'Was the whole establishment a sham?' he asked himself. 'The mushroom of a single night which should disappear before morning?'

Watching a favourable opportunity, Brackenbury dashed upstairs to the higher regions of the house. It was as he had expected. He ran from room to room, and saw not a stick of furniture nor so much as a picture on the walls. Although the house had been painted and papered, it was not only uninhabited at present, but plainly had never been inhabited at all. The young officer remembered with astonishment its specious, settled, and hospitable air on his arrival. It was only at a prodigious cost that the imposture could have been carried out upon so great a scale.

Who, then, was Mr Morris? What was his intention in thus playing the householder for a single night in the remote west of London? And why did he collect his visitors at hazard from the streets?

Brackenbury remembered that he had already delayed too long, and hastened to join the company. Many had left during his absence; and counting the Lieutenant and his host, there were not more than five persons in the drawing-room—recently so thronged. Mr Morris greeted him, as he re-entered the apartment, with a smile, and immediately rose to his feet.

'It is now time, gentlemen,' said he, 'to explain my purpose in decoying you from your amusements. I trust you did not find the evening hang very dully on your hands; but my object, I will confess it, was not to entertain your leisure, but to help myself in an unfortunate necessity. You are all gentlemen,' he continued, 'your appearance does you that much justice, and I ask for no better security. Hence, I speak it without concealment, I ask you to render me a dangerous and delicate service; dangerous because you may run the hazard of your lives, and delicate because I must ask an absolute discretion upon all that you shall see or hear. From an utter stranger the request is almost comically extravagant; I am well aware of this; and I would add at once, if there be anyone present who has heard enough, if there be one among the party who recoils from a dangerous confidence and a piece of Quixotic devotion to he knows not whom—here is my hand ready, and I shall wish him goodnight and God-speed, with all the sincerity in the world.'

A very tall, black man, with a heavy stoop, immediately responded to this appeal.

'I commend your frankness, sir,' said he; 'and, for my part, I go. I make no reflections; but I cannot deny that you fill me with suspicious thoughts. I go myself, as I say; and perhaps you will think I have no right to add words to my example.'

'On the contrary,' replied Mr Morris, 'I am obliged to you for all you say. It would be impossible to exaggerate the gravity of my proposal.'

'Well, gentlemen, what do you say?' said the tall man, addressing the others. 'We have had our evening's frolic; shall we go homeward peaceably in a body? You will think well of my suggestion in the morning, when you see the sun again in innocence and safety.'

The speaker pronounced the last words with an intonation which added to their force; and his face wore a singular expression, full of gravity and significance. Another of the company rose hastily, and, with some appearance of alarm, prepared to take his leave. There were only two who held their ground, Brackenbury and an old red-nosed cavalry Major; but these two preserved a nonchalant demeanour, and, beyond a look of intelligence which they rapidly exchanged, appeared entirely foreign to the discussion that had just been terminated.

Mr Morris conducted the deserters as far as the door, which he closed upon their heels; then he turned round disclosing a countenance of mingled relief and animation, and addressed the two officers as follows:

'I have chosen my men like Joshua in the Bible,' said Mr Morris, 'and I now believe I have the pick of London. Your appearance pleased my hansom cabmen; then it delighted me; I have watched your behaviour in a strange company, and under the most unusual circumstances: I have studied how you played and how you bore your losses; lastly, I have put you to the test of a staggering announcement, and you received it like an invitation to dinner. It is not for nothing,' he cried, 'that I have been for years the companion and the pupil of the bravest and wisest potentate in Europe.'

'At the affair of Bunderchang,' observed the Major, 'I asked for twelve volunteers, and every trooper in the ranks replied to my appeal. But a gaming party is not the same thing as a regiment under fire. You may be pleased, I suppose, to have found two, and two who will not fail you at a push. As for the pair who ran away, I count them among the most pitiful hounds I ever met with. Lieutenant Rich,' he added, addressing Brackenbury, 'I have heard much of you of late; and I cannot doubt but you have also heard of me. I am Major O'Rooke.'

And the veteran tendered his hand, which was red and tremulous, to the young Lieutenant.

'Who has not?' answered Brackenbury.

'When this little matter is settled,' said Mr Morris, 'you will think I have sufficiently rewarded you; for I could offer neither a more valuable service than to make him acquainted with the other.'

'And now,' said Major O'Rooke, 'is it a duel?'

'A duel after a fashion,' replied Mr Morris, 'a duel with unknown and dangerous enemies, and, as I gravely fear, a duel to the death. I must ask you,' he continued, 'to call me Morris no longer: call me, if you please, Hammersmith; my real name, as well as that of another person to whom I hope to present you before long, you will gratify me by not asking and not seeking to discover for yourselves. Three days ago the person of whom I speak disappeared suddenly from home; and, until this morning, I received no hint of his situation. You will fancy my alarm when I tell you that he is engaged upon a work of private justice. Bound by an unhappy oath, too lightly sworn, he finds it necessary, without the help of law, to rid the earth of an insidious and bloody villain. Already two of our friends, and one of them my own born brother, have perished in the enterprise. He himself, or I am much deceived, is taken in the same fatal toils. But at least he still lives and still hopes, as this billet sufficiently proves.'

And the speaker, no other than Colonel Geraldine, proffered a letter, thus conceived:—

Major Hammersmith,—On Wednesday, at 3 A.M., you will be admitted by the small door to the gardens of Rochester House, Regent's Park, by a man who is entirely in my interest. I must request you not to fail me by a second. Pray bring my case of swords, and, if you can find them, one or two gentlemen of conduct and discretion to whom my person is unknown. My name must not be used in this affair.

T. GODALL.

'From his wisdom alone, if he had no other title,' pursued Colonel Geraldine, when the others had each satisfied his curiosity, 'my friend is a man whose directions should implicitly be followed. I need not tell you, therefore, that I have not so much as visited the neighbourhood of Rochester House; and that I am still as wholly in the dark as either of yourselves as to the nature of my friend's dilemma. I betook myself, as soon as I had received this order, to a furnishing contractor, and, in a few hours, the house in which we now are had assumed its late air of festival. My scheme was at least original; and I am far from regretting an action which has procured me the services of Major O'Rooke and Lieutenant Brackenbury Rich. But the servants in the street will have a strange awakening. The house which this evening was full of lights and visitors they will find uninhabited and for sale tomorrow morning. Thus even the most serious concerns,' added the Colonel, 'have a merry side.'

'And let us add a merry ending,' said Brackenbury.

The Colonel consulted his watch.

'It is now hard on two,' he said. 'We have an hour before us, and a swift cab is at the door. Tell me if I may count upon your help.'

'During a long life,' replied Major O'Rooke, 'I never took back my hand from anything, nor so much as hedged a bet.'

Brackenbury signified his readiness in the most becoming terms; and after they had drunk a glass or two of wine, the Colonel gave each of them a loaded revolver, and the three mounted into the cab and drove off for the address in question.

Rochester House was a magnificent residence on the banks of the canal. The large extent of the garden isolated it in an unusual degree from the annoyances of neighbourhood. It seemed the *parc aux cerfs* of some great nobleman or millionaire. As far as could be seen from the street, there was not a glimmer of light in any of the numerous windows of the mansion; and the place had a look of neglect, as though the master had been long from home.

The cab was discharged, and the three gentlemen were not long in discovering the small door, which was a sort of postern in a lane between two garden walls. It still wanted ten or fifteen minutes of the appointed time; the rain fell heavily, and the adventurers sheltered themselves below some pendent ivy, and spoke in low tones of the approaching trial.

Suddenly Geraldine raised his finger to command silence, and all three bent their hearing to the utmost. Through the continuous noise of the rain, the steps and voices of two men became audible from the other side of the wall; and, as they drew nearer, Brackenbury, whose sense of hearing was remarkably acute, could even distinguish some fragments of their talk.

'Is the grave dug?' asked one.

'It is,' replied the other; 'behind the laurel hedge. When the job is done, we can cover it with a pile of stakes.'

The first speaker laughed, and the sound of his merriment was shocking to the listeners on the other side.

'In an hour from now,' he said.

And by the sounds of the steps it was obvious that the pair had separated, and were proceeding in contrary directions.

Almost immediately after the postern door was cautiously opened, a white face was protruded into the lane, and a hand was seen beckoning to the watchers. In dead silence the three passed the door, which was immediately locked behind them, and followed their guide through several garden alleys to the kitchen entrance of the house. A single candle burned in the great paved kitchen, which was destitute of the customary furniture; and as the party proceeded to ascend from thence by a flight of winding stairs, a prodigious noise of rats testified still more plainly to the dilapidation of the house.

Their conductor preceded them, carrying the candle. He was a lean man, much bent, but still agile; and he turned from time to time and admonished silence and caution by his gestures. Colonel Geraldine followed on his heels, the case of swords under one arm, and a pistol ready in the other. Brackenbury's heart beat thickly. He perceived that they were still in time; but he judged from the alacrity of the old man that the hour of action must be near at hand; the circumstances of this adventure were so obscure and menacing, the place seemed so well chosen for the darkest acts, that an older man than Brackenbury might have been pardoned a measure of emotion as he closed the procession up the winding stair.

At the top the guide threw open a door and ushered the three officers before him into a small apartment, lighted by a smoky lamp and the glow of a modest fire. At the chimney corner sat a man in the early prime of life, and of a stout but courtly and commanding appearance. His attitude and expression were those of the most unmoved composure; he was smoking a cheroot with much enjoyment and deliberation, and on a table by his elbow stood a long glass of some effervescing beverage, which diffused an agreeable odour through the room.

'Welcome,' said he, extending his hand to Colonel Geraldine. 'I knew I might count on your exactitude.'

'On my devotion,' replied the Colonel, with a bow.

'Present me to your friends,' continued the first; and, when that ceremony had been performed, 'I wish, gentlemen,' he added, with the most exquisite affability, 'that I could offer you a more cheerful programme; it is ungracious to inaugurate an acquaintance upon serious affairs; but the compulsion of events is stronger than the obligations of good-fellowship. I hope and believe you will be able to forgive me this unpleasant evening; and for men of your stamp it will be enough to know that you are conferring a considerable favour.'

'Your Highness,' said the Major, 'must pardon my bluntness. I am unable to hide what I know. For some time back I have suspected Major Hammersmith, but Mr Godall is unmistakable. To seek two men in London unacquainted with Prince Florizel of Bohemia was to ask too much at Fortune's hands.'

'Prince Florizel!' cried Brackenbury in amazement.

And he gazed with the deepest interest on the features of the celebrated personage before him.

'I shall not lament the loss of my incognito,' remarked the Prince, 'for it enables me to thank you with the more authority. You would have done as much for Mr Godall, I feel sure, as for the Prince of Bohemia; but the latter can perhaps do more for you. The gain is mine,' he added, with a courteous gesture.

And the next moment he was conversing with the two officers about the Indian army and the native troops, a subject on which, as on all others, he had a remarkable fund of information and the soundest views.

There was something so striking in this man's attitude at a moment of deadly peril that Brackenbury was overcome with respectful admiration; nor was he less sensible to the charm of his conversation or the surprising amenity of his address. Every gesture, every intonation, was not only noble in itself, but seemed to ennoble the fortunate mortal for whom it was intended; and Brackenbury confessed to himself with enthusiasm that this was a sovereign for whom a brave man might thankfully lay down his life.

Many minutes had thus passed, when the person who had introduced them into the house, and who had sat ever since in a corner, and with his watch in his hand, arose and whispered a word into the Prince's ear.

'It is well, Dr Noel,' replied Florizel, aloud; and then addressing the others, 'You will excuse me, gentlemen,' he added, 'if I have to leave you in the dark. The moment now approaches.'

Dr Noel extinguished the lamp. A faint, grey light, premonitory of the dawn, illuminated the window, but was not sufficient to illuminate the room; and when the Prince rose to his feet, it was impossible to distinguish his features or to make a guess at the nature of the emotion which obviously affected him as he spoke. He moved towards the door, and placed himself at one side of it in an attitude of the wariest attention.

'You will have the kindness,' he said, 'to maintain the strictest silence, and to conceal yourselves in the densest of the shadow.'

The three officers and the physician hastened to obey, and for nearly ten minutes the only sound in Rochester House was occasioned by the excursions of the rats behind the woodwork. At the end of that period, a loud creak of a hinge broke in with surprising distinctness on the silence; and shortly after, the watchers could distinguish a slow and cautious tread approaching up the kitchen stair. At every second step the intruder seemed to pause and lend an ear, and during these intervals, which seemed of an incalculable duration, a profound disquiet possessed the spirit of the listeners.

Dr Noel, accustomed as he was to dangerous emotions, suffered an almost pitiful physical prostration; his breath whistled in his lungs, his teeth grated one upon another, and his joints cracked aloud as he nervously shifted his position.

At last a hand was laid upon the door, and the bolt shot back with a slight report. There followed another pause, during which Brackenbury could see the Prince draw himself together noiselessly as if for some unusual exertion. Then the door opened, letting in a little more of the light of the morning; and the figure of a man appeared upon the threshold and stood motionless. He was tall, and carried a knife in his hand. Even in the twilight they could see his upper teeth bare and glistening, for his mouth was open like that of a hound about to leap. The man had evidently been over the head in water but a minute or two before; and even while he stood there the drops kept falling from his wet clothes and pattered on the floor.

The next moment he crossed the threshold. There was a leap, a stifled cry, an instantaneous struggle; and before Colonel Geraldine could spring to his aid, the Prince held the man, disarmed and helpless, by the shoulders.

'Dr Noel,' he said, 'you will be so good as to relight the lamp.'

And relinquishing the charge of his prisoner to Geraldine and Brackenbury, he crossed the room and set his back against the chimney-piece. As soon as the lamp had kindled, the party beheld an unaccustomed sternness on the Prince's features. It was no longer Florizel, the careless gentleman; it was the Prince of Bohemia, justly incensed and full of deadly purpose, who now raised his head and addressed the captive President of the Suicide Club.

'President,' he said, 'you have laid your last snare, and your own feet are taken in it. The day is beginning; it is your last morning. You have just swum the Regent's Canal; it is your last bathe in this world. Your old accomplice, Dr Noel, so far from betraying me, has delivered you into my hands for judgment. And the grave you had dug for me this afternoon shall serve, in God's Almighty Providence, to hide your own just doom from the curiosity of mankind. Kneel and pray, sir, if you have a mind that way; for your time is short, and God is weary of your iniquities.'

The President made no answer either by word or sign; but continued to hang his head and gaze sullenly on the floor, as though he were conscious of the Prince's prolonged and unsparing regard.

'Gentlemen,' continued Florizel, resuming the ordinary tone of his conversation, 'this is a fellow who has long eluded me, but whom, thanks to Dr Noel, I now have tightly by the heels. To tell the story of his misdeeds would occupy more time than we can now afford; but if the canal had contained nothing but the blood of his victims, I believe the wretch would have been no drier than you see him. Even in an affair of this sort I desire to preserve the forms of honour. But I make you the judges, gentlemen—this is more an execution than a duel; and to give the rogue his choice of weapons would be to push too far a point of etiquette. I cannot afford to lose my life in such a business,' he continued, unlocking the case of swords; 'and as a pistol-bullet travels so often on the wings of chance, and skill and courage may fall by the most trembling marksman, I have decided, and I feel sure you will approve my determination, to put this question to the touch of swords.'

When Brackenbury and Major O'Rooke, to whom these remarks were particularly addressed, had each intimated his approval, 'Quick, sir,' added Prince Florizel to the President, 'choose a blade and do not keep me waiting; I have an impatience to be done with you for ever.'

For the first time since he was captured and disarmed the President raised his head, and it was plain that he began instantly to pluck up courage.

'Is it to be stand up?' he asked eagerly, 'and between you and me?'

'I mean so far to honour you,' replied the Prince.

'Oh, come!' cried the President. 'With a fair field, who knows how things may happen? I must add that I consider it handsome behaviour on your Highness's part; and if the worst comes to the worst I shall die by one of the most gallant gentlemen in Europe.'

And the President, liberated by those who had detained him, stepped up to the table and began, with minute attention, to select a sword. He was highly elated, and seemed to feel no doubt that he should issue victorious from the contest. The spectators grew alarmed in the face of so entire a confidence, and adjured Prince Florizel to reconsider his intention.

'It is but a farce,' he answered; 'and I think I can promise you, gentlemen, that it will not be long a-playing.'

'Your Highness will be careful not to overreach,' said Colonel Geraldine.

'Geraldine,' returned the Prince, 'did you ever know me fail in a debt of honour? I owe you this man's death, and you shall have it.'

The President at last satisfied himself with one of the rapiers, and signified his readiness by a gesture that was not devoid of a rude nobility. The nearness of peril, and the sense of courage, even to this obnoxious villain, lent an air of manhood and a certain grace.

The Prince helped himself at random to a sword.

'Colonel Geraldine and Doctor Noel,' he said, 'will have the goodness to await me in this room. I wish no personal friend of mine to be involved in this transaction. Major O'Rooke, you are a man of some years and a settled reputation—let me recommend the President to your good graces. Lieutenant Rich will be so good as to lend me his attentions: a young man cannot have too much experience in such affairs.'

'Your Highness,' replied Brackenbury, 'it is an honour I shall prize extremely.'

'It is well,' returned Prince Florizel; 'I shall hope to stand your friend in more important circumstances.'

And so saying he led the way out of the apartment and down the kitchen stairs.

The two men who were thus left alone threw open the window and leaned out, straining every sense to catch an indication of the tragical events that were about to follow. The rain was now over; day had almost come, and the birds were piping in the shrubbery and on the forest trees of the garden. The Prince and his companions were visible for a moment as they followed an alley between two flowering thickets; but at the first corner a clump of foliage intervened, and they were again concealed from view. This was all the Colonel and the physician had an opportunity to see, and the garden was so vast, and the place of combat evidently so remote from the house, that not even the noise of sword-play reached their ears.

'He has taken him towards the grave,' said Dr Noel, with a shudder.

'God,' cried the Colonel, 'God defend the right!'

And they awaited the event in silence, the Doctor shaking with fear, the Colonel in an agony of sweat. Many minutes must have elapsed, the day was sensibly broader, and the birds were singing more heartily in the garden before a sound of returning footsteps recalled their glances towards the door. It was the Prince and the two Indian officers who entered. God had defended the right.

'I am ashamed of my emotion,' said Prince Florizel; 'I feel it a weakness unworthy of my station, but the continued existence of that hound of Hell had begun to play upon me like a disease, and his death has more refreshed me than a night of slumber. Look, Geraldine,' he continued, throwing his sword upon the floor, 'there is the blood of the man who killed your brother. It should be a welcome sight. And yet,' he added, 'see how strangely we men are made! my revenge is not yet five minutes old, and already I am beginning to ask myself if even revenge be attainable on this precarious stage of life. The ill he did, who can undo it? The career in which he amassed a huge fortune (for the house itself in which he stayed belonged to him)—that career is now a part of the destiny of mankind forever; and I might weary myself making thrusts in carte until the crack of judgment, and Geraldine's brother would be none the less dead, and a thousand other innocent persons would be none the less dishonoured and debauched! The existence of a man is so small a thing to take, so mighty a thing to employ! Alas!' he cried, 'is there anything in life so disenchanting as attainment?'

'God's justice has been done,' replied the Doctor. 'So much I behold. The lesson, your Highness, has been a cruel one for me; and I await my own turn with deadly apprehension.'

'What was I saying?' cried the Prince. 'I have punished, and here is the man beside us who can help me to undo. Ah, Doctor Noel! you and I have before us many a day of hard and honourable toil; and perhaps, before we have done, you may have more than redeemed your early errors.'

'And in the meantime,' said the Doctor, 'let me go and bury my oldest friend.'

The Bottle Imp

Note.—Any student of that very unliterary product, the English drama of the early part of the century, will here recognise the name and the root idea of a piece once rendered popular by the redoubtable O. Smith. The root idea is there and identical, and yet I hope I have made it a new thing. And the fact that the tale has been designed and written for a Polynesian audience may lend it some extraneous interest nearer home.—R. L. S.

So Keawe took the bottle up and dashed it on the floor till he was weary; but it jumped on the floor like a child's ball, and was not injured.

'This is a strange thing,' said Keawe. 'For by the touch of it, as well as by the look, the bottle should be of glass.'

'Of glass it is,' replied the man, sighing more heavily than ever; 'but the glass of it was tempered in the flames of Hell.'

THERE WAS a man of the Island of Hawaii, whom I shall call Keawe; for the truth is, he still lives, and his name must be kept secret; but the place of his birth was not far from Honaunau, where the bones of Keawe the Great lie hidden in a cave. This man was poor, brave, and active; he could read and write like a schoolmaster; he was a first-rate mariner besides, sailed for some time in the island steamers, and steered a whaleboat on the Hamakua coast. At length it came in Keawe's mind to have a sight of the great world and foreign cities, and he shipped on a vessel bound to San Francisco.

This is a fine town, with a fine harbour, and rich people uncountable; and, in particular, there is one hill which is covered with palaces. Upon this hill Keawe was one day taking a walk with his pocket full of money, viewing the great houses upon either hand with pleasure. 'What fine houses these are!' he was thinking, 'and how happy must those people be who dwell in them, and take no care for the morrow!' The thought was in his mind when he came abreast of a house that was smaller than some others, but all finished and beautified like a toy; the steps of that house shone like silver, and the borders of the garden bloomed like garlands, and the windows were bright like diamond; and Keawe stopped and wondered at the excellence of all he saw. So stopping, he was aware of a man that looked forth upon him through a window so clear that Keawe could see him as you see a fish in a pool upon the reef. The man was elderly, with a bald head and a black beard; and his face was heavy with sorrow, and he bitterly sighed. And the truth of it is, that as Keawe looked in upon the man, and the man looked out upon Keawe, each envied the other.

All of a sudden, the man smiled and nodded, and beckoned Keawe to enter, and met him at the door of the house.

'This is a fine house of mine,' said the man, and bitterly sighed. 'Would you not care to view the chambers?'

So he led Keawe all over it, from the cellar to the roof, and there was nothing there that was not perfect of its kind, and Keawe was astonished.

'Truly,' said Keawe, 'this is a beautiful house; if I lived in the like of it, I should be laughing all day long. How comes it, then, that you should be sighing?'

'There is no reason,' said the man, 'why you should not have a house in all points similar to this, and finer, if you wish. You have some money, I suppose?'

'I have fifty dollars,' said Keawe; 'but a house like this will cost more than fifty dollars.'

The man made a computation. 'I am sorry you have no more,' said he, 'for it may raise you trouble in the future; but it shall be yours at fifty dollars.'

'The house?' asked Keawe.

'No, not the house,' replied the man; 'but the bottle. For, I must tell you, although I appear to you so rich and fortunate, all my fortune, and this house itself and its garden, came out of a bottle not much bigger than a pint. This is it.'

And he opened a lockfast place, and took out a round-bellied bottle with a long neck; the glass of it was white like milk, with changing rainbow colours in the grain. Withinsides something obscurely moved, like a shadow and a fire.

'This is the bottle,' said the man; and, when Keawe laughed, 'You do not believe me?' he added. 'Try, then, for yourself. See if you can break it.'

So Keawe took the bottle up and dashed it on the floor till he was weary; but it jumped on the floor like a child's ball, and was not injured.

'This is a strange thing,' said Keawe. 'For by the touch of it, as well as by the look, the bottle should be of glass.'

'Of glass it is,' replied the man, sighing more heavily than ever; 'but the glass of it was tempered in the flames of Hell. An imp lives in it, and that is the shadow we behold there moving: or so I suppose. If any man buy this bottle the imp is at his command; all that he desires—love, fame, money, houses like this house, ay, or a city like this city—all are his at the word uttered. Napoleon had this bottle, and by it he grew to be the king of the world; but he sold it at the last, and fell. Captain Cook had this bottle, and by it he found his way to so many islands; but he, too, sold it, and was slain upon Hawaii. For, once it is sold, the power goes and the protection; and unless a man remain content with what he has, ill will befall him.'

'And yet you talk of selling it yourself?' Keawe said.

'I have all I wish, and I am growing elderly,' replied the man. 'There is one thing the imp cannot do—he cannot prolong life; and, it would not be fair to conceal from you, there is a drawback to the bottle; for if a man die before he sells it, he must burn in Hell forever.'

'To be sure, that is a drawback and no mistake,' cried Keawe. 'I would not meddle with the thing. I can do without a house, thank God; but there is one thing I could not be doing with one particle, and that is to be damned.'

'Dear me, you must not run away with things,' returned the man. 'All you have to do is to use the power of the imp in moderation, and then sell it to someone else, as I do to you, and finish your life in comfort.'

'Well, I observe two things,' said Keawe. 'All the time you keep sighing like a maid in love, that is one; and, for the other, you sell this bottle very cheap.'

'I have told you already why I sigh,' said the man. 'It is because I fear my health is breaking up; and, as you said yourself, to die and go to the devil is a pity for anyone. As for why I sell so cheap, I must explain to you there is a peculiarity about the bottle. Long ago, when the Devil brought it first upon earth, it was extremely expensive, and was sold first of all to Prester John for many millions of dollars; but it cannot be sold at all, unless sold at a loss. If you sell it for as much as you paid for it, back it comes to you again like a homing pigeon. It follows that the price has kept falling in these centuries, and the bottle is now remarkably cheap. I bought it myself from one of my great neighbours on this hill, and the price I paid was only ninety dollars. I could sell it for as high as eighty-nine dollars and ninety-nine cents, but not a penny dearer, or back the thing must come to me. Now, about this there are two bothers. First, when you offer a bottle so singular for eighty odd dollars, people suppose you to be jesting. And second—but there is no hurry about that—and I need not go into it. Only remember it must be coined money that you sell it for.'

'How am I to know that this is all true?' asked Keawe.

'Some of it you can try at once,' replied the man. 'Give me your fifty dollars, take the bottle, and wish your fifty dollars back into your pocket. If that does not happen, I pledge you my honour I will cry off the bargain and restore your money.'

'You are not deceiving me?' said Keawe. The man bound himself with a great oath.

'Well, I will risk that much,' said Keawe, 'for that can do no harm.' And he paid over his money to the man, and the man handed him the bottle.

'Imp of the bottle,' said Keawe, 'I want my fifty dollars back.' And sure enough he had scarce said the word before his pocket was as heavy as ever.

'To be sure this is a wonderful bottle,' said Keawe.

'And now good morning to you, my fine fellow, and the Devil go with you for me!' said the man.

'Hold on,' said Keawe, 'I don't want any more of this fun. Here, take your bottle back.'

'You have bought it for less than I paid for it,' replied the man, rubbing his hands. 'It is yours now; and, for my part, I am only concerned to see the back of you.' And with that he rang for his Chinese servant, and had Keawe shown out of the house.

Now, when Keawe was in the street, with the bottle under his arm, he began to think. 'If all is true about this bottle, I may have made a losing bargain,' thinks he. 'But perhaps the man was only fooling me.' The first thing he did was to count his money; the sum was exact—forty-nine dollars American money, and one Chili piece. 'That looks like the truth,' said Keawe. 'Now I will try another part.'

The streets in that part of the city were as clean as a ship's decks, and though it was noon, there were no passengers. Keawe set the bottle in the gutter and walked away. Twice he looked back, and there was the milky, round-bellied bottle where he left it. A third time he looked back, and turned a corner; but he had scarce done so, when something knocked upon his elbow, and behold! it was the long neck sticking up; and as for the round belly, it was jammed into the pocket of his pilot-coat.

'And that looks like the truth,' said Keawe.

The next thing he did was to buy a cork-screw in a shop, and go apart into a secret place in the fields. And there he tried to draw the cork, but as often as he put the screw in, out it came again, and the cork as whole as ever.

'This is some new sort of cork,' said Keawe, and all at once he began to shake and sweat, for he was afraid of that bottle.

On his way back to the port-side, he saw a shop where a man sold shells and clubs from the wild islands, old heathen deities, old coined money, pictures from China and Japan, and all manner of things that sailors bring in their sea-chests. And here he had an idea. So he went in and offered the bottle for a hundred dollars. The man of the shop laughed at him at the first, and offered him five; but, indeed, it was a curious bottle—such glass was never blown in any human glassworks, so prettily the colours shone under the milky white, and so strangely the shadow hovered in the midst; so, after he had disputed awhile after the manner of his kind, the shop-man gave Keawe sixty silver dollars for the thing, and set it on a shelf in the midst of his window.

'Now,' said Keawe, 'I have sold that for sixty which I bought for fifty—or, to say truth, a little less, because one of my dollars was from Chili. Now I shall know the truth upon another point.'

So he went back on board his ship, and, when he opened his chest, there was the bottle, and had come more quickly than himself. Now Keawe had a mate on board whose name was Lopaka.

'What ails you?' said Lopaka, 'that you stare in your chest?'

They were alone in the ship's forecastle, and Keawe bound him to secrecy, and told all.

'This is a very strange affair,' said Lopaka; 'and I fear you will be in trouble about this bottle. But there is one point very clear—that you are sure of the trouble, and you had better have the profit in the bargain. Make up your mind what you want with it; give the order, and if it is done as you desire, I will buy the bottle myself; for I have an idea of my own to get a schooner, and go trading through the islands.'

'That is not my idea,' said Keawe; 'but to have a beautiful house and garden on the Kona Coast, where I was born, the sun shining in at the door, flowers in the garden, glass in the windows, pictures on the walls, and toys and fine carpets on the tables, for all the world like the house I was in this day—only a storey higher, and with balconies all about like the King's palace; and to live there without care and make merry with my friends and relatives.'

'Well,' said Lopaka, 'let us carry it back with us to Hawaii; and if all comes true, as you suppose, I will buy the bottle, as I said, and ask a schooner.'

Upon that they were agreed, and it was not long before the ship returned to Honolulu, carrying Keawe and Lopaka, and the bottle. They were scarce come ashore when they met a friend upon the beach, who began at once to condole with Keawe.

'I do not know what I am to be condoled about,' said Keawe. 'Is it possible you have not heard,' said the friend, 'your uncle—that good old man—is dead, and your cousin—that beautiful boy—was drowned at sea?'

Keawe was filled with sorrow, and, beginning to weep and to lament, he forgot about the bottle. But Lopaka was thinking to himself, and presently, when Keawe's grief was a little abated, 'I have been thinking,' said Lopaka. 'Had not your uncle lands in Hawaii, in the district of Kau?'

'No,' said Keawe, 'not in Kau; they are on the mountainside—a little way south of Hookena.'

'These lands will now be yours?' asked Lopaka.

'And so they will,' says Keawe, and began again to lament for his relatives.

'No,' said Lopaka, 'do not lament at present. I have a thought in my mind. How if this should be the doing of the bottle? For here is the place ready for your house.'

'If this be so,' cried Keawe, 'it is a very ill way to serve me by killing my relatives. But it may be, indeed; for it was in just such a station that I saw the house with my mind's eye.'

'The house, however, is not yet built,' said Lopaka.

'No, nor like to be!' said Keawe; 'for though my uncle has some coffee and ava and bananas, it will not be more than will keep me in comfort; and the rest of that land is the black lava.'

'Let us go to the lawyer,' said Lopaka; 'I have still this idea in my mind.'

Now, when they came to the lawyer's, it appeared Keawe's uncle had grown monstrous rich in the last days, and there was a fund of money.

'And here is the money for the house!' cried Lopaka.

'If you are thinking of a new house,' said the lawyer, 'here is the card of a new architect, of whom they tell me great things.'

'Better and better!' cried Lopaka. 'Here is all made plain for us. Let us continue to obey orders.'

So they went to the architect, and he had drawings of houses on his table.

'You want something out of the way,' said the architect. 'How do you like this?' and he handed a drawing to Keawe.

Now, when Keawe set eyes on the drawing, he cried out aloud, for it was the picture of his thought exactly drawn.

'I am in for this house,' thought he. 'Little as I like the way it comes to me, I am in for it now, and I may as well take the good along with the evil.'

So he told the architect all that he wished, and how he would have that house furnished, and about the pictures on the wall and the knick-knacks on the tables; and he asked the man plainly for how much he would undertake the whole affair.

The architect put many questions, and took his pen and made a computation; and when he had done he named the very sum that Keawe had inherited.

Lopaka and Keawe looked at one another and nodded.

'It is quite clear,' thought Keawe, 'that I am to have this house, whether or no. It comes from the Devil, and I fear I will get little good by that; and of one thing I am sure, I will make no more wishes as long as I have this bottle. But with the house I am saddled, and I may as well take the good along with the evil.'

So he made his terms with the architect, and they signed a paper; and Keawe and Lopaka took ship again and sailed to Australia; for it was concluded between them they should not interfere at all, but leave the architect and the bottle imp to build and to adorn that house at their own pleasure.

The voyage was a good voyage, only all the time Keawe was hold-ing in his breath, for he had sworn he would utter no more wishes, and take no more favours from the Devil. The time was up when they got back. The architect told them that the house was ready, and Keawe and Lopaka took a passage in the *Hall*, and went down Kona way to view the house, and see if all had been done fitly according to the thought that was in Keawe's mind.

Now the house stood on the mountainside, visible to ships. Above, the forest ran up into the clouds of rain; below, the black lava fell in cliffs, where the kings of old lay buried. A garden bloomed about that house with every hue of flowers; and there was an orchard of papaia on the one hand and an orchard of breadfruit on the other, and right in front, toward the sea, a ship's mast had been rigged up and bore a flag. As for the house, it was three storeys high, with great chambers and broad balconies on each. The windows were of glass, so excellent that it was as clear as water and as bright as day. All manner of furniture adorned the chambers. Pictures hung upon the wall in golden frames: pictures of ships, and men fighting, and of the most beautiful women, and of singular places; nowhere in the world are there pictures of so bright a colour as those Keawe found hang-ing in his house. As for the knick-knacks, they were extraordinary fine; chiming clocks and musical boxes, little men with nodding heads, books filled with pictures, weapons of price from all quarters of the world, and the most elegant puzzles to entertain the leisure of a solitary man. And as no one would care to live in such chambers, only to walk through and view them, the balconies were made so broad that a whole town might have lived upon them in delight; and Keawe knew not which to prefer, whether the back porch, where you got the land breeze, and looked upon the orchards and the flowers, or the front balcony, where you could drink the wind of the sea, and look down the steep wall of the mountain and see the *Hall* going by once a week or so between Hookena and the hills of Pele, or the schooners plying up the coast for wood and ava and bananas.

When they had viewed all, Keawe and Lopaka sat on the porch. 'Well,' asked Lopaka, 'is it all as you designed?'

'Words cannot utter it,' said Keawe. 'It is better than I dreamed, and I am sick with satisfaction.'

'There is but one thing to consider,' said Lopaka; 'all this may be quite natural, and the bottle imp have nothing whatever to say to it. If I were to buy the bottle, and got no schooner after all, I should have put my hand in the fire for nothing. I gave you my word, I know; but yet I think you would not grudge me one more proof.'

'I have sworn I would take no more favours,' said Keawe. 'I have gone already deep enough.'

'This is no favour I am thinking of,' replied Lopaka. 'It is only to see the imp himself. There is nothing to be gained by that, and so nothing to be ashamed of; and yet, if I once saw him, I should be sure of the whole matter. So indulge me so far, and let me see the imp; and, after that, here is the money in my hand, and I will buy it.'

'There is only one thing I am afraid of,' said Keawe. 'The imp may be very ugly to view; and if you once set eyes upon him you might be very undesirous of the bottle.'

'I am a man of my word,' said Lopaka. 'And here is the money betwixt us.'

'Very well,' replied Keawe. 'I have a curiosity myself. So come, let us have one look at you, Mr Imp.'

Now as soon as that was said, the imp looked out of the bottle, and in again, swift as a lizard; and there sat Keawe and Lopaka turned to stone. The night had quite come, before either found a thought to say or voice to say it with; and then Lopaka pushed the money over and took the bottle.

'I am a man of my word,' said he, 'and had need to be so, or I would not touch this bottle with my foot. Well, I shall get my schooner and a dollar or two for my pocket; and then I will be rid of this devil as fast as I can. For to tell you the plain truth, the look of him has cast me down.'

'Lopaka,' said Keawe, 'do not you think any worse of me than you can help; I know it is night, and the roads bad, and the pass by the tombs an ill place to go by so late, but I declare since I have seen that little face, I cannot eat or sleep or pray till it is gone from me. I will give you a lantern and a basket to put the bottle in, and any picture or fine thing in all my house that takes your fancy;—and be gone at once, and go sleep at Hookena with Nahinu.'

'Keawe,' said Lopaka, 'many a man would take this ill; above all, when I am doing you a turn so friendly, as to keep my word and buy the bottle; and for that matter, the night and the dark, and the way by the tombs, must be all tenfold more dangerous to a man with such a sin upon his conscience, and such a bottle under his arm. But for my part, I am so extremely terrified myself, I have not the heart to blame you. Here I go then; and I pray God you may be happy in your house, and I fortunate with my schooner, and both get to heaven in the end in spite of the Devil and his bottle.'

So Lopaka went down the mountain; and Keawe stood in his front balcony, and listened to the clink of the horse's shoes, and watched the lantern go shining down the path, and along the cliff of caves where the old dead are buried; and all the time he trembled and clasped his hands, and prayed for his friend, and gave glory to God that he himself was escaped out of that trouble.

But the next day came very brightly, and that new house of his was so delightful to behold that he forgot his terrors. One day followed another, and Keawe dwelt there in perpetual joy. He had his place on the back porch; it was there he ate and lived, and read the stories in the Honolulu newspapers; but when anyone came by they would go in and view the chambers and the pictures. And the fame of the house went far and wide; it was called *Ka-Hale Nui*—the Great House—in all Kona; and sometimes the Bright House, for Keawe kept a Chinaman, who was all day dusting and furbishing; and the glass, and the gilt, and the fine stuffs, and the pictures, shone as bright as the morning. As for Keawe himself, he could not walk in the chambers without singing, his heart was so enlarged; and when ships sailed by upon the sea, he would fly his colours on the mast.

So time went by, until one day Keawe went upon a visit as far as Kailua to certain of his friends. There he was well feasted; and left as soon as he could the next morning, and rode hard, for he was impatient to behold his beautiful house; and, besides, the night then coming on was the night in which the dead of old days go abroad in the sides of Kona; and having already meddled with the Devil, he was the more chary of meeting with the dead. A little beyond Honaunau, looking far ahead, he was aware of a woman bathing in the edge of the sea; and she seemed a well-grown girl, but he thought no more of it. Then he saw her white shift flutter as she put it on, and then her red holoku; and by the time he came abreast of her she was done with her toilet, and had come up from the sea, and stood by the track-side in her red holoku, and she was all freshened with the bath, and her eyes shone and were kind. Now Keawe no sooner beheld her than he drew rein.

'I thought I knew everyone in this country,' said he. 'How comes it that I do not know you?'

'I am Kokua, daughter of Kiano,' said the girl, 'and I have just returned from Oahu. Who are you?'

'I will tell you who I am in a little,' said Keawe, dismounting from his horse, 'but not now. For I have a thought in my mind, and if you knew who I was, you might have heard of me, and would not give me a true answer. But tell me, first of all, one thing: Are you married?'

At this Kokua laughed out aloud. 'It is you who ask questions,' she said. 'Are you married yourself?'

'Indeed, Kokua, I am not,' replied Keawe, 'and never thought to be until this hour. But here is the plain truth. I have met you here at the roadside, and I saw your eyes, which are like the stars, and my heart went to you as swift as a bird. And so now, if you want none of me, say so, and I will go on to my own place; but if you think me no worse than any other young man, say so, too, and I will turn aside to your father's for the night, and tomorrow I will talk with the good man.'

Kokua said never a word, but she looked at the sea and laughed.

'Kokua,' said Keawe, 'if you say nothing, I will take that for the good answer; so let us be stepping to your father's door.'

She went on ahead of him, still without speech; only sometimes she glanced back and glanced away again, and she kept the strings of her hat in her mouth.

Now, when they had come to the door, Kiano came out on his verandah, and cried out and welcomed Keawe by name. At that the girl looked over, for the fame of the great house had come to her ears; and, to be sure, it was a great temptation. All that evening they were very merry together; and the girl was as bold as brass under the eyes of her parents, and made a mock of Keawe, for she had a quick wit. The next day he had a word with Kiano, and found the girl alone.

'Kokua,' said he, 'you made a mock of me all the evening; and it is still time to bid me go. I would not tell you who I was, because I have so fine a house, and I feared you would think too much of that house and too little of the man that loves you. Now you know all, and if you wish to have seen the last of me, say so at once.'

'No,' said Kokua; but this time she did not laugh, nor did Keawe ask for more.

This was the wooing of Keawe; things had gone quickly; but so an arrow goes, and the ball of a rifle swifter still, and yet both may strike the target. Things had gone fast, but they had gone far also, and the thought of Keawe rang in the maiden's head; she heard his voice in the breach of the surf upon the lava, and for this young man that she had seen but twice she would have left father and mother and her native islands. As for Keawe himself, his horse flew up the path of the mountain under the cliff of tombs, and the sound of the hoofs, and the sound of Keawe singing to himself for pleasure, echoed in the caverns of the dead. He came to the Bright House, and still he was singing. He sat and ate in the broad balcony, and the Chinaman wondered at his master, to hear how he sang between the mouthfuls. The sun went down into the sea, and the night came; and Keawe walked the balconies by lamplight, high on the mountains, and the voice of his singing startled men on ships.

'Here am I now upon my high place,' he said to himself. 'Life may be no better; this is the mountain top; and all shelves about me toward the worse. For the first time I will light up the chambers, and bathe in my fine bath with the hot water and the cold, and sleep alone in the bed of my bridal chamber.'

So the Chinaman had word, and he must rise from sleep and light the furnaces; and as he wrought below, beside the boilers, he heard his master singing and rejoicing above him in the lighted chambers. When the water began to be hot the Chinaman cried to his master; and Keawe went into the bathroom; and the Chinaman heard him sing as he filled the marble basin; and heard him sing, and the singing broken, as he undressed; until of a sudden, the song ceased. The Chinaman listened, and listened; he called up the house to Keawe to ask if all were well, and Keawe answered him 'Yes', and bade him go to bed; but there was no more singing in the Bright House; and all night long, the Chinaman heard his master's feet go round and round the balconies without repose.

Now the truth of it was this: as Keawe undressed for his bath, he spied upon his flesh a patch like a patch of lichen on a rock, and it was then that he stopped singing. For he knew the likeness of that patch, and knew that he was fallen in the Chinese Evil.

Now, it is a sad thing for any man to fall into this sickness. And it would be a sad thing for anyone to leave a house so beautiful and so commodious, and depart from all his friends to the north coast of Molokai between the mighty cliff and the sea-breakers. But what was that to the case of the man Keawe, he who had met his love but yesterday, and won her but that morning, and now saw all his hopes break, in a moment, like a piece of glass?

Awhile he sat upon the edge of the bath; then sprang, with a cry, and ran outside; and to and fro, to and fro, along the balcony, like one despairing.

'Very willingly could I leave Hawaii, the home of my fathers,' Keawe was thinking. 'Very lightly could I leave my house, the high-placed, the many-windowed, here upon the mountains. Very bravely could I go to Molokai, to Kalaupapa by the cliffs, to live with the smitten and to sleep there, far from my fathers. But what wrong have I done, what sin lies upon my soul, that I should have encountered Kokua coming cool from the sea-water in the evening? Kokua, the soul ensnarer! Kokua, the light of my life! Her may I never wed, her may I look upon no longer, her may I no more handle with my loving hand; and it is for this, it is for you, O Kokua! that I pour my lamentations!'

Now you are to observe what sort of a man Keawe was, for he might have dwelt there in the Bright House for years, and no one been the wiser of his sickness; but he reckoned nothing of that, if he must lose Kokua. And again, he might have wed Kokua even as he was; and so many would have done, because they have the souls of pigs; but Keawe loved the maid manfully, and he would do her no hurt and bring her in no danger.

A little beyond the midst of the night, there came in his mind the recollection of that bottle. He went round to the back porch, and called to memory the day when the Devil had looked forth; and at the thought ice ran in his veins.

'A dreadful thing is the bottle,' thought Keawe, 'and dreadful is the imp, and it is a dreadful thing to risk the flames of Hell. But what other hope have I to cure my sickness or to wed Kokua? What!' he thought, 'would I beard the Devil once, only to get me a house, and not face him again to win Kokua?'

Thereupon he called to mind it was the next day the *Hall* went by on her return to Honolulu. 'There must I go first,' he thought, 'and see Lopaka. For the best hope that I have now is to find that same bottle I was so pleased to be rid of.'

Never a wink could he sleep; the food stuck in his throat; but he sent a letter to Kiano, and about the time when the steamer would be coming, rode down beside the cliff of the tombs. It rained; his horse went heavily; he looked up at the black mouths of the caves, and he envied the dead that slept there and were done with trouble; and called to mind how he had galloped by the day before, and was astonished. So he came down to Hookena, and there was all the country gathered for the steamer as usual. In the shed before the store they sat and jested and passed the news; but there was no matter of speech in Keawe's bosom, and he sat in their midst and looked without on the rain falling on the houses, and the surf beating among the rocks, and the sighs arose in his throat.

'Keawe of the Bright House is out of spirits,' said one to another. Indeed, and so he was, and little wonder.

Then the *Hall* came, and the whaleboat carried him on board. The after-part of the ship was full of Haoles who had been to visit the volcano, as their custom is; and the midst was crowded with Kanakas, and the forepart with wild bulls from Hilo and horses from Kau; but Keawe sat apart from all in his sorrow, and watched for the house of Kiano. There it sat, low upon the shore in the black rocks, and shaded by the cocoa palms, and there by the door was a red holoku, no greater than a fly, and going to and fro with a fly's busyness. 'Ah, queen of my heart,' he cried, 'I'll venture my dear soul to win you!'

Soon after, darkness fell, and the cabins were lit up, and the Haoles sat and played at the cards and drank whiskey as their custom is; but Keawe walked the deck all night; and all the next day, as they steamed under the lee of Maui or of Molokai, he was still pacing to and fro like a wild animal in a menagerie.

Towards evening they passed Diamond Head, and came to the pier of Honolulu. Keawe stepped out among the crowd and began to

ask for Lopaka. It seemed he had become the owner of a schooner—
none better in the islands—and was gone upon an adventure as far
as Pola-Pola or Kahiki; so there was no help to be looked for from
Lopaka. Keawe called to mind a friend of his, a lawyer in the town (I
must not tell his name), and inquired of him. They said he was
grown suddenly rich, and had a fine new house upon Waikiki shore;
and this put a thought in Keawe's head, and he called a hack and
drove to the lawyer's house.

The house was all brand new, and the trees in the garden no
greater than walking-sticks, and the lawyer, when he came, had the
air of a man well pleased.

'What can I do to serve you?' said the lawyer.

'You are a friend of Lopaka's,' replied Keawe, 'and Lopaka
purchased from me a certain piece of goods that I thought you might
enable me to trace.'

The lawyer's face became very dark. 'I do not profess to misunder-
stand you, Mr Keawe,' said he, 'though this is an ugly business to be
stirring in. You may be sure I know nothing, but yet I have a guess, and
if you would apply in a certain quarter I think you might have news.'

And he named the name of a man, which, again, I had better not
repeat. So it was for days, and Keawe went from one to another, finding everywhere new clothes and carriages, and fine new houses and
men everywhere in great contentment, although, to be sure, when
he hinted at his business their faces would cloud over.

'No doubt I am upon the track,' thought Keawe. 'These new
clothes and carriages are all the gifts of the little imp, and these glad
faces are the faces of men who have taken their profit and got rid of
the accursed thing in safety. When I see pale cheeks and hear sighing, I shall know that I am near the bottle.'

So it befell at last that he was recommended to a Haole in Beritania
Street. When he came to the door, about the hour of the evening
meal, there were the usual marks of the new house, and the young
garden, and the electric light shining in the windows; but when the
owner came, a shock of hope and fear ran through Keawe; for here
was a young man, white as a corpse, and black about the eyes, the
hair shedding from his head, and such a look in his countenance as
a man may have when he is waiting for the gallows.

'Here it is, to be sure,' thought Keawe, and so with this man he nowise veiled his errand. 'I am come to buy the bottle,' said he.

At the word, the young Haole of Beritania Street reeled against the wall.

'The bottle!' he gasped. 'To buy the bottle!' Then he seemed to choke, and seizing Keawe by the arm carried him into a room and poured out wine in two glasses.

'Here is my respects,' said Keawe, who had been much about with Haoles in his time. 'Yes,' he added, 'I am come to buy the bottle. What is the price by now?'

At that word the young man let his glass slip through his fingers, and looked upon Keawe like a ghost.

'The price,' says he; 'the price! You do not know the price?'

'It is for that I am asking you,' returned Keawe. 'But why are you so much concerned? Is there anything wrong about the price?'

'It has dropped a great deal in value since your time, Mr Keawe,' said the young man stammering.

'Well, well, I shall have the less to pay for it,' says Keawe. 'How much did it cost you?'

The young man was as white as a sheet. 'Two cents,' said he.

'What?' cried Keawe, 'two cents? Why, then, you can only sell it for one. And he who buys it—' The words died upon Keawe's tongue; he who bought it could never sell it again, the bottle and the bottle imp must abide with him until he died, and when he died must carry him to the red end of Hell.

The young man of Beritania Street fell upon his knees. 'For God's sake buy it!' he cried. 'You can have all my fortune in the bargain. I was mad when I bought it at that price. I had embezzled money at my store; I was lost else; I must have gone to jail.'

'Poor creature,' said Keawe, 'you would risk your soul upon so desperate an adventure, and to avoid the proper punishment of your own disgrace; and you think I could hesitate with love in front of me. Give me the bottle, and the change which I make sure you have all ready. Here is a five-cent piece.'

It was as Keawe supposed; the young man had the change ready in a drawer; the bottle changed hands, and Keawe's fingers were no sooner clasped upon the stalk than he had breathed his wish to be a clean man. And, sure enough, when he got home to his room, and stripped himself before a glass, his flesh was whole like an infant's. And here was the strange thing: he had no sooner seen this miracle, than his mind was changed within him, and he cared naught for the Chinese Evil, and little enough for Kokua; and had but the one thought, that here he was bound to the bottle imp for time and for eternity, and had no better hope but to be a cinder for ever in the flames of Hell. Away ahead of him he saw them blaze with his mind's eye, and his soul shrank, and darkness fell upon the light.

When Keawe came to himself a little, he was aware it was the night when the band played at the hotel. Thither he went, because he feared to be alone; and there, among happy faces, walked to and fro, and heard the tunes go up and down, and saw Berger beat the measure, and all the while he heard the flames crackle, and saw the red fire burning in the bottomless pit. Of a sudden the band played 'Kiki-au-ao'; that was a song that he had sung with Kokua, and at the strain courage returned to him.

'It is done now,' he thought, 'and once more let me take the good along with the evil.'

So it befell that he returned to Hawaii by the first steamer, and as soon as it could be managed he was wedded to Kokua, and carried her up the mountainside to the Bright House.

Now it was so with these two, that when they were together, Keawe's heart was stilled; but so soon as he was alone he fell into a brooding horror, and heard the flames crackle, and saw the red fire burn in the bottomless pit. The girl, indeed, had come to him wholly; her heart leapt in her side at sight of him, her hand clung to his; and she was so fashioned from the hair upon her head to the nails upon her toes that none could see her without joy. She was pleasant in her nature. She had the good word always. Full of song she was, and went to and fro in the Bright House, the brightest thing in its three storeys, carolling like the birds. And Keawe beheld and heard her with delight, and then must shrink upon one side, and weep and groan to think upon the price that he had paid for her; and then he must dry his eyes, and wash his face, and go and sit with her on the broad balconies, joining in her songs, and, with a sick spirit, answering her smiles.

There came a day when her feet began to be heavy and her songs more rare; and now it was not Keawe only that would weep apart, but each would sunder from the other and sit in opposite balconies with the whole width of the Bright House betwixt. Keawe was so sunk in his despair, he scarce observed the change, and was only glad he had more hours to sit alone and brood upon his destiny, and was not so frequently condemned to pull a smiling face on a sick heart. But one day, coming softly through the house, he heard the sound of a child sobbing, and there was Kokua rolling her face upon the balcony floor, and weeping like the lost.

'You do well to weep in this house, Kokua,' he said. 'And yet I would give the head off my body that you (at least) might have been happy.'

'Happy!' she cried. 'Keawe, when you lived alone in your Bright House, you were the word of the island for a happy man; laughter and song were in your mouth, and your face was as bright as the sunrise. Then you wedded poor Kokua; and the good God knows what is amiss in her—but from that day you have not smiled. Oh!' she cried, 'what ails me? I thought I was pretty, and I knew I loved him. What ails me that I throw this cloud upon my husband?'

'Poor Kokua,' said Keawe. He sat down by her side, and sought to take her hand; but that she plucked away. 'Poor Kokua,' he said, again. 'My poor child—my pretty. And I had thought all this while to spare you! Well, you shall know all. Then, at least, you will pity poor Keawe; then you will understand how much he loved you in the past—that he dared Hell for your possession—and how much he loves you still (the poor condemned one), that he can yet call up a smile when he beholds you.'

With that, he told her all, even from the beginning.

'You have done this for me?' she cried. 'Ah, well, then what do I care!'—and she clasped and wept upon him.

'Ah, child!' said Keawe, 'and yet, when I consider of the fire of Hell, I care a good deal!'

'Never tell me,' said she; 'no man can be lost because he loved Kokua, and no other fault. I tell you, Keawe, I shall save you with these hands, or perish in your company. What! you loved me, and gave your soul, and you think I will not die to save you in return?'

'Ah, my dear! you might die a hundred times, and what difference would that make?' he cried, 'except to leave me lonely till the time comes of my damnation?'

'You know nothing,' said she. 'I was educated in a school in Honolulu; I am no common girl. And I tell you, I shall save my lover. What is this you say about a cent? But all the world is not American. In England they have a piece they call a farthing, which is about half a cent. Ah! sorrow!' she cried, 'that makes it scarcely better, for the buyer must be lost, and we shall find none so brave as my Keawe! But, then, there is France; they have a small coin there which they call a centime, and these go five to the cent or thereabout. We could not do better. Come, Keawe, let us go to the French islands; let us go to Tahiti, as fast as ships can bear us. There we have four centimes, three centimes, two centimes, one centime; four possible sales to come and go on; and two of us to push the bargain. Come, my Keawe! kiss me, and banish care. Kokua will defend you.'

'Gift of God!' he cried. 'I cannot think that God will punish me for desiring aught so good! Be it as you will, then; take me where you please: I put my life and my salvation in your hands.'

Early the next day Kokua was about her preparations. She took Keawe's chest that he went with sailoring; and first she put the bottle in a corner; and then packed it with the richest of their clothes and the bravest of the knick-knacks in the house. 'For,' said she, 'we must seem to be rich folks, or who will believe in the bottle?' All the time of her preparation she was as gay as a bird; only when she looked upon Keawe, the tears would spring in her eye, and she must run and kiss him. As for Keawe, a weight was off his soul; now that he had his secret shared, and some hope in front of him, he seemed like a new man, his feet went lightly on the earth, and his breath was good to him again. Yet was terror still at his elbow; and ever and again, as the wind blows out a taper, hope died in him, and he saw the flames toss and the red fire burn in Hell.

It was given out in the country they were gone pleasuring to the States, which was thought a strange thing, and yet not so strange as the truth, if any could have guessed it. So they went to Honolulu in the *Hall*, and thence in the *Umatilla* to San Francisco with a crowd of Haoles, and at San Francisco took their passage by the mail brigantine, the *Tropic Bird*, for Papeete, the chief place of the French in the south islands. Thither they came, after a pleasant voyage, on a fair day of the Trade Wind, and saw the reef with the surf breaking, and Motuiti with its palms, and the schooner riding within-side, and the white houses of the town low down along the shore among green trees, and overhead the mountains and the clouds of Tahiti, the wise island.

It was judged the most wise to hire a house, which they did accordingly, opposite the British Consul's, to make a great parade of money, and themselves conspicuous with carriages and horses. This it was very easy to do, so long as they had the bottle in their possession; for Kokua was more bold than Keawe, and, whenever she had a mind, called on the imp for twenty or a hundred dollars. At this rate they soon grew to be remarked in the town; and the strangers from Hawaii, their riding and their driving, the fine holokus and the rich lace of Kokua, became the matter of much talk.

They got on well after the first with the Tahitian language, which is indeed like to the Hawaiian, with a change of certain letters; and as soon as they had any freedom of speech, began to push the bottle. You are to consider it was not an easy subject to introduce; it was not easy to persuade people you were in earnest, when you offered to sell them for four centimes the spring of health and riches inexhaustible. It was necessary besides to explain the dangers of the bottle; and either people disbelieved the whole thing and laughed, or they thought the more of the darker part, became overcast with gravity, and drew away from Keawe and Kokua, as from persons who had dealings with the Devil. So far from gaining ground, these two began to find they were avoided in the town; the children ran away from them screaming, a thing intolerable to Kokua; Catholics crossed themselves as they went by; and all persons began with one accord to disengage themselves from their advances.

Depression fell upon their spirits. They would sit at night in their new house, after a day's weariness, and not exchange one word, or the silence would be broken by Kokua bursting suddenly into sobs. Sometimes they would pray together; sometimes they would have the bottle out upon the floor, and sit all evening watching how the shadow hovered in the midst. At such times they would be afraid to go to rest. It was long ere slumber came to them, and, if either dozed off, it would be to wake and find the other silently weeping in the dark, or, perhaps, to wake alone, the other having fled from the house and the neighbourhood of that bottle, to pace under the bananas in the little garden, or to wander on the beach by moonlight.

One night it was so when Kokua awoke. Keawe was gone. She felt in the bed and his place was cold. Then fear fell upon her, and she sat up in bed. A little moonshine filtered through the shutters. The room was bright, and she could spy the bottle on the floor. Outside it blew high, the great trees of the avenue cried aloud, and the fallen leaves rattled in the verandah. In the midst of this Kokua was aware of another sound; whether of a beast or of a man she could scarce tell, but it was as sad as death, and cut her to the soul. Softly she arose, set the door ajar, and looked forth into the moonlit yard. There, under the bananas, lay Keawe, his mouth in the dust, and as he lay he moaned.

It was Kokua's first thought to run forward and console him; her second potently withheld her. Keawe had borne himself before his wife like a brave man; it became her little in the hour of weakness to intrude upon his shame. With the thought she drew back into the house.

'Heaven!' she thought, 'how careless have I been—how weak! It is he, not I, that stands in this eternal peril; it was he, not I, that took the curse upon his soul. It is for my sake, and for the love of a crea-ture of so little worth and such poor help, that he now beholds so close to him the flames of Hell—ay, and smells the smoke of it, lying without there in the wind and moonlight. Am I so dull of spirit that never till now I have surmised my duty, or have I seen it before and turned aside? But now, at least, I take up my soul in both the hands of my affection; now I say farewell to the white steps of Heaven and the waiting faces of my friends. A love for a love, and let mine be equalled with Keawe's! A soul for a soul, and be it mine to perish!'

She was a deft woman with her hands, and was soon apparelled. She took in her hands the change—the precious centimes they kept ever at their side; for this coin is little used, and they had made provision at a Government office. When she was forth in the avenue clouds came on the wind, and the moon was blackened. The town slept, and she knew not whither to turn till she heard one coughing in the shadow of the trees.

'Old man,' said Kokua, 'what do you here abroad in the cold night?'

The old man could scarce express himself for coughing, but she made out that he was old and poor, and a stranger in the island.

'Will you do me a service?' said Kokua. 'As one stranger to another, and as an old man to a young woman, will you help a daughter of Hawaii?'

'Ah,' said the old man. 'So you are the witch from the eight islands, and even my old soul you seek to entangle. But I have heard of you, and defy your wickedness.'

'Sit down here,' said Kokua, 'and let me tell you a tale.' And she told him the story of Keawe from the beginning to the end.

'And now,' said she, 'I am his wife, whom he bought with his soul's welfare. And what should I do? If I went to him myself and offered to buy it, he would refuse. But if you go, he will sell it eagerly; I will await you here; you will buy it for four centimes, and I will buy it again for three. And the Lord strengthen a poor girl!'

'If you meant falsely,' said the old man, 'I think God would strike you dead.'

'He would!' cried Kokua. 'Be sure He would. I could not be so treacherous—God would not suffer it.'

'Give me the four centimes and await me here,' said the old man.

Now, when Kokua stood alone in the street, her spirit died. The wind roared in the trees, and it seemed to her the rushing of the flames of Hell; the shadows tossed in the light of the street lamp, and they seemed to her the snatching hands of evil ones. If she had had the strength, she must have run away, and if she had had the breath she must have screamed aloud; but, in truth, she could do neither, and stood and trembled in the avenue, like an affrighted child.

Then she saw the old man returning, and he had the bottle in his hand.

'I have done your bidding,' said he. 'I left your husband weeping like a child; tonight he will sleep easy.' And he held the bottle forth.

'Before you give it me,' Kokua panted, 'take the good with the evil—ask to be delivered from your cough.'

'I am an old man,' replied the other, 'and too near the gate of the grave to take a favour from the Devil. But what is this? Why do you not take the bottle? Do you hesitate?'

'Not hesitate!' cried Kokua. 'I am only weak. Give me a moment. It is my hand resists, my flesh shrinks back from the accursed thing. One moment only!'

The old man looked upon Kokua kindly. 'Poor child!' said he, 'you fear; your soul misgives you. Well, let me keep it. I am old, and can never more be happy in this world, and as for the next—'

'Give it me!' gasped Kokua. 'There is your money. Do you think I am so base as that? Give me the bottle.'

'God bless you, child,' said the old man.

Kokua concealed the bottle under her holoku, said farewell to the old man, and walked off along the avenue, she cared not whither. For all roads were now the same to her, and led equally to Hell. Sometimes she walked, and sometimes ran; sometimes she screamed out loud in the night, and sometimes lay by the wayside in the dust and wept. All that she had heard of Hell came back to her; she saw the flames blaze, and she smelt the smoke, and her flesh withered on the coals.

Near day she came to her mind again, and returned to the house. It was even as the old man said—Keawe slumbered like a child. Kokua stood and gazed upon his face.

'Now, my husband,' said she, 'it is your turn to sleep. When you wake it will be your turn to sing and laugh. But for poor Kokua, alas! that meant no evil—for poor Kokua no more sleep, no more singing, no more delight, whether in Earth or Heaven.'

With that she lay down in the bed by his side, and her misery was so extreme that she fell in a deep slumber instantly.

Late in the morning her husband woke her and gave her the good news. It seemed he was silly with delight, for he paid no heed to her distress, ill though she dissembled it. The words stuck in her mouth, it mattered not; Keawe did the speaking. She ate not a bite, but who was to observe it? for Keawe cleared the dish. Kokua saw and heard him, like some strange thing in a dream; there were times when she forgot or doubted, and put her hands to her brow; to know herself doomed and hear her husband babble, seemed so monstrous.

All the while Keawe was eating and talking, and planning the time of their return, and thanking her for saving him, and fondling her, and calling her the true helper after all. He laughed at the old man that was fool enough to buy that bottle.

'A worthy old man he seemed,' Keawe said. 'But no one can judge by appearances. For why did the old reprobate require the bottle?'

'My husband,' said Kokua, humbly, 'his purpose may have been good.'

Keawe laughed like an angry man.

'Fiddle-de-dee!' cried Keawe. 'An old rogue, I tell you; and an old ass to boot. For the bottle was hard enough to sell at four centimes; and at three it will be quite impossible. The margin is not broad enough, the thing begins to smell of scorching—brrr!' said he, and shuddered. 'It is true I bought it myself at a cent, when I knew not there were smaller coins. I was a fool for my pains; there will never be found another: and whoever has that bottle now will carry it to the pit.'

'O my husband!' said Kokua. 'Is it not a terrible thing to save oneself by the eternal ruin of another? It seems to me I could not laugh. I would be humbled. I would be filled with melancholy. I would pray for the poor holder.'

Then Keawe, because he felt the truth of what she said, grew the more angry. 'Heighty-teighty!' cried he. 'You may be filled with melancholy if you please. It is not the mind of a good wife. If you thought at all of me, you would sit shamed.'

Thereupon he went out, and Kokua was alone.

What chance had she to sell that bottle at two centimes? None, she perceived. And if she had any, here was her husband hurrying her away to a country where there was nothing lower than a cent. And here—on the morrow of her sacrifice—was her husband leaving her and blaming her.

She would not even try to profit by what time she had, but sat in the house, and now had the bottle out and viewed it with unutterable fear, and now, with loathing, hid it out of sight.

By-and-by, Keawe came back, and would have her take a drive. 'My husband, I am ill,' she said. 'I am out of heart. Excuse me, I can take no pleasure.'

Then was Keawe more wroth than ever. With her, because he thought she was brooding over the case of the old man; and with himself, because he thought she was right, and was ashamed to be so happy.

'This is your truth,' cried he, 'and this your affection! Your husband is just saved from eternal ruin, which he encountered for the love of you—and you can take no pleasure! Kokua, you have a disloyal heart.'

He went forth again furious, and wandered in the town all day. He met friends, and drank with them; they hired a carriage and drove into the country, and there drank again. All the time Keawe was ill at ease, because he was taking this pastime while his wife was sad, and because he knew in his heart that she was more right than he; and the knowledge made him drink the deeper.

Now there was an old brutal Haole drinking with him, one that had been a boatswain of a whaler, a runaway, a digger in gold mines, a convict in prisons. He had a low mind and a foul mouth; he loved to drink and to see others drunken; and he pressed the glass upon Keawe. Soon there was no more money in the company.

'Here, you!' says the boatswain, 'you are rich, you have been always saying. You have a bottle or some foolishness.'

'Yes,' says Keawe, 'I am rich; I will go back and get some money from my wife, who keeps it.'

'That's a bad idea, mate,' said the boatswain. 'Never you trust a petticoat with dollars. They're all as false as water; you keep an eye on her.'

Now, this word struck in Keawe's mind; for he was muddled with what he had been drinking.

'I should not wonder but she was false, indeed,' thought he. 'Why else should she be so cast down at my release? But I will show her I am not the man to be fooled. I will catch her in the act.'

Accordingly, when they were back in town, Keawe bade the boatswain wait for him at the corner, by the old calaboose, and went forward up the avenue alone to the door of his house. The night had come again; there was a light within, but never a sound; and Keawe crept about the corner, opened the back door softly, and looked in. There was Kokua on the floor, the lamp at her side; before her was a milk-white bottle, with a round belly and a long neck; and as she viewed it, Kokua wrung her hands.

A long time Keawe stood and looked in the doorway. At first he was struck stupid; and then fear fell upon him that the bargain had been made amiss, and the bottle had come back to him as it came at San Francisco; and at that his knees were loosened, and the fumes of the wine departed from his head like mists off a river in the morning. And then he had another thought; and it was a strange one, that made his cheeks to burn.

'I must make sure of this,' thought he.

So he closed the door, and went softly round the corner again, and then came noisily in, as though he were but now returned. And, lo! by the time he opened the front door no bottle was to be seen; and Kokua sat in a chair and started up like one awakened out of sleep.

'I have been drinking all day and making merry,' said Keawe. 'I have been with good companions, and now I only come back for money, and return to drink and carouse with them again.'

Both his face and voice were as stern as judgment, but Kokua was too troubled to observe.

'You do well to use your own, my husband,' said she, and her words trembled.

'O, I do well in all things,' said Keawe, and he went straight to the chest and took out money. But he looked besides in the corner where they kept the bottle, and there was no bottle there.

At that the chest heaved upon the floor like a sea-billow, and the house span about him like a wreath of smoke, for he saw he was lost now, and there was no escape. 'It is what I feared,' he thought. 'It is she who has bought it.'

And then he came to himself a little and rose up; but the sweat streamed on his face as thick as the rain and as cold as the wellwater.

'Kokua,' said he, 'I said to you today what ill became me. Now I return to carouse with my jolly companions,' and at that he laughed a little quietly. 'I will take more pleasure in the cup if you forgive me.'

She clasped his knees in a moment; she kissed his knees with flowing tears.

'O,' she cried, 'I asked but a kind word!'

'Let us never one think hardly of the other,' said Keawe, and was gone out of the house.

Now, the money that Keawe had taken was only some of that store of centime pieces they had laid in at their arrival. It was very sure he had no mind to be drinking. His wife had given her soul for him, now he must give his for hers; no other thought was in the world with him.

At the corner, by the old calaboose, there was the boatswain waiting.

'My wife has the bottle,' said Keawe, 'and, unless you help me to recover it, there can be no more money and no more liquor tonight.'

'You do not mean to say you are serious about that bottle?' cried the boatswain.

'There is the lamp,' said Keawe. 'Do I look as if I was jesting?'

'That is so,' said the boatswain. 'You look as serious as a ghost.'

'Well, then,' said Keawe, 'here are two centimes; you must go to my wife in the house, and offer her these for the bottle, which (if I am not much mistaken) she will give you instantly. Bring it to me here, and I will buy it back from you for one; for that is the law with this bottle, that it still must be sold for a less sum. But whatever you do, never breathe a word to her that you have come from me.'

'Mate, I wonder are you making a fool of me?' asked the boatswain.

'It will do you no harm if I am,' returned Keawe.

'That is so, mate,' said the boatswain.

'And if you doubt me,' added Keawe, 'you can try. As soon as you are clear of the house, wish to have your pocket full of money, or a bottle of the best rum, or what you please, and you will see the virtue of the thing.'

'Very well, Kanaka,' says the boatswain. 'I will try; but if you are having your fun out of me, I will take my fun out of you with a belaying pin.'

So the whaler-man went off up the avenue; and Keawe stood and waited. It was near the same spot where Kokua had waited the night before; but Keawe was more resolved, and never faltered in his purpose; only his soul was bitter with despair.

It seemed a long time he had to wait before he heard a voice singing in the darkness of the avenue. He knew the voice to be the boatswain's; but it was strange how drunken it appeared upon a sudden.

Next, the man himself came stumbling into the light of the lamp. He had the Devil's bottle buttoned in his coat; another bottle was in his hand; and even as he came in view he raised it to his mouth and drank.

'You have it,' said Keawe. 'I see that.'

'Hands off!' cried the boatswain, jumping back. 'Take a step near me, and I'll smash your mouth. You thought you could make a cat's-paw of me, did you?'

'What do you mean?' cried Keawe.

'Mean?' cried the boatswain. 'This is a pretty good bottle, this is; that's what I mean. How I got it for two centimes I can't make out; but I'm sure you shan't have it for one.'

'You mean you won't sell?' gasped Keawe.

'No, SIR!' cried the boatswain. 'But I'll give you a drink of the rum, if you like.'

'I tell you,' said Keawe, 'the man who has that bottle goes to Hell.'

'I reckon I'm going anyway,' returned the sailor; 'and this bottle's the best thing to go with I've struck yet. No, sir!' he cried again, 'this is my bottle now, and you can go and fish for another.'

'Can this be true?' Keawe cried. 'For your own sake, I beseech you, sell it me!'

'I don't value any of your talk,' replied the boatswain. 'You thought I was a flat; now you see I'm not; and there's an end. If you won't have a swallow of the rum, I'll have one myself. Here's your health, and goodnight to you!'

So off he went down the avenue towards town, and there goes the bottle out of the story.

But Keawe ran to Kokua light as the wind; and great was their joy that night; and great, since then, has been the peace of all their days in the Bright House.

The Sinking Ship

'Fast, Mr Spoker?' asked the Captain. 'The expression is a strange one, for time (if you will think of it) is only relative.'

'SIR,' SAID the first lieutenant, bursting into the Captain's cabin, 'the ship is going down.'

'Very well, Mr Spoker,' said the Captain; 'but that is no reason for going about half-shaved. Exercise your mind a moment, Mr Spoker, and you will see that to the philosophic eye there is nothing new in our position: the ship (if she is to go down at all) may be said to have been going down since she was launched.'

'She is settling fast,' said the first lieutenant, as he returned from shaving.

'Fast, Mr Spoker?' asked the Captain. 'The expression is a strange one, for time (if you will think of it) is only relative.'

'Sir,' said the lieutenant, 'I think it is scarcely worth while to embark in such a discussion when we shall all be in Davy Jones's Locker in ten minutes.'

'By parity of reasoning,' returned the Captain gently, 'it would never be worth while to begin any inquiry of importance; the odds are always overwhelming that we must die before we shall have brought it to an end. You have not considered, Mr Spoker, the situation of man,' said the Captain, smiling, and shaking his head.

'I am much more engaged in considering the position of the ship,' said Mr Spoker.

'Spoken like a good officer,' replied the Captain, laying his hand on the lieutenant's shoulder.

On deck they found the men had broken into the spirit-room, and were fast getting drunk.

'My men,' said the Captain, 'there is no sense in this. The ship is going down, you will tell me, in ten minutes: well, and what then? To the philosophic eye, there is nothing new in our position. All our lives long, we may have been about to break a blood-vessel or to be struck by lightning, not merely in ten minutes, but in ten seconds; and that has not prevented us from eating dinner, no, nor from putting money in the Savings Bank. I assure you, with my hand on my heart, I fail to comprehend your attitude.'

The men were already too far gone to pay much heed.

'This is a very painful sight, Mr Spoker,' said the Captain.

'And yet to the philosophic eye, or whatever it is,' replied the first lieutenant, 'they may be said to have been getting drunk since they came aboard.'

'I do not know if you always follow my thought, Mr Spoker,' returned the Captain gently. 'But let us proceed.'

In the powder magazine they found an old salt smoking his pipe.

'Good God,' cried the Captain, 'what are you about?'

'Well, sir,' said the old salt, apologetically, 'they told me as she were going down.'

'And suppose she were?' said the Captain. 'To the philosophic eye, there would be nothing new in our position. Life, my old ship-mate, life, at any moment and in any view, is as dangerous as a sinking ship; and yet it is man's handsome fashion to carry umbrellas, to wear indiarubber over-shoes, to begin vast works, and to conduct himself in every way as if he might hope to be eternal. And for my own poor part I should despise the man who, even on board a sinking ship, should omit to take a pill or to wind up his watch. That, my friend, would not be the human attitude.'

'I beg pardon, sir,' said Mr Spoker. 'But what is precisely the difference between shaving in a sinking ship and smoking in a powder magazine?'

'Or doing anything at all in any conceivable circumstances?' cried the Captain. 'Perfectly conclusive; give me a cigar!'

Two minutes afterwards the ship blew up with a glorious detonation.

The Yellow Paint

'That is none of my business,' said the physician.

IN A certain city there lived a physician who sold yellow paint. This was of so singular a virtue that whoso was bedaubed with it from head to heel was set free from the dangers of life, and the bondage of sin, and the fear of death for ever. So the physician said in his prospectus; and so said all the citizens in the city; and there was nothing more urgent in men's hearts than to be properly painted themselves, and nothing they took more delight in than to see others painted. There was in the same city a young man of a very good family but of a somewhat reckless life, who had reached the age of manhood, and would have nothing to say to the paint: 'Tomorrow was soon enough,' said he; and when the morrow came he would still put it off. So he might have continued to do until his death; only, he had a friend of about his own age and much of his own manners; and this youth, taking a walk in the public street, with not one fleck of paint upon his body, was suddenly run down by a water-cart and cut off in the heyday of his nakedness. This shook the other to the soul; so that I never beheld a man more earnest to be painted; and on the very same evening, in the presence of all his family, to appropriate music, and himself weeping aloud, he received three complete coats and a touch of varnish on the top. The physician (who was himself affected even to tears) protested he had never done a job so thorough.

Some two months afterwards, the young man was carried on a stretcher to the physician's house.

'What is the meaning of this?' he cried, as soon as the door was opened. 'I was to be set free from all the dangers of life; and here have I been run down by that self-same water-cart, and my leg is broken.'

'Dear me!' said the physician. 'This is very sad. But I perceive I must explain to you the action of my paint. A broken bone is a mighty small affair at the worst of it; and it belongs to a class of accident to which my paint is quite inapplicable. Sin, my dear young friend, sin is the sole calamity that a wise man should apprehend; it is against sin that I have fitted you out; and when you come to be tempted, you will give me news of my paint.'

'O!' said the young man, 'I did not understand that, and it seems rather disappointing. But I have no doubt all is for the best; and in the meanwhile, I shall be obliged to you if you will set my leg.'

'That is none of my business,' said the physician; 'but if your bearers will carry you round the corner to the surgeon's, I feel sure he will afford relief.'

Some three years later, the young man came running to the physician's house in a great perturbation. 'What is the meaning of this?' he cried. 'Here was I to be set free from the bondage of sin; and I have just committed forgery, arson and murder.'

'Dear me!' said the physician. 'This is very serious. Off with your clothes at once.' And as soon as the young man had stripped, he examined him from head to foot. 'No,' he cried with great relief, 'there is not a flake broken. Cheer up, my young friend, your paint is as good as new.'

'Good God!' cried the young man, 'and what then can be the use of it?'

'Why,' said the physician, 'I perceive I must explain to you the nature of the action of my paint. It does not exactly prevent sin; it extenuates instead the painful consequences. It is not so much for this world, as for the next; it is not against life; in short, it is against death that I have fitted you out. And when you come to die, you will give me news of my paint.'

'O!' cried the young man, 'I had not understood that, and it seems a little disappointing. But there is no doubt all is for the best: and in the meanwhile, I shall be obliged if you will help me to undo the evil I have brought on innocent persons.'

'That is none of my business,' said the physician; 'but if you will go round the corner to the police office, I feel sure it will afford you relief to give yourself up.'

Six weeks later, the physician was called to the town gaol.

'What is the meaning of this?' cried the young man. 'Here am I literally crusted with your paint; and I have broken my leg, and committed all the crimes in the calendar, and must be hanged tomorrow; and am in the meanwhile in a fear so extreme that I lack words to picture it.'

'Dear me!' said the physician. 'This is really amazing. Well, well; perhaps, if you had not been painted, you would have been more frightened still.'

*Faith, Half-Faith
and No Faith At All*

'We find the proofs of our religion in the works of nature,' said he, and beat his breast.

IN THE ancient days there went three men upon pilgrimage; one was a priest, and one was a virtuous person, and the third was an old rover with his axe.

As they went, the priest spoke about the grounds of faith.

'We find the proofs of our religion in the works of nature,' said he, and beat his breast.

'That is true,' said the virtuous person.

'The peacock has a scrannel voice,' said the priest, 'as has been laid down always in our books. How cheering!' he cried, in a voice like one that wept. 'How comforting!'

'I require no such proofs,' said the virtuous person.

'Then you have no reasonable faith,' said the priest.

'Great is the right, and shall prevail!' cried the virtuous person. 'There is loyalty in my soul; be sure, there is loyalty in the mind of Odin.'

'These are but playings upon words,' returned the priest. 'A sackful of such trash is nothing to the peacock.'

Just then they passed a country farm, where there was a peacock seated on a rail; and the bird opened its mouth and sang with the voice of a nightingale.

'Where are you now?' asked the virtuous person. 'And yet this shakes not me! Great is the truth, and shall prevail!'

'The devil fly away with that peacock!' said the priest; and he was downcast for a mile or two.

But presently they came to a shrine, where a Fakeer performed miracles.

'Ah!' said the priest, 'here are the true grounds of faith. The peacock was but an adminicle. This is the base of our religion.'

And he beat upon his breast, and groaned like one with colic.

'Now to me,' said the virtuous person, 'all this is as little to the purpose as the peacock. I believe because I see the right is great and must prevail; and this Fakeer might carry on with his conjuring tricks till doomsday, and it would not play bluff upon a man like me.'

Now at this the Fakeer was so much incensed that his hand trembled; and, lo! in the midst of a miracle the cards fell from up his sleeve.

'Where are you now?' asked the virtuous person. 'And yet it shakes not me!'

'The devil fly away with the Fakeer!' cried the priest. 'I really do not see the good of going on with this pilgrimage.'

'Cheer up!' cried the virtuous person. 'Great is the right, and shall prevail!'

'If you are quite sure it will prevail,' says the priest. 'I pledge my word for that,' said the virtuous person.

So the other began to go on again with a better heart.

At last one came running, and told them all was lost: that the powers of darkness had besieged the Heavenly Mansions, that Odin was to die, and evil triumph.

'I have been grossly deceived,' cried the virtuous person.

'All is lost now,' said the priest.

'I wonder if it is too late to make it up with the Devil?' said the virtuous person.

'O, I hope not,' said the priest. 'And at any rate we can but try. But what are you doing with your axe?' says he to the rover.

'I am off to die with Odin,' said the rover.

The House of Eld

'Ah, poor souls, if they but knew the joys of being fettered!'

SO SOON as the child began to speak, the gyve was riveted; and the boys and girls limped about their play like convicts. Doubtless it was more pitiable to see and more painful to bear in youth; but even the grown folk, besides being very unhandy on their feet, were often sick with ulcers.

About the time when Jack was ten years old, many strangers began to journey through that country. These he beheld going lightly by on the long roads, and the thing amazed him. 'I wonder how it comes,' he asked, 'that all these strangers are so quick afoot, and we must drag about our fetter?'

'My dear boy,' said his uncle, the catechist, 'do not complain about your fetter, for it is the only thing that makes life worth living. None are happy, none are good, none are respectable, that are not gyved like us. And I must tell you, besides, it is very dangerous talk. If you grumble of your iron, you will have no luck; if ever you take it off, you will be instantly smitten by a thunderbolt.'

'Are there no thunderbolts for these strangers?' asked Jack.

'Jupiter is longsuffering to the benighted,' returned the catechist.

'Upon my word, I could wish I had been less fortunate,' said Jack. 'For if I had been born benighted, I might now be going free; and it cannot be denied the iron is inconvenient, and the ulcer hurts.'

'Ah!' cried his uncle, 'do not envy the heathen! Theirs is a sad lot! Ah, poor souls, if they but knew the joys of being fettered! Poor souls, my heart yearns for them. But the truth is they are vile, odious, insolent, ill-conditioned, stinking brutes, not truly human—for what is a man without a fetter?—and you cannot be too particular not to touch or speak with them.'

After this talk, the child would never pass one of the unfettered on the road but what he spat at him and called him names, which was the practice of the children in that part.

It chanced one day, when he was fifteen, he went into the woods, and the ulcer pained him. It was a fair day, with a blue sky; all the birds were singing; but Jack nursed his foot. Presently, another song began; it sounded like the singing of a person, only far more gay; at the same time there was a beating on the earth. Jack put aside the leaves; and there was a lad of his own village, leaping, and dancing and singing to himself in a green dell; and on the grass beside him lay the dancer's iron.

'O!' cried Jack, 'you have your fetter off!'

'For God's sake, don't tell your uncle!' cried the lad.

'If you fear my uncle,' returned Jack, 'why do you not fear the thunderbolt?'

'That is only an old wives' tale,' said the other. 'It is only told to children. Scores of us come here among the woods and dance for nights together, and are none the worse.'

This put Jack in a thousand new thoughts. He was a grave lad; he had no mind to dance himself; he wore his fetter manfully, and tended his ulcer without complaint. But he loved the less to be deceived or to see others cheated. He began to lie in wait for heathen travellers, at covert parts of the road, and in the dusk of the day, so that he might speak with them unseen; and these were greatly taken with their wayside questioner, and told him things of weight. The wearing of gyves (they said) was no command of Jupiter's. It was the contrivance of a white-faced thing, a sorcerer, that dwelt in that country in the Wood of Eld. He was one like Glaucus that could change his shape, yet he could be always told; for when he was crossed, he gobbled like a turkey. He had three lives; but the third smiting would make an end of him indeed; and with that his house of sorcery would vanish, the gyves fall, and the villagers take hands and dance like children.

'And in your country?' Jack would ask.

But at this the travellers, with one accord, would put him off; until Jack began to suppose there was no land entirely happy. Or, if there were, it must be one that kept its folk at home; which was natural enough.

But the case of the gyves weighed upon him. The sight of the children limping stuck in his eyes; the groans of such as dressed their ulcers haunted him. And it came at last in his mind that he was born to free them.

There was in that village a sword of heavenly forgery, beaten upon Vulcan's anvil. It was never used but in the temple, and then the flat of it only; and it hung on a nail by the catechist's chimney. Early one night, Jack rose, and took the sword, and was gone out of the house and the village in the darkness.

All night he walked at a venture; and when day came, he met strangers going to the fields. Then he asked after the Wood of eld and the house of sorcery; and one said north, and one south; until Jack saw that they deceived him. So then, when he asked his way of any man, he showed the bright sword naked; and at that the gyve on the man's ankle rang, and answered in his stead; and the word was still *Straight on*. But the man, when his gyve spoke, spat and struck at Jack, and threw stones at him as he went away; so that his head was broken.

So he came to that wood, and entered in, and he was aware of a house in a low place, where funguses grew, and the trees met, and the steaming of the marsh arose about it like a smoke. It was a fine house, and a very rambling; some parts of it were ancient like the hills, and some but of yesterday, and none finished; and all the ends of it were open, so that you could go in from every side. Yet it was in good repair, and all the chimneys smoked.

Jack went in through the gable; and there was one room after another, all bare, but all furnished in part, so that a man could dwell there; and in each there was a fire burning, where a man could warm himself, and a table spread where he might eat. But Jack saw nowhere any living creature; only the bodies of some stuffed.

'This is a hospitable house,' said Jack; 'but the ground must be quaggy underneath, for at every step the building quakes.'

He had gone some time in the house, when he began to be hungry. Then he looked at the food, and at first he was afraid; but he bared the sword, and by the shining of the sword, it seemed the food was honest. So he took the courage to sit down and eat, and he was refreshed in mind and body.

'This is strange,' thought he, 'that in the house of sorcery there should be food so wholesome.'

As he was yet eating, there came into that room the appearance of his uncle, and Jack was afraid because he had taken the sword.

But his uncle was never more kind, and sat down to meat with him, and praised him because he had taken the sword. Never had these two been more pleasantly together, and Jack was full of love to the man.

'It was very well done,' said his uncle, 'to take the sword and come yourself into the House of Eld; a good thought and a brave deed. But now you are satisfied; and we may go home to dinner arm in arm.'

'O, dear, no!' said Jack. 'I am not satisfied yet.'

'How!' cried his uncle. 'Are you not warmed by the fire? Does not this food sustain you?'

'I see the food to be wholesome,' said Jack; 'and still it is no proof that a man should wear a gyve on his right leg.'

Now at this the appearance of his uncle gobbled like a turkey.

'Jupiter!' cried Jack, 'is this the sorcerer?'

His hand held back and his heart failed him for the love he bore his uncle; but he heaved up the sword and smote the appearance on the head; and it cried out aloud with the voice of his uncle; and fell to the ground; and a little bloodless white thing fled from the room.

The cry rang in Jack's ears, and his knees smote together, and conscience cried upon him; and yet he was strengthened, and there woke in his bones the lust of that enchanter's blood. 'If the gyves are to fall,' said he, 'I must go through with this, and when I get home I shall find my uncle dancing.'

So he went on after the bloodless thing. In the way, he met the appearance of his father; and his father was incensed, and railed upon him, and called to him upon his duty, and bade him be home, while there was yet time. 'For you can still,' said he, 'be home by sunset; and then all will be forgiven.'

'God knows,' said Jack, 'I fear your anger; but yet your anger does not prove that a man should wear a gyve on his right leg.'

And at that the appearance of his father gobbled like a turkey.

'Ah, heaven,' cried Jack, 'the sorcerer again!'

The blood ran backward in his body and his joints rebelled against him for the love he bore his father; but he heaved up the sword, and plunged it in the heart of the appearance; and the appearance cried out aloud with the voice of his father; and fell to the ground; and a little bloodless white thing fled from the room.

The cry rang in Jack's ears, and his soul was darkened; but now rage came to him. 'I have done what I dare not think upon,' said he. 'I will go to an end with it, or perish. And when I get home, I pray God this may be a dream, and I may find my father dancing.'

So he went on after the bloodless thing that had escaped; and in the way he met the appearance of his mother, and she wept. 'What have you done?' she cried. 'What is this that you have done? O, come home (where you may be by bedtime) ere you do more ill to me and mine; for it is enough to smite my brother and your father.'

'Dear mother, it is not these that I have smitten,' said Jack; 'it was but the enchanter in their shape. And even if I had, it would not prove that a man should wear a gyve on his right leg.'

And at this the appearance gobbled like a turkey.

He never knew how he did that; but he swung the sword on the one side, and clove the appearance through the midst; and it cried out aloud with the voice of his mother; and fell to the ground; and with the fall of it, the house was gone from over Jack's head, and he stood alone in the woods, and the gyve was loosened from his leg.

'Well,' said he, 'the enchanter is now dead, and the fetter gone.' But the cries rang in his soul, and the day was like night to him. 'This has been a sore business,' said he. 'Let me get forth out of the wood, and see the good that I have done to others.'

He thought to leave the fetter where it lay, but when he turned to go, his mind was otherwise. So he stooped and put the gyve in his bosom; and the rough iron galled him as he went, and his bosom bled.

Now when he was forth of the wood upon the highway, he met folk returning from the field; and those he met had no fetter on the right leg, but, behold! they had one upon the left. Jack asked them what it signified; and they said, 'That was the new wear, for the old was found to be a superstition.' Then he looked at them nearly; and there was a new ulcer on the left ankle, and the old one on the right was not yet healed.

'Now, may God forgive me!' cried Jack. 'I would I were well home.'

And when he was home, there lay his uncle smitten on the head, and his father pierced through the heart, and his mother cloven through the midst. And he sat in the lone house and wept beside the bodies.

MORAL:

Old is the tree and the fruit good,
Very old and thick the wood.
Woodman, is your courage stout?
Beware! the root is wrapped about
Your mother's heart, your father's bones;
And like the mandrake comes with groans.

The Touchstone

He had two sons; and the younger son was a boy after his heart, but the elder was one whom he feared.

THE KING was a man that stood well before the world; his smile was sweet as clover, but his soul withinsides was as little as a pea. He had two sons; and the younger son was a boy after his heart, but the elder was one whom he feared. It befell one morning that the drum sounded in the dun before it was yet day; and the King rode with his two sons, and a brave array behind them. They rode two hours, and came to the foot of a brown mountain that was very steep.

'Where do we ride?' said the elder son.

'Across this brown mountain,' said the King, and smiled to himself.

'My father knows what he is doing,' said the younger son.

And they rode two hours more, and came to the sides of a black river that was wondrous deep.

'And where do we ride?' asked the elder son.

'Over this black river,' said the King, and smiled to himself.

'My father knows what he is doing,' said the younger son.

And they rode all that day, and about the time of the sunsetting came to the side of a lake, where was a great dun.

'It is here we ride,' said the King; 'to a King's house, and a priest's, and a house where you will learn much.'

At the gates of the dun, the King who was a priest met them; and he was a grave man, and beside him stood his daughter, and she was as fair as the morn, and one that smiled and looked down.

'These are my two sons,' said the first King.

'And here is my daughter,' said the King who was a priest.

'She is a wonderful fine maid,' said the first King, 'and I like her manner of smiling.'

'They are wonderful well-grown lads,' said the second, 'and I like their gravity.'

And then the two Kings looked at each other, and said, 'The thing may come about.'

And in the meanwhile the two lads looked upon the maid, and the one grew pale and the other red; and the maid looked upon the ground smiling.

'Here is the maid that I shall marry,' said the elder. 'For I think she smiled upon me.'

But the younger plucked his father by the sleeve. 'Father,' said he, 'a word in your ear. If I find favour in your sight, might not I wed this maid, for I think she smiles upon me?'

'A word in yours,' said the King his father. 'Waiting is good hunting, and when the teeth are shut the tongue is at home.'

Now they were come into the dun, and feasted; and this was a great house, so that the lads were astonished; and the King that was a priest sat at the end of the board and was silent, so that the lads were filled with reverence; and the maid served them smiling with downcast eyes, so that their hearts were enlarged.

Before it was day, the elder son arose, and he found the maid at her weaving, for she was a diligent girl. 'Maid,' quoth he, 'I would fain marry you.'

'You must speak with my father,' said she, and she looked upon the ground smiling, and became like the rose.

'Her heart is with me,' said the elder son, and he went down to the lake and sang.

A little after came the younger son. 'Maid,' quoth he, 'if our fathers were agreed, I would like well to marry you.'

'You can speak to my father,' said she; and looked upon the ground, and smiled and grew like the rose.

'She is a dutiful daughter,' said the younger son, 'she will make an obedient wife.' And then he thought, 'What shall I do?' and he remembered the King her father was a priest; so he went into the temple, and sacrificed a weasel and a hare.

Presently the news got about; and the two lads and the first King were called into the presence of the King who was a priest, where he sat upon the high seat.

'Little I reck of gear,' said the King who was a priest, 'and little of power. For we live here among the shadow of things, and the heart is sick of seeing them. And we stay here in the wind like raiment drying, and the heart is weary of the wind. But one thing I love, and that is truth; and for one thing will I give my daughter, and that is the trial stone. For in the light of that stone the seeming goes, and the being shows, and all things besides are worthless. Therefore, lads, if ye would wed my daughter, out foot, and bring me the stone of touch, for that is the price of her.'

'A word in your ear,' said the younger son to his father. 'I think we do very well without this stone.'

'A word in yours,' said the father. 'I am of your way of thinking; but when the teeth are shut the tongue is at home.' And he smiled to the King that was a priest.

But the elder son got to his feet, and called the King that was a priest by the name of father. 'For whether I marry the maid or no, I will call you by that word for the love of your wisdom; and even now I will ride forth and search the world for the stone of touch.' So he said farewell, and rode into the world.

'I think I will go, too,' said the younger son, 'if I can have your leave. For my heart goes out to the maid.'

'You will ride home with me,' said his father.

So they rode home, and when they came to the dun, the King had his son into his treasury. 'Here,' said he, 'is the touchstone which shows truth; for there is no truth but plain truth; and if you will look in this, you will see yourself as you are.'

And the younger son looked in it, and saw his face as it were the face of a beardless youth, and he was well enough pleased; for the thing was a piece of a mirror.

'Here is no such great thing to make a work about,' said he; 'but if it will get me the maid I shall never complain. But what a fool is my brother to ride into the world, and the thing all the while at home!'

So they rode back to the other dun, and showed the mirror to the King that was a priest; and when he had looked in it, and seen himself like a King, and his house like a King's house, and all things like themselves, he cried out and blessed God. 'For now I know,' said he, 'there is no truth but the plain truth; and I am a King indeed, although my heart misgave me.' And he pulled down his temple, and built a new one; and then the younger son was married to the maid.

In the meantime the elder son rode into the world to find the touchstone of the trial of truth; and whenever he came to a place of habitation, he would ask the men if they had heard of it. And in every place the men answered: 'Not only have we heard of it, but we alone, of all men, possess the thing itself, and it hangs in the side of our chimney to this day.' Then would the elder son be glad, and beg for a sight of it. And sometimes it would be a piece of mirror, that showed the seeming of things; and then he would say, 'This can never be, for there should be more than seeming.' And sometimes it would be a lump of coal, which showed nothing; and then he would say, 'This can never be, for at least there is the seeming.' And sometimes it would be a touchstone indeed, beautiful in hue, adorned with polishing, the light inhabiting its sides; and when he found this, he would beg the thing, and the persons of that place would give it him, for all men were very generous of that gift; so that at the last he had his wallet full of them, and they chinked together when he rode; and when he halted by the side of the way he would take them out and try them, till his head turned like the sails upon a windmill.

'A murrain upon this business!' said the elder son, 'for I perceive no end to it. Here I have the red, and here the blue and the green; and to me they seem all excellent, and yet shame each other. A murrain on the trade! If it were not for the King that is a priest and whom I have called my father, and if it were not for the fair maid of the dun that makes my mouth to sing and my heart enlarge, I would even tumble them all into the salt sea, and go home and be a King like other folk.'

But he was like the hunter that has seen a stag upon a mountain, so that the night may fall, and the fire be kindled, and the lights shine in his house; but desire of that stag is single in his bosom.

Now after many years the elder son came upon the sides of the salt sea; and it was night, and a savage place, and the clamour of the sea was loud. There he was aware of a house, and a man that sat there by the light of a candle, for he had no fire. Now the elder son came in to him, and the man gave him water to drink, for he had no bread; and wagged his head when he was spoken to, for he had no words.

'Have you the touchstone of truth?' asked the elder son and when the man had wagged his head, 'I might have known that,' cried the elder son. 'I have here a wallet full of them!' And with that he laughed, although his heart was weary.

And with that the man laughed too, and with the fuff of his laughter the candle went out.

'Sleep,' said the man, 'for now I think you have come far enough; and your quest is ended, and my candle is out.'

Now when the morning came, the man gave him a clear pebble in his hand, and it had no beauty and no colour; and the elder son looked upon it scornfully and shook his head; and he went away, for it seemed a small affair to him.

All that day he rode, and his mind was quiet, and the desire of the chase allayed. 'How if this poor pebble be the touchstone, after all?' said he: and he got down from his horse, and emptied forth his wallet by the side of the way. Now, in the light of each other, all the touchstones lost their hue and fire, and withered like stars at morning; but in the light of the pebble, their beauty remained, only the pebble was the most bright. And the elder son smote upon his brow. 'How if this be the truth?' he cried, 'that all are a little true?' And he took the pebble, and turned its light upon the heavens, and they deepened about him like the pit; and he turned it on the hills, and the hills were cold and rugged, but life ran in their sides so that his own life bounded; and he turned it on the dust, and he beheld the dust with joy and terror; and he turned it on himself, and kneeled down and prayed.

'Now, thanks be to God,' said the elder son, 'I have found the touchstone; and now I may turn my reins, and ride home to the King and to the maid of the dun that makes my mouth to sing and my heart enlarge.'

Now when he came to the dun, he saw children playing by the gate where the King had met him in the old days; and this stayed his pleasure, for he thought in his heart, 'It is here my children should be playing.' And when he came into the hall, there was his brother on the high seat and the maid beside him; and at that his anger rose, for he thought in his heart, 'It is I that should be sitting there, and the maid beside me.'

'Who are you?' said his brother. 'And what make you in the dun?'

'I am your elder brother,' he replied. 'And I am come to marry the maid, for I have brought the touchstone of truth.'

Then the younger brother laughed aloud. 'Why,' said he, 'I found the touchstone years ago, and married the maid, and there are our children playing at the gate.'

Now at this the elder brother grew as grey as the dawn. 'I pray you have dealt justly,' said he, 'for I perceive my life is lost.'

'Justly?' quoth the younger brother. 'It becomes you ill, that are a restless man and a runagate, to doubt my justice, or the King my father's, that are sedentary folk and known in the land.'

'Nay,' said the elder brother, 'you have all else, have patience also; and suffer me to say the world is full of touchstones, and it appears not easily which is true.'

'I have no shame of mine,' said the younger brother. 'There it is, and look in it.'

So the elder brother looked in the mirror, and he was sore amazed; for he was an old man, and his hair was white upon his head; and he sat down in the hall and wept aloud.

'Now,' said the younger brother, 'see what a fool's part you have played, that ran over all the world to seek what was lying in our father's treasury, and came back an old carle for the dogs to bark at, and without chick or child. And I that was dutiful and wise sit here crowned with virtues and pleasures, and happy in the light of my hearth.'

'Methinks you have a cruel tongue,' said the elder brother; and he pulled out the clear pebble and turned its light on his brother; and behold the man was lying, his soul was shrunk into the smallness of a pea, and his heart was a bag of little fears like scorpions, and love was dead in his bosom. And at that the elder brother cried out aloud, and turned the light of the pebble on the maid, and, lo! she was but a mask of a woman, and withinsides she was quite dead, and she smiled as a clock ticks, and knew not wherefore.

'O, well,' said the elder brother, 'I perceive there is both good and bad. So fare ye all as well as ye may in the dun; but I will go forth into the world with my pebble in my pocket.'

The Poor Thing

'Be plain with me,' said the man, 'and tell me your name and of your nature.'

'My name,' quoth the other, 'is not yet named, and my nature not yet sure.'

THERE WAS a man in the islands who fished for his bare belly-ful, and took his life in his hands to go forth upon the sea between four planks. But though he had much ado, he was merry of heart; and the gulls heard him laugh when the spray met him. And though he had little lore, he was sound of spirit; and when the fish came to his hook in the mid-waters, he blessed God without weighing. He was bitter poor in goods and bitter ugly of counte-nance, and he had no wife.

It fell in the time of the fishing that the man awoke in his house about the midst of the afternoon. The fire burned in the midst, and the smoke went up and the sun came down by the chimney. And the man was aware of the likeness of one that warmed his hands at the red peats.

'I greet you,' said the man, 'in the name of God.'

'I greet you,' said he that warmed his hands, 'but not in the name of God, for I am none of His; nor in the name of Hell, for I am not of Hell. For I am but a bloodless thing, less than wind and lighter than a sound, and the wind goes through me like a net, and I am broken by a sound and shaken by the cold.'

'Be plain with me,' said the man, 'and tell me your name and of your nature.'

'My name,' quoth the other, 'is not yet named, and my nature not yet sure. For I am part of a man; and I was a part of your fathers, and went out to fish and fight with them in the ancient days. But now is my turn not yet come; and I wait until you have a wife, and then shall I be in your son, and a brave part of him, rejoicing manfully to launch the boat into the surf, skilful to direct the helm, and a man of might where the ring closes and the blows are going.'

'This is a marvellous thing to hear,' said the man; 'and if you are indeed to be my son, I fear it will go ill with you; for I am bitter poor in goods and bitter ugly in face, and I shall never get me a wife if I live to the age of eagles.'

'All this have I come to remedy, my father,' said the Poor Thing; 'for we must go this night to the little isle of sheep, where our fathers lie in the dead-cairn, and tomorrow to the earl's hall, and there shall you find a wife by my providing.'

So the man rose and put forth his boat at the time of the sunsetting; and the Poor Thing sat in the prow, and the spray blew through his bones like snow, and the wind whistled in his teeth, and the boat dipped not with the weight of him.

'I am fearful to see you, my son,' said the man. 'For methinks you are no thing of God.'

'It is only the wind that whistles in my teeth,' said the Poor Thing, 'and there is no life in me to keep it out.'

So they came to the little isle of sheep, where the surf burst all about it in the midst of the sea, and it was all green with bracken, and all wet with dew, and the moon enlightened it. They ran the boat into a cove, and set foot to land; and the man came heavily behind among the rocks in the deepness of the bracken, but the Poor Thing went before him like a smoke in the light of the moon. So they came to the dead-cairn, and they laid their ears to the stones; and the dead complained withinsides like a swarm of bees: 'Time was that marrow was in our bones, and strength in our sinews; and the thoughts of our head were clothed upon with acts and the words of men. But now are we broken in sunder, and the bonds of our bones are loosed, and our thoughts lie in the dust.'

Then said the Poor Thing: 'Charge them that they give you the virtue they withheld.'

And the man said: 'Bones of my fathers, greeting! for I am sprung of your loins. And now, behold, I break open the piled stones of your cairn, and I let in the moon between your ribs. Count it well done, for it was to be; and give me what I come seeking in the name of blood and in the name of God.'

And the spirits of the dead stirred in the cairn like ants; and they spoke: 'You have broken the roof of our cairn and let in the moon between our ribs; and you have the strength of the still-living. But what virtue have we? what power? or what jewel here in the dust with us, that any living man should covet or receive it? for we are less than nothing. But we tell you one thing, speaking with many voices like bees, that the way is plain before all like the grooves of launching: So forth into life and fear not, for so did we all in the ancient ages.' And their voices passed away like an eddy in a river.

'Now,' said the Poor Thing, 'they have told you a lesson, but make them give you a gift. Stoop your hand among the bones without drawback, and you shall find their treasure.'

So the man stooped his hand, and the dead laid hold upon it many and faint like ants; but he shook them off, and behold, what he brought up in his hand was the shoe of a horse, and it was rusty.

'It is a thing of no price,' quoth the man, 'for it is rusty.'

'We shall see that,' said the Poor Thing; 'for in my thought it is a good thing to do what our fathers did, and to keep what they kept without question. And in my thought one thing is as good as another in this world; and a shoe of a horse will do.'

Now they got into their boat with the horseshoe, and when the dawn was come they were aware of the smoke of the earl's town and the bells of the Kirk that beat. So they set foot to shore; and the man went up to the market among the fishers over against the palace and the Kirk; and he was bitter poor and bitter ugly, and he had never a fish to sell, but only a shoe of a horse in his creel, and it rusty.

'Now,' said the Poor Thing, 'do so and so, and you shall find a wife and I a mother.'

It befell that the Earl's daughter came forth to go into the Kirk upon her prayers; and when she saw the poor man stand in the market with only the shoe of a horse, and it rusty, it came in her mind it should be a thing of price.

'What is that?' quoth she.

'It is a shoe of a horse,' said the man.

'And what is the use of it?' quoth the Earl's daughter.

'It is for no use,' said the man.

'I may not believe that,' said she; 'else why should you carry it?'

'I do so,' said he, 'because it was so my fathers did in the ancient ages; and I have neither a better reason nor a worse.'

Now the Earl's daughter could not find it in her mind to believe him. 'Come,' quoth she, 'sell me this, for I am sure it is a thing of price.'

'Nay,' said the man, 'the thing is not for sale.'

'What!' cried the Earl's daughter. 'Then what make you here in the town's market, with the thing in your creel and nought beside?'

'I sit here,' says the man, 'to get me a wife.'

'There is no sense in any of these answers,' thought the Earl's daughter; 'and I could find it in my heart to weep.'

By came the Earl upon that; and she called him and told him all. And when he had heard, he was of his daughter's mind that this should be a thing of virtue; and charged the man to set a price upon the thing, or else be hanged upon the gallows; and that was near at hand, so that the man could see it.

'The way of life is straight like the grooves of launching,' quoth the man. 'And if I am to be hanged let me be hanged.'

'Why!' cried the Earl, 'will you set your neck against a shoe of a horse, and it rusty?'

'In my thought,' said the man, 'one thing is as good as another in this world and a shoe of a horse will do.'

'This can never be,' thought the Earl; and he stood and looked upon the man, and bit his beard.

And the man looked up at him and smiled. 'It was so my fathers did in the ancient ages,' quoth he to the Earl, 'and I have neither a better reason nor a worse.'

'There is no sense in any of this,' thought the Earl, 'and I must be growing old.' So he had his daughter on one side, and says he: 'Many suitors have you denied, my child. But here is a very strange matter that a man should cling so to a shoe of a horse, and it rusty; and that he should offer it like a thing on sale, and yet not sell it; and that he should sit there seeking a wife. If I come not to the bottom of this thing, I shall have no more pleasure in bread; and I can see no way, but either I should hang or you should marry him.'

'By my troth, but he is bitter ugly,' said the Earl's daughter. 'How if the gallows be so near at hand?'

'It was not so,' said the Earl, 'that my fathers did in the ancient ages. I am like the man, and can give you neither a better reason nor a worse. But do you, prithee, speak with him again.'

So the Earl's daughter spoke to the man. 'If you were not so bitter ugly,' quoth she, 'my father the Earl would have us marry.'

'Bitter ugly am I,' said the man, 'and you as fair as May. Bitter ugly I am, and what of that? It was so my fathers—'

'In the name of God,' said the Earl's daughter, 'let your fathers be!'

'If I had done that,' said the man, 'you had never been chaffering with me here in the market, nor your father the Earl watching with the end of his eye.'

'But come,' quoth the Earl's daughter, 'this is a very strange thing, that you would have me wed for a shoe of a horse, and it rusty.'

'In my thought,' quoth the man, 'one thing is as good—'

'O, spare me that,' said the Earl's daughter, 'and tell me why I should marry.'

'Listen and look,' said the man.

Now the wind blew through the Poor Thing like an infant crying, so that her heart was melted; and her eyes were unsealed, and she was aware of the thing as it were a babe unmothered, and she took it to her arms, and it melted in her arms like the air.

'Come,' said the man, 'behold a vision of our children, the busy hearth, and the white heads. And let that suffice, for it is all God offers.'

'I have no delight in it,' said she; but with that she sighed.

'The ways of life are straight like the grooves of launching,' said the man; and he took her by the hand.

'And what shall we do with the horseshoe?' quoth she.

'I will give it to your father,' said the man; 'and he can make a kirk and a mill of it for me.'

It came to pass in time that the Poor Thing was born; but memory of these matters slept within him, and he knew not that which he had done. But he was a part of the eldest son; rejoicing manfully to launch the boat into the surf, skilful to direct the helm, and a man of might where the ring closes and the blows are going.

The Song of the Morrow

The sea foam ran to her feet, and the dead leaves swarmed about her back, and the rags blew about her face in the blowing of the wind.

THE KING of Duntrine had a daughter when he was old, and she was the fairest King's daughter between two seas; her hair was like spun gold, and her eyes like pools in a river; and the King gave her a castle upon the sea beach, with a terrace, and a court of the hewn stone, and four towers at the four corners. Here she dwelt and grew up, and had no care for the morrow, and no power upon the hour, after the manner of simple men.

It befell that she walked one day by the beach of the sea, when it was autumn, and the wind blew from the place of rains; and upon the one hand of her the sea beat, and upon the other the dead leaves ran. This was the loneliest beach between two seas, and strange things had been done there in the ancient ages. Now the King's daughter was aware of a crone that sat upon the beach. The sea foam ran to her feet, and the dead leaves swarmed about her back, and the rags blew about her face in the blowing of the wind.

'Now,' said the King's daughter, and she named a holy name, 'this is the most unhappy old crone between two seas.'

'Daughter of a King,' said the crone, 'you dwell in a stone house, and your hair is like the gold: but what is your profit? Life is not long, nor lives strong; and you live after the way of simple men, and have no thought for the morrow and no power upon the hour.'

'Thought for the morrow, that I have,' said the King's daughter; 'but power upon the hour, that have I not.' And she mused with herself.

Then the crone smote her lean hands one within the other, and laughed like a sea-gull. 'Home!' cried she. 'O daughter of a King, home to your stone house; for the longing is come upon you now, nor can you live any more after the manner of simple men. Home, and toil and suffer, till the gift come that will make you bare, and till the man come that will bring you care.'

The King's daughter made no more ado, but she turned about and went home to her house in silence. And when she was come into her chamber she called for her nurse.

'Nurse,' said the King's daughter, 'thought is come upon me for the morrow, so that I can live no more after the manner of simple men. Tell me what I must do that I may have power upon the hour.'

Then the nurse moaned like a snow wind. 'Alas!' said she, 'that this thing should be; but the thought is gone into your marrow, nor is there any cure against the thought. Be it so, then, even as you will; though power is less than weakness, power shall you have; and though the thought is colder than winter, yet shall you think it to an end.'

So the King's daughter sat in her vaulted chamber in the masoned house, and she thought upon the thought. Nine years she sat; and the sea beat upon the terrace, and the gulls cried about the turrets, and wind crooned in the chimneys of the house. Nine years she came not abroad, nor tasted the clean air, neither saw God's sky. Nine years she sat and looked neither to the right nor to the left, nor heard speech of any one, but thought upon the thought of the morrow. And her nurse fed her in silence, and she took of the food with her left hand, and ate it without grace.

Now when the nine years were out, it fell dusk in the autumn, and there came a sound in the wind like a sound of piping. At that the nurse lifted up her finger in the vaulted house.

'I hear a sound in the wind,' said she, 'that is like the sound of piping.'

'It is but a little sound,' said the King's daughter, 'but yet is it sound enough for me.'

So they went down in the dusk to the doors of the house, and along the beach of the sea. And the waves beat upon the one hand, and upon the other the dead leaves ran; and the clouds raced in the sky, and the gulls flew widdershins. And when they came to that part of the beach where strange things had been done in the ancient ages, lo! there was the crone, and she was dancing widdershins.

'What makes you dance widdershins, old crone?' said the King's daughter; 'here upon the bleak beach, between the waves and the dead leaves?'

'I hear a sound in the wind that is like a sound of piping,' quoth she. 'And it is for that that I dance widdershins. For the gift comes that will make you bare, and the man comes that must bring you care. But for me the morrow is come that I have thought upon, and the hour of my power.'

'How comes it, crone,' said the King's daughter, 'that you waver like a rag, and pale like a dead leaf before my eyes?'

'Because the morrow has come that I have thought upon, and the hour of my power,' said the crone; and she fell on the beach, and, lo! she was but stalks of the sea tangle, and dust of the sea sand, and the sand lice hopped upon the place of her.

'This is the strangest thing that befell between two seas,' said the King's daughter of Duntrine.

But the nurse broke out and moaned like an autumn gale. 'I am weary of the wind,' quoth she; and she bewailed her day.

The King's daughter was aware of a man upon the beach; he went hooded so that none might perceive his face, and a pipe was underneath his arm. The sound of his pipe was like singing wasps, and like the wind that sings in windlestraw; and it took hold upon men's ears like the crying of gulls.

'Are you the comer?' quoth the King's daughter of Duntrine.

'I am the comer,' said he, 'and these are the pipes that a man may hear, and I have power upon the hour, and this is the song of the morrow.' And he piped the song of the morrow, and it was as long as years; and the nurse wept out aloud at the hearing of it.

'This is true,' said the King's daughter, 'that you pipe the song of the morrow; but that ye have power upon the hour, how may I know that? Show me a marvel here upon the beach, between the waves and the dead leaves.'

And the man said, 'Upon whom?'

'Here is my nurse,' quoth the King's daughter. 'She is weary of the wind. Show me a good marvel upon her.'

And, lo! the nurse fell upon the beach as it were two handfuls of dead leaves, and the wind whirled them widdershins, and the sand lice hopped between.

'It is true,' said the King's daughter of Duntrine, 'you are the comer, and you have power upon the hour. Come with me to my stone house.'

So they went by the sea margin, and the man piped the song of the morrow, and the leaves followed behind them as they went.

Then they sat down together; and the sea beat on the terrace, and the gulls cried about the towers, and the wind crooned in the

chimneys of the house. Nine years they sat, and every year when it
fell autumn, the man said, 'This is the hour, and I have power in it';
and the daughter of the King said, 'Nay, but pipe me the song of the
morrow.' And he piped it, and it was long like years.

Now when the nine years were gone, the King's daughter of
Duntrine got her to her feet, like one that remembers; and she looked
about her in the masoned house; and all her servants were gone; only
the man that piped sat upon the terrace with the hand upon his face;
and as he piped the leaves ran about the terrace and the sea beat
along the wall. Then she cried to him with a great voice, 'This is the
hour, and let me see the power in it.' And with that the wind blew off
the hood from the man's face, and, lo! there was no man there, only
the clothes and the hood and the pipes tumbled one upon another in
a corner of the terrace, and the dead leaves ran over them.

And the King's daughter of Duntrine got her to that part of the
beach where strange things had been done in the ancient ages; and
there she sat her down. The sea foam ran to her feet, and the dead
leaves swarmed about her back, and the veil blew about her face in
the blowing of the wind. And when she lifted up her eyes, there
was the daughter of a King come walking on the beach. Her hair was
like the spun gold, and her eyes like pools in a river, and she had no
thought for the morrow and no power upon the hour, after the
manner of simple men.

Select Bibliography

Abrahamson, R. L. '"I never read such an impious book": re-examining Stevenson's Fables', *Journal of Stevenson Studies*, Volume 4 (Stirling, 2007)

Balderston, Daniel *Borges's Frame of Reference: The Strange Case of Robert Louis Stevenson* (Princeton University PhD, 1981)

Balderston, Daniel 'A Projected Stevenson Anthology (Buenos Aires, 1968–70)', *Variaciones Borges* 23 (Pittsburgh, 2007)

Bell, Ian *Dreams of Exile: Robert Louis Stevenson: A Biography* (London, 1993)

Bell-Villada, Gene H. *Borges and His Fiction: A Guide to His Mind and Art* (North Carolina, 1981)

Blyth, R.H. *Zen in English Literature and Oriental Classics* (Tokyo, 1942)

Borges, Jorge Luis *A Universal History of Infamy* (London, 1973)

Borges, Jorge Luis *Fictions* (London, 2000)

Borges, Jorge Luis *Labyrinths: Selected Stories and Other Writings* (London, 2000)

Borges, Jorge Luis *The Aleph* (London, 2000)

Borges, Jorge Luis *The Total Library: Non-Fiction 1922–1986* (London, 2001)

Borges, Jorge Luis & Adolfo Bioy Casares *Extraordinary Tales* (London, 1973)

Di Giovanni, Norman Thomas, Daniel Halpern & Frank MacShane (eds) *Borges on Writing* (London, 1974)

Dury, Richard 'Robert Louis Stevenson's Critical Reception' at: http://www.robert-louis-stevenson.org/richard-dury-archive/critrec.htm (accessed June 2017)

Fielding, Penny (ed.) *The Edinburgh Companion to Robert Louis Stevenson* (Edinburgh, 2010)

Galchen, Rivka 'Borges on Pleasure Island', *New York Times*, 27 June
    2010

Harman, Clare *Robert Louis Stevenson: A Biography* (London, 2010)

Reid, Alastair *Oases: Poems and Prose* (Edinburgh, 1997)

Rodriguez Monegal, Emir *Jorge Luis Borges: A Literary Biography*
    (New York, 1978)

Stevenson, Robert Louis *The Works of Robert Louis Stevenson*,
    Tusitala Edition (London, 1923–4)

Stevenson, Robert Louis *Fables* (Glasgow, 2012)

Swearingen, Roger G. *The Prose Writings of Robert Louis Stevenson:
    A Guide* (London, 1980)

Wilson, Jason *Jorge Luis Borges* (London, 2006)

Acknowledgements

THANK YOU to Edinburgh International Book Festival, who chose me to be one of the five Scottish writers for their Outriders project exploring the Americas, which was supported through the Scottish Government's Edinburgh Festivals Expo Fund. My trip to Argentina was vivid, memorable, enlightening. I met a great many wonderful people there, some of whom influenced my reading of Borges and of Stevenson (not to mention inspiring elements of my next novel). In Scotland, I thank: Nick Barley and Cat Tyre of EIBF; Jenny Niven of Creative Scotland. In Argentina, I thank: Maria Kodama; Valeria Zamparolo and Maria Ines Lopez Vicente of the British Council, Argentina; Mariana Enriquez; Gabriela Adamo of Filba; Ernesto Montequin; Gloria Silva at Villa Ocampo; Mabel Mayol and Ana Quiroga, Museo Nacional de Bellas Artes; staff at the Biblioteca Miguel Cané; Billy Suárez; Mariano Tenconi Blanco; staff at the Hotel Montecassino, Capilla del Monte.

Thank you to Professor Daniel Balderston, whose essay first sparked my enthusiasm for bringing this volume together. When I emailed Professor Balderston as a professional and personal courtesy, seeking his blessing for this project, he responded in the most gracious and generous manner.

Thank you to everyone at Birlinn/Polygon, especially: Neville Moir, Alison Rae, Vikki Reilly, Edward Crossan, Jim Hutcheson.

Thank you to Rosanna Al-Mulla and Karl Magee, Archives and Special Collections, University Library, University of Stirling.

Thank you to staff at the National Library of Scotland, Edinburgh.

Thank you to Duncan Jones, Association for Scottish Literary Studies, Glasgow.

Thank you to my Creative Writing colleagues at the University of Stirling: Kathleen Jamie, Chris Powici, Liam Murray Bell.

Thank you to my agent, Joanna Swainson, of Hardman & Swainson.

Thank you to all my friends, old and new, in Scotland, Argentina and beyond.

A Note on the Editor

KEVIN MACNEIL is an award-winning writer from the Outer Hebrides now lecturing in Creative Writing at the University of Stirling. He is an acclaimed novelist, poet, editor and screenwriter. He co-wrote Hamish: The Movie and his books include *A Method Actor's Guide to Jekyll and Hyde* and *The Brilliant & Forever*, short-listed for the Saltire Fiction of the Year Award.